T0271507

THE SEA CEMETERY

Aslak Nore

THE SEA CEMETERY

Translated from the Norwegian by
Deborah Dawkin

MACLEHOSE PRESS
QUERCUS·LONDON

First published as *Havets kirkegård* by H. Aschehoug & Co., Oslo, in 2021

First published in Great Britain in 2024 by

MacLehose Press
An imprint of Quercus Editions Limited
Carmelite House
50 Victoria Embankment
London EC4Y 0DZ

An Hachette UK company

This translation has been published with the financial support of NORLA

The moral right of Aslak Nore to be
identified as the author of this work has been
asserted in accordance with the Copyright,
Designs and Patents Act, 1988.

Deborah Dawkin asserts her moral right to be identified
as the translator of the work.

A CIP catalogue record for this book is available
from the British Library.

ISBN (HB) 978 1 52942 435 5
ISBN (TPB) 978 1 52942 436 2
ISBN (Ebook) 978 1 52942 440 9

This book is a work of fiction. Names, characters,
organisations, places and events are
either the product of the author's imagination
or are used fictitiously. Any resemblance to
actual persons, living or dead, events or
particular places is entirely coincidental.

10 9 8 7 6 5 4 3 2 1

Typeset by Jouve (UK), Milton Keynes
Printed and bound in Great Britain by Clays Ltd, Elcograf S.p.A.

Papers used by Quercus Books are from well-managed forests and other
responsible sources.

DOCTOR ABROAD

**Hans Falck has saved thousands of lives.
At the price of forgetting his own kids' birthdays.**

By John O. Berg

Lebanon, September 1982. Dusk. A young doctor walks with hurried steps through the Shatila refugee camp in Beirut. In his right hand he holds a large red first-aid bag. In the crook of his other arm, he carries a newborn baby wrapped in a blanket.

Hans Falck is surrounded by the smell of gunpowder and excrement, a stench he will encounter often over the next few decades, one that will always remind him of that evening in Shatila. A militia of Christian Phalangists has entered the camp. Their mission: to find the militant Palestinians hiding there. The slaughter has begun. The Phalangists spare nobody. Around him he hears scattered voices, screams and gunshots.

A rocket streaks across the sky, and a split second later the buildings are drenched in an unreal silver-grey light. Hans stops. Between the heaps of rubbish, boxes of war rations and spirit bottles lie the dead: young men with their genitals hacked off, pregnant women with their bellies sliced open, children, babies. Some twenty metres away to the left, he sees a cluster of people: women shielding their children, men in tight embraces, each with a small bullet hole in their forehead. All executed at close range.

The rocket fizzles out and the light vanishes like a switch has been flipped. Towards the camp's southern exit, he can make out the silhouettes of the single-storey buildings that have been blown apart, and behind their ruins an iron ring of militiamen.

He hears the quiet, penetrating sound of the baby's cries. Taking shelter behind a dustbin, he sinks to his knees and tries to rock the child.

Can anyone see him? No, he is well hidden.

But he must do something, or the infant will be taken from him. Hans unzips the large first-aid bag. He chucks out some bottles of saline solution and alcohol, together with a folding stretcher that takes up too much space, and catheters, stethoscopes and blood pressure monitors, whose sharp edges could injure the baby's head.

There's a bottle of Johnnie Walker Black Label in the side pocket. A gift from the Palestinian leadership, with whom he met. He knows, without actually knowing, that they are all dead now.

Hans opens the bottle and dips his finger into the whisky, then lets the baby inhale the fumes, before poking his fingertip into its little mouth. The baby sucks on it with the inexplicable strength of a newborn, then gives a little whimper before going quiet. Carefully Hans makes a bed of cloths and blankets in the bottom of the bag, then lowers the little body onto it, covering it with tourniquets and thin bandages. Then he zips the bag closed.

Hans Falck takes the bag and starts to walk towards the soldiers. He is already known for his charm, in the words of one colleague he "can seduce anyone from a tax official to a top politician". On this hideous night in 1982, Dr Falck is facing his greatest test. He must deliver a newborn baby from a massacre.

Lebanon, summer 2006. It is almost twenty-five years since the massacres in the Palestinian refugee camps shook the world. Much water has passed under the bridge since then, yet much is unchanged: Lebanon is still at war and Hans Falck is as energetic and boyishly charming as he was in the seventies, when as a young Bergen shipping magnate's son he checked out the ladies, dressed as an ordinary worker and declared that come the revolution he would put his father's companies under collective ownership.

"But the probate courts got there first," Falck says, flashing a smile at the famous Palestinian actress who is coming his way in the bar of the Mayflower, the legendary hotel where he often stays when he's in Beirut.

"We just call him Hans Saqr," says the young woman, blushing. "*Saqr* is the Arabic for 'falcon', or *falck* in Norwegian."

Hans orders two Johnnie Walkers without ice. "Have to drink the PLO's favourite tipple." He raises his crystal glass. "To the living, the dead and the oppressed!"

The latter is, of course, a group to which nobody could claim Hans belongs. He descends from the powerful Falck family, who played such a prominent role in Norway throughout the twentieth century as shipowners, public benefactors and politicians. His grandfather, Thor Falck – known by the family as "Big Thor" – was a famous shipowner who died in the Hurtigruten shipping disaster during the war and was posthumously awarded the War Cross with Sword for his role in organising resistance efforts against German forces along the coast.

The Falck family has, since his death, been split in two. The Bergen Falcks, to which Hans belongs, reside on an estate south of Fana. Malicious tongues have consistently claimed that they suffered an injustice when the family's fortunes were divided. Might we see future inheritance disputes between the Oslo and Bergen branches?

"Absolutely not, I can vouch for that," Hans insists. "As a communist I am utterly opposed to the institution of inheritance. Nothing does so much to entrench inequality."

He smiles. "Besides, losing our fortune has been a *good* thing. A blessing. The wealthy go through life fearful that everything will be taken from them one day. Only when you've lost everything are you free."

The same cannot be said of the so-called Oslo branch of the Falck empire. Hans's uncle, Olav, is a former Minister of Defence and leader of the influential SAGA Group, with its headquarters at Rederhaugen, outside the capital. Said to be worth approximately 10 billion kroner, Olav prefers to remain in the shadows, but has influence that cannot be measured in money.

Do we see echoes here of the classic schism in Norwegian history, between the entrepreneurial communities along our coastline and the administrative elites in Oslo?

"We Bergenites aren't overly interested in the capital," Hans says, laughing. "Put it this way: when I fly to the Continent or the Middle East, I never stop off in Oslo if I can avoid it."

Bergen patriot, idealistic radical, champagne socialist. Hans Falck can be described in many ways. No matter the occasion, he always seems to have a good answer and a roguish smile lurking. But according to those who truly know him, Hans is like a Russian doll: when one layer is removed, another appears. He is on first-name terms with half the Middle East, from top politicians to taxi drivers on Hamra Street, yet he remains a mystery to his nearest and dearest. The man whose infectious laugh now echoes across the hotel foyer has seen more suffering than any Norwegian of his generation, yet he seems strangely unaffected. The doctor who is famed far beyond medical circles for saving thousands of innocent lives in the world's worst conflict areas has forgotten his own kids' birthdays more than once. The feminist who walks at the front of International Women's Day marches is candid about his infidelity to the women in his life. But even here he has an answer: "To rephrase Hemingway: I like communists

4

when they're doctors, but when they're priests, I hate them. I'm just a human being like anyone else."

Is there anything that can ruffle him?

Well, yes, it seems so.

The question of whether Hans Falck has ever actually loved anyone, other than the world's oppressed and his own reflection. For the first time his gaze falters and he shifts in his chair. He may not give me a direct answer, but perhaps he answers nevertheless.

Lebanon, September 1982. The stink of alcohol hits hard even at a distance. Preferable to the smell of death, Hans thinks. The young militiamen, eyes swimming, kerchiefs over their noses, aim their rifles at him. Behind him he hears gunshots, screams, then silence.

"We're carrying out an operation against Palestinian terrorists," says the Lebanese Phalangist officer. "As a foreigner you were given the opportunity to leave the camp before it started."

He lights a cigarette. "The fact you didn't take it indicates that you're with the militant groups yourself."

Some of the youngest soldiers, most likely teenagers, step forward menacingly.

"I was assisting at a birth," Hans answers.

"Today's babies are tomorrow's terrorists," says the officer, spitting out the words. "Where's the kid?"

Hans notices that his palms are so wet with sweat that the bag is about to slip from his grasp. One peep from the baby and they're both dead.

"I don't know," Hans says. "The last thing I saw was that the maternity clinic was stormed."

"What country are you from?"

"Norway . . . a Christian country . . . Israel-friendly . . . close ties."

The officer grins and exchanges a few words with a comrade. He nods. "You can go."

Hans breathes a sigh of relief.

"After we've checked the bag."

What to do now? Hans gently puts it down on the ground. Carefully opens the zip. The militiamen lean over him. The baby's face is hidden. But Hans notices that the blanket is moving a little with the child's breathing.

Can anyone else see it?

Hans takes the bottle of Johnnie Walker and holds it up to the officer.

"You need this more than I do," he says.

The Phalangist examines the label. Fortunately, the soldiers seem unsuspicious of the bag. The officer grabs the bottle. "Get lost," he says.

Hans's hands are shaking so hard he can barely close the zip. Feeling numb he passes between two lines of Phalangist soldiers as though walking a gauntlet, heading towards freedom, comforted that if they fire now they will shoot each other. He drives back to the Mayflower Hotel, the same hotel he is sitting in now on a deep leather sofa, twenty-five years later, a dark shadow slipping across his confident face.

"So, what happened to the child?"

"I left it in someone else's care. I promised the mother never to reveal its identity. And that's a promise I intend to keep. But I hope the child has a better life than she did."

PART I
HIGH CLIFF

1

A FALCON READY FOR FLIGHT

Their grandmother had always predicted that the family estate would go under before she did. What she meant – whether she was declaring herself immortal or putting a curse on her descendants – nobody really knew. Vera Lind was not a writer for nothing, but of all the stories she ever told, none frightened Sasha more.

She had been baptised Alexandra Falck. It was their grandmother who had insisted on calling her Sasha or Sashenka – little Sasha – when she was a child, after the Russian great-grandfather none of them had even seen a picture of.

Tortured by insomnia Sasha had risen early, flinging on a navy-blue polo neck and tweed blazer. It was important when faced with unpleasant duties to be formally attired. She had discovered that one of the PhD interns at the foundation's archive, which she headed up, had viewed the annual reports for 1969 and 1970. This was a violation of the confidentiality agreement he had signed, and Sasha did not take such breaches of trust lightly.

His snooping was disconcerting enough, but worse, it felt like a symptom of something more, like the changing mood in the air when one season shifts to another: stories that had long been hidden were about to rise to the surface.

What had Grandma meant when she said that the truth and family loyalty stood in conflict?

Sasha locked up the old gatekeeper's lodge where she and her family lived. The girls were staying at a cabin with friends. Mads was away on business in Asia. Early in their marriage he had hinted that it might be a bit stifling to live on the estate, which was not only home to the family's company headquarters but to several family members. Sasha had been furious, the way we are when somebody points out an obvious truth about something we love.

But moving was out of the question.

Rederhaugen lay a short boat trip west of the capital. Sasha walked up the tree-lined avenue towards the fountain at the fork in the driveway. The frost had laid a veil of pale pastel shades over the landscape. An icy wind stroked her face, cutting straight through her jacket. She shuddered involuntarily.

She had lived here all her life, yet she still found herself overcome by love and devotion for the place. It was her world. The estate and the family were one, an extension of herself: the gently sloping rocks to the west, where she had bathed as a child; the jetties and boathouses on the southern tip; the immaculate lawn, emerald green in the summer, that swept down into a thick coniferous forest, which ended abruptly at a cliff edge to the east, where Vera's writing cottage lay.

From the fountain, now drained for the winter, she followed the gravel path up to the white three-storey mansion that presided over the estate from a grassy hill, with colonnades, large bay windows, intricate wrought-iron balconies and a round tower topped with crenels.

She was conservative by nature. Change always filled her with trepidation. Once, during a quarrel, Mads had pointed out that someone with Sasha's background – she and her two siblings were set to inherit what was perhaps Norway's most beautiful private estate, as well as a billion-kroner company and humanitarian foundation – had little to gain from any revolutionary upheaval. True enough, but her conservatism went deeper than that: when it came to it, family was all that mattered.

For Sasha, family came first, and whenever its most powerful figures were in conflict – her grandmother and her dominating father, for example, who had lived on the same estate for half a century without really talking – it was her job to keep things on an even keel.

She let herself into the sunken doorway at the back of the main house. From there, she continued through the library and into her office. A postcard lay in her in tray, postmarked Finse 1222: *Don't forget our trip over the Hardanger Glacier. Love you, M.*

Such little surprises were typical of Mads. She was touched that he had gone to the trouble of buying a post-card in Finse and sending it before he left. When she was younger, Sasha would have dismissed it as a cynical ploy to impress her. Now she understood it as love.

She sat down in the brown Eames chair.

As the chief archivist of the SAGA Foundation, she was personally responsible for any permanent employees and PhD interns. She opened her diary. *Meeting: 08.00–08.10.* She looked at the clock. Fifteen minutes to go. She was dreading it.

During the last year she had been overseeing the preparations for an ambitious collaborative project with the Bundesarchiv in Freiburg: the Abteilung Militärarchiv. Often, when she mentioned the initiative to outsiders, their eyes would glaze over. Archives weren't sexy, but

Sasha could not have been less bothered. For her, history came to life in old letters and brief telegrams. And it was a job that satisfied her need for order and objectivity. True, her grandmother always said that history was no more objective than a novel, but that was just one of her many provocative statements.

Sasha's work with the German archives involved collating and digitising the records of the hundreds of thousands of German soldiers stationed on Norwegian soil in World War II. Relatives and historians would now be able to search for names, dog tag numbers and the like, and access any available information. The logistical challenges were enormous, but her father was keen for the foundation to be better known in Germany.

There was a knock at the door, then another, but she waited until it was precisely eight to reply.

"Yes?"

Sindre Tollefsen stepped in tentatively. His clothes were worn, and his hairline had receded such that only a wispy tuft on top of his head remained. He surveyed her uneasily, a mild, slightly evasive expression in his eyes. They were probably the same age.

"Take a seat," she said. He complied. She thought about all the people her father must have sent packing.

How did he cope with it?

"As you know," she said, clearing her throat, "the SAGA Foundation has been collaborating with the university for some time, giving PhD students an opportunity to use our archives for their research. A partnership based on mutual trust. You've made some important contributions to Norwegian war history as well as to our project with the German military archive."

He swallowed and his sharp Adam's apple moved in his throat. Sasha had been very excited about Tollefsen's doctoral project. He was researching the little-known story of anti-Nazi resistance within the Wehrmacht on Norwegian soil. It was groundbreaking stuff.

"But there was one *absolute* precondition," Sasha continued, "to which you signed up when you were given access to our archives: a duty of confidentiality regarding the German soldiers and anything related to SAGA or the Falck family."

Only now did the gravity of the situation seem to hit the doctoral researcher. "How did you know . . .?"

"I'm not about to discuss our internal security procedures," she answered.

The system, which had been set up by Rederhaugen's security chief, was modelled on that used by Norway's health service, and allowed her to see who had entered the archives. After her unsettling conversation with Vera the day before, Sasha had viewed some digitised documents and spotted Tollefsen's username in the log. She hated the thought of someone digging about in her family's affairs. In this, she resembled her father.

"You went into SAGA's annual reports from 1969 and 1970," she said. "These are internal documents, of no relevance to either your research or the public."

"Of no relevance to the public?" The student raised his voice.

"Correct," said Sasha. "As you may know, our family is very selective in its dealings with the press. You won't ever have read any 'at home with' features on the Falcks, and you never will. Loyalty and discretion are our hallmarks."

13

She tapped a ballpoint pen on the leather-topped desk.

"Anyway, you have abused our trust, and your place here and access to the archives are therefore withdrawn with immediate effect."

His lower lip trembled. "Are you kicking me out?"

She nodded. "I'm afraid so."

Contrary to her expectation, he did not get up, but sat in silence, a contorted smile on his face.

"Do you know why I read the two reports?"

"No. Neither am I interested."

"Because Vera Lind's life story is relevant to my research. It ties in with the fallacious story your family has woven around itself."

She took a deep breath, resisting the temptation to answer in kind. "Our time is up," she said abruptly, nodding towards the door.

The researcher got up to go, before turning back. "I thought you were different from the others, Sasha Falck. But you're just as cowardly. Even more so, if that's possible. I have no desire to work for a foundation that takes the truth for its motto, but stands for the opposite. Ask your grandmother what really happened in 1970."

The door slammed behind him.

Sasha sat, staring up at the ceiling. Vera, again. Truth and loyalty? 1970? In line with her character – considerate and diplomatic in her own view, self-effacing and agreeable in that of her siblings – Sasha visited her grandmother once every week in her writing cottage at High Cliff.

She had been there the previous day.

As always Sasha had brought fresh pastries, and as always her grandmother had provided a glass of red wine and a cigarette while Sasha read a chapter to her from one of her favourite novels. At first, they did not deviate from their usual routine, but then the conversation took a new turn.

"The family are planning to mark the seventy-fifth anniversary of the ferry disaster later this year," Sasha had said in a tentative voice. "We've chartered a Hurtigruten ship and we're going to the site of the wreck."

Her grandmother turned to her slowly. "I need another cigarette, Sashenka dear."

"I thought it might be nice for you to join us," Sasha went on. "Maybe you could talk a bit about what actually happened."

"Talk?"

"You've never spoken about it."

It was typical of her grandmother's generation to keep traumatic events to themselves. The accident had taken her husband and come close to taking her newborn son.

"It would probably do me good," said Vera. "But I'm not so sure you'd want to hear what I have to say."

"Of course we would. It's a long time since the war, we can handle the truth."

Her grandmother surveyed her through the smoke.

"*We?*" she said, shaking her head. "You've always been so loyal to the family, Sashenka. That's an admirable trait. But sometimes loyalty and the search for truth collide. I won't be going on any chartered Hurtigruten, that's for certain. But do you want to know what really happened that day?"

Sasha nodded.

"Well, now's not the time, Sashenka. But when it is, you'll have to be prepared for everything to come crashing down."

Nothing more was said, but when Sasha was about to leave, her grandmother asked her to order her a cab into town and to walk with her through the forest to the crossroads.

"But you never go out nowadays, Grandma," she said.

"Well, I am now, Sashenka dear," her grandmother said sharply. "It's not as if I'm under a Guardianship Order!"

Sasha swallowed hard. She wasn't used to being put in her place by Vera. It had stayed with her as she walked back through the forest and for the rest of the day.

Where Vera had gone in the cab, Sasha still had no idea, but it was time to find out.

Sitting at the side door was Jazz, the family guard dog. The instant he caught sight of her, he rose onto his hind legs in greeting.

"What's up?" she whispered, scratching him behind the ears. Jazz barked impatiently. He was a Belgian Malinois, a dog with a long black nose and coffee-coloured coat like a German Shepherd, but with shorter fur, a slimmer body and a straighter back than his German relatives. Jazz was as affectionate as a puppy and brave as a wolf. He could be trained for anything. He climbed trees like a cat. When presidents needed protection or terrorists apprehending, a Malinois always led the way.

Sasha hurried after the dog across the lawn and into the forest. She knew every root and rock on the path, the entire geography of the estate was imprinted on her body: a soft carpet of spruce needles leading to a sloping rock that got slippery when it rained; the bone-smooth roots around the water-lily-covered tarn; the two axe-shaped boulders that formed a pass. As children they had been forbidden to enter the Devil's Forest.

Suddenly the landscape opened out, and the vegetation ended abruptly in a steep drop, with Grandma's cottage a few metres to the left.

Sasha felt a little gust of wind and a twinge of vertigo. Jazz bounded up the rock slab steps to the front door. He rose on two legs again and barked.

Sasha gently tapped the horseshoe knocker.

No answer.

"Grandma?"

She opened the door; it creaked lightly.

"Vera, are you here?"

A stale, closed-in smell hit her. The parquet floor gave way slightly underfoot as she walked past the crammed bookshelves towards the bedroom. She opened the door. The bed was made, a white lace coverlet laid over the duvet. A photograph on the wall showed her father as a baby in Vera's arms on the Hurtigruten ship. It always moved her, giving her a sense that the world and time were interconnected.

When she was younger, tears had filled the eyes of old folk at the mere sight of her, because she was so like her grandmother. She could see it herself. The upper lip that turned down slightly at the corners of the mouth, giving her a naturally melancholic, aristocratic air, which many interpreted as arrogance. The pearly, unblemished skin that contrasted with her hair, which like her grandmother's was mahogany brown with a hint of red. Their eyes were also similar: framed by sharp cheekbones and heavy, dark eyebrows, they slanted gently upward from the root of the nose, with azure-blue irises. She was in her early thirties now, "the time when women are most beautiful", as her older cousin, the womaniser and male chauvinist Dr Falck, liked to say.

She closed the bedroom door gently and went into the kitchenette. Everything was neat and tidy. In the fridge Sasha found the shopping she had brought over the day before. She opened a cupboard over the kitchen counter.

She was about to close it when she noticed how the sunlight shone on a row of stem glasses on the top shelf. Three of them were slightly misty. Sasha took one down and felt it with her fingertip. A few drops still clung to the glass, and the rim was damp, as if it had been rinsed only recently. Jazz whimpered and shoved his strong neck against her hip.

She went outside. The dog bounded off towards High Cliff, stopping abruptly as if slamming on the brakes, then padded to the edge with his nose to the ground, as though he was trying to tell her something.

High Cliff had an overhang, partially covered with junipers and other shrubs, making it hard to see what was below. About ten metres downhill there was a little skerry, connected to the mainland at low tide by a strip of pebbles and sand that guided water into a shallow bay filled with shells, seaweed and mud.

She leaned out to look. Putting her arm around Jazz's neck, she crouched down. The low sun stung her eyes. Still unable to see properly, she got onto her hands and knees, and groped her way to the edge of the rugged outcrop, spruce needles pricking her palms, ripples on the bay below.

Her grandmother lay face down in the water, swaying gently on the surface, like a buoy, or a forgotten inflatable toy. Sunlight sparkled around her, and her body was encircled by a wreath of red jellyfish. *Draugspy*, Vera had called them – the spew of the *draug*, the headless harbinger of death by drowning. On the back of her green quilt vest, Sasha could make out the Falck coat of arms, a falcon preparing to take flight, and through the water's ruffled surface its outstretched wings seemed to move.

2

DON'T TELL YOUR FATHER
HOW TO . . .

Olav Falck flung his bathrobe onto a bench and walked naked across the jetty. It was oddly cold for the time of year. The frost-covered planks stuck to the soles of his feet. The air was minus seven, the water was two or maybe three degrees. The jetty lay next to a red-painted boathouse in a bay concealed by jagged rocks on either side. As usual he checked for jellyfish. Then dived out.

His blood vessels contracted to protect his body's vital organs. He lay on his back, his winter-shrunken dick floating to the surface, until he had control of his breathing and could stare up at the clear blue sky. Olav had been an all-season swimmer for as long as he could remember, since before it was fashionable. That babies instinctively held their breath underwater was an accepted fact, but it also suited the heroic story he liked to tell about himself. For Olav Falck, life was a test of manhood. And he had fought for his own from the outset.

But life had been good to him. Now, in his seventy-fifth year, he was still medication-free, although his cardiologist had strongly advised him not to bathe in cold water without supervision. Not that he gave two hoots about that; if he was going to die, it should be in the sea. Ice bathing was his only addiction.

There were challenges even now, of course, like who would take over when he stepped down. But generally the same thing applied to the family business as to the country in which they lived. It was no longer a matter of *building*, but of managing.

Only after a good while did he climb up the jetty steps and feel the light prickling sensation as the blood flowed back into his fingers and toes, like heat from a wood burner spreading through a cold room.

On the jetty Olav delivered a few rhythmic jabs and uppercuts at the air. He was fond of classic athletics. When the Olympics or World Championships were on, he might even cancel meetings to watch an important event. He liked the boxing best of all. He was nineteen in 1959 when Ingemar Johansson beat Floyd Patterson; he followed the golden age of the 1960s and 70s with an eagle eye and often had ringside seats for title fights in Las Vegas.

Few things irritated him more than Norway's ban on professional boxing, yet another example of Norwegian nanny-stateism. Yes, it involved an element of risk, but what was life without risk? Life was good because it was tough. Without pain there was no joy.

He hurried along the path through the frozen patch of forest that separated the bay from the garden, and over the lawn towards his father's bust, sculpted in bronze and set on a plinth of untreated granite, made by one of the country's leading sculptors. A glow of sunlight lit the sculpture's forehead; an epitaph engraved below read: *To live on in the hearts we leave behind is not to die. Thor S. Falck 03.11.1903–23.10.1940.* Although Olav had lost his father as a baby and had no memory of him, he was filled with humility for the dynasty of which he was a part.

21

He went in through the basement entrance at the back of the rose tower. After a scalding hot shower in the changing room, he went up the rose tower's winding staircase and into his office. He checked his diary. No appointments for the rest of the day. Excellent, he could write the speech he had been pondering for so long. With a working title of "Pioneers of the Resistance Movement", its starting point would be his father. As the director of a large Bergen shipping company responsible for several Hurtigruten ferries, "Big Thor" had organised spying missions targeting the German invaders and sent fishing boats across the North Sea to smuggle radio transmitters back from Britain.

Olav's speech would also touch on the underwater mines that had been laid by the British along Norway's coast. That his father had lost his life to one of these, rather than to German weaponry, was something of an irony.

Olav had formulated only a few sentences when there was a knock on the door.

"Sverre?" Olav said. "What are you doing here?"

Olav's eldest son was in his mid-thirties, and as the years passed it was getting increasingly difficult to deny their growing resemblance. Like Olav, he was tall and athletic, his long, tanned face with narrow, inquisitive eyes dominated by a large, hooked nose, described by malicious tongues as the "falcon beak".

Sverre had left his usual conservative Savile Row tweed in the wardrobe today, and was wearing an ostentatious black shirt with an embroidered floral pattern. His obsequious expression was accompanied by an uncharacteristic joviality.

"I thought we might have a little chat," Sverre said.

"No walk-ins, thank you, Sverre. I'm enjoying my view of the fjord today, and my clear diary while I write my speech about Father."

"It's about the diving expedition down to the shipwreck during the conference," Sverre continued. "I've got someone here I want you to meet."

Sverre was project manager for the SAGA Arctic Challenge planned for later that year. So far he had done a pretty good job. The chartering of a Hurtigruten vessel to take a bevy of international thinkers past the site of the 1940 tragedy and through Lofoten and Vesterålen represented everything the SAGA Foundation stood for. It was quintessentially Norwegian but also attractive to foreigners.

"Ah," Olav sighed. "The two of you had better come in."

Sverre's companion wore a wine-coloured velvet blazer that intruded on Olav's field of vision like a bolt of red cloth.

"Has fancy dress season come early this year?" he said.

He recognised the man, of course. Olav did not despise the upstarts who had popped up on the country's rich lists in recent years – in fact, he rather enjoyed seeing how their shamelessness made the tweed knickerbocker-wearing classes squirm. And nobody liked his bling more than Ralph Rafaelsen.

Olav sent for coffee while he tried to ascertain the power balance between his son and Rafaelsen. In recent years the media had hailed Rafaelsen as an enterprising, risk-seeking guy. He had established a huge salmon farm in his home town and had continued to expand the business ever since.

"So, you've come to talk about a shipwreck dive?" Olav said, looking at each in turn. "You're the one with the diving suit?"

The plan was that when the Hurtigruten ship came to the site of the ferry disaster, a diver would descend to the wreck, three hundred metres down, in a specially made suit, his progress transmitted live to the conference participants.

"Correct," Rafaelsen said, looking him in the eye. "Though calling it a diving suit is like calling a space shuttle a plane."

"Or marketing your fish as 'Atlantic wild salmon'?" Olav said. "Those limp creatures of yours have as much in common with the proud Atlantic salmon as a poodle does with a wolf."

Rafaelsen laughed. "This suit is revolutionary. It's an atmospheric diving suit, so we avoid the problem of decompression sickness at great depth. The pilot – this is more like a one-man submarine – remains unaffected by the pressure. There's only one of its kind in Norway. And it's mine. The dive will be a great addition to the conference."

As Rafaelsen expounded on the technicalities of this wonderful contraption, Olav barely bothered to listen. He was a generalist. He had never understood the nerdish obsession with detail.

To his great annoyance, Sverre seemed to fawn on Rafaelsen, despite being his senior by about ten years; he nodded eagerly at his every word, laughing at his crass northern jokes.

Sverre's flawed character was the main reason why Olav was still, at the age of seventy-five, CEO of the SAGA Group, a company that *Kapital* magazine had valued at twelve billion kroner. The income from his real estate company and capital investments might underpin the family's cash flow, but these days he had only disdain for venture capitalists, shopkeepers and small-time investors. He preferred to focus on the SAGA Foundation, of which he was chair of the board. The money had to keep rolling in, of course, but SAGA had an entirely different mission: to promote the country's history. Some had billions on their balance sheets, others had cultural capital. Only SAGA had both.

Nonetheless, Olav would not have stayed on well past retirement age had SAGA merely contented itself with conferences and scholarships, like most non-profits of its kind. From the earliest post-war years the family's companies had been interlinked with Norway's secret services, first with the anti-communist Occupation Preparedness programme known as "Stay Behind", and later as . . . No, it was a long and complicated story. Intelligence work of this kind did not bring in money, or public recognition. On the contrary, it could threaten his other businesses. But it gave Olav something more valuable – a sense of being relevant. And before he could consider stepping down, he would have to initiate his eventual successor – who according to the statute must be one of his children – into the complexities of the situation.

There were good reasons why he was still at the helm of this ship.

"Sounds good." Olav cut Rafaelsen off halfway through a description of the special underwater cameras. "We'll do it."

"There's one more thing," Sverre said, clearly about to launch into something else.

Olav smiled. "I've got all day."

"As you probably know," Sverre began, and Olav noted a hesitation in his voice, "we've invited lots of high-profile guests to the conference. They've all accepted, they all want to go to Lofoten. We still have pulling power. Some have billions on the ledger, others have cultural capi—"

"Get to the point," Olav said.

"I've just had confirmation that the Saudi royal family will be represented," Sverre said. "The crown prince himself may drop by in his private plane."

"Bodø has Norway's longest airstrip," added Rafaelsen. "The U2 Dragonfly landed there in 1960, so a private jet isn't a problem."

Sverre looked at his companion. "Ralph and I have talked about offering something extra for the younger VIPs. Ralph has contacts in the helicopter squadrons up here. We can hire a few helicopters, land on the Hurtigruten ship in the afternoon, and fly some of the guests over Lofoten to Rafaelsen's villa in Vesterålen, then back to the ship the next morning."

"A little bonus, you might say," Rafaelsen said.

The Saudi royal family . . . hired helicopters . . . Rafaelsen's villa . . . The words crowded in Olav's head like the nightmares that had sometimes overwhelmed him as a child.

He sat in silence a while, his head inclined, before opening his mouth.

"May I say something?"

"That's why we're here," Sverre said.

Olav cleared his throat. "When I was last at the Dorchester in London, I got chatting with the doorman. He asked me why I wasn't staying in the Falcks' usual suite."

At the mention of the hotel, Olav observed his son bite his lip, as though he knew what was coming. Olav smiled and continued. " 'Oh,' I said to the doorman, 'I prefer a standard room, as long as the view is good, even though I'm a . . . ' "

He paused, as if searching for the word.

" '. . . a wealthy man.' 'But your son always takes the suite,' the doorman said. 'Yes,' I replied, 'but he's the *son* of a wealthy man.' "

He looked sternly at Sverre, who sat in silence, shame-faced. Rafaelsen sniggered quietly. Olav turned his gaze on him.

"Norway's a good country to be prosperous in. Most Norwegians don't have anything against people with money; on the contrary they admire people with guts and entrepreneurial spirit. And our laws protect our interests well. But it's a delicate balance. Just as we admire diligence and skill, we abhor decadence and dissolution. We never had much of an aristocracy, and certainly not since the Nobility Act of 1821, when titles and privileges were abol-ished. When you're handling wealth in Norway – if you want to make your mark as something more than a mere investor – you'd do better *not* to fight the unions and hire undeclared and underpaid Poles to build your houses."

Now it was Rafaelsen's turn to look like a schoolboy caught red-handed in a sweet shop. A great deal had been written about the working conditions when he built his gigantic villa in Vesterålen.

"Managing wealth in Norway requires an understand-ing of the Norwegian model," Olav said. "You must acknowledge tripartite cooperation, and the benefits of the compressed wage structure, which means getting drunk with shop stewards and union leaders. This is the true Norwegian model. We ensure that ordinary, honest folk have a good life; we pay them well so they can go for

a holiday in the sun, buy a new car and take out a mort-
gage to buy their own home. In return we get a people who
respect us, who don't vote for troublemakers or storm our
properties. All these ideas of yours for the Hurtigruten
trip – the bloody Saudis, the helicopters and this knees-up
on your property – are in breach of this unspoken
contract."

"I get it," said Rafaelsen. "Don't tell your father how
to—"

He was interrupted by someone knocking.

"We're busy," Olav said.

His secretary stuck her head in anyway.

"Are you deaf?" Olav said, irritably.

"I'm terribly sorry, but it's important."

"It had better be."

He was reaching for his coffee cup, but the expression
on her face as she entered the room made him stop.

"The meeting's over," he said to Sverre and Rafaelsen,
who looked at each other in confusion as they got up
and left.

"What's happened?" Olav asked when he was alone
with his secretary. Deep down he already knew the answer.

3

NO MAN'S LAND

American Interrogation Centre, unknown location
in the Middle East

When Johnny Berg was led into the brightly lit room
between two guards, he remembered what his mentor, an
elderly officer who went by the initials HK, had once
warned him: the worst thing about torture is not the pain
itself, but the anticipation.

He had no idea where he was. They had moved him
from one prison camp to another before he ended up in
American custody. The weeks, the months after his arrest
by the Kurdish militia were as shrouded as a mountain in
a snowstorm, when we can't tell where the earth ends and
the sky begins, when minutes are like hours, and hours are
like minutes.

The guards had removed his balaclava before they
pushed him into the room, as if to let him see what awaited
him. The fluorescent lights in the ceiling sliced into his eyes.
Hard rock music burst from the speakers at full volume.

In the middle of the room there was a sloping bench
with leather straps on both sides, together with a black
woollen hood and a neatly folded towel. Further into the
room, two men in balaclavas, grey fleece jackets and military boots were waiting. Against the wall stood two
watering cans.

The music stopped.

No, thought Johnny, his heart pounding, tell me this is an exercise, a dream, anything, just let me slip away, this is worse than death.

"Yahya Sayyid Al-Jabal?" one of the men said in a broad American accent. "That's your name?"

Johnny didn't answer.

"I asked you a question," said the man, a touch louder.

"No, sir," Johnny said. "My name is John Omar Berg."

"Nationality?"

"Norwegian."

"OK," the man said through his balaclava, still no aggression in his voice. "We have some questions we need answered."

The other man, also masked, but more powerfully built, took over. He spoke in an everyday tone, as though talking about repairing a washing machine, with a typical southern states drawl.

"We can do this in one of two ways. You'll prefer the first."

Johnny stared at the rugged grey stone wall.

"You travelled into Iraq and Syria under the name Al-Jabal," the heavier guy continued. "According to Kurdish self-government authorities you registered at the border crossing in Erbil on September 12th last year. But now you're saying that Al-Jabal isn't your name?"

Johnny closed his eyes again, leaned his head back and put his hands over his face.

"I can't go into the details of my mission," he said. "But it can be confirmed by my superiors."

The Americans pressed on. "What were you doing here?"

What was his vow of confidentiality worth now? Nothing. "I was there, er, to take out a Norwegian foreign fighter."

"What was his name?"

"His name was Abu Fellah, and the Norwegian authorities can confirm what I'm saying."

In the past year, large numbers of Western Muslims had streamed into the region to help build the newly declared "caliphate". The alarm had gone off in the security services. The fear now was that these battle-hardened malcontents would decide to return to their homelands.

The man shook his head slowly, his facial features taking vague shape under his balaclava. "We've made enquiries. Neither Norway nor any other allies can confirm this wild story of yours."

Johnny felt his throat tighten; breathing seemed impossible. Everything came to an end, even the luck that had kept him alive so far. For ten years he had worked for the Norwegian intelligence services in the world's most dangerous places – Afghanistan, Libya and Iraq. He had been awarded medals for his service. It had often been a close-run thing, but *God is Norwegian*, wasn't that what they said?

Bullshit.

"I'll ask you again," the interrogator continued. "What were you doing here?"

After years of service, he was burned out and disillusioned. The Middle East was going to hell anyway, whether the West intervened or not. Their efforts were either pointless or making a bad situation worse.

A year ago he had been contacted by an officer who asked him to undertake an assignment outside official channels. A mission of the greatest national importance, for which there was no political will in Norway, the "nation of peace". His job was to travel to Kurdistan, pick up a US weapon purchased at the bazaar in the capital, link up with a former US special forces soldier who was fighting IS down there, and cross no man's land to the IS-controlled town where Fellah lived. The fact that he was going without the nation's blessing was never made explicit.

Memories of what had happened came back to him in flashes, images flitting across his retina, accompanied by sweats and palpitations. The low house, tinted green through the night optics, the air-conditioned rooms, the dusty carpets, the muffled shots and the gaze of two small children in the hallway outside.

No, Johnny could not deal with that particular image. He pushed it away.

They had been discovered just before they reached the tall grass in no man's land. They had accomplished their mission, but the American was shot and killed. Johnny fled, but when he got back to the Kurdish side, he was arrested by the Kurdish militia. Exactly what had happened was impossible to say. He assumed IS had put it out over the radio that one of their own had disappeared. It was revenge for what he had done; it was common knowledge that the warring parties listened in to each other's communications, there was a good chance the Kurds would take him for the missing IS fighter.

It worked. The Kurds took him to an internment camp for terrorists, before letting the Americans take over. Which was why he was here, in this windowless room, with a man who did not believe his story.

It dawned on him how hopeless his situation was. His mission had been unofficial, *deniable,* and those on the Norwegian side who could have spoken up for him had not. He was just a dark-haired Norwegian with brown skin and Arab roots, who had apparently lost faith in the West's military actions.

The Norwegian authorities could give him medals for bravery. His hand might be shaken by generals, government ministers and even royalty. But deep down he knew he would always be a foreigner in their eyes. All brown Norwegians knew that. When you were brave in battle or scored for the national team, you were one hundred per cent Norwegian. But when things went wrong, you were nothing but that little dago, darkie, muzzy, chink, the fourteen-year-old forced to run from the neo-Nazis and hide in a bush, teeth chattering. Norwegians loved the integrated, ingratiating foreigners who went skiing in the winter, sang and waved the flag on May 17th and ate pork ribs on Christmas Eve, but they also liked to have their prejudices confirmed: *We should have known he couldn't be trusted.*

He was the perfect scapegoat.

The Americans pulled a tight black hood over his head. They laid him out on the sloping bench. Then one of them fastened the straps over the three diagonal scars on his chest, so he was unable to move.

Apart from the sloshing sound as the watering cans were lifted from the floor, it was silent. Everything was black. He felt the lukewarm water being poured over his face, before it ran down into the black hood and slowly filled his nostrils.

He held his breath. Held it until his lungs screamed and his intestines twisted in pain. Then he blacked out.

He thought of Ingrid. Since he had become a father, it was only the dreams of his daughter that kept him alive when things got rough. Sometimes she felt so close he could stroke her dark, shoulder-length hair. She sat beside him on the edge of his metal bed among the orange-clad prisoners, dangling her little legs, with grazed knees and grubby toes, or placed her dolls in elaborate rows against the cell wall and combed their hair or scolded them. She was so close when she padded over to the washbasin with her soft baby steps to brush her teeth with pink tooth-paste, then she was suddenly gone, like a mirage on a desert road. She was his flesh and blood, she had his features, a mixture of Norwegian and something foreign, whose true origins even he did not know.

The human instinct not to breathe water into one's lungs is so strong that it overrides the fear of running out of oxygen.

When he finally gave in, he had no idea whether he was breathing in or out, only that his airways were filling with water and that he was drowning, as helpless as someone trapped in the depths of a sinking ship. The instinct not to breathe underwater was also strong enough to make him say anything, absolutely anything, to get away.

Nobody could hold out against this.

Who was responsible for his lying here? That the mission had gone wrong was on him, but for the men who had issued the order to fail to lift a finger was unforgivable. If he ever found those responsible, he would devote the rest of his life to ensuring that they would endure the same thing, that they would have to lie here, on a wooden bench in a dark cellar, and feel the water running into their airways.

"I . . . I . . ."

The two men lifted him into a sitting position. Johnny drew breath and roared in fear and pain.

"My name is John Omar Berg, I worked in the Marines and as an intelligence officer. Using the name . . . Yahya Al-Jabal . . . I came here to join Islamic State."

"Excellent. Take him back to the Kurds."

4

WHAT KIND OF PROSE IS THIS?

Olav had returned from his morning swim and was standing with one foot up on the bench rubbing Spenol into his inside thigh when he heard his son outside.

On the morning he got news of the death, he had realised at once what had happened. He had always known deep down that his mother would take her own life. He had known it for seventy-five years. Waited for it. Heard her screams in the night as a child. Hoped they would stop. His mother had ended her days in the water, just as his father had.

There were only four days to go before the funeral and there was still a lot to organise. He had to keep control, maintain the status quo. It was Vera who had established Rederhaugen and laid the foundations for SAGA's position. Her death could trigger fresh questions that might lead back to the dark years, and from there open the abyss onto the war.

No. Olav took a deep breath.

One thing at a time, he thought. He must address the questions surrounding his mother's death in the same way he solved any problem, calmly and systematically.

He had furnished the family lawyer, Siri Greve, with full powers to collect Vera's will from the Oslo courthouse.

She was due back any minute now, and he feared what it might contain.

In recent years he had talked to his mother only once a year, on his birthday at the end of July, and she had always cried. In Olav's view their conflict had one clear cause. Where for him family was paramount, she had always put herself first.

He was torn from his thoughts when the door opened behind him. He saw Sverre in the misted-up mirror. The older Sverre got, the more he looked like old pictures of himself, but there was something weak and evasive in his personality that a photograph could not capture, like the difference between a real Rolex and a good copy.

"You here?" he said, continuing to rub the Spenol into his thigh. He had thought that the armed forces would lick his son into shape and prepare him for the duties that awaited him at SAGA. It had not gone that way: Sverre had come home from his tour abroad pale and shaking.

His son nodded, seemingly uneasy at the sight of him naked.

"The pastor sent me an email last night with a draft of the eulogy. I've printed it out."

Olav wrapped a towel round his waist, took the printout and started reading.

"*Vera Lind has left this mortal coil,*" he read. "Sverre?" he said, waving the document in the air. "What the hell is this?"

His son stared down at the wet floor.

"*She has laid down her burden* . . . What kind of prose is this? This is dross, Sverre! Mother was an author. Language was her tool. She would rather have cut off her right hand than write such a piece!"

"An author?" Sverre objected. "It's nearly fifty years since she published anything. And those are the pastor's words, not mine."

"Do I look like I give a shit about Norwegian priests? A bunch of godless, lesbian socialists the lot of them. Your job was to provide a few bullet points about Vera that not even a priest could get wrong. This is worthless trash."

Olav screwed the speech into a ball and flung it in the bin.

"I'll ask Alexandra to arrange another meeting with the pastor. If she's not up to it, we'll get someone else. Or get Alexandra to write it herself."

"You asked me, not Sasha," Sverre said glumly.

Olav sprayed his neck with cologne.

"The Danes export bacon, the French export wine, and Norway exports oil and salmon. You understand? If we had to infiltrate a war zone and take out a Taliban leader at a thousand metres with a sniper rifle, I would of course ask you. I have huge respect for what you did in Afghanistan, Sverre."

His son didn't answer.

"We all have our own talents. Dear old Adam Smith would call it a division of labour. It was wrong of me to ask you in the first place." He smiled. "My mistake."

Sverre stared at him with dark eyes. It irritated Olav massively that his son never retaliated. He was clearly offended now, though Olav had only told the truth. You had to in the long run.

Olav had raised Sverre as his heir apparent from when he was little. He often threw the terrified boy into cold water, where he screamed and thrashed about like a fish on a line. If he took a few years to get over this tough treatment, that was his issue. Olav had expected him to see the value of "cold-water habituation" as he got older, but he never did.

Olav had always assumed he would step down as SAGA CEO and the foundation's chair at the usual retirement age. But time flew by without his finding the right moment or a worthy heir. He informed his children and colleagues that seventy was the new pensionable age. But come his splendid birthday party, attended by the king and prime minister, Olav had raised his glass and declared that after much reflection he had decided to "extend his term" yet again.

He was well within his rights, both formally and legally. SAGA's articles of association gave him the right to extend his term of office indefinitely. And without him, the family would just be another of those wealthy old dynasties with massive properties, a stack of debts and no cash flow.

"It was an attempt to say something about someone who meant something to us," Sverre said. "Not a prime minister's New Year speech."

Olav put an arm round his son's shoulders. "The New Year speech is always ghastly. Norwegian politicians' speeches are about as passionate as committee reports."

"I've no plans to be a politician."

"Good. Politicians are elected for a few years, get a taste for power, then vanish into oblivion. Look at the people I served in government with. All forgotten, bar the odd exception. A has-been politician is as sad a sight as a bankrupt TV star or a drug-addicted ex-athlete. But you're a survivor, Sverre. A boxer with a granite chin. If you're going take over here someday, you'll have to handle worse criticism than this. When I was defence minister, the vultures were circling me twenty-four hours a day. Life is a struggle, Sverre, life is an ice bath; you either drag yourself ashore or you drown. Come on, now."

They stepped into the corridor. A winding staircase at the end led up to Olav's office in the rose tower. Instead, they took the staircase opposite it to the library, where the family were now gathering to go through the issues and duties related to Vera's death.

Siri Greve was leaning against the rough brick wall at the top of the stairs. As usual she was wearing a figure-hugging suit that emphasised her long legs, in a marine blue that contrasted with her wavy blonde hair.

From the look she gave him, Olav knew things were serious.

"Go ahead, Sverre. Give me a moment with Siri," he said, waving his son away.

Sverre disappeared without a word as Olav crossed the granite floor.

"You look like the bearer of bad news."

"I'm afraid this could get complicated," Siri said.

"The settlement of an estate is never easy," he said, as if trying to postpone the discomfort.

"The will has gone."

Olav stood with his hands in his pockets. A bad taste rose up from his throat, a feeling that he was no longer in control.

He had steeled himself for unpleasant surprises in the will, but not for this.

"A will doesn't just vanish," he said. "I thought it was in safekeeping with the Oslo County Court?"

"Quite right. Vera Lind left her will at the courthouse decades ago," Siri replied.

"But then it should just be a matter of getting access to it?"

"The probate officer has confirmed in writing that your mother already signed for the will," said Siri, waving a piece of paper. "Vera fetched it the day she committed suicide."

Olav ran two fingers over the tip of his nose and mouth before they landed under his chin. "Mother fetches her will, then goes and throws herself off High Cliff?"

"It's hard to comprehend," Siri said. "But yes."

He put his hands back in his pockets and began to pace up and down the landing.

"What's the worst-case scenario here?"

This was his customary approach, his trade secret: whenever nuclear weapons experts or climate scientists gave lectures at SAGA, Olav asked how bad it *could* get, and based his strategies on that.

"Vera may have wanted to get rid of the will, that's one possibility. Worst-case scenario, she's written a new, legally binding will, one that benefits other branches of the family."

"Hans and the bloody Bergen crowd," muttered Olav.

The Oslo branch of the family, first under Vera's bohemian influence and later under his own supervision, had grown hugely wealthy on the various income streams from the SAGA Group. The foundation had added something yet more valuable: influence. How long would it last?

"Well, that's how things stand now." Siri nodded towards the library. "Clock's ticking. Shall we?"

5

SUBSTANTIAL ASSETS

"The question is where the deceased should be laid to rest."

This was something Sasha had strong feelings about. She raised a hand. The funeral director was a plump, red-faced middle-aged man in a dark suit.

Four days had passed since she had discovered her grandmother's body, and the image of her that morning – on her stomach on the shore, her quilted vest with its coat of arms stained dark green in the water – had come to her every day and night since. Sasha had never found a dead person before; she had never even seen one.

But she could handle trauma. Worse by far were the feelings of guilt that washed over her now. Vera had behaved oddly from the moment Sasha asked the naive and idiotic question about whether she might consider talking about the shipwreck. And she had ended it all that night.

"How about Æreslunden at Our Saviour's?" suggested Sverre.

"That's lost its shine," murmured Olav. "Either it's full, or it's gone out of fashion with the dead."

"Daddy," said Sasha sharply. "You can't talk like that."

"Father's in Vestre cemetery," Olav continued. "Vestre's not bad. A joint grave would be the most natural thing."

"I don't agree," Sasha said.

All eyes turned to her. Their meeting was being held in the library's atrium, a bright, circular room around five metres in diameter. Sunlight penetrated the long, narrow window that went all the way around the room, blinding her where she sat. The ceiling was dominated by biblical motifs from the Books of Kings. Beneath the window, shelves reached down to a finely polished light granite floor, and there were reading areas with deep chairs in the centre of the room, where the family now sat.

"What's the basis for your disagreement?" asked Olav.

"I'd suggest a memorial grove at High Cliff," his daughter said. "Grandma's ashes should be scattered over the fjord here."

The funeral director blinked nervously and noted it down. "Over the fjord. Right."

Olav ignored him and glanced over at the lawyer. "Siri, where does the law stand on this idea?"

"It's possible in theory, as long as the ash isn't scattered over a densely populated area or an area of the sea with heavy traffic from leisure boats."

The funeral director moved on to the practicalities of the funeral itself: the mahogany-stained cherrywood coffin, which photograph of Vera to use in the memorial programme, the hiring of musicians for the church service and reception.

"How about the Sølvguttene Choir?" Olav asked. "I want them in the church."

The funeral director hesitated. "They're very popular. I think it'll be difficult at short notice."

"OK," Olav said irritably, glancing down at his Rolex Daytona watch, fastened with a ski strap in red, white and blue. "I'll phone the conductor myself. My son will call your office if we have any more questions."

The man nodded and hurried out.

It was "typical Daddy" to humiliate people like that, but Sasha had lived with it for so long that she barely gave it a thought. One day in the sauna under Rederhaugen, Siri, despite being ten years her senior, had invited Sasha to join her women's network to stand up against the old greybeard's domination of the family.

They should have asked Grandma to join their group too, she being the original feminist, but nobody had ventured to do so. Not that she would have agreed to such a thing. And it was too late now anyway.

Olav cleared his throat. "The aim of our little gathering here, besides dealing with the practicalities of the funeral, is to keep you informed of the legal questions surrounding the administration of Vera's estate. Andrea is still in Sweden, but she'll be home as soon as possible."

Sverre threw a meaningful glance in Sasha's direction; the two siblings were never as close as when they discussed their little sister's irresponsible character. Andrea was the product of her father's short-lived affair in the nineties with a blue-blooded, alcoholic Swedish socialite.

"Alexandra, is Mads coming back early from Asia?" Olav asked.

Sasha shook her head.

When she had told her husband about her grandmother's death, his immediate thought had been to book the first flight home, but she had persuaded him not to. Mads was generally her closest confidant, but it was as though Vera's death made her gravitate towards her flesh and blood. He had only ever known Vera superficially.

Her suicide was an intimate family affair in which he had no place.

"I dissuaded him. But he'll be here for the funeral."

"Good. They're rather important meetings he's attending out there," Olav said. He looked at the others in turn.

"For those of you who may be wondering, we've been in close dialogue with the police since the death. They've followed standard procedure: completed a crime scene investigation, looked through her phone records and interviewed those of us who were here. They've ruled out any possibility of foul play and closed the investigation. That goes without saying, of course, but it's a relief nonetheless."

He glanced over at Siri Greve, with the look of someone sharing a secret. Perhaps Vera had thrown a few hand grenades in her will?

"I want an update on the will," said Sverre.

Sometimes her brother came out with a flash of incisive clarity, but to Sasha's surprise both Siri and her father reacted with fumbling discomfort.

"There are certain complications attached to Mother's will," Olav said.

"Complications?" Sasha and Sverre said in chorus.

"Well," said Siri Greve.

"The will has not surfaced," Olav said. "I've just been informed that Mother picked it up from the courthouse on the day she took her life."

Silence filled the atrium.

For Sasha it was like being hit with a hammer on the back of the head. She felt utterly dazed.

What the fuck? Did this new information make her more guilty, or less? Not in the legal sense of the word, but morally. It was impossible to say. It was just so weird. To reward one person, or disinherit another, was at least a logical response to shifting family dynamics.

But to remove your will and then take your own life?

It made no sense. And she was unable to shake off the feeling that this all stemmed from what she had said.

"But why?" said Sverre.

"I don't know. One hypothesis is that she didn't want to leave a will at all," Olav said. "Why else would she pick it up?"

"What does this mean legally?" continued his son.

Siri Greve got up. Her family had acted as legal representatives for the Falck family for generations. Olav had little trust in outsiders. And Siri not only had the right pedigree, she was also an outstanding lawyer who had been a partner in a leading firm before Olav had lured her over to SAGA.

"The rules of intestacy, that is, if the testator has not left a valid will, favour the living heirs, in this case Olav. Thus far, we're operating on the hypothesis that Vera intended to leave a will, but it has not yet come to light. To understand what's really at stake, we need to be clear about what Vera actually owned, and what she had no claim over."

"What about SAGA?" said Sverre.

"Vera did not own SAGA. Its assets are regulated separately. You know the details. Olav controls the company, and each of the three children owns a smaller share. The same applies to the Bergen branch of the family. As you know, the existing shareholders have first refusal in the event of a sale. So, you needn't worry about the SAGA Group."

"Father knew how important it was to allow the family to maintain control over time," Olav added, nodding.

Like the Falck patriarchs before him, Olav had always been obsessed with his legacy. When, as a new grandfather, he visited Sasha in the hospital after Camilla was born, he had lifted the little bundle in his arms and said: "A new generation. There's nothing more beautiful!"

Siri looked at the others. "Vera's estate, whether it's decided by statutory inheritance rules or by testamentary inheritance, primarily comprises the family properties: Hordnes in Bergen, the Hunting Lodge up at Ustaoset and of course Rederhaugen. We're talking about substantial assets here."

Substantial assets was the understatement of the day; even the so-called Hunting Lodge was in reality an entire summer estate.

"Just out of interest," said Sverre, "how much are these properties worth?"

Siri smiled politely. Sasha could see how irritating she found her brother. "Well. It's easy to estimate the price of a two-bed apartment or an even a villa, because the market's so big and there's constant turnover. But the Hunting Lodge, Hordnes and Rederhaugen? These are three of the country's most unique properties, worth whatever a potential buyer is willing to pay. And there aren't many such buyers."

Sverre leaned forward in his chair. "Have any of you talked to the Bergenites?"

"No doubt they held a begging bowl out to Mother," said Olav.

Money had been tight for the Bergen branch of the family during the shipping crisis of the seventies. The old

47

Hordnes estate out near Fana Fjord had been on the verge of a forced sale. Vera bought the property and let them live there for a peppercorn rent, but their cash flow was, according to Olav, so limited that they could barely pay their electricity bills.

"Are you worried that Vera may have left one or more of the properties to the Bergen branch?" said Sasha.

"It's one possibility," Siri said.

Olav got up and began to pace about the atrium restlessly.

"Hans and the Bergen side knew that Vera was still registered as the owner of our properties. Hans chases after any bit of skirt, and now he's tried his wicked ways on an eccentric ninety-five-year-old. It's hard to find a better definition of the word *depraved*."

Even the closest families could lose their powers of reason in the face of an inheritance dispute. But Sasha had thought hers would be able to maintain some dignity. How naive she had been. At times, it was exhausting to be a Falck.

"Those are terrible accusations, Daddy," she said. "We have no idea what's happened here. This is speculation and worst-case spiralling."

"Hans and the Bergen lot have been out to get us since before you were born, Sasha. They've never got over how badly they played their cards back in the seventies."

"It's still just speculation," Sasha said. "We've got a few days before the funeral. If Vera really did collect her will, it must be here somewhere."

"OK, Alexandra. I want you to go systematically through her things at High Cliff," said Olav.

Sasha nodded dutifully.

"Why the rush to find it?" Sverre asked. "Isn't a will irrevocable no matter what?"

"Information is power," Siri said, smiling at Sasha over the table.

Olav turned to his daughter again. "Please let me know the moment you find it."

"Shouldn't we try talking to Hans?" said Sasha. "Perhaps he knows something."

"I doubt he'll be available," said Olav. "He's off somewhere with no phone coverage as usual."

6

DO WE HAVE A DEAL?

The front, Iraqi Kurdistan

"Last chance to go back," the driver said in broken English, lighting a cigarette from the glow of the previous one. "It is too dangerous."

"Keep driving," said Hans Falck, rolling down the window of the old pickup.

The road into the prison zigzagged between caltrops, concrete blocks, armoured vehicles and sandbag defences. Kurdish special forces kitted out in silver-grey American camouflage uniforms stood guard, slapping themselves to keep warm in the cold desert wind.

The dirty grey Land Rover rolled slowly towards the first checkpoint. A soldier in a balaclava and Kevlar helmet indicated for the car to stop; another checked the boot and inside the vehicle for weapons and bombs, then looked under the chassis with a mirror. Then he waved them on down the dusty road.

At the next checkpoint, just a hundred metres on, Hans was ordered out of the car. Dense smoke rose from a rusty oil barrel, settling like a blanket and mixing with the smell of firewood and spiced lamb. This was the smell of the Middle East.

A female soldier ordered Hans to take off his mountain boots, vest and jacket, then searched him and scanned him with a metal detector. She had dark features, with eyes that smouldered in her narrow face.

"What is your business here in the prison?"

"I'm here to talk to your boss," Hans replied, smiling.

She did not return his smile, but led him into a guard-house. At the back of the bare room, behind a metal desk under the red Kurdish star on its yellow background, sat a portly officer in a green work uniform a size too small. Hans put his ID documents on the table, together with his international doctor's pass and a letter of introduction.

The prison director took his time as he leafed through the papers and scratched his beard.

"Let me see now . . . Afghanistan in the 1980s, Lebanon, Gaza, Bosnia, Iraq, Syria. But mostly Kurdistan. I see you are many years a friend to our cause. Co-author, it says, of a field manual to anaesthetics used by doctors in war zones worldwide. An impressive career, Mr Hans."

Hans nodded unenthusiastically.

"But our prison has been inspected by doctors from the Red Crescent many times," the director continued. "They found nothing to criticise here. We treat our enemies better than they treat us. We are civilised people, not beasts. You know the dangers of coming in? If there is trouble, it is not guaranteed we can save you."

"That's a risk I'm willing to take." Hans took a sip of his tea, sweet as syrup. "I have permission from the Norwegian authorities to treat a Norwegian prisoner."

He was still unable to bring himself to use the name Yahya Al-Jabal in reference to Johnny Berg; the man for whom he had been searching for several months now, ever since HK had whispered to him that he had disappeared in Syria.

"An extremely dangerous individual, subject to the strictest security," the director explained. "We got him from the Americans, after they gave him a good going-over. Most of our Western prisoners are uneducated men with a history of petty crime. Riff-raff, scum, sadists, crooks, yes, but not the sharpest knives, as they say. Al-Jabal is different. His background is in the Norwegian special forces, from what I understand. Speaks Arabic and some Kurdish and knows enough about our culture to pass as a sympathiser. May I ask why exactly Al-Jabal needs to be seen by you?"

"The Hippocratic oath demands that I treat everyone, friend or enemy," Hans replied calmly, sipping his tea. "I'm concerned about his health."

Berg was, according to the Norwegian authorities, presumed dead. But Hans's old friend in the service had heard a rumour that he was rotting in a Kurdish jail accused of being a jihadist. The situation here made him uneasy. The Kurds had always, and not without reason, felt betrayed and stabbed in the back by their foreign allies. Their paranoia had only grown in recent years, when they had been left to hold the front line almost single-handedly against the Islamists.

The prison director got up and went into a side room, the smell of his sweat settling over the room like a cloud. After what seemed like an eternity he returned.

"I am sorry, Mr Hans," he said. "I've discussed it, but it's not possible."

Hans settled back in the chair, with his hands serving as a headrest. A "no" down here was not the same as in Europe.

"Call the health minister in Erbil and explain the situation," Hans said. He searched his phone for the contact and handed it to the prison director. "He's a good friend."

The man stared at the screen for a long time, without a word, before handing back the mobile.

"Call him yourself."

Hans rang the number but got through to an answering machine. He cursed under his breath.

"It is impossible," the director of the prison repeated, dropping another sugar cube in his tea.

Hans took a deep breath and played his last card. "I came to the Sinjar mountains last summer, just after the massacres and the ethnic cleansing, as one of a handful of Western doctors. I don't know if you followed it in the international press, but if you're in any doubt about my loyalty to those who fight so bravely against the jihadists, I'd say in all modesty that I've done more for the Kurdish cause than most. Give me a little time with the prisoner, and you have one problem less in your prison before nightfall."

The director stared at him for a long time.

"OK, Mr Hans," he said, at last. "You have one hour."

The prison was built in grey concrete, with narrow gun slits and small, high glassless windows.

It was just days since Vera had called him. Hans had always liked her. Their close bond went back to the spring of 1970, when Hans was a high school student and Vera was working on a manuscript that had taken her to the old Falck estate by Fana Fjord. A manuscript that had never been published.

Vera had called two days before committing suicide, and he had thought afterwards that she seemed somewhat preoccupied and doom-laden, the way people often are before they make a fateful decision.

They had talked for almost ten minutes, and she said there were things she could not discuss over the phone.

That was the last he heard from her.

There was something rotten about it all, and this was another reason to find and talk to Johnny Berg. It might seem strange that a young Norwegian jailed for being a foreign soldier could play a part in an inheritance dispute surrounding a ninety-five-year-old author. But that was the way of it.

A guard unlocked an iron gate and let him in. Two sluice gates beyond that, and he was standing before the prisoners' accommodation unit.

He was led along a corridor of cells, the stench of sweat and excreta and rotten meat growing stronger the further they went. A shard of light fell from a small window high on the wall onto bare turquoise and white walls. Through the hatches he could see the prisoners, all wearing orange jumpsuits. The cells were clearly overcrowded. A smell of disease and untreated infections choked the air, evidence of a lack of drugs and medical equipment. Hans glimpsed prisoners limping about with severed limbs, and others who looked on the verge of death.

As a doctor, Hans was used to almost everything, but when the guard opened the final door, he almost vomited.

The cell might be designed for about twenty people, but there had to be several times that number crammed in here. Undernourished old men with bird-like ribcages sat playing cards with young boys with amputated limbs, a teenager crooned a doleful song in something resembling Flemish, others coughed and tended to their wounds, applying tourniquets or dirty bandages. A man with a patch over one eye swung across the floor on crutches. Some of the prisoners tried to make eye contact with Hans and shouted, "*Sahafi!*" – journalist – while others ran their index fingers across their throats on seeing him.

The smell was strongest deep inside the room. Here, it stank of death. Around the French toilet in the floor hung towels and jackets.

"He's over there," said the guard, pointing. He kicked a young man who was sitting in the lotus position. "Get up, Al-Jabal!"

Johnny was sitting near a turquoise brick wall with his eyes closed and palms up, as though in meditation. Like his fellow inmates, he was wearing an orange prisoner uniform, of the type IS dressed their hostages in before execution. The Kurds' way of sticking two fingers up at IS, no doubt. Even though his symmetrical face was grey and emaciated, Johnny was a beautiful boy. Or man: he was in his early thirties now. A lightly arched nose ended in broad lips, sharp cheekbones protruded over a thick beard, and his dark, greasy hair lay over his shoulders. He opened his eyes. Johnny gazed up at Hans for a long time. It was impossible to gauge his mental state from his expression.

Hans had a clear memory of the last time they had met. During the Israeli bombing of Lebanon in 2006, Johnny Berg, then a young freelance journalist, had interviewed him. A good interview, one of the better ones. Hans had not suspected that Berg was working in intelligence back then, but he was certain now.

"I've come to examine you," Hans said. "Good to see you again. That was a great article."

Johnny held his gaze for some time, still without saying a word. Then he closed his eyes again and breathed calmly through his nose.

The Kurdish soldier looked around nervously; they had started to attract attention from the other prisoners.

Although Johnny was thin and malnourished, you could see that he had once been very fit. He had three long, diagonal scars across his ribcage, and just below the shoulder there were two healed bullet holes where the skin was slightly darker.

Hans measured Johnny's resting pulse, his heart rhythm and blood pressure, before taking a blood sample from his middle finger.

"Listen to me now," said Hans, placing his hands over the young man's hands. "When I was your age, I took every overseas assignment I could get. But I'm getting old now. Did you ever hear of anyone saying on their deathbed that they regretted not having made more money or taken more undercover assignments in the Middle East?"

"Why are you saying this?" Johnny said.

"You have a daughter."

Finally, Johnny looked up.

"Don't make the same mistake I did," Hans continued. "I'll demand your release as a Norwegian on grounds of ill health. The Kurds will be more than happy to get rid of a foreign fighter and disease carrier."

"Why are you helping me?" asked Johnny after a long pause.

"My Hippocratic oath."

"You know that's a load of crap," Johnny said, shaking his head.

"You've been the subject of a gross injustice."

"True. But that's not why you're here."

"Johnny, Johnny! I can see you're not giving up. Alright," Hans said, "you're going to do me a favour when you get back to Norway. I won't go into detail now, but that's my offer. Freedom, in exchange for you doing me a favour."

The prisoner tilted his head, as if thinking about it.

"You still have your supporters in Norway," Hans continued. "People who thought you were dead and are shocked at how you've been treated. Two police officers will escort you to Norway. Do as I say, and you'll be in European airspace before nightfall."

"How can I trust you?" Johnny said, looking up with his clear green eyes.

"You can't", said Hans. "But I don't see that you've got much choice in your current situation. Do we have a deal?"

7

A TOAST! TO MOTHER!

On the evening before the funeral, Sasha heard footsteps outside the writing cottage on High Cliff. Shortly afterwards, someone rapped the horseshoe knocker hard on the heavy wooden door, but before she could open it, the door was flung open and a figure made its entrance in the dark.

Olav was dressed in knee-high wellingtons, a fleece and overtrousers with leather patches on the knees.

He stepped across the creaking floor. "Have you found anything from Mother yet, Alexandra?"

Ever since Sasha was a little girl there had always been something of the fairy tale about her visits to Grandma. Yes, the objective world existed, even for Vera, but it was the world of engineers, physicists and doctors, and was far less interesting to her than our descriptions of it. It was the stories we had told each other around the campfire from ancient times that made us human, stories that eventually became books, books that found their way onto Vera's bookshelves at High Cliff, a timeless world her father had now shaken her out of.

She had spent the last few days in this room. She had shunted the kids off to school in the mornings and ensured that a babysitter was there for them in the afternoon. She had been home briefly today, however, to dig out some clothes for the funeral: black velvet dresses and patent leather shoes for the girls, a dark suit with matching tie for Mads. His plane would land just hours before it began, and he would be pleased to find an outfit hanging up and ready to go. They both liked to make little gestures to show they cared. But other than that she had been at High Cliff.

To search through every single book in any large library was a challenge, and Vera's collection was massive. The walls of her little writing room were lined with what Sasha estimated to be a hundred metres of bookshelves. And then there were the taped-up cardboard boxes down in the potato cellar and the numerous files of correspondence with her publisher.

Her fingertips felt as if they had been sanded smooth by all the books she had leafed through. Some were signed by fellow authors, some well known, others less so. There were countless novels, books on history, sociology and economics, as well as more esoteric writings about myths and astrology. Out of their pages rose the memories.

"I've found everything imaginable," Sasha said. "Apart from the will."

"I called the courthouse," said her father, "to check that Mother really *did* collect the will and that Siri wasn't misleading us. But there's no doubt."

"Don't you trust Siri?" Sasha asked.

Her father smiled. "More than most. But, then again, she's not family."

It was getting dark, the surface of the fjord was bluish black like oil. Far away, on the other side, she saw some faint lights on the crest of the hill that rose from the water's edge, and behind that a grey evening sky.

"Are you feeling sad, Alexandra?"

Her father looked at her with the sensitive and open gaze that he had now and then, which conjured childhood feelings of security and deep affection, memories of creeping up into his lap.

"Yes," she said, looking away. "I suppose I am."

Sasha had always been the apple of Grandma's eye. When she was small, Vera used to give her ten kroner in pocket money. Sverre had to settle for five, or nothing, because Sasha was the only one in the family who understood literature and stories. Only she had the finely tuned gaze and quiet power that a writer needed to possess. Sasha always took pride in this and had never understood why her grandmother stopped writing.

One memory kept coming back to her. She could not have been more than ten or eleven years old, but she could picture it vividly. They were reading a Greek myth, about Iris, the messenger of the gods, when Grandma suddenly pricked up her ears. They heard a noise outside. It grew louder. It sounded like a baby crying, a wailing, piercing sound. Grandma had started to cry.

"Why are you crying?" Sasha asked. "It's just cats mating."

Grandma had looked at Sasha. "It may just be that to other people. But not for us. For a writer, truth is the image reality creates in the mind. Where you might think of a cat, I think of a child in pain. And it can be just as true."

Olav was leafing through a scrapbook of old newspaper cuttings. "It goes without saying that Mother kept all her reviews," he said with bittersweet sadness, reading some aloud. "'A measured and confident debut'. 'Dark and magnificent from our new coastal bard'."

The two collections of short stories Verd Lind published in the fifties were well received without attracting much attention. It was only later, when a couple of her stories were put on the national curriculum, that they became cult classics. During the sixties she wrote a series of suspense novels and was hailed as "Norway's Daphne du Maurier". They had sold well before her literary production dried up suddenly in about 1970.

"How famous was Grandma really?"

"Not as famous as she thought she ought to be," said Olav, laughing.

"It's strange that she stopped writing," Sasha said.

Her father did not answer, but went into the kitchenette and dug out a dusty bottle of aquavit. He filled two shot glasses, sat at the end of the desk, and pushed one towards her.

"Did you know it was the Germans who built this cottage when they requisitioned Rederhaugen?"

Sasha sipped the aquavit. It made her shudder.

"After the war Vera decided to turn it into a writing cottage," he continued. "The log walls and notched corners at the front are all part of those improvements. But you can still see the original materials in the wall facing the forest."

He pointed, but Sasha interrupted him. "I know almost nothing about that time. Grandma barely talked about it, and neither did you."

Olav took a swig of aquavit and stared dolefully at her.

"Because it hurt."

"Hurt?" She gazed straight into her father's furrowed face, where a deep line had appeared above his bushy eyebrows.

"How best to describe it?" He glanced uneasily out of the window. "Mother wasn't a mother the way you are. She was distant. Warm and cold all at once. I was largely left in the care of a governess when she was away. She went to the south of France for the whole winter once. A whole winter . . . She *had* to write, she said. I remember how I cried the day she left. I was nine years old. Can you imagine? I stood there on the platform of Østbane station and wept."

Sasha saw a little Olav standing on a long platform with the train rolling slowly out of the station. She put her hand on his.

"Mother used to scream at night," he continued. "It was long before the refurbishment. The main house was empty and cold back then, and very echoey, so her cries reverberated through the corridors to the room where I lay. She screamed, without warning. Every night she sat up in bed and screamed."

"Didn't she get any help?"

"She didn't want it. And there wasn't the same awareness about these things as there is now. Once when I was twelve, maybe thirteen, I couldn't take it any longer. I stood on the mezzanine in the main house with a rope round my neck. I thought I would be free if I threw myself over the railings. That death was just a step away. That death was black, that death was nothing."

"Oh, Daddy," Sasha said, stroking his shoulder.

"Things got better. They always get better, Alexandra. Next morning I woke up with an extraordinary feeling. Yes, I was still terrified about what Mother might do, as I was all throughout my life. But I was free. Something inside me had recognised that we shape our own destiny."

There was so much Sasha wanted to ask, but she was too overwhelmed by what he had just said.

"Only when you were growing did I experience the same fear again. You were the spitting image of her in old photographs. I didn't want you to have a life like hers. And you didn't turn out like her, Alexandra. You have the qualities my forebears were known for. Yes, perhaps you're like me on a good day. You're intelligent and visionary, of course, but you have something else too, something more important. You have character. Values. Loyalty. You're calm under pressure. You think twice before you talk, and let people guess what you're thinking."

Sasha smiled at her father. It was almost pathological. He only ever saw himself though other people's eyes. He constantly saddled others with his own emotions, the atmosphere in any room was dependent on his mood. And yet she loved him, in a way that couldn't be compared to how she felt for anyone else. Not Mads, not her siblings. Not even her love for her children; it was so much less complex.

"I found a book about the sinking of the Hurtigruten ferry," she said, picking up *Writings About the Princess Ragnhild Shipwreck*. "There's a chapter on the marine investigation at the Salten District Court that took place the day after the disaster."

"It makes for painful reading," said Olav, leafing through it. He put on the reading glasses that hung around his neck and read aloud. "'With the explosion the ship was lifted out of the water, so the captain was thrown in the air and landed on the bridge deck. He got back onto his knees, but was immediately flung down again, falling onto his left side. The captain assumes the explosion was due to a mine. He adds that he had never experienced this before. He did, however, witness torpedoing in the last war, and this explosion did not unfold in the same way. He bases his conclusion that it was a mine on the deep thudding'—"

"But are we really so sure it was?" asked Sasha.

"As sure as we can be when it comes to historical events. Everyone who's ever written about it draws the same conclusion. And look what Captain Brækhus says here."

He read on slowly: " 'The captain is of the opinion that everything points to this as the cause. It seems likely that the accident site lies in a minefield laid by the British on April 8, 1940.' "

"To think the British were responsible for Grandfather's death," said Sasha.

Olav nodded. "But on the positive side, Alexandra, just imagine: my mother leaped into that freezing cold sea with me in her arms. If she hadn't, I wouldn't be sitting here tonight."

He smiled. "And neither would you."

Sasha had not felt this close to her father for a long time.

"The last time I saw Grandma," she confided, "I asked her if she'd speak about the Hurtigruten disaster."

A shadow fell across his face. "Mother was a storyteller, not a historian."

"I'm worried that it might be my question that made her throw herself off that cliff."

"No, Alexandra," said Olav. This time it was he who placed a hand on hers. "A murder can have a simple motive, love or hate. The motive for suicide is life itself. And Mother's life was *never* your responsibility."

"There are so many unanswered questions about Grandma," Sasha said. "Not only where she's hidden her will, of course, but who she really was, where she came from, why she stopped writing."

His face hardened. "Listen, Mother's life is a maze. If you get lost in it, you'll never find your way out again." He held her gaze for a long time before breaking into a smile. "A toast! To Mother!"

After a while he got up and put the glasses on the kitchen counter.

"Are you on course for tomorrow's eulogy?"

Sasha nodded. "I think so."

"It'll be good to have the funeral over and done. With it a chapter will close in our family's history. No matter how alluring the secrets of Vera's life may appear – and as with most myth-makers it will look very exciting on the surface – you must promise me one thing, Alexandra."

Sasha felt herself go cold. "And what's that?"

"That you won't look under that rock. Because if you do, everything we've built here could come crashing down."

8

THE WAR CROSS WITH
TWO SWORDS

The prosecution requested that the prison meeting take place behind closed doors, for reasons of national security. Their submission was accepted.

Lawyer Jan I. Rana sat next to the accused. John Omar Berg, or Johnny Berg, as he introduced himself, had arrived in the country just days before, after being escorted out of Kurdistan. His face was still emaciated, and his cheekbones very pronounced, making him look almost lizard-like. But his long black hair was combed back now, and hung neatly down over the back of a traditional Norwegian knitted sweater.

Dressing villains in knitwear, particularly Marius sweaters, might seem cynical. But clichés were clichés because they worked, according to Rana.

The judge was a tall, phlegmatic man in dark dress. With what Rana took to be six generations' confidence from the villas and orchards of West Oslo, he read out the prosecution's requests. These included four weeks in custody with a ban on communication and visits, in accordance with Section 133 of the Penal Code regarding terrorist organisations, and Section 136 regarding travel for terrorist purposes.

"Does the defendant, John Omar Berg, plead guilty or not guilty?" asked the judge, with affected nonchalance.

"Not guilty," Jan I. Rana said.

"Right. Then we'll hear from the prosecution first," said the judge, clearing his throat.

A blonde woman in her late thirties stood up.

"On September 12, 2014, John Omar Berg lands in the Kurdish city of Erbil. This much we know. We also know that he has, over the past few years, expressed an increasingly extreme world view, as shown in an email dated July 23 of that year. I quote: 'I am so disgusted by the role of the West in the Middle East that I feel like enlisting with IS. At least they have some guts,' end quote. Berg has a clear aim: he plans to join this terrorist organisation."

She paused. Rana looked over at Johnny, who was as impassive as a waxwork. There was a serenity to him that Rana had never seen before in anyone sitting in a courtroom, like a Tibetan monk who had meditated non-stop for ten years.

"Therefore, Berg clearly has terrorist intentions," the police lawyer continued. "On the day in question he crosses the front line of the northern Iraqi city of Tel Skuf to meet like-minded Norwegians, who live in a village controlled by Islamic State, among them a wanted Norwegian jihadist and foreign fighter Abu Fellah. What happens when John Berg meets Fellah, no one knows. What *is* known, however, through foreign intelligence, is that he is arrested by Kurdish Peshmerga militia the next morning."

The police lawyer turned to the judge. "The reason the prosecution finds custody vital in this particular case is because of the severity of the charge. But it also has its basis in who John Omar Berg is and his military background."

The judge already seemed bored with the police lawyer's pedestrian speech. She blended in with the
courtroom's minimalist furnishings, thought Rana.

"Berg," she continued, "is a trained Marine Hunter
who worked in the armed forces for a number of years,
with the highest security clearances. That a person with
such a background should decide to join a terrorist organisation increases the gravity of any travel as a foreign
fighter. He represents a terrorist threat. There are multiple reasons, therefore, as to why he must be held in
custody: we know from other European countries that
several prisoners released from the prison in which Berg
was held are presently under investigation for planning
terrorist activities. Furthermore, the prosecution con-
siders the risk of the spoliation of evidence as real and
imminent in this case. Finally, it would be interpreted as
offensive to the public sense of justice if he were to be
released."

With this, she concluded her submission, closed her
document case, and sat down with her hands clasped
neatly in her lap.

Jan I. Rana straightened his tie and dark suit jacket.

His birth name was Mohammed Iqbal Rana, a name
that lent itself to being shortened to Mo-I-Rana, the name
of a town in the far north of Norway, making him an easy
butt of other boys' jokes. The young Mo-I-Rana soon realised that if he was to get anywhere in life, he would have
to stop mugging the local toffs behind Tåsen shopping
centre and play on the Norwegian team. Besides which,
half of Oslo would soon be called Mohammed. He needed
a Norwegian name. He considered Tormod. Or perhaps
Bjørn. But they sounded fake. Totally alien to him.

Then he discovered that Jan was Norway's most common name. And also the Persian word for soul.

A perfect name.

Jan I. Rana became a bookworm. He kept himself to himself at law school. The ambitious Pakistanis who eventually took over the faculty regarded him as a lower life form. To the well-heeled students from the elegant villas he was just another foreigner, a kid from the concrete estates on the east side of Oslo. He could never be one of them. A Stang or Falsen, a Lütken or Stoud Platou, Smith, Collett, or Bull . . . Their lineage went back to the aristocracy, all of them Eidsvoll men and Supreme Court justices. In fact, his own pedigree could be traced back to the Indian Rajput, to the warrior caste, but to a Norwegian that meant nothing.

Instead, Jan I. Rana began to cultivate the image of a man with Norwegian working-class roots. He boasted to the female law students in the beer cellar that his ancestors were railwaymen who built the Bergen line, and that Rana was a common name among Swedes and seventeenth-century Finnish migrants. Pretty soon his suspicions were confirmed; most of his fellow students were lazy and ignorant. They'd believe anything so long as your story was interesting and detailed enough.

Eventually he realised that his background was an advantage. Old friends always needed defence lawyers, and new generations followed on their heels. The caliphate proved a gold mine for him; he should have sent the caliph a company Christmas card every year, since it was his twisted ideology that earned him a living. Which was why he had dropped everything when the celebrity doctor, Hans Falck, had called Rana & Andenæs to ask him to defend an "innocent Norwegian suspect" accused of being a foreign fighter.

Yeah, right, Rana had thought.

With most people accused of being foreign fighters, it was simply a matter of repeating the usual fiction that they had gone out to help women and children, and hope that the prosecution did not have too much evidence to the contrary. John Omar Berg, as he was called, was not interested in that. He had handed Rana a note with the initials "HK" and a phone number. The man behind the initials had given such a strong response that Rana looked forward to presenting the case.

"The prosecution is absolutely right on several points," he began. "John Berg trained as a Marine Hunter, the toughest military unit in the armed forces. It is also correct that Berg worked in the armed forces for some years, and that he crossed the front line over to Islamic State territory. And yes, he has written emails that could be interpreted as supporting IS. And yes, he spent time as a prisoner in a prison with links to terrorist plots. But does that mean that the case is cut and dried? That John Berg should and must be imprisoned?"

Rana looked at the police lawyer and then at the judge. The rhetorical pause that followed was long enough to elicit their interest.

"There's just one problem with the prosecution's story," Rana continued. "And that is: what did Berg do in his years in the armed forces? He worked for the intelligence service."

Rana proceeded to outline Berg's activities in the years from 2006 to 2010, when he was in Afghanistan. "At huge risk to himself, John Berg reveals networks whose sole purpose is to make bombs intended to kill Norwegian soldiers. He's good at what he does. He's outstanding. He is awarded medals for bravery, the War Cross with One Sword, then with Two Swords.

"*Two* Swords," he repeated.

He paused once more. "Only Gunnar Sønsteby has ever been more highly decorated. Berg saves Norwegian lives, defends Norwegian interests. With time, his responsibilities grow. He secures Afghan government ministers, defectors from Iran's Revolutionary Guards and Russian politicians as his sources. In Libya, he works in the tactical air support team, that is, he reconnoitres the territory and reports enemy coordinates to Norwegian and allied fighter planes. And yes – he eventually has moral qualms over the fact that this job results in the loss of civilian life.

"So, what does John Berg do then? Does he defect? No, he does the honourable thing; he informs his superiors of his moral doubts. He goes through the proper channels. He remains loyal, but not obedient.

"For a while we hear nothing more about Berg. He is now a father. He is exhausted from everything he's been through. Tests conducted by the armed forces' chief medical officer reveal that he has symptoms of PTSD. This is the price Berg has paid to defend Norway. But what happens then?"

Rana scratched his head. This was the crux of his defence. "Yes, what then? John Berg gets on a plane to the Kurdish city of Erbil, just as my learned colleague has told us. But what she has failed to offer is anything of substance regarding Berg's motivation for that journey. Yes, she's found an email containing an offhand comment. We would, I suggest to the court, expect at least some evidence of internet radicalisation, or contact with Islamist leaders at home and abroad, or logistical communications about travel or living arrangements. But in John Berg's case? Nothing at all!"

To his satisfaction Rana noticed that the judge had leaned forward a little in his chair.

"Were I prosecuting with such scant evidence, I might have suggested that this was, in itself, proof of how cunning and professional 'Jihadist Berg' is. Perhaps he did something that no known foreign fighter in any Western country has managed to do before: perhaps he went completely under the radar before his departure. Well, if that were the case, unlikely as it is, this court would still find it difficult to sentence him. There's simply no evidence to indicate any intention to join a terrorist organisation. We can say his decision to travel to a country on the government travel warning list was naive. Although again, Berg has also worked in a journalistic capacity, and may have travelled there to report on events. We simply don't know. And that's the point.

"Finally, may I remind the court, that the terms of custody explicitly state that the probability that the accused has done what he is accused of must outweigh any probability to the contrary. Nothing that the prosecution has presented indicates that this is the case. Permit me, therefore, to shed some light here, and to suggest what Berg was *actually* doing."

The police lawyer looked up.

"John Berg was working for the intelligence service," Rana said.

She looked at him suspiciously.

"Berg is *deniable*. What does that mean here? Well, as the court will know, espionage between states is usually regulated by the Vienna Convention. In short, the convention says that if we discover that a foreign power is using diplomats to spy on us, we don't punish those diplomats, we expel them. But people who are 'deniable' enjoy no such luxury."

He paused briefly.

"Yahya Al-Jabal was Berg's cover name in the service. When Berg crossed the front line and went into an IS-controlled area, it was not to join a terrorist organisation. On the contrary: his intention was to do what John Berg has done so brilliantly for all these years. The very thing that has earned him awards for bravery. To protect Norway. To make sure that people like you and I, law-abiding tax-payers, can sleep safely in our beds at night."

How he loved it when the words fell into well-formed sentences that led to a technical knockout.

"And forgive me, but the amount of dirty laundry that will be hung out in public revealing Berg's role as an operator is not something I would relish, were I on the prosecution team."

"Are you finished?" the judge said.

"Just one final word, if I may, Your Honour," said Rana. "John Berg is not only innocent of this charge. He is a hero. A Norwegian hero. While executing his duties *for* Norway, he was abandoned in one of the worst places on the planet, a prison for terrorists, war criminals and jihadists in Syria, and the Norwegian authorities did not lift a finger. And this, Your Honour, is the real crime here."

With that Rana sat down.

The prosecution stood up, to make one last brief comment: "As regards the War Cross with Sword, Your Honour: this award can be withdrawn if the recipient proves unworthy of it. We have recommended that the minister rescind John Berg's, although this decision can only be made by Royal Command, by the King-in-Council."

For the first time during the proceedings Rana noticed a reaction in Johnny. When the War Cross and the king were mentioned, he sat bolt upright, and the colour left his lips. He looked as though he was going to shout something, but he restrained himself.

"Is everyone finished now?" the judge said, yawning as he looked at his watch.

He left the courtroom to deliberate. Rana glanced over at Johnny Berg, who seemed calm again, with his hands in his lap and an inward-looking gaze.

Things were moving quickly now. The judge returned to deliver his decision:

"The court finds that conditions for the charges against the defendant – Section 133 regarding terrorist organisations, and Section 136 regarding travel for terrorist purposes – are not sufficiently met. John O. Berg is released."

Chairs scraped as everyone got up.

Rana turned to Johnny Berg and winked. "There's a table reserved at the Theatercafé, and the champagne's on ice. Shall we go over?"

9

THE DOCTOR'S WARM HANDS

Olav walked across the lawn with his hands deep in his pockets. The service had been a reminder of his own mortality. Funerals and obituaries came thick and fast these days, like road signs as you approached a city. It was inescapable: life was a lemming march and Olav was approaching the precipice. Death was whipping up forces he could no longer control.

Thankfully the formal condolence line outside the church was done with. The worst excesses in the pastor's address had been weeded out. Minibuses had driven right up to the church entrance with the less mobile guests. From the balcony a hired string quartet and an internationally known opera singer had given a rendition of Schubert's "Ave Maria".

Olav had sent a personal note to the king requesting his company at the funeral. In the past, the monarch would sometimes drop in at Rederhaugen, to eat fish balls and watch *Dagsrevyen* while his bodyguards waited in the car. There was status in knowing the king on those terms, and he rarely seemed as content as when he could put his feet on the table and have a beer and cigarette out of the spotlight. He had not responded to the invitation, however.

The time had come to talk to Hans. The sound of the string quartet, now installed on the mezzanine, echoed through Rederhaugen, blending with the hum of voices and the clinking of silver spoons against porcelain. Although Olav had squeezed more hands in his lifetime than most, he loathed large gatherings.

He slipped through the reception rooms at the side of the large hall, nodding graciously left and right. There were people here he had not seen in years, a pageant of faces from his mother's life and his own, most furrowed and ravaged by time.

Why were they all here? What did they want? His children often accused him of holding a cynical view of human nature, but Olav knew better; he was just a realist.

He greeted Johan Grieg, his mother's old publisher and a SAGA board member, pale and stoic from his long battle with Addison's Disease. Johan had once been a friend and brother-in-arms, but wasn't it the destiny of all friendships to endure as shadows of what they had been?

Sitting at a nearby table were some old politicians. Olav had voted Labour all his life. Not that he really liked the Labour Party. He had nothing but contempt for what he considered to be their debating club sensibilities. But there had to be some grown-ups in the room over at party headquarters. And what other choice did one have? The Right? Villa owners and angry little shopkeepers whom he despised almost as much as the minor parties, which one couldn't take seriously anyway.

But where had Hans got to? Olav continued through the hall, past the bay window and into the music room where he heard a woman's voice with a Nordland accent call out.

"Falck. I just wanted to say how much I admire you."

His mood was instantly lifted by the compliment. He turned and walked towards her.

"That's so nice to hear on a day like this."

Standing before him was an elegant, short-haired woman in her seventies, wearing a necklace over a black polo neck. A pained expression had suddenly appeared on her face.

"Oh, forgive me, Olav Falck! My condolences, of course. Your good works have not gone unnoticed . . ."

He stared at her in confusion.

"How embarrassing," she continued. "I thought you were *Hans* Falck."

Only now did Olav spot Hans, as he emerged from behind a pillar a metre or so away. He walked towards the woman with light, springy steps, took her small hand in his large, sinewy doctor's hands and looked deep into her eyes. Personal boundaries clearly did not exist for him.

"Thank you so much, my dear. Do I hear a hint of a Lofoten accent?"

"Moskenes," she said, blushing.

"Oh, I *love* you northerners!" Hans proclaimed, flinging his arms open so wide that people turned to look. "I've often thought during my travels how the hospitality and life-wisdom in the north of Norway reminds me of the Middle East. You're so very different from southerners, thank God."

"I know that you worked as a duty doctor in Flakstad long ago. My father was a doctor up there and he knew Vera Lind."

"Are we talking about the great Dr Schultz?"

Olav grew restless, as he always did when the people around him were better informed than himself. *Dr Schultz.* His mother had mentioned that name before things had gone sour between them.

"Yes, he was my father."

"May he rest in peace," said Hans. "A legendary doctor. A radical, a humanist who devoted his career to improving the lives of the poor in a time before prosperity and the welfare state. Dr Schultz was a role model for me and for every radical and socially aware doctor in the seventies."

The woman was clearly touched by his compliments, while Olav tried to hide his envy. He was increasingly being approached by people who asked if he was related to Hans Falck. There had been a time when the opposite was true. Hans had been a buffoon, a womanising, self-aggrandising, poor little rich boy. He was still a buffoon in Olav's eyes, but in recent years he had become a folk hero for his work in the world's conflict zones. Hans had been the first Westerner to expose the IS massacres in Sinjar-fjellet. He gave the appearance of being upset by the horrors he witnessed, but Olav was sure he enjoyed the attention.

Olav liked to point out that Hans Falck's sympathy for the world's oppressed was inversely proportional to his concern for his nearest and dearest, spread about the country and across generations as they were.

"And, I'll say this much," the woman continued, still addressing Hans. "You were absolutely right to turn down the St Olav's Medal."

"But of course. We socialists have a long tradition of turning down these bourgeois titles. There's a principle at stake."

Had Hans really turned down the St Olav?

Olav himself was irked by the fact that the Borgerdåds Medal – the highest award of all – was no longer given out.

"There's nothing sillier than refusing the St Olav's Medal," Olav countered. His comment fell on stony ground. "Didn't you accept honorary Kurdish citizenship?"

"And the Lebanese Order of the Cedar," Hans said, winking at the woman.

She whispered something in his ear, nodded politely at Olav and disappeared.

"My sons couldn't be here today, Olav, but everyone sends their condolences," Hans said when they were alone.

"May I have a word?" Olav said, showing Hans into a hallway dominated by French chicken-wire cabinets filled with Japanese porcelain.

Where he still had something over Hans was his grip on the family's properties. Hans might have a way with the ladies (which looked increasingly pathetic as he grew older), and a certain humanitarian capital, but his branch of the family was broke. The courts had taken everything from his father Per Falck, although Vera's intervention had enabled the Bergen branch to continue living at Hordnes, and Olav had given them seats on the foundation's board as well as symbolic shares in SAGA Group. It was better to have them on the inside. It was the ultimate humiliation, of course, and by now there were so many mouths to feed that Hans's SAGA dividend did not go very far.

"We need to talk about the inheritance," said Olav.

"There we're in total agreement."

Olav leaned on the wall and surveyed his relative.

"Oh? I thought you communists were against that particular institution."

"What do you want, Olav?" said Hans.

"You may have heard that no will has surfaced since Mother died. We know that she picked it up from the

79

courthouse on the day she took her life. But we've found nothing among her belongings here at Rederhaugen, which points to her having destroyed it. Meaning that her estate will be administered in accordance with the Inheritance Act."

"I don't know how much contact you had with your mother over the years. But if you'd talked to her, you'd know that Vera and I had a very close relationship, going back to 1970, when she spent the winter in Bergen working on a book."

"If *you* genuinely knew my mother, you'd know that her funeral is not an appropriate time to make such insinuations."

"Your mother always preferred the truth," Hans said. "That was one of the things I valued about her. She rang me recently. Two days before her death, in fact. Said she wanted to talk to me, one to one, to discuss the inheritance."

A crooked smile appeared on Hans's sun-lined face.

"Vera may, of course, have disposed of her will, as you say. But it's just possible that your family has powerful reasons to keep her last testament from ever seeing the light of day. To rid yourselves of a document that would in all likelihood result in you losing property and having to distribute assets to others."

Through the half-open doors, Olav heard the murmur of voices. Hans came up close to him and placed a hand on his. It really was just as warm as all the rumours said.

Hans turned and left, and Olav observed how he melted into the crowd with a sprightly step. How old he felt.

10

WHO ARE WE?

"Who are we?" began Sasha.

She was looking out at the guests at the memorial reception, first at those seated at low tables around the log fire, then at those who had settled into the sofas in the bay window with its view over the fjord.

"Who are we?" she repeated. "As individuals and as a nation? This is a question to which I've given much thought since Grandma's death. It is the existential question that underpins all others. Who was Vera?"

As planned, this opening caught her audience's attention. She held her father's gaze. It was something he might have written himself. A conscious choice on her part. It was her father who had taught her how to give a speech. He, and Vera.

"The name we give our country is derived from the word *norvegr*, which means 'road to the north'.

"One such *norvegr* is the shipping route that runs along the entire length of our long coastline. Who are we? A hardy people from a land that was unforgiving, where our forebears survived on what the coast could offer. For hundreds of years sailors and traders exchanged goods along this route. Grandma's journey from the poverty in which she grew up, to the privileges of the family of which she became a part, is the story of Norway in the last century. And this sea route is central to it. It was along this coast that Vera travelled south as a young woman."

She paused.

"So, who was Vera? Grandma rarely talked about herself. A characteristic many of her generation share. So, as I sat searching for these words after her death, I often wished that I'd asked her more about her homestead. That I'd asked her about her father, the Russian Pomor merchant she never met, about her mother who raised her single-handedly on Yttersia, Lofoten, in the twenties and thirties. But that's something many of you will recognise. We go through life like sleepwalkers, and we don't realise what we've got until it's too late."

She stopped to take a sip of her wine. "It might seem paradoxical that a private person like Vera could be so dedicated to storytelling, to writing the books that brought her such public acclaim, which according to the critic Øystein Rottem stood 'at the crossroads between grounded coastal naturalism, un-Norwegian decadence and timeless mythology'. But I believe the opposite was true. Books were her escape from reality as a girl and remained so until her death. On the flying carpet of literature, she had the freedom to go wherever she pleased."

Her audience nodded quietly, and Sasha knew the moment had come to turn a corner in her speech.

"Or so it seemed. Vera Lind began her life in a poor fishing village and ended it here at Rederhaugen. She survived a dramatic shipwreck, which claimed her husband's life, by leaping out into the waves with her small baby in her arms. It was a tragedy that would shape the rest of her life, as well as our lives, the lives of those who came after her. If she hadn't jumped with little Olav – my father – in her arms and been borne up by the waves, none of *this* would have happened. I have a lot to thank you for, dear Grandma, but I shall begin and end here. May you find peace."

The audience burst into spontaneous applause. She could feel her cheeks burning, and she gripped her glass harder, as if she needed it to keep balance. Olav came over and embraced her.

"You have no idea how much I value those words, Alexandra dear," he whispered.

She thanked him and wriggled out of his hold. She felt hollow, as though she were an actress in her father's theatrical show. Feeling a desperate need for a cigarette, she picked up a shawl and made her way between the guests, who patted her on the shoulder and complimented her.

"Sasha?" said a voice, as she reached the double doors to the veranda.

She turned and clasped Grandma's old editor by both wrists, thin and adorned with ivory-coloured bangles. "Ruth, how lovely to see you."

Ruth Mendelsohn was an elegant retiree with wavy, silvery hair and intelligent, penetrating eyes under two arched eyebrows.

"Beautiful speech, my dear. But did you believe it yourself?"

"What do you mean?" Sasha asked, opening the door to the conservatory, and going out onto the terrace to light her cigarette.

"Vera talked so much about you," Ruth said. "She often said that you were the only person in the family who understood what she did, and what drove her. I see you're a closet smoker too. Do you have one spare?"

Sasha held out the pack and offered her a light.

"Why would I lie?"

Slightly bent-backed, Ruth walked towards the bust of Big Thor and stopped at the chain that cordoned off the frozen rose bed.

"Because the truth is too difficult," she said. "Isn't that always the reason people avoid it?"

"What do you mean?" asked Sasha, warily.

"It's been an age since I was last at High Cliff," said Ruth. "Shall we go over?"

Sensing that Ruth had something to tell her, Sasha led her around the main house and down to the crossroads, where they took the path into the forest towards High Cliff. Minutes later they were standing at the cliff edge. Ruth stared uneasily down at the beach and into the shallow water below. The breeze was stronger out here, and colder.

"Did you know that the suicide rate among Holocaust survivors was lower than in the general population?" she said. "Among the authors, on the other hand – those who wrote about the Holocaust – the opposite is true. Jean Améry, Tadeusz Borowski, Paul Celan, Jerzy Kosinski, Joseph Wulf and Primo Levi. They survived the Holocaust, but they all committed suicide, often decades later. Why?"

Sasha felt a cold draught through her thin clothes.

"Either because writers are more sensitive by nature, or because writing means reliving the pain."

Ruth nodded.

"Precisely. The myth of Vera is exactly as you told it. The storytelling dreamer. A mad artist brought low by psychological problems and writer's block."

"I didn't quite mean it that way," said Sasha.

"During all the years I worked with her, Vera talked about wanting to write something other than crime fiction or macabre short stories. A book about the Hurtigruten ferry disaster and what happened during the war. Does the title *The Sea Cemetery* mean anything to you?"

Sasha had a sudden feeling that this was something she ought to have known about. Luckily her blushes were hidden in the twilight. There was something alluring yet morbid about that title. Sea and soil, water and death.

"Do you want to come in?"

Ruth nodded, and Sasha showed her into the cold, dark cottage. The furniture formed shadowy silhouettes around them; they might have frightened her once. She flicked the old-fashioned light switch on.

"At the end of 1969, the time was finally ripe," continued Ruth. "All through the winter of 1970 Vera sat in the old Falck estate in Bergen and wrote."

"Are you saying that Grandma worked on a last book, one that was never published, while staying with the Bergenites?" Sasha protested. "That can't be true. She never mentioned it. And they hated Grandma. Understandably, after she wrecked their parents' marriage."

"Well, I visited her at Hordnes, that's the name of the estate, yes? She wanted to write a tribute to the coastal culture she was born into, with the voyage on the Hurtigruten at the centre of the narrative. But that was just the backdrop. She wanted to write an alternative story about the war. A story that broke with conventional notions of friends and enemies, guilt and shame. The wartime heroes were still alive back then, Sasha."

The feeling of having been kept in the dark made Sasha numb all over. Not knowing was more painful than any lies that might be unearthed.

"No one in the family has ever read this manuscript," she said quietly.

"Neither have I," said Ruth.

"What do you mean?"

"It was seized by the security police before I had the chance."

"What?" Sasha exclaimed, letting the shock sink in before protesting. "That's crazy! Norway isn't Stalinist Russia. We're not like that."

"As you asked in your speech: *Who are we?*"

Ruth enunciated the words meaningfully.

"But what could the manuscript contain, for it to be seized like that?"

"I don't know, Sasha. Really, I don't. But there's something the authorities never knew. There was another copy, which we smuggled out of the publishing house in an old edition of *The Count of Monte Cristo* and handed over to Vera out here at High Cliff. She deposited it at the Oslo courthouse, as security of sorts, before things got really dark for her."

Deposited it at the *courthouse* . . . Suddenly Sasha understood what the old editor was telling her.

"Grandma was at the courthouse on the day she took her own life," Sasha said. "We thought it was to fetch her will, but she must have been after her manuscript."

The other woman nodded.

"Perhaps *The Sea Cemetery* is Vera's will and testament? I remember your grandmother saying that every will is a form of testament. That every testament is a novel, and every novel a testament."

"The book must be here somewhere," she said, going over to the shelves. "I mean *The Count of Monte Cristo.*"

They found it by the foot of the wing-back armchair where Grandma always sat. Sasha weighed it in her hand. It was unusually light.

"That's it," said Ruth, looking over her shoulder.

Sasha opened it. At the bottom of its hollowed centre were some typed and numbered pages. She read the first line:

Dearest Sashenka

She looked over at Ruth. "I'd prefer to read this alone. I'm sure you understand."

"That's much too short to be the manuscript," said Ruth. "It looks like a letter."

"Yes. But why would Vera hide a letter for me inside a book instead of leaving it on her desk?"

For the first time that evening Ruth Mendelsohn broke into a smile. "Your grandmother was a crime writer. Surely that's answer enough? And what troubled her most in relation to the family at the time, and perhaps to the very end, was the feeling of not being believed. You would never have found this letter if I hadn't told you the story of the manuscript."

"Perhaps."

All Sasha wanted now was to go home and read it in peace.

"History is power. You all know that here at Rederhaugen. Control the narrative, and you wield the power. Others have dictated the official story for long enough. Perhaps it's time to let Vera speak for herself?"

Sasha stared through the window at the horizon. Far in the distance she could see the light of a motorboat.

"Read your letter," Ruth said quietly. "And tell Vera's story. That would make her proud."

"I'm not so sure," Sasha said, remembering her father's words. "Certain stones ought not be turned over. Everything we've built here could come crashing down."

Ruth's tone grew more assertive.

"I've lived long enough to know, Sasha Falck. The world will keep turning even if you give your grandmother redress for the injustice she suffered."

Johnny Berg left the celebrations at the Theatercafé early. He walked across the city square and headed down to Aker Brygge harbour.

Just as his text had promised, Hans Falck was waiting for him in a white motorboat at the end of the pier. Wearing a tie and white shirt under his dark, knee-length overcoat, he seemed overdressed for the occasion, like a guy wearing patent leather Oxfords at a New Year's Eve party. Johnny stepped aboard and shook his hand.

"So, the trial went according to plan?"

Johnny nodded. "Luckily, the press wasn't there."

He had not seen Hans since that day in the Kurdish jail. Although he suited a field doctor's uniform better than a formal suit, the energy was the same.

"Good to be home?"

"Never as good as you think it'll be."

"What we fear most is never as bad as we fear, and what we hope for is never as good. That's how it is. Great we could meet. I've come straight from a funeral at Rederhaugen. I got the caretaker to put a boat out on the water for me. Shall we take her for a spin?"

Johnny stood next to Hans Falck in the sleek *skjærgård-sjeep*. The doctor put the boat into plane and took a gentle left turn so the silhouettes of the Oscarshall Summer Palace and the Fram Museum rose against the twilight sky to their right.

A while later he slowed down.

"You see over there?" Hans said, pointing.

A wall of grey rock stretched like a natural fortress along the water's edge and a few hundred metres inland, ending in coniferous forest on the cliffs above.

"That's Rederhaugen."

"Yes, I recognise it," Johnny replied. He could see lights on in some of the windows. Rising above the trees was a tower with a pennant flying on top.

"It was built by my great-grandfather," Hans continued. "His ambition was to build a property in Bergen that could compete with Christian Michelsen's Gamlehaugen. He was a competitive man and a Bergen patriot through and through. But when he couldn't find a suitable plot of land, he bought this place in addition to the Fana estate. Rederhaugen is one of the few examples of Gothic architecture in Norway."

"The fewer castles, the better for ordinary people, that's a law of nature," Johnny said.

"You're a radical," Hans said, smiling broadly. "Good man."

"So were you when we talked in Beirut. And now you're telling me about some old aristocrat who wanted to build castles in Norway. Is your socialism just a ploy to attract the ladies?"

Hans smiled. "I am a socialist and I will be until the day I die. But I'm a family man too. A Falck. The older

I get, the more important the passing of generations is to me. You'll feel the same one day."

"I doubt it," said Johnny, lighting a cigarette away from the wind.

"Do you know Olav Falck?"

"I know *of* him."

Hans glanced across the water, where a veil of mist had settled. "It was precisely because of my concern for the family name and its lasting reputation that I contacted you. SAGA is a nest of vipers, something for which Olav bears full responsibility."

"Charitable organisations run by rich, privileged do-gooders may be irritating," said Johnny, "but how much harm can an organisation that focuses on Norwegian history, peace in the Middle East and authoritarian hybrid regimes in Eastern Europe really do?"

"Olav and SAGA have two aspects. The one you're describing, the squeaky-clean surface, is just a front, a cover for espionage and the use of military force beyond parliamentary control."

Despite himself, Johnny's curiosity was piqued.

"That's not uncommon in intelligence," he admitted. "There are plenty of examples of institutions and straw companies that are fig leaves for espionage. But is this more than an allegation?"

"Well," Hans said, putting the boat into neutral, "it so happens I talked at great length with the person responsible for Rederhaugen becoming an intelligence centre. She regretted it later and wanted to talk about what she'd done. That's whose funeral I've just come from. Have you heard of Vera Lind?"

"Not really." Johnny tapped his cigarette over the side.

"Vera was a well-known author in her time, back in the fifties and sixties. In 1970, while I was still living on the family estate in Bergen, Vera spent a winter there. She was consulting the archives to find out the truth about what happened to the family during the war. More specifically, when a Hurtigruten ferry was sunk in 1940. Her manuscript was so contentious it was seized and burned by the security police."

"Fascinating," said Johnny. "Not that I quite see what I can bring to this."

"I'm hiring you to write my biography."

Johnny turned to him. "You're fucking kidding me, Hans. A biography? About you?"

Hans grinned and shook his head.

"I can claim, in all humility, to have lived a very interesting life, and you wrote a very good portrait of me."

This was getting stranger and stranger. Johnny had imagined many reasons for their meeting, but not this.

"Why not write it yourself?"

Hans chuckled. "Rederhaugen shuts up like a clam. They never give outsiders the time of day, least of all me. But if a biographer asks for a little off-the-record gossip about Hans Falck's women, then you'll see them talk alright."

"I'm sure," Johnny admitted. "But what are you really after?"

"A death always has a destabilising effect on a family. Olav's a control freak who rules with an iron fist. Vera Lind was his mother, and she left a will, whose contents it is, to put it bluntly, in my interests to ascertain. The problem is, she took all knowledge of it to her grave."

"You want me to help you in an inheritance dispute?"

"It involves significant sums. I've good reason to think that my side of the family was well provided for in that will. We're talking properties worth hundreds of millions, maybe more. I want you to find the whereabouts of Vera Lind's will and determine its contents."

"And how am I to do that?"

"Olav has a daughter called Alexandra, everyone else calls her Sasha. She's the company's archivist. Quite brilliant. A carbon copy of her grandmother, but daddy's little girl nonetheless. She's always been torn between Vera's literary sensibilities and Olav's power games. Your job is to make her believe that you can help her find the will. She'll lead us to it."

"I still can't believe you came all the way to Kurdistan to rope me into an inheritance row."

"I didn't. But we've both worked in the Middle East, Johnny."

The boat bobbed up and down.

"You're aware that we get to know things out in the field that we'd never hear at home. I've got a wide network of sources in Kurdistan. We'll go into detail later, but my contacts have indicated to me that the operation in which you were involved can be traced back through bank transfers and straw companies to the SAGA Foundation here in Norway. Not so long ago I learned that Olav lobbied actively, through his significant contacts in politics and the security service, *against* your return to Norway."

Johnny sighed. "But why? I don't even know him."

"But you know things that present a threat to SAGA and to Olav."

"Like what?"

Hans stared at him with a fatherly, slightly condescending gaze. "You still don't get it? When you did that last job in the Middle East, you weren't working for the Norwegian secret services, as I understand you have in the past. They'd never have let you carry out such a dangerous and politically toxic assignment. And if they had, they'd have pulled you out the day you were captured. No, John Omar Berg, you were, without knowing it, working for SAGA. And your employer left you in the lurch."

Hans looked inland towards Rederhaugen. "There's a direct link between what happened to Vera in 1970 and what happened to you. You both knew things that could reveal the dark side of SAGA; a historical thread runs through the post-war period, leading back to the Hurtigruten shipwreck in the war." He put the boat into gear. "Can you see now that we have a common interest in this? My branch of the family gets its rightful share of the inheritance, and you get the man who was willing to let you rot in a prison cell."

The scintillating scent of a mission filled Johnny's nostrils, but he said nothing.

"You'll remember, we made a deal." Hans Falck fixed him with his gaze. "Which still stands. And something else: the chief of the armed forces is a good friend of mine. I'm aware of the problems apropos your daughter. We don't live in a corrupt country, Johnny, but it's possible that someone will glance through those medical records of yours, with – how should I put it? – a degree of interest. With whatever consequences that might have for your parental access rights. One way or the other. And you will of course get your fair cut too if you succeed."

He accelerated and swung the boat in a large arc, ensuring that Johnny got a last glimpse of the Rederhaugen tower. There was light in one of the windows.

When Sasha came back to the main house, the memorial reception was over. She helped some girls in white shirts clear the tables, while Olav directed two interns who were carrying a table upstairs. From the kitchen hallway, she could hear glasses and plates being stacked.

Andrea, her little sister, had arrived that morning, just in time for the funeral. They had barely talked.

"I'm so fucking glad to be here," Andrea said, hugging her. "I was on Svalbard with no internet when Grandma died – I had to book the most expensive one-way ticket ever. And as we came over the north of Norway a hurricane blew up. Luckily I'd popped a Valium before take-off, and the turbulence just felt like a good massage in the spa. I'm pretty fucked now, but it was the right thing to do."

"Daddy said you were in Sweden," Sasha said.

"I'm always in Sweden when he asks."

Sasha laughed. Andrea was in her early twenties and taller than her sister, athletic in a boyish way, with straight, broad shoulders, narrow hips and long, well-defined arms. Her androgynous look was heightened by her short, dark hair and the baggy clothes she always wore.

Their father came towards them. "A little gathering, everyone!"

Sasha had had enough family get-togethers for one day, she was eager to get home and read her grandmother's letter. Olav had undone his top button and rolled up his sleeves, and was leaning on a low display cabinet. His three children gathered around it.

"An intense day, wouldn't you say?" Olav said, running his fingers through his grey hair.

They all nodded and stood in silence. It was true, a funeral was surprisingly tiring. Sasha drew a finger over the glass top, which was covered with a thin layer of dust. *DS* Prinsesse Ragnhild. *In the service of Nordenfjeldske Steamship Company 1931–1940,* read the engraving. She gazed down at the intricate model of the Hurtigruten ferry. The decks, the pipes, the bridge, the lifeboats, the prow and poop deck. For an instant she pictured the passengers – businessmen and emissaries, fishermen and workers, sailors and helmsmen – as they stood at the ticket kiosk or enjoyed the view from the rails. And Vera, twenty years old and a new mother. She could think of nothing but *The Sea Cemetery.*

"I just want to say how much I appreciate the way you all stepped up today. Andrea, for the wonderful Caspian caviar and foie gras. Sverre, for handling the logistics."

"Hoorah, a medal for logistics!" groaned Andrea.

"Amateurs think war is about strategy, experts know it's about logistics," Olav said. "Smile, Sverre!"

Olav turned towards Sasha. "Alexandra, dear Alexandra, thank you for your speech. It means more than you can know."

The reception had clearly aroused his sentimental side. Sasha just wanted it all to be over. Olav reached his arms around Sverre and Andrea and leaned forward over the glass so he was almost touching foreheads with Sasha.

"D'you remember how we used to talk about being a flat back four? Us versus the world. Alexandra and Andrea on the wings, and Sverre and I in central defence. I don't trust any of the guests today beyond the four of us. Not one of them. They can smile and offer all the condolences they want; they'd rob us and stab us in the back given half a chance."

No one said anything.

"Family," said Olav. "The eternal passing of generations, the direct line of descent. Nothing else matters. Everything else is trivial when it comes down to it."

Sasha had barely given the girls or Mads a thought since Grandma's death, and certainly not since finding the letter and talking to Ruth. But she was suddenly filled with longing for her own family, for their voices, their smell.

"Well, that's all," Olav said, releasing them. "Thank you."

"Drinks in the blue room?" asked Andrea.

Sverre agreed; he was always up for a drink.

"Sorry," Sasha said. "Mads landed today, and I barely got to talk to him during the funeral. And the kids have been rather neglected since Grandma died. Another time."

Andrea and her brother disappeared upstairs. Sasha turned off the lights and went outside. Alone at last. It was a cold, clear night. Jazz came bounding out of the darkness. She walked back home.

Mads was sitting at the rustic oak table, his tie loosened, sipping a glass of red wine. He was nearly forty, and the years had given his face a lived-in look that made him more attractive than ever. Two frown lines divided his brow, there was a hint of grey in his three-day stubble, and his folded shirtsleeves revealed powerful, sinewy forearms, doubtless the result of long hours in the gym.

Giving him a quick kiss, she walked over to the kitchen counter and poured herself a glass of wine.

"Are the girls asleep?"

"They were totally shattered," Mads said, "after dashing up and down those long corridors all afternoon. Camilla said funerals were almost as fun as Christmases and birthdays. Margot asked about death."

She laughed, and without saying anything Mads got up and took her in his arms. They stood like that for a long time.

"It's great to have you back," she whispered.

"Maybe we should go away. Just the four of us?" he said tenderly. "I need a break. How about a trip to France?"

Sasha slipped from his embrace. "Can I ask you something, Mads?"

"Sure."

"Do you ever regret choosing SAGA over politics?"

When they first met, her husband was seen as a political rising star, but one Sunday shortly after their marriage, her father had talked him round. The future lay with SAGA at Rederhaugen, not with "a Social Democrat Party on a life support machine". His father-in-law regarded it as a sporting triumph whenever he got former politicians to join the company, and Mads, who came from a family with no money, had doubtless been tempted by the steep rise in earnings associated with a move into the private sector.

"I'm not sure there would still be an *us* if I'd stayed in politics," Mads said.

"What do you mean?"

"It was all-consuming. I still have to travel a lot, but I have regular working hours. Politics is a drug – you forget the people round you. Like an author I suppose, like Vera."

"There were things Vera kept from us."

"What do you mean?"

She went over to the window, opened it and lit a cigarette. He usually hated her smoking. This time he said nothing, just came up beside her and leaned on the windowsill.

She sighed.

"Daddy wants me to let Grandma's secrets rest. But Vera's old editor wants me to get to the bottom of the mystery surrounding the last manuscript she wrote. What should I do?"

"Olav's instincts are generally sound."

"That's your answer?"

"Was it really a question?" Mads tilted his head and looked at her. "I think you know the answer yourself. I'll support you whatever, Sasha, so long as you do what's right for you."

She gave him a gentle kiss on the forehead. "Do I tell you enough that I love you?"

"Feel free to say it more often."

She flicked her cigarette out in the darkness and went into the other room. She picked up Grandma's letter.

My dear Sashenka,

If you find this letter, I know that you've talked to somebody I trust. That's why I left it here, rather than as a farewell letter for everybody to see. Only somebody who knows what happened to me in 1970 could possibly find this. A little security measure, you might say.

These are the people who supported me against those who wanted to silence me. My version of what took place during the war didn't fit with the official story as told by the nation and its war heroes. Little did I know that I would never be able to write again after what happened. That I'd be condemned to 2,340 weeks or some 16,380 days of writer's block.

I found myself thinking about this during our conversation yesterday. The family are marking the 75th anniversary of the Hurtigruten disaster, and you wanted my version of events.

But memories are like a cat that slips out of your grasp when you try to stroke its fur, but creeps into your bedroom at night to lie on top of you, purring.

I still have the photograph of Olav and myself, standing at the rail on the Hurtigruten ferry after its departure from Bergen, just days before the accident. I hold it up to the light. How much of a person's essence remains constant through their lives? How much is left of Olav, or of myself?

You're tired of hearing it, Sasha, but you look so like me in that picture. You – the only one in the family who inherited my interest in literature. You could sit for hours when you were little, listening to all my ghost stories from the north.

But I'm not writing this to you to reminisce. This family has, in my opinion, degenerated under Olav's leadership. We are perhaps more prosperous than ever, but morally we are bankrupt.

I could give you a long list of examples, on both a political and personal plane, but I shall content myself with saying that I have stated my case in more detail elsewhere. You may have an inkling that this can be traced back to *events that took place during the war and to the sinking of the Prinsesse Ragnhild. This accident remains a cancerous tumour that has never been removed. To a large extent this is my fault and my responsibility. Although I had my reasons.*

The family stands at a crossroads now, Sasha. You can go on living by the motto on the Falck coat of arms, Familia Ante Omnia, and put family before everything, even when such loyalty conflicts with the truth.

The powerful men in this family have put loyalty over truth for too long. Loyalty to the family, to a fixed idea of Norway and Norwegian history. They have forced their narrative through, and when someone confronts them about it, they respond with rage, just as powerful people who take their privileges for granted always do.

I'm hoping it will be you who dares to challenge this. If you want to find the truth, you will. But you must be prepared for it to prove very painful.

I should be saying this to you face to face, but I don't have the strength. Or the courage. Death doesn't frighten me. Its only power is the pain it inflicts on those left behind, and even that diminishes with age.

Paradoxically, it ceases at the moment of its happening. Death exists only for the living.

V.L.

PART II
THE ROSE WINDOW

11

IT'S COMING HOME
THAT'S HARD

A few days after his conversation with Hans, Johnny Berg walked across a secluded cobbled square in central Oslo, found the brass plaque engraved with the words GRIEG FORLAG, and rang the bell. The heavy door opened; armoured glass, he noted. Standing in the foyer, he examined the paintings and photographs of the publisher's pantheon of dead authors.

Vera Lind's picture must have been taken some time during the sixties, as she had that combination of bright, youthful eyes and the beginnings of lines about the mouth that is so characteristic of the age she would have been back then, her mid-forties.

"So, you're fascinated by Vera Lind too?" said a voice behind him.

Hans Falck strode across the foyer and embraced him warmly. "Glad you could make it. I've got a couple of days before I have to return to Kurdistan."

"My days are pretty quiet," Johnny said.

He had spent the last few days wandering about the city, this way and that, past the apartment in Bjølsen where he grew up, and the Sagene Barbershop where Zolly his football coach had worked, which had retained its old name but was now a hipster bar. The ground floor of the old apartment block in Løkka where he had squatted as a sixteen-year-old, and where he and his friends had read radical classics and listened to ska while they planned how to chase off the neo-Nazis, was now home to an estate agent. It was unavoidable perhaps: the city made him melancholy, the way every home town does, when places and memories merge into each other, until we can no longer separate them out.

He was free – freed from the world's worst jail. He should be happy. So why wasn't he? He found himself missing his time behind walls. Not the beatings, of course, or the torture and disease. No, he missed dreaming of freedom. The world's prisons are full of dreamers. It's the only luxury no institution can take from its inmates. And now the dreams were gone, and only reality remained.

He had nothing to do, and so he got nothing done. But Hans had called him that day and asked him to come to the publishing house.

"Did you get hold of the chief medical officer? A good man."

Johnny nodded. He had been seen and had tests run the day before.

"I'm going back to get the results later today."

Their conversation was interrupted when the publisher made his entrance. Peder Grieg was a tall, thin man of about forty, with a strong jawline that hinted at vigour and determination. After his last meeting with Hans, Johnny had made a few enquiries about the Grieg family. Peder, who was now head of the publishing house, lacked his father's charm, but was said to have better control over the bottom line.

"Hans!" said Grieg, in a tone no doubt meant to be jovial. "And this must be Johnny Berg? Follow me, chaps."

They walked into an immaculate office dominated by leather furnishings and a handsome lacquered desk. Peder indicated a space on the sofa, while two staff members – a woman and a man who seemed totally at one with the culture – brought in the contracts.

Ignoring the offer of a seat, Hans Falck stood looking at the drawings of all the previous publishers in the Grieg family. "A Johan and a Peder every other generation since the 1800s, isn't that right?"

"Since 1842," Peder agreed.

"One Johan Grieg squanders the company's money, then the next generation's Peder has to earn it back, before Johan the younger can squander it again, leaving another Peder to save the stumps." Hans winked. " 'Johan's Curse' – isn't that what they call it?"

"Well," Peder said humourlessly, "the industry's constantly changing – we do our best to stay at the forefront. And I have no sons, so there'll be no 'Johan's Curse' hanging over the next generation."

He settled back in his chair. "As you know, Hans, I am sceptical about handing the responsibility for your biography to an author with such limited experience as Berg here."

"If my old mentors in the Middle East had applied that logic when I was a newly qualified GP, thousands of war-wounded kids would have died." Hans smiled mischievously. "Johnny has something most experienced writers lack: talent and grit."

"Well," said Peder, "as publishers we stand by our authors. We want your biography." He turned to Johnny and fixed him with a critical gaze. "May I ask how you propose to begin this book?"

"Certainly," said Johnny, clearing his throat. Hans had declined to mention this scepticism the last time they had met. It was a real problem, since without the backing of the publisher their plan was redundant, and he could forget about interviewing the Falck family at Rederhaugen. "How many prime ministers' memoirs have you published in recent years?"

"Three," said Peder Grieg, suddenly a little uncertain. "And one by the former High Commissioner for Refugees."

"How did they sell?" asked Johnny.

"We're talking about books that shed light on us as a nation!" exclaimed the publisher. "Grieg Forlag tells the story of Norway. This has always been our ambition and it still is."

"The only people who read those books are political commentators," Johnny continued. "They're launched in your foyer with a fanfare, only to disappear from people's consciousness and collect dust in a warehouse before being used as kindling. Nobody's interested in the stories of these self-righteous moralists."

The staff raised their eyebrows and exchanged glances, but Peder scratched his head uneasily and nodded, as if inviting Johnny to continue.

"Some writers believe that the way to the reader's heart is glorifying the subject and glossing over their faults. I intend to tackle this biography using my subject's own method."

"What method might that be?" the editor asked sceptically.

"I shall seduce the reader as Hans seduces his women," Johnny said, sending a glance Falck's way. "We're talking about a man who is capable of charming everyone and anyone. How? Because Hans is always honest, even about his weaknesses, about how his achievements have come at the expense of his family and children, and the women he left sitting at home while he was unfaithful. A war, no matter how awful, is never the hardest thing – no, the hardest thing is to come home. But despite all his weaknesses, all the darkness, Hans is a man who allows us to dream, to seek something greater than ourselves."

The patronising glances had given way to expectant stares. The staff around the low coffee table were listening with interest.

"When I interviewed Hans some years ago, he told me a story. His biography will begin in a Lebanese refugee camp in 1982. Hans has just left the only woman he has ever loved. He's running through a hail of bullets with a defenceless baby in his arms, surrounded by militia who want him and the child dead. After this opening, we'll return to Bergen in 1970, where a young shipowner's son and radical high school student meets someone who will inspire him to dream of greater things." Johnny lowered his voice. "Her name is Vera Lind."

Peder Grieg took a deep breath and raised his eyebrows. "And you consider yourself capable of telling this story?"

"Yes," Johnny said seriously. "Because, without overstating it, these are feelings and dilemmas I have experienced myself. I know a bit about how we sacrifice our children and family when we work in a war zone. And this – a combination of the familiar and the extraordinary – is the way to people's hearts, whether they be Hans's mistresses or his readers."

Peder looked at his watch and chuckled with satisfaction as he pushed the contract across the table. "I've heard enough, Johnny Berg. The job is yours. Fifty-fifty, divided between the two of you. We'll provide an advance and cover your travel expenses in the Middle East, against receipts. Hans, do you have anything to add before we sign?"

"Tell the truth," Hans said to Johnny. "Just don't make me boring."

Hans was fired up when they emerged and suggested they go for a drink. Johnny declined and headed towards Kvadraturen. He felt a superficial pleasure at the little show he had just put on, but it was quickly wearing off. Such displays had once been his bread and butter, but as he crossed Grev Wedel's square he felt empty, like a clown who takes off his make-up after a performance.

He was let into the Gamle Logen and went quickly up the wide, carpeted staircase until he reached an office door in the eaves marked NATIONAL MILITARY MEDICAL OUTPATIENT CLINIC. A doctor stuck his head out and smiled affably. "John Berg? Come in."

Leading him through to a messy office, with a poster that read, REACH OUT TO A VETERAN, he rattled on about his old friend Hans Falck, then offered Johnny a seat.

"Right, it was that fMRI scan you did," he said, in a tone that sounded ominously thoughtful.

The doctor put two pictures before him. They were neural scans, that much Johnny could see. "Here you see a brain that has not been exposed to explosion trauma. Note the difference in the tissue . . ."

He pointed to an area at the bottom right of the image. "On the healthy brain this area resembles a crab's claw, d'you see?"

With his elbows on the table and hands folded, he leaned over the desk. "There's no easy way to say this. You're looking at what we doctors call a TBI. A Traumatic Brain Injury."

"A brain injury?" Johnny swallowed.

"You worked in the special forces?"

"That was a long time ago. I've been working in a mainly civilian capacity for the last few years."

"In a civilian capacity," said the consultant, scratching his chin. "Research from the US shows a strong correlation between TBIs and operators who have been exposed to various kinds of explosions over a long period – door-breaching, roadside bombs, that sort of thing. Have you suffered from insomnia or depression in recent years?"

Johnny hesitated for a moment. "Occasionally," he said. "Hasn't everybody?"

"These are just some of the common symptoms. TBI doesn't necessarily result in a reduced quality of life," he said. "But it's important you think carefully and answer the question honestly. We know that TBIs have psychological effects, similar to those of post-traumatic stress disorder. Irritation, depression, anger, erectile dysfunction."

And so it continued. A brain injury. Brain damage. A hole in the head. Hole in the heart. He felt wretched. When at last he was finished, the doctor surveyed him with a kindly and intelligent gaze.

"I've worked here for a good few years," he said. "We've tried very hard to improve the conditions for our veterans. Yes, the special commands have their own routines, but the principles are the same. They're simple enough: honest debriefings during and after assignments. Nothing's off limits when we talk here. And peer support is vital. We take care of each other – and of our boys."

He took a swig of his coffee. "Look, I know there are things you can't or won't tell me. But do you have anyone you can talk to about what you've experienced?"

Johnny felt something seep up from his stomach into his throat. "No," he said. "Not really."

"Let me say this," the doctor continued. "You can get along alright with this TBI. What I think you need, though, is someone to talk to. You'll find we're all here for each other at the clinic."

Johnny could not say why – perhaps it was the idea of being part of something, the doctor's kindness, or having bottled everything up for so long – but he began to talk. "I was away when my daughter was born," he said, looking down. "Stuck in the Libyan desert, directing fire for our bombers. Got to know about it three days later. My team-mate Grotle and I celebrated with a swig of whisky in our tent. All I wanted was to go home. I was sure everything would be fine if only I could just get home."

"It's a major event in anyone's life," the doctor said with empathy. "So that's not hard to understand."

"I came home. Everything was fine at first. It's calm and peaceful in a house with a newborn baby, like a church, kind of sacred, everyone talking in whispers. And my girl-friend was so beautiful, she was glowing. I felt so close to them both. Like I'd never leave them again. But there was this underlying feeling. It was the betrayal. That I'd gone off on an assignment instead of being there for the birth."

He could taste the tears rising.

"And then my anger at what I'd been a part of. We'd worked as forward air controllers from the ground. The

coordinates I gave the bombers caused the deaths of innocent Libyans. And for what? Libya didn't improve, it got
worse. I'd worked like that for ten years, and for what? It
didn't bear thinking about."

"The research literature talks about something we now
call moral injury," said the doctor. "People who've not
been in any physical danger – drone pilots, for example, in
an American desert – can nonetheless suffer long-term
effects. You've clearly faced danger, but I think this is what
we're looking at."

"I stopped giving a shit," Johnny continued. "I didn't
show up for work, smoked weed all day. My missus threw
me out. We were meant to have fifty-fifty custody at first,
but things got complicated. So it went down to weekends.
But when she and her new man, a fucking security service
bodyguard, turned up at my place and I was lying on the
sofa stoned while my daughter slept, she put her foot down.
From then on, I only got to see her under supervision."

The doctor leaned forward. "Then what did you do?"

"The only thing I could. I went abroad again. To the
only place I felt safe. Did what I was meant to do and got
arrested because of a misunderstanding. A seven-month
absence from my daughter on top of everything else – well,
it didn't help my case, put it that way. I don't get to see her
at all now. And that was the court's decision before . . ."
He peered cautiously at the fMRI results. ". . . these
papers that show I have, um . . . brain damage."

"You're saying what most veterans say," said the doctor.
"It isn't the assignments themselves that are the hardest
part, no matter how dramatic they are. It's coming home."

12

WE HAVE SURVIVED SHIPWRECKS AND FAMILY DIVISION

Before Vera's death, Olav had put out a tender for the restoration of the rose tower at the east wing of the main house. He had found a reputable builder, under whose command a team of surly workers erected scaffolding, before shrouding the tower in a snow-white mesh.

The problem was that the wooden panels on the roof near the crenels were so rotten that water from the recent heavy rains and snowfall had leaked into the top floor where the rose window was. Besides this, the old stained-glass window was now very fragile. It was a miracle it had held out through the storms. The worry was that the water would find its way into his office below.

There was a knock at the door. Olav was standing at the window of his office, staring out through the hazy scaffolding mesh. It was late. He was wearing his tan penny loafers as usual. He had given a pair to Alexandra, and to his joy she wore them all the time. He leaned over the radiator. It was nice and warm; he was feeling the cold more with age. Alexandra had always obeyed him. She was loyal. Family came before everything, as it should.

"Yes," he called out.

Siri's face appeared in the shadows at the doorway. She came in and poured herself some water from the carafe.

"You wanted to talk to me," she said.

He offered her a glass of wine, but no, she was driving.

"So, the will hasn't surfaced," Olav half asked, half stated.

His lawyer did not answer, but stood quietly, leaning against the sideboard, observing him thoughtfully.

"I have to admit that I don't fully understand what's at stake here," she said.

"It's gone," Olav replied sharply. "What is it you don't understand?"

"Vera was listed as the owner of the family's properties, and you're worried she may have given some of them away?"

Olav scratched his bushy eyebrows thoughtfully. "Take a seat, Siri."

It was meant to sound like both an invitation and a command. Siri sat on the sofa and placed one leg over the other. Olav took some books from the shelf and laid them on the low coffee table.

"These are Mother's books, or some of them," he said in a teacherly tone. "Interesting in the main, albeit forgotten. Who remembers a novel or short story collection fifty years later? They're confined to the literary graveyard."

He noticed that Siri was shifting impatiently on the sofa.

"I'll get to the point," he said. "I first got wind of the fact that Mother was working on a completely different project in the winter of 1970. Mother was in Bergen, and somebody I knew at her publishing house told me they had high hopes for a manuscript about the Hurtigruten disaster during the war."

Olav took a swig of red wine. "I can't say I was over-joyed. I knew the kind of traumatic memories it might

113

bring up. But freedom of expression is everything, as our constitution states, and if that was what she wanted to write about, she was within her rights."

Siri nodded. Like most lawyers, she adhered to principle, an occupational weakness that could get on Olav's nerves, though the Greve family's pedantic streak made them well suited to handling legally binding documents, of which Rederhaugen had many.

"Anyway, it soon became apparent that there were complications surrounding her new manuscript," he continued. "Mother, God rest her soul, had managed to incur the wrath of the secret police. *How* exactly, I've no idea, but it was clear that Grieg could publish a book containing baseless allegations against people who weren't around to defend themselves, my father among them. Mother took it all very badly, she saw enemies around every corner, ghosts in broad daylight. The mental problems she'd always lived with only got worse."

"Well, confiscating a manuscript is an extreme use of power," said Siri.

Olav sighed. "It wasn't that which caused her breakdown, it was all the trauma that had never been addressed. She was admitted to Blakstad. Those were dark years. You know the story."

"I still can't see any connection with the will."

"A few years later it came to my attention that the manuscript was still in existence. That Mother had left it with the courthouse as a sort of testament."

Siri nodded, as if she finally understood. "You mean Vera's last will and testament was a literary manuscript and not a legally binding document?"

"Lord only knows," Olav said. "Perhaps it was both."

"And you're worried that it's gone astray and could be published?"

"We've survived shipwrecks, smear campaigns and family division. And we'll get through this. But yes, that's my worry."

"Who knows about this?"

"God knows. I've barely spoken to my mother in fifty years. But since we're talking about a manuscript, the first person to come to mind is Johan Grieg, her publisher."

Siri stared at him thoughtfully. "Talk to Johan. Make it clear to him he's not to mention this to anyone."

Olav nodded in silence. Siri got up and left the room and he closed the door after her. His steps were as heavy as his breathing. He felt so old. Was it because he was no longer a son, and only a father? He slumped back in his chair and put his feet up on the desk. History weighed on him like a yoke.

He reached for his mobile and searched for Johan Grieg. It was a long time since they'd talked on the phone.

Vera's old publisher answered at the third ring, with the questioning voice of someone who can see who is calling but is reluctant to identify themselves. "Hello? Who's that?"

Such a frail voice. Grieg had really gone downhill lately.

"It's Olav. Olav Falck. I've got a question, Johan."

"Yes, it would be surprising if you'd called to reminisce about the old days," Grieg said.

"When, apart from the funeral, have you visited Rederhaugen recently?"

"I don't remember."

"But I do," said Olav. "It was on the day Mother took her life. You attended a dinner here."

There was a short silence on the other end. "Is this some sort of interrogation?"

"You arrived at the usual time and left rather early."

Olav smiled with satisfaction at his own reflection in the window. Johan had always been weak under pressure, and was no less so now, ill as he was.

"I haven't the strength to go creeping around Rederhaugen at night," Grieg sighed. "Least of all to Vera's cottage."

That was undeniably true, Olav thought, but also a deft diversionary tactic on the publisher's part.

"Do you have Mother's manuscript?"

He heard Grieg sigh again.

"You were my mother's publisher and very fond of her," Olav continued. "Besides, you've always had a guilty conscience about what happened in 1970."

"This is absurd," Grieg said, breathing heavily. "This is *your* family, *your* trauma, and you're accusing me. You know very well that if any of this were the case, you'd have been the first person I'd contact. I've always stood by the Falck family."

"Let it stay that way," said Olav. "Not a word to anyone."

He hung up.

13

GUARDIANSHIP ORDER

Sasha woke with a start.

The radio alarm on her bedside table showed 03:43. Mads was sleeping with his muscular back towards her. She was exhausted and simultaneously wide awake. She turned onto her other side and closed her eyes again, but knew at once that she would not be getting any more sleep.

Almost a week had passed since the funeral. During the mornings she had worked diligently in the SAGA archive, spending the afternoons with her family in the lodge. The state of emergency caused by her grandmother's death was being slowly displaced by the repetitive normality of daily life. She had obeyed her father's warning not to look further into her grandmother's story. Well . . . almost.

Her T-shirt was damp with sweat. She sat on the edge of the bed and stroked Mads's back with her index finger. He grunted something inaudible, but fell instantly back to sleep.

She normally slept through the night like a child. But these were not normal times. Grandma Vera had confided in her in the form of a letter, just before taking her own life, and she had hidden it in a place only those initiated into the events of 1970 would find it. She shuddered with a mix of excitement and fear.

Sasha went into the bathroom, flung her sweaty T-shirt into the laundry basket, got dressed and went out into the living room. She liked being up at night, the gentle hum of household appliances, the soft light from the other side of the fjord creeping in through the window. She shoved her feet into a pair of shoes and went outside. The night threw a blast of winter cold at her; spring was still waiting in the wings. The darkness made her more aware of the sounds around her, like an animal, and her sharpened senses prompted freewheeling thoughts.

She lit a cigarette and whistled for Jazz. Unusually, he did not come. Thoughts of Vera's death threatened to overwhelm her, like a complicated mathematical equation she could not figure out. She climbed up onto a mossy outcrop overlooking the bathing area and stood gazing out across the fjord.

A while later she jumped down and jogged through the little forest and past the moonlit statue of Big Thor and the tall bay windows of the main house behind it.

Quietly, so as not to wake anyone, she crept back into the house, sat at the table and opened the Mac. Mads had sent her some links to hotels and chateaus in Provence before going to bed. That could wait. Somebody named John Berg wanted to interview her for "a planned biography of Hans Falck for Grieg Forlag, *strictly off-the-record*". Sasha laughed to herself and wrote a short reply: *Only if it's unauthorised.* She sent it before she could think better of it.

Not that it mattered. No way would she spill family secrets to some journalist.

The last email was from Blakstad Hospital. Despite her promise to her father, she had tried to call them, but when no one picked up, she'd sent an email about the possibility of viewing Vera Lind's records.

The short, dismissive answer was signed by the hospital's head of communications. Few things annoyed Sasha as much as a stubborn adherence to the rules. She was formulating a sharp reply when she heard footsteps in the hallway.

"Sasha?" said Mads sleepily.

"Why are you awake at this hour?" she asked.

"Why are *you* awake? You think I haven't noticed? You've barely slept this past week."

"Sit down, Mads. There's something I have to tell you."

He poured himself a glass of water and sat opposite her, his hands cupped over hers. Long ago she had fallen for his charisma and eloquence as a young rising star in politics, but it was his caring side she loved him for now. Like most people, Mads had spent his years as a student presenting as who he wanted to be, and these family years being who he was in reality.

"Is it about Vera and the question you asked me?"

"I found a letter from her," said Sasha. "I haven't said anything to Daddy, or to Sverre or Andrea."

He took a breath and nodded. "What was it about?"

"A suicide note, more or less."

He stretched his hands above his head. "You should give it to the police."

"No," she said, irritated by his answer. "This isn't a matter for the police. It's not against the law to take your own life."

"What about Olav?"

She stared at him across the table. "Grandma was furious with Daddy. That's why she wrote the letter. She asked me to find out the truth about the family and what happened during the war – and later on too. I'm worried Grandma knew something about SAGA that I'd rather not find out."

Mads got up and went over to the kitchen counter. He poured two glasses of wine.

"Why are you telling me this?" he asked at last.

"Because it's so damned lonely dealing with this alone!"

He sat down again. "So, what are you going to do?"

Sasha explained briefly that she was thinking of taking the boat out to Blakstad, where Vera had been hospitalised in the seventies, to get her records. "You still support me?"

Mads smiled. "I wouldn't want to be the one to stand in your way."

Sasha didn't answer but felt her heart sink at his tone. This was not something he was keen to dig about in.

"I'm going to bed," he said. "Probably a good idea if you did too."

Next morning, she followed the path from the lodge along the seafront. She crossed the beach below the house and walked up the gently sloping rocks to higher ground. An overgrown path took her behind the Snøhetta-designed auditorium, blasted into the hillside for SAGA's twenty-fifth anniversary, and then on through the forest until the bay came into view, with its jetty and boathouse.

Sasha did not indulge in many luxuries. Thinking about it now, there was just the one: a 1968 Riva Aquarama in a rich mahogany, a runabout that was blingy in a way that she associated with new money, in sharp contrast to the moderation she usually showed. But she loved the boat. She often came down here in the winter just to feel the polished wood and the graceful, perfect shape of the hull, and as soon as there was a hint of spring in the air, she would have a specialist prepare it for the season and bring it out of the boathouse, here on the southern headland. If the Renaissance masters had designed boats, Sasha told herself, the result would be an Aquarama.

As she walked down towards the jetty, she saw Olav with the gardener, who was helping him carry some jerrycans over to his Grimsøy sailboat. The Aquarama was bobbing up and down at the water's edge.

She always preferred to travel by sea if she had the choice, whether she wanted to go to the city centre in the east or to Nesodden in the south, or beyond the fjord to the west, where Blakstad Hospital lay. To say they had given her the cold shoulder would be an understatement, but things generally fell into place when you met with people face to face.

"You're taking the Riva out early this year!" Olav shouted. "Too early, I'd say. Where are you off to?"

She shrugged. "Just taking a trip."

Sasha stepped into the boat. Sitting on the cream-coloured leather seats and turning the ignition always reminded her of driving a sports car. Not a bad comparison: the power came from two twelve-cylinder Lamborghini engines. She reversed and took a gentle swing to the right before accelerating westwards. The spring sun warmed her face, forcing a smile.

Half an hour later she slowed down, cruising calmly in towards a winter-deserted pier and moored. From there she took a path through a copse until Blakstad came into view.

The buildings were a mix of the tasteful garden-city architecture popular when the asylum was first built in the early 1900s, and the soulless brick structures of the post-war years. She hurried through the wide doors of the administration block.

Like many people in her profession, the head of communications was a former journalist. Sasha thought she recognised her from a short-lived chat show some years back.

"Alexandra Falck, I assume?" the woman said brusquely.

Sasha nodded.

"Your request has been considered. And rejected. We can't open medical records to outsiders. We're dealing with what can be very sensitive material."

The impatience and rage Sasha felt over such inflexibility matched only that of her father.

"You must be aware that there are cases where this duty of confidentiality can be waived," she said, controlling her temper. "If, for example, information is required for research. I manage the archives at the SAGA Foundation."

The head of communications smiled icily. "Then I suggest you make a formal application."

"And I'm not merely a researcher, in this case. I'm related to the patient. Not long ago, Vera, my grandmother, took her own life. I'll remind you that relatives may also access old medical records."

The head of communications hesitated, and in that moment Sasha knew she had won.

"Very well. You have two hours."

The woman led Sasha past reception and downstairs to a basement corridor lined with discarded hospital equipment: beds, walking frames, stethoscopes, catheters, slings and stretchers. She unlocked an unmarked metal door. The distinctive smell of old paper hit Sasha. The light flickered before settling, and dust motes danced as they crossed the room. There were shelves on all sides stacked high with cardboard boxes, each labelled with a year.

"What was the name and time frame?" asked the woman.

"Vera Margrethe Lind," Sasha replied. "Born in 1920, admitted in the spring of 1970. I don't know the exact date, but no earlier than the end of April or the beginning of May."

The woman indicated a shelf. "Lind . . . let's see now."

She ran her fingertips over the boxes, pulled out a box and handed it to Sasha. "Here are your folders. You can't sit here. I'll find you a room. You've got experience of reading official documents?"

Sasha smiled. "It's my job."

She was shown into a side room. She placed the documents on a small veneer table, shut the door and started to read.

Vera had been admitted on May 2, 1970, after a "gradual deterioration of her mental health that culminated in a psychotic episode with subsequent suicide attempts at her place of residence".

She had been thoroughly examined in May 1970 by psychiatrist Finn Butenschøn, who after extensive consultations concluded that she was suffering from "deep trauma, probably caused by lack of attachment relationships in childhood and a shipping accident in the north of Norway during the war" that "radically reduced her mental capacities and her ability to function in society".

Sasha stopped and took a breath. None of this was exactly new or surprising to her, but in a patient assessment dated May 27, Butenschøn had added something that took her aback: "The patient's condition has, in the

opinion of the undersigned, worsened, because of a grandiose narcissistic self-image expressed in delusionary
thoughts about her own greatness, combined with persecutory delusions. She is convinced that known figures in
Norwegian public life and her own family want to harm
her. This is further expressed in repeated claims that she
has written a work that was 'burned in the forest' because
it contained information that could change 'Norwegian
history'."

Sasha got up and leaned against the wall in the cramped
room. *Known figures in Norwegian public life and her own
family?*

In the Falck family these were often the same thing.

She sat down again and continued reading. It was clear
that the hospital psychiatrists had done a thorough job.
Butenschøn had been in contact with a Dr Schultz in
Lofoten, "whose medical records from the patient's childhood align with her current presentation".

Damn it! They weren't in the file. She'd have to look
into that.

Vera had exhibited externalising behaviours, particularly
in the first year. In October 1970, the nurses had "sought
emergency authorisation" to use what was referred to as
"mechanical force". She had tried to commit suicide repeatedly, once by going on hunger strike in the winter of 1971
and then, in one particularly grotesque incident on July 27
of the same year, she "made a noose out of her blouse, rubbed
soap on the floor and tried to hang herself from the door
handle. This attempt was averted by an auxiliary nurse".

Here Sasha sat, in the basement of the same building,
forty-five years later. A sense of claustrophobia flooded
over her, as though she herself was being held down by

mechanical force. She ran to the door, and, half convinced she was locked in an isolation cell, seized the handle.

The door swung open onto the empty basement. The only sound was from a whirring fan. She stood there gasping for breath with the taste of salt tears in her mouth.

Was she crying over Vera's tragic past? Yes, probably, but these were also tears of rage at being kept in the dark, at her own ignorance, at those who had never told her about this, and at herself, for never asking.

She leaned against the wall. "You are not Grandma," she said aloud to herself. "You are the archivist for the SAGA Foundation."

It helped. When she had calmed down, she sat at the table again. Bit by bit the drama and intensity in the entries waned. In the late winter of 1972, the situation was stable enough for Vera to be allowed to take longer walks outside the hospital building.

Her constant companion, Finn Butenschøn, was full of praise.

"Having observed the patient for more than two years," he wrote in his last entry, dated June 6, 1972, "we can confirm that the situation has stabilised, especially with regard to externalising behaviours/suicidal tendencies, which have largely disappeared."

Nonetheless, he raised a warning finger: "It is, however, my firm opinion that we have not got to the bottom of the megalomaniacal tendencies and persecutory delusions which the patient continues to exhibit. This may be a question to be taken into account by the Court of Protection when assessing the patient for a possible Guardianship Order due to mental incapacity. Please refer to the family lawyer, August Greve Jr."

Sasha had seen enough. She returned the folders to their box, thanked everyone in reception and walked down to her tethered boat.

Mental Incapacity. Guardianship Order. The words came like a cold wind from an age of forced sterilisations and lobotomies.

"Where do I go from here?" she asked herself, with the boat in plane over the cold fjord. When she saw the tower at Rederhaugen on the horizon, the answer came to her. It was too early to confront her father. Siri Greve, on the other hand, was the daughter of the lawyer who had represented the Falcks in the Guardianship Order case. If anyone knew anything, and Siri knew most things, it was her.

Sasha moored the boat and headed for the main house.

14

LA SÉDUCTION

The doorbell rang through his dream. Johnny opened his eyes and sat up. He had fallen asleep on the sofa. A few half-empty boxes of pad thai stood on the table among soft drinks bottles, ice-cream tubs, screwed-up kitchen roll and soft lumps of Moroccan hash. He had fallen off the wagon big time. A hangover from cannabis was different from one caused by alcohol. Not throbbing, but heavy and numbing, like waking up from a general anaesthetic.

The doorbell rang again. The last few days' rampage was coming back to him in vague glimpses. A dealer in a doorway in Fredensborg, a noisy karaoke bar in Trondheimsveien, a strip club behind Rådhuset. Where had it started? Yes, he knew alright. It had begun in Gamle Logen.

The doorbell rang for the third time. Johnny went over to the intercom. He heard the main door thunder in the stairwell a couple of floors below, and heavy footsteps coming up the stairs.

"Who is it?" said Johnny, standing inside his front door.

"Open the door. It's me."

HK's voice was distinctive as always. A powerful baritone with the lazy, musical tones of a taxi driver from Oslo East combined with something more refined, rather like the man himself.

Johnny opened up. HK must have lost ten kilos since his time as head of Section. It suited him. And his trim white beard contrasted with his skin, which had gained a healthy, ruddy tinge from life in retirement. Only the deep-set, wolf-grey eyes were the same. They hugged each other.

"You look pretty good," said HK.

"I'm still standing. But you look younger every time."

The older man smiled warmly.

"Retirement! The minute we leave the Section we feel younger. Meanwhile the lives of the chaps in active service are measured in dogs' years. We'll be the same age soon."

Johnny had to smile.

Coming up behind HK was a red-faced giant of a man. "Grotle!" exclaimed Johnny, giving his old partner a bear hug.

"Christ, you look awful, Johnny," growled Grotle, holding him by the shoulders with his huge, iron-hard hands. Johnny could see now that his colleague had aged and looked more drawn. He was over fifty, with a weather-beaten face and untidy hair that was beginning to thin. The wild ginger-grey beard was shorter than in Afghanistan, where it was whispered that Grotle could have been state governor of Faryab by mere virtue of his height and barn-door shoulders. If there was something the Afghans respected, it was physical prowess, and this West Country guy was as strong as a polar bear. He was a trained clearance diver, one of Norway's best, and when they had worked together in the Section, it was said that Grotle had webbed feet.

"Hell, it's good to see you, Johnny. I really thought you were done for," Grotle continued.

"Do you still live on your houseboat?" Johnny asked.

"Don't come ashore more than I have to," Grotle said with a wink. "But when HK told me you were back and in a bad way, I had to come."

"Wait out here," Johnny said anxiously. "I want to clean up a bit first."

The two men ignored him and stepped into his apartment.

HK glanced at the coffee table, then at Grotle, then at Johnny. "So, that's what it's come to."

He fixed Johnny with the look of a resigned father who finds that the home-alone party has got out of hand. "We've gotta do something about this, Johnny, don't you think?"

Johnny hesitated for a second, then nodded reluctantly.

They cleaned the entire apartment, vacuumed and aired it, and scrubbed the kitchen and bathroom, where Grotle held the lumps of Moroccan hash pointedly over the toilet.

"Wait," Johnny protested. "It could be good to hang on to that."

"Even better to be rid of it," said Grotle, flushing it down.

Job done, they sat in the kitchen with a steaming hot cup of coffee each.

"I was afraid for you, Johnny," Grotle said. "But I was fucking pissed off too. You didn't give a toss about orders. You started to operate on your own and dragged the rest of us into the shit with you. You spent too much time watching anti-US lectures on YouTube and you smoked too much hash."

"We should never have bombed Libya," Johnny said. "And I quit smoking hash. Before this little spree."

"You know your problem?" Grotle's eyes had softened. "You take all the world's problems on your shoulders. I agree that Libya wasn't too smart."

"Not too smart?" said Johnny. "Innocent people were killed, the power balance in the Middle East was turned upside down by people who had no idea what they were doing. The gates of hell were opened."

Grotle looked at him sternly. "You were just an operative, for fuck's sake, not the bloody foreign minister. Politicians decide policy, we implement it. That's better than the alternative."

The giant got up and headed for the front door. "I've got a flight back up north to catch. Enjoy yourselves. Call if there's anything, Johnny. You'll find me in Ramsund mostly. But any more fucking nonsense and I'll personally cut off your balls."

HK and Johnny bought some chicken and herbs for a coq au vin from the delicatessen in Bygdøy Allé, and a couple of rich Burgundies from the *vinmonopol*. With the smell of garlic, bacon, herbs and red wine rising from the pan, Johnny's apartment felt almost cosy.

"I'd forgotten what a good cook you are," Johnny said, as his older friend stirred some cognac into the sauce.

"I picked up a lot in Lebanon. The French guys always ate well, even on tough assignments." HK smiled across the kitchen counter. "They taught me how to cook – and how to gather intelligence."

HK's past was shrouded in mist, just like his private life. Johnny knew he lived in a gay relationship with a retired government adviser and had begun his career as an intelligence officer in the Norwegian UN battalion in Lebanon in the early eighties, but that was it.

"The French really knew that part of the Middle East. But they taught me something else too, something essential for anybody working in intelligence."

"Charm?" Johnny smiled. HK had instilled its importance on Johnny when he was leading his operations unit.

"You've not forgotten everything, then!" HK winked. "Say what you want about those hunky Trøndelag cross-country skiers in our elite units; they're not exactly *charmant*."

HK liked to throw in a few French words after a glass or two.

"People think the art of seduction is about getting a person into bed. And it goes without saying that it can be. But *la séduction* is essentially about power. About getting what we want by stealth rather than force. That's the most important thing the French taught me."

"Wasn't it in Lebanon that you got to know Hans Falck?" asked Johnny.

"Beirut," HK said, cautiously. "Summer of '82. I can say with absolute certainty, because that was when the Israelis attacked."

There was a pause as Johnny let him think in peace.

"Hans was working in a Palestinian refugee camp south of the city. Total workaholic, very clever, and even more arrogant and full of himself back then than now. There were rumours that he was in a relationship with a leader of one of the most infamous armed Palestinian groups."

"Hans told me a *slightly* different version of that story," said Johnny.

"There were *rumours*," HK repeated. "Hans had a wife back in Norway, but he's always lived like a bachelor the moment he crosses into foreign territory. And he certainly spent a lot of time with the Palestinian militias back then. But we'll never know the truth, one way or another, since Mouna Khouri, as she was called, was killed in the massacres in the refugee camps. That was September '82. A month I'll never forget."

He seemed suddenly distant. "Shall we eat now?"

While Johnny helped himself to chicken casserole, he told HK what the chief medical officer had said. HK listened attentively.

"And in the middle of all this, I've had a job offer."

"What? You mean someone is actually prepared to hire you?" HK said with a gravelly laugh.

"Hans Falck wants me to write his biography."

HK was about to take a sip, but he stopped midway.

"Well, I never," he said, clearing his throat. "What was your answer?"

"I said yes. The contract's signed."

"Well, that's a rather unexpected move from our friend Hans Falck."

"He told me that it was Olav Falck and SAGA who were behind my last assignment," said Johnny.

"I should never have retired," sighed HK. "That operation was utter madness. We'd never have done anything like that when I was in charge of the Section."

"But he also told me that the assignment was part of something Olav and SAGA have been doing throughout the post-war years. That my story was the latest chapter in something that could bring the entire foundation down.

And if Olav Falck's to blame for Norway's failure to rescue me in Kurdistan, I'm not going to object."

"Interesting," murmured HK. "Revenge is a powerful driving force, now as always." He stroked his fingers slowly over his chin. "Are you aware of the kind of trail you're following here, Johnny old chap? Smarter journalists than you have tried, with nothing to show for it."

"I'm better placed than them to investigate this."

HK paused for a long time before answering. "I worked with Olav in the old days, before he established SAGA. We were frogmen together. From there he went into the service, and I went into police surveillance. We got on well. Our minds worked the same way. More concerned with questions of strategy than monitoring Maoist students – or I was, at least. In the end, we had a falling-out. It was probably inevitable."

"Why?"

"We were both concerned with national security, but in different ways. My loyalties have always been with the Constitution, while Olav is willing to use means to protect the country that flout its principles. That's the difference between us. Olav is an extreme pragmatist – he's power-hungry and ruthless."

Johnny took another sip. "And this mode of thinking shaped SAGA?"

"From top to bottom!" said HK. "SAGA was part of the so-called Stay Behind Network. Old resistance fighters from the war and other pillars of the community who weren't prepared to lay down their arms initiated the building of a secret, private army in case of Soviet invasion. They were found in every Western European country, including Norway. Rederhaugen was used as a weapons depot during the Cold War."

"But weren't they exposed in the seventies?" Johnny remembered the story vaguely.

"Many were," said HK. "But not all. Rederhaugen was a perfect depot. The Germans occupied it during the war and dug tunnels under it and built bomb shelters. Good, strong cement walls. After the war large quantities of weapons and equipment were brought there, and the old German Wehrmacht generals were flown in to show the locals all the fortifications and defences they had built in case of Soviet invasion. Nobody exposed the fact that the Falck family and SAGA were storing weapons at Rederhaugen."

HK took a breath. "Although, there was one person who tried to tell the truth. Olav's mother. An author named Vera Lind, who passed away recently."

Johnny nodded. There it was again: SAGA and Vera Lind.

"Hans mentioned she left a will that hasn't been found."

"I've no idea about that, but what's certain is that Lind's manuscript was confiscated. I was involved in the investigation myself."

For the first time that evening Johnny got the feeling that often popped up when he talked to HK, that nothing could surprise the old warhorse. "What are you saying? Have you read the manuscript?"

"No, I never read it. But the Lind investigation is behind the enmity between Olav and me, and ultimately why I left the surveillance service. I couldn't support the suppression of free speech and the destruction of someone's life under the auspices of 'national security'. For Olav, the

Falck dynasty's mission is to manage the official historical narrative about Norway. Anyone who challenges this, and thereby SAGA, is made to suffer. As Vera Lind was in 1970.

"And . . ." HK continued quietly, "it seems that may include you, Johnny."

Johnny swallowed. His hands were sweaty and he felt his heart thump.

"As I neared retirement age," HK continued, "influential people in intelligence and military circles began discussing whether Norway's 'toolkit' was sufficient to counter the threat of terrorism. I was kept well out of it, but I know it was Martens Magnus, the Head of the MoD's special forces unit, who was the main instigator of SB 2.0. That is, Stay Behind for a new era."

Johnny nodded.

"It was Magnus's people who recruited me for this assignment."

"And you were naive or worn down enough to say yes," said HK. "Countries like France, the USA, Britain and Israel kill state enemies unashamedly. It's not even a secret. In Norway it's a political impossibility. We don't do that sort of thing. But what do you do when a psychopath like Abu Fellah stands in the desert and boasts that Norway's streets will be flooded with blood, with the resources and logistics from IS to make it happen?"

Johnny hid his face in his hands; that was precisely how it had been.

"Well," HK continued patiently, "then you ask the Americans if they have a Predator drone to spare. But if they're all in use, or the target escapes detection, then you call in ground forces. Not officially, of course. You contact the only man in the kingdom with the ability to carry out this task, whose appearance allows him to blend right into the Middle East, and who's got himself entangled in some sort of trouble, so he has no choice but to carry out a 'black' operation. A lethal weapon the armed forces spent 30 million kroner to train; a man called John Omar Berg."

He stared at Johnny. "Who better to ask?"

Johnny lit a cigarette and took a deep drag. "I was loyal," he said, at last. "I'd never have said anything, not until I found out they were prepared to leave me in that jail. Martens Magnus is one thing. But do you know whether Olav Falck is really behind this? As Hans claims?"

"Olav's smart," HK said gravely. "He never gets his hands dirty. No threats or violence were involved when he destroyed his mother. Instead, he became her caring guardian! And, likewise, when it emerged that you were stuck in Kurdistan, and I set heaven and earth in motion to get you out, Olav rang me."

Here HK switched to what was doubtless a credible imitation of the old patriarch's gravelly tones: " 'Berg was the best,' he said. 'A national hero. It's shameful that as a nation we couldn't offer him proper support after all his troubles. It was bound to go wrong. But you know, HK, how intransigent our government is when it comes to bringing foreign fighters home.' Those were his exact words. It's not my style to tell people to go to hell, Johnny, but I came close. Olav has learned that power in Norway isn't exercised in plain sight, it's shrouded in morality and altruism. But the issue was the same: both you and Vera Lind were sitting on stories that challenged their narrative about the kind of nation Norway is, stories that could sink the Falck family and SAGA if they came out."

HK lifted his glass and looked at him. "Cheers, Johnny. This is your chance. Play your cards right, and it could mean the fall of Olav and SAGA. Once and for all."

Their eyes met. Johnny's old boss smiled enigmatically. He reciprocated.

"Do as Hans suggests, look up Olav's daughter. There was, if I'm not mistaken, talk of a security service inform-ant back in 1970; perhaps there's somebody out there who can be leaned on. I'll see what I can find in the archives."

HK lit a pipe. The warm smell of tobacco smoke evoked images from the past. The day all those years ago when HK had come to Ramsund to recruit Johnny. The time he'd given each of his young recruits a ten-kroner note and told them to get to Trondheim. Walking together down Afghan backstreets.

"What are you thinking about, Johnny? You seem distracted."

"It's strange but when you lit your pipe, I found myself thinking about . . ."

". . . the past?" said HK. "No other part of the brain is more strongly linked to our memory than the olfactory system."

Johnny nodded, suddenly overwhelmed by a feeling of melancholy.

"Which is why the perfumes of ex-girlfriends should be banned."

HK smiled.

"Exactly. How's Rebecca?"

"OK, I think. Her new man is a security service body-guard with four children from a previous marriage, a finishers' T-shirt for the Norseman Triathlon and a black belt in parenting."

HK's eyes were blurry from so many glasses of wine. He played a Jacques Brel song and put an arm around Johnny's shoulder. "We'll fix that when the time's right. You're a good man, Johnny, a good man."

HK had switched to brandy and raised his glass.

"A toast to Hans as well, for getting you to write his biography. Literature and espionage are both about seduction. Conjuring a reality, which we trick the enemy – or the reader – into believing in, until they no longer see that they've been duped. That, my friend, is *la séduction*."

15

WOMAN TO WOMAN

In the basement of the main house, beyond the changing rooms, was a swimming pool, with sunloungers and hot tubs, all bathed in a turquoise light.

Sasha went into the ladies' changing room and then out into the pool area. There was a faint whiff of chlorine, and the waves made by the figure swimming past splashed lightly over the tiles.

Siri Greve had swum at national junior level and still put in as many sessions as she could. She had not yet noticed Sasha, who was watching her elegant movements, the breath drawn rhythmically on each third stroke on alternate sides, the goggles and tight black cap giving her an unreal appearance. Sasha sat at the end of the pool to wait.

"Sasha?" said Siri, catching her breath, when she stopped a few lengths later. She pushed her goggles up onto her forehead. "What are you doing here?"

"I've been texting you the past few days."

"I'm sorry." The lawyer swung herself up out of the water. "Don't take it personally. A bit of a set-to on one of the boards I sit on. Middle-aged white men, you know how it is."

It was hardly a surprise that Siri Greve had not replied to Sasha's texts. When she wasn't swimming or working at SAGA, she was dashing between board meetings. The rise in female representation on company boards was not just beneficial to gender equality, but also to Siri Jacqueline Greve. If perennial "board-hopping" and Chanel-feminism had a face, it was hers. But had it been Sasha's father, the patriarch, trying to reach her, the response time would doubtless have been cut in half.

"We need to talk about Vera," Sasha said.

"How about in the sauna?"

It was not a question, and though reluctant, Sasha followed Siri's V-shaped back. It was in the sauna beneath Rederhaugen that Siri held court, gathering her large network of high-achieving women from the fields of politics, culture and business. Sasha had occasionally been invited to join them. She, too, according to Siri, needed a counterweight to the "self-obsessed, megalomaniacal" men of Rederhaugen. Here, in the sauna, Sasha listened to the latest gossip about incoming ministerial advisors, impotent braggards and open marriages consumed by jealousy, all of which seemed be the network's favourite subjects, guaranteed to make eyes light up with schadenfreude.

Sasha undressed and took a quick cold shower. Siri Greve was already sitting on the top bench, unostentatiously naked. She threw a scoop of water onto the glowing rocks and the steam rose pitilessly towards the ceiling, making it hard to breathe for a few seconds.

"So, Sasha. What's happened since we last spoke?"

Sasha started to recount the details from the records at Blakstad. The problem with Siri was that Sasha was never sure where her loyalties lay. Over the years, and particularly since she'd joined the network, they had become friends of sorts, and Siri had been happy to openly discuss her various lovers with her ("the operations chief was a five out of ten in bed; too good-looking for anyone to dare to teach him"). There had been many after her divorce, including a well-known financier who had cheated on her so often she had no tears left to cry.

At the same time this woman was her father's secret weapon and closest ally, backed by the weighty history of three generations of collaboration between the Greves and Falcks. It was Olav who paid her salary, and Sasha knew full well that people rarely cut the umbilical cord with their benefactors without good reason.

"A Guardianship Order," Siri mused, staring into the steamy air, when Sasha had finished. "I'm no expert, but as far as I remember, a new, updated guardianship law was introduced some years ago, following the ratification of a UN convention on the rights of disabled people. Any person placed under a Guardianship Order must give their written consent. Although there are, of course, exceptions, where a person may still be deprived of legal capacity."

"Precisely! And I want to find out what happened when Grandma's case came before the courts. Something doesn't fit. Your father was our family lawyer at the time – you've got to help me find the transcripts. He must have kept a record of everything, don't you think?"

Siri Greve passed her hands over her Restylane-smooth forehead and down over her cheeks. "I can't do that." She took a deep breath. "A confidentiality agreement was the first thing I signed when I started working for SAGA. My father engrained it into me from childhood: 'You can disagree violently with the Falcks, you can challenge them, shout at them in the back room if needed. But you can never break your vow of confidentiality.'"

Sasha looked straight into Siri Greve's eyes. "I'm a Falck."

"But not all Falcks are equal. You know I want to help you, Sasha. Woman to woman, right? I can set up a meeting with Olav and put your case to him."

"No," Sasha said, feeling herself boil up inside. "You're not to mention any of this to Daddy."

"What makes you think I'd be willing to set aside my loyalty to Olav?"

Sasha felt her cheeks burn. If she wanted to take this any further, she would need to muster some of her father's ruthlessness. And her grandmother's nose for a mystery.

"Do you remember telling me what the worst thing about your divorce was, Siri? It wasn't the money, or the sense of failure, or even the children," said Sasha. "It was not knowing about all his infidelities."

As usual she did not mention Siri's ex by name; he was the *unmentionable*. "The feeling of being kept in the dark. Well, that's how I feel now. I stand up there on the podium like a bloody mascot and give a speech about the importance of knowing our history, and I don't even know my own family's history."

Siri's eyes were wide.

"There's a big difference—"

"No," Sasha interrupted, "I'm not finished. You hold court for your high-powered feminists down here in the sauna. That's all well and good. But what do you call a lone female writer having her manuscript confiscated and being threatened into silence by powerful men if not a story of female oppression? I don't know what happened to Vera, either in 1970 or more recently, but I'll find out."

"But Olav . . .?"

"Daddy thinks there's a conflict between Vera's story and the family. But he's wrong. Honesty always beats sweeping things under the carpet."

Siri broke into a smile. She seemed both surprised and impressed.

"Daddy doesn't have many years left at the helm. When the next chapter in our history is written, might it not be an idea to be on good terms with the person who takes over? Woman to woman?"

"My oh my!" said Siri.

"Shall we go up?" Sasha said, jumping down onto the cool floor.

Apart from two portrait paintings – one of her father, August Greve Jr, the other of August Greve the elder – Siri's office was furnished in a contemporary style, with not a Chesterfield or heavy oak desk in sight. The modern sofas, chairs and modest desk were in muted tones of coffee and cream, lit by cylindrical lamps that cast a golden light. Sasha followed Siri's fresh fragrance across the floor.

The lawyer unlocked a door onto a dusty little room filled with shelves that could be moved using a manual crank. With swift, decisive movements she pulled out a shelf, and after running her slender fingers over the brown files, took one out.

"This isn't the first time you've taken this out," Sasha said. "I can see you've known this story all along."

Siri didn't answer. "There's a ton of correspondence in here, but I think I know what you're looking for. Are you sure you want to hear this?"

Sasha nodded and reached for the file, but Siri began to read aloud from it.

"Guardianship Hearing, May 28, 1970. 'The court has, on the recommendation of Blakstad Hospital and at the request of Vera M. Lind's closest relative and heir, issued herewith a Guardianship Order for three years. This is in accordance with the Act of 28 November 1898, which permits a person to be deprived of legal capacity if it be deemed necessary to prevent said person from putting their assets or other financial interests at risk of significant depreciation.'"

"Enough," said Sasha, and Siri stopped. Sasha felt the ground shake under her, and put her head in her hands. This was too shocking to contemplate.

Closest relative and heir. It could be none other than Olav who had requested that his mother be deprived of her legal capacity and put under a Guardianship Order.

Vera, her grandmother, crazy, yes, now and then, but also her hero and guiding star, deemed mentally incapacitated, her grandma, who sat in her wing-back chair with a novel in her lap, Vera, placed under a Guardianship Order by the person closest to her.

"It was Daddy," she mumbled, feeling a chill run through her.

"Yes, of course it was Olav," Siri said in an unsentimental tone. "What do you expect a man like Olav to do when his mother is psychotic and suicidal?"

"So, what happened in those three years?" Sasha asked. She would have liked to discuss Siri's remark, but not now.

"June, 1973. The Guardianship Order will be extended by a further two years," the lawyer read tonelessly.

"But Vera was discharged from Blakstad the year before!" Sasha felt herself losing control for the first time. She was so furious she was trembling. What had they been up to?

"It may be of little consolation," Siri said, "but Vera regained legal capacity in 1975, according to the court documents. Meaning that the properties – Rederhaugen, Hordnes and the Hunting Lodge – were returned to her ownership. But we've already discussed that."

What had Olav taken from her? And how could Sasha get further with her investigation? She said nothing, closing her eyes. She could no longer run from the truth.

"You can't say I didn't warn you," Siri Greve said.

16

WE NEED A SNIPER

Sverre was walking across the lawn in front of the main house when he heard a loud bang.

He jumped. The sound always took him back to that day on a dusty mountain road when the bullets penetrated the armour plating on their vehicle, when they slammed on the brakes and leaped out under the cover of a smoke grenade, before throwing themselves into a ditch and returning the Taliban's fire.

It was nine years since he had first flown over Afghanistan. Every day he missed the tingling feeling when – after a brief stopover in Turkey – he woke up on the chartered plane that was used for the last leg of their journey. He could still picture the landscape: sun-scorched fields, deserts and snow-white mountains far in the distance. *Hindu Kush.* Just the name sounded romantic, like a place out of one of the adventure books he had devoured as a boy. All around him his comrades lay sleeping with open mouths, stretched out on the wooden benches. He still felt moved by the mere thought of them: his squad, his team, his partner.

The noise he had just heard lacked the sting of live ammunition. An airgun, perhaps?

It was three years since Sverre had left the armed forces, and for three years he had regretted it. Naturally it was his father who had got him to leave. The military was good for building character, Olav said, but it was no place to stay unless you wanted to become "a drunken major and a regular at the brothels in South Sudan". More important duties, he insisted, called at Rederhaugen. So Sverre had become vice-president of SAGA, with an office under his father's. And from then on it was the top position in SAGA he longed for.

He worked most evenings, as well as weekends and holidays. When he went jogging it was invariably with a leadership skills podcast in his ears. He had set himself a goal. Every day he would do at least one thing – big or small – to bring him closer to the top job. Hard work and a systematic approach would bring its rewards over time.

But something had gone awry. His father's "tenure" had been repeatedly extended, and Olav seemed to favour other contenders. With his grandmother's death and all the uncertainty around the inheritance, everything was up in the air again.

A cold wind pierced his thin white shirt and tweed jacket. On the pathway near Big Thor's bust he slipped on an ice patch and lay floundering on the ground, cursing.

The sea came into view through the forest. Sasha's two daughters were down on the jetty, with a couple of older boys, one of whom was waving a rifle over his head. On the headland at the far end of the bay a seagull was staggering about. It had been shot.

"What the hell are you doing?" shouted Sverre.

"He was just showing us how to shoot an air rifle," Margot said, pointing at the gangly boy with the gun. "Now the seagull's flown off and it's too far away."

"Can't you see it's bleeding?" Camilla said indignantly.

"It's against the law to shoot seagulls," Sverre said sternly. "Give me that rifle."

With an ashamed look the boy handed it over.

"The bird's hurting," Camilla said.

The seagull was seventy to eighty metres away. Sverre took off his jacket, rested the butt of the rifle in his shoulder groove. It took nothing more to feel free. He aimed. It was a long time since he had fired an airgun, or any gun at all. The bird managed to take wing, quickly gaining height above them. It was all down to the breathing now: inhale, exhale, empty the lungs, pull the trigger gently. Sverre fired. The bird dropped to the ground, as lifeless as a clay pigeon.

"Shit, what a shot!" gasped the boys. "Are you a sharpshooter or something?"

Sverre calmly lowered the rifle and pointed at Sasha's girls. "You two go up to the main building. And you," he said to the boys. "Bury the bird. You'll find a shovel in the boathouse. And no, I'm not a sharpshooter, I'm a *sniper*."

He was on his way back to the main house when he heard a voice coming from the forest behind him.

"Good work, Sverre Falck."

He turned and found himself staring into two narrow eyes in a thin, weathered face that gave the impression its owner had spent years in a poncho shelter.

"Martens!" he said. "What are you doing here?"

Sverre had known of Martens Magnus long before he had begun to visit his father informally, but his feeling that he was a fawning leech had only grown stronger over the years. Olav and MM, as he was often referred to, had become fast friends. Olav had even secured Martens, thirty years his junior, a place on SAGA's board. MM had been an officer in the Marine Hunters, which Sverre had dreamed of joining since he was a boy. At Vera's funeral he had spotted Martens in his uniform with the winged logo emblazoned on his chest, an honour which Sverre coveted.

Now MM was dressed in civilian clothes, a dark wool coat and boots polished to a shine.

"I didn't get to offer you my condolences at the funeral," he said, stretching his hand out for an iron handshake. "But it was a thoroughly good send-off."

Sverre put his hands in his pockets, kicked at the gravel on the path and nodded.

It was not altogether true that Sverre had been totally cut off from the armed forces since leaving. A year ago, Martens Magnus had come to him to ask if he would do a little courier job. A flight to the Middle East, a visit to a local bank and then a meeting. A mission for Norway, he could say nothing more. Naturally Sverre had taken him up on it. And once more he had felt alive, no longer a sleepwalker drifting through the days.

"I wonder if you've got a minute?" Martens said. "There's something I want to discuss with you."

"My office?"

"Good idea."

Together they walked over to the main house and up the winding staircase. The Marine officer's footsteps disappeared into the scarlet-coloured rug that Sverre had bought in Afghanistan, and which lay between the heavy teak desk and the built-in bookcases. Leather-bound historical works dominated the room, along with

149

military plaques, framed medals and an antelope's head on the wall. The sea glinted through the high, arched windows.

"Very elegant," said Martens, nodding. "You've got a smarter office than your father."

"You haven't seen anything yet!" Sverre smiled proudly, opening a smaller door that led to a walk-in wardrobe, where a row of freshly pressed shirts and suit jackets hung in front of a wide gun cabinet. He tapped in a code and opened it. The rifles stood neatly arranged. Sverre selected one and brought it out into the office.

"A Purdey, for big-game hunting in Africa, engraved with the Falck coat of arms."

"Not bad, eh," Martens said, weighing it in his hands with the confidence of an expert. "Olav's latest interest is in big game hunting. I'm trying to convince him that kind of thing is passé."

Sverre smiled.

"By the way," said Martens, stroking the stock. "On the day your grandmother died and we had dinner here, did you notice anything unusual? Was anyone acting strangely?"

What was strange was that Martens would ask him such a question.

"Has my father sent you to cross-examine me?" he asked.

Martens smiled. "No. Quite the contrary, in fact. I've been hearing good reports about you. Your old boss in the sniper squad is a colleague of mine, a good friend. Says you were a team player. And an outstanding marksman, of course. As you know, the snipers and the Marine Hunters have close ties."

Sverre had failed in the last round of the selection process for Marine Hunter Command, one of the world's top special forces. It ranked as his greatest defeat. Now he felt a tingling down his spine.

"As you may know," continued Martens, "we're running operations in Afghanistan. We're setting up a task force now. But we're short on snipers. A clusterfuck of illnesses, injuries and other unfortunate circumstances."

Sverre's chest swelled. "Sad to hear it."

"Long story short," said MM, "we need a sniper. You're not a Marine Hunter, but you've got the skills and experience. And you take the initiative, we like that. How about it?"

"Hmm. It's an honour to be asked," said Sverre, running his fingertips tenderly over the butt of the Purdey. "Let me think it over."

"Sure." Martens picked up his coat and gave Sverre a firm handshake. "But don't think too long. We start preparations shortly."

He paused in the doorway. "And, Sverre, while I've got you one to one. You've not heard anything about Johnny Berg from your veteran friends lately?"

"Johnny Berg?" Naturally he knew the name. Berg was a legend to everyone in the more operational units within the forces. "I thought he flipped out and disappeared in the Middle East?"

"He's back," said Martens. "Tell me if you come across him. And get back to me about the assignment ASAP."

Sverre stood on the Uzbek carpet decorated with warriors and mythical creatures. He was done playing second fiddle around here. In the military, at least, he could be himself.

But something else came to him too: jagged flashes of gunfire, telltale wires at the roadside, the flash of light before the Iveco in front was thrown into the air, the taste of earth and sand in his mouth, the smoke, the 12.7 that smacked tracer bullets into the mountains, the smell of ammunition, petrol and burnt flesh.

Yes, he had been frightened, but he missed that fear. Something civilians would never understand. And now Martens Magnus had prescribed him a medicine for that loss, the only medicine he knew would work.

17

THEY'VE GOT TO BE WIPED OUT

Front line, Kurdistan

The hospital was on the Kurdish side of the front line, so close that IS could strike at them at any moment. Hans Falck told the driver to stop in front of the main entrance and got out. A dilapidated two-storey brick building, sunflower-yellow, surrounded by cypresses and withered palms, with a dusty-brown patch of garden at the front.

It was chaos in the reception area. The police academy on the other side of the city had been hit by terrorists the day before. Independent sources had reported many dead and injured. Old women in headscarves and traditional dress sat wailing on the bench along the wall, while military guards, several of them women in dark-green camouflage uniforms, tried to keep order. Hans looked out over the waiting room. People were limping about on old crutches, with dirty, blood-soaked bandages on newly amputated limbs, while young mothers hushed their crying infants.

Hans was welcomed and shown round the hospital by a Norwegian nurse from Drammen, who immediately told him that her parents were Yazidis, a minority group who had been living in the region for thousands of years before the jihadists had started their ethnic cleansing of "devil worshippers", as they called them.

There was a low rumbling sound in the distance.

"Just the coalition forces bombing terrorist positions on the other side of the line," she said, with a shrug. "Nothing to worry about."

They descended a stairway to the basement. She explained that the most vulnerable sections were down there in case of an attack: the X-ray department and the intensive care and maternity units. It must have been the latter into which she led him next, since the sweet scent of baby poo mingled with the smell of disinfectant.

A girl with tousled raven-black hair sat propped up in bed, breastfeeding an infant.

"What a beautiful baby!" Hans smiled, stroking the little one gently on the cheek.

The infant reminded him of his daughter Marte when she was born, the only one of his children's births he had attended. The nurse stopped to talk to one of the women lying there.

"All the women here are Yazidis, like my parents," she told him. "And these babies are all the result of mass rapes. The girl who is breastfeeding was abducted and sold at a slave market in Mosul before she managed to escape. By which time she was pregnant. You have contacts in the international press, Dr Falck, and a platform. The world needs to know what's happening here."

Hans Falck grabbed her hands and stared deep into her eyes. "The world will know. And, please, call me Hans."

Hans Falck had seen more than his fair share of atrocities: Christian militias slaughtering civilians in the Lebanese camps, the Soviets in Afghanistan, the Turks in Kurdistan, the Israelis in Gaza, Assad in Aleppo. The list was endless. But terror was generally a means to an end.

With IS everything was turned on its head. They made no attempt to hide what they were doing here. Quite the contrary, they broadcast it far and wide. The atrocities were an end in themselves. Their stated goals – conquering Rome or taking over the world – were clearly just a means of getting people to join them.

The rumbling sound was getting louder; the bombers were clearly getting closer.

"I'd like you to take a look at Mike's injuries," said the nurse.

"Mike?"

"He's Norwegian. A friend to the cause who was injured during an attack last week. Are you on Instagram?"

"No," said Hans.

"Mike is big on there. NordicSNIPER has a hundred and fifty thousand followers from all over the world. He finances his Peshmerga squad through crowdfunding and private donations."

Mike was lying on an iron bed, a bandaged leg on top of the blanket. He explained, with a reserved, inward-looking gaze, that he had been hit in the leg by shrapnel. But the infection was subsiding now, and he would soon go back to the front.

Hans noticed, however, that the entrance wound was still infected and the scab was dark in colour.

"We should probably make a little incision here. D'you need anaesthetic?"

Mike shook his head. "Go ahead."

Hans made a deep incision on the side of the calf with a scalpel. Mike didn't make a sound.

"I hear you've been working for the Kurds for years," said Mike looking up. "Respect!"

Unlike the other high-profile doctors he knew in the international arena – Mads Gilbert, Hans Husum, Marianne Mjaaland to name a few, with whom he had a rather complicated relationship – Hans Falck had a special interest in Kurdistan. He had felt an affinity for the Kurds ever since the early eighties when he took his first trip into the mountains with the guerrilla fighters of the Kurdistan Workers' Party, the PKK.

"How did you end up here?"

"Same as all the others." Mike hesitated. "Couldn't just sit there and watch the terrorists slaughtering my people. Told the forces that I was coming here to look after my sick father, bought kit with my discharge payment and left."

"And what did they say?"

"You want to hear the truth?" said Mike.

"I'm a conscientious objector myself," Hans said. "I'm under no illusions about the military."

"They made my life hell. They couldn't get at me, so they went after the folks round me. The boys in my old squad got a rollicking if they liked my Insta posts. My girlfriend, who's in the army, was told to dump me or get out."

Hans put a tourniquet on Mike's leg.

"I'm a Norwegian patriot, that's what they don't get. You don't fight Daesh by sending a couple of transport planes and a bloody troop of paramedics to Iraq. The Norwegians don't understand a thing about this war."

"This isn't our war," said Hans.

Mike looked hard at him. "Oh yes, it is. If we don't stop the enemy here, all Europe will burn. Jihadism is a cancer. A plague. The jihadists have gotta be wiped out, each and every one. This is all about the wider defence of Norway, can't you see that?"

"You really believe that?" said Hans. The other man nodded.

"When I was back home, I was called in to meet with the intelligence crowd in Akershus. I told them straight: I'm going back, but if you need intelligence, just contact me. I don't want any money for it. But I heard nothing. Until months later. Then I was contacted by some Norwegian guy from the armed forces, who wanted to offer financial support to my unit."

"Your group survives on crowdfunding?"

"That's right. Anyway, I met the guy down here in town, and he said that the money came with a little condition. I had to get hold of a handgun and put it in a safe deposit box in Erbil. 'OK,' I said, 'I can fix that.'"

"Who was this Norwegian?"

Mike clasped his hands behind his head and fixed Hans with his gaze.

"I don't want to say. But it was someone I knew from the forces. The point is that the guy who got the handgun off me was arrested soon afterwards, in no man's land near the front by a neighbouring Kurdish group. They'd talked to their contacts in Norwegian intelligence, who said he was a well-known jihadist, a former Marine Hunter who'd converted and gone over to the terrorists. Total bullshit. It was the Norwegians who'd sent him in to kill the jihadists, then they left him in the lurch for the same crime."

"How d'you know that?" objected Hans, who felt that the conversation was about to take a very different turn. But it was often like that here in the Middle East: compatriots talked openly about things that were strictly under wraps at home.

"Because the Kurds seized the weapon he had on him," said Mike. "Same serial number as the one I'd procured. I checked. I tried to get him released, but the Americans had him by then. That's how they do it. They use you when it suits them, then leave you in the shit."

Hans looked thoughtful, his eyes roaming the dilapidated ward.

"Who are *they*?"

"You know," Mike continued calmly, "if you work for the Peshmerga down here, Western special forces and intelligence often come along. British, French, Americans, others. They all want information about Daesh terrorists from their respective countries, and they don't hide the fact that their aim is to take them out. That they've got to die. Norwegians don't say these things. We're just here to drill wells and build girls' schools. But, of course, we're doing exactly the same thing as everybody else. We kill terrorists, but it's not politically acceptable. My guess is that the operator who was abandoned did this job for Norway as a freelancer. Meaning it couldn't be traced back to the authorities. But that's just speculation."

"I know the guy," said Hans. "He's back in Norway. But I need to know who it was you met from the armed forces."

"That's not how it works, mate," Mike said, shaking his head. "Tell him to come down here himself and meet me. Then I'll explain everything."

They heard a shrill whistling noise, and a second later the walls shook so hard that the plaster fell off, while scissors and scalpels danced on the trolley next to the bed.

"Artillery!" Mike cried, throwing himself out of his bed and limping out of the room and down the hall. With Hans following fast on his heels, the Norwegian Kurd shouted: "Gotta get the babies into the bunker!"

The whistling and crashing were getting closer, as though a halfwit giant were trampling the building above to smithereens. A huge bang made the walls tremble.

"Over here!" yelled the Norwegian nurse, holding a screaming baby in one arm and pulling a hospital bed with the other.

The bomb room was built of concrete and large enough to house a dozen beds. An emergency power generator stood in one corner. It reeked of diesel. Mike sat slumped against a wall, not moving.

The mothers' screams competed with the piercing cries of their newborn infants. Hans waved his arms to help them find the way. The air was hot and thick, insulation material drifted to the floor like sawdust. The ceiling light flickered before it fizzled out and everything went black.

A bomb landed straight above them. The room shook like a plane flying through turbulence, the local nurses lifted their arms into the air and prayed to Allah.

Then it went quiet.

Moments later they heard the reassuring rumble of the bomber planes in the distance.

"I think Daesh is done for the day," said Mike, still slumped against the wall.

Hans nodded. "Seems like it."

"You see what I mean now?" Mike said. "They've got to be wiped out. To the last man."

18

DADDY'S BEEN AT THE HELM
FOR TOO LONG

From the window of the lodge, Sasha could see that the girls were playing outside. She put the folder of documents down on the table and sent a message on the sibling group chat:

Meet now? It's about Grandma.

She had been relatively young when she became a mother, first with Camilla and two years later with Margot. Perhaps because she talked less about her children than most people she knew, she saw herself as a capable mother. Not just that; she loved her children more than anything in the world and would die for them without hesitation. Yet she had always thought of motherhood as something that had to be done, a duty, a means of continuing the family line. Naturally there had been the all-consuming years with brain fog from breastfeeding and interrupted sleep, especially since she despised the whole au pair thing, so common in these parts. But that was over now. The fears she had felt for the children slowly loosened their grip. They lost their milk teeth and started asking questions about death, the universe and their place in the world.

Andrea texted back first: *I'm in between jobs, haha, so I have time now.*

More and more the girls lived their own lives; Camilla with her dresses and princesses, Margot with her books. The melancholy expressed by many of her friends over their children's growing independence was alien to Sasha. Perhaps because she was born that way, or perhaps it was because her own mother had died so young, leaving her and Sverre to be raised by Olav, a father she admired and adored, though his parenting style, distant and authoritarian, was very different from her generation's ideals.

My office in 20 minutes? replied Sverre.

Either way, with the girls being more grown-up now, she had more time to do her own thing. She had already made more headway with Vera's story. After the Blakstad Hospital and Guardianship Order shock, Sasha had systematically gone through all the SAGA Foundation's internal reports from the years around 1970. Her findings had made her sure of one thing: she had to present this to her siblings.

Mads made an entrance wearing a tracksuit and gave her a quick kiss.

"I've barely seen you in the last few days."

"I know." Sasha nodded. "I've been working."

"You've seemed a bit off lately. What have you discovered?"

Looking watchfully out the window, Sasha told him about the medical records at Blakstad and the declaration of incapacity. Mads listened in silence.

"So, if I understand you correctly," he said at last, "you're suggesting that Olav kept his mother under a Guardianship Order for several years in the seventies."

"I'm not *suggesting*," said Sasha. She found his pointedly sceptical formulations provocative. "It's a *fact*."

"I don't know anyone more attached to their father than you are," said Mads. "He's even your boss. And he was Vera's guardian."

"That's right."

"He must have had a good reason," Mads said thoughtfully. "Think of all the responsibilities your father's taken on. First, he has to assume the role of guardian when his mother becomes psychotic, then his wife dies of cancer and he raises you and Sverre and Andrea on his own, while running a company. The man's a force of nature."

Sasha had not thought about it that way. But, however true it rang, his reasoning lacked one crucial component, namely an explanation as to why her father had applied for his mother to be declared incapacitated – his own mother – and what that had to do with the manuscript of *The Sea Cemetery*.

Mads looked at her sternly. "Olav asked you to stop digging into Vera's past."

"I've already broken that promise."

He took a deep breath. "Have I ever really told you what it was like joining the Falcks? Since the moment I met your family, I dreamed of being accepted by you all. Not because you were rich and powerful."

He turned towards her. "But because you *were* a family. With skeletons in the closet, absolutely, but who hasn't got a few? A family who drank and quarrelled and had lunch together every Sunday. I only had my mother. You won't like what I'm about to say now." His voice was calm and decisive. "Your family and Rederhaugen are the two most valuable things in your life, Sasha. You mustn't forget that."

"Exactly! I can't bear to think how the truth of what happened to Grandma was kept hidden from us."

"But maybe it was for the sake of the family? You've no idea what might happen if you defy Olav's advice and start digging about in old board reports."

"Why are you taking Daddy's side?" she yelled.

"Mummy? Why are you yelling?" asked Margot. The girls were suddenly standing in the doorway.

"Grown-ups quarrel sometimes," she said, stroking her daughter's hair. Sasha took a deep breath. Her husband's cowardice made her angry. But her findings had presented her with a choice: going solo, or seeking an alliance. For now, she had plumped for the latter.

She walked quickly over to Sverre's office, knocked and opened the door without waiting for an answer. Andrea and Sverre were there already, each draped on the armrests of one of the sofas arranged in front of the bookshelves, talking in hushed tones. So, they had understood she was serious. The military paraphernalia and framed medals that lined the walls made it look like an old man's office.

"So, Sasha," Sverre said, looking up. "What's up?"

Andrea lit a cigarette and flicked her straight dark hair.

"You can smoke out the window," her brother said, opening the arched window that overlooked the lawn with the sea behind it. A low sun was glowing red over the hills in the west.

"But you're a man of the past, Sverre," said Andrea. "In your world, women don't have the vote, gays are all paedophiles, Churchill's just taken over from Chamberlain and the British are being evacuated from Dunkirk. The smoking ban can't possibly apply in your office."

Listening to her little sister, Sasha found her comments even more irrelevant and inane than usual. "It's good we could meet. I've something important to discuss with you both."

Andrea stubbed out her cigarette. Sverre said nothing.

"No doubt we're all affected by Grandma's death and her missing will," Sasha continued, noticing how terribly serious she sounded. "As the family's archivist, I have taken it upon myself to dig a little into her past. I've discovered some things that . . . well . . . that could have consequences for all three of us."

She put the old reports on the coffee table.

"These are SAGA's board reports from 1969 and 1970," she explained. Her siblings looked at her quizzically.

"Hang on," her little sister said. "I don't follow."

"Neither do I," said Sverre.

"A few days ago, I went to Blakstad Hospital."

"Grandma did a stint out there, didn't she?" Andrea said in a tone that annoyed Sasha. "You're not an artist unless you've fought with a few inner demons."

"She became psychotic in the spring of 1970," Sasha said, meeting her sister's gaze and trying to talk calmly and patiently. "Two years of suicide attempts and the use of 'mechanical force' before she was discharged."

She could see her words were having an effect on them both. Andrea's broad smile froze and Sverre went as stiff as a waxwork.

"The next thing I discovered was that Grandma was put under a Guardianship Order. Do you know what that means? She was deprived of her legal capacity. Arguably the strongest constraints that can be enforced in Norway. Grandma had a guardian. And that guardian was our father. Not just while she was hospitalised, but in the years that followed, until the order was lifted in 1975."

"Shit," said Andrea.

Sverre took a deep breath, tipped his head back and stared at the stucco ceiling.

"Nobody has ever told us about this. Last night I went through SAGA's internal reports," Sasha continued, tapping the yellowing papers on the table, "to see what significance this might have for Grandma's estate and her control over the family's companies."

They were both leaning forward in their chairs now.

"We're all familiar with the story of SAGA's founding," said Sasha. "With some of the money from the sale of our share in the Falck shipping company, Daddy and Vera established a company and foundation in 1965 that would later become SAGA. The foundation's articles of association are clear."

She picked up a document and read: " 'It falls to the founders of the foundation, Vera Margrethe Lind and Olav Theodor Falck, to choose and dismiss other board members, and also to extend their positions on the board, without the time limits that apply to the other board members, so long as they have full legal capacity.' "

"I didn't even know Grandma was on the board," said Andrea, whose interest was now reluctantly piqued.

"Of course she had a seat on the board," Sasha said. "Vera gave Daddy a rather generous advance on his inheritance, so to speak. The fortune was sunk into a billion-kroner non-profit foundation, but on *one* condition: she would have a hand on SAGA's tiller for as long as she wanted."

Sasha opened the report from the following year. "Take a look," she said to Sverre. "This is from June 1970, five years later. Changes have now been made to the board.

There are still *three* signatories. But look who they are this time! Here's Daddy, here's August Greve Jr. But no Vera. Instead, we have her publisher, Johan Grieg."

"Grandma was in Blakstad," Sverre objected. "So, it's hardly surprising."

Sasha waved the document in front of him so that the brittle pages almost came apart. "The devil is in the detail. Look at the articles of association. It now says: 'As the founder of SAGA it is given to Olav Falck to extend his role without the time limit applicable to other board members. Neither can he be unseated.' '*He*' versus '*they*', and '*his* role' versus '*their* role'. Minute linguistic details, with major consequences. And why is Vera Lind left out? Well, that gets mentioned very briefly on page 13. See here."

With her brother and sister craning over her shoulder, she read the passage.

" 'Vera Lind left the board after disagreements with the other members.' Nothing more. But surely the statutes can't change without her approval? Well, there was one exception. Because in June of 1970 Vera no longer has what we call *legal capacity*. The declaration of her incapacity, the removal of her legal ability to act, was the only way to kick her out of SAGA."

"But why?" said Sverre. "Why go to such lengths?"

"Because," Sasha replied slowly, "Vera had been working on a new book that year. I know it was called *The Sea Cemetery*, but what it contained, I've no idea. Vera had a secret so great that Olav was willing to do anything to prevent her from revealing it. Forget the 'will and testament' that's gone astray. The real testament is *The Sea Cemetery*."

"Good Lord," Sverre exclaimed, leaning on the window ledge.

"I need something strong," Andrea said, pouring whisky into three crystal glasses.

"Listen now, both of you," said Sasha. "I've spent my life doing what was expected of me," she continued. "What Daddy expected of me. I'm done with covering up everything that's happened in this family. But I can't do this on my own. I need your help."

"With what, exactly?" Andrea asked.

"There'll be a time after Daddy. We should be prepared. It's up to us to deliver the truth about SAGA. And we have to find out what that is. Daddy's been at the helm for far too long," said Sasha calmly. "We all have seats on the board and a share in the business. It's time for him to step down. He's lied to us. If he doesn't step down, we'll have to force him."

There was silence. Sverre looked distinctly uncomfortable, Andrea peered up at the ceiling towards their father's office, as though he could hear what they were saying. And he probably could; he could hear everything.

"Have you any idea what you're setting in motion here?" Andrea said at last, chasing an ice cube round her glass. "This is mutiny!"

"Perhaps. Are you in?"

Sasha glared at her little sister.

"Are you in?"

Andrea tapped idly at the Falck coat of arms on the heavy crystal glass. "I'm not sure. There can be reasons why certain secrets, or truths, never come out. Daddy knows that. If you go on with this and challenge him directly, this family will be eaten up by conflict and inheritance disputes, like so many others."

She took a deep breath. "I'm saying no."

Sasha felt more contempt for her sister in that moment than she could ever remember. Not just for her spinelessness, but because she always hid it behind her flyaway style.

"Duly noted," Sasha said, turning to her brother.

"Sverre?"

She knew, of course, that he had always fostered the dream, however unrealistic, of following in his father's footsteps as the CEO of SAGA. She made no mention of the way her own ambitions had been affected by the last few days.

He sat in thought for a while, before clearing his throat.

"I'm off to Afghanistan with the Marine Hunters."

He spoke with barely disguised pride. "So, there won't be any power struggles for me right now. I haven't mentioned it to Father, so please don't say anything before I see him tomorrow."

"Congratulations," Sasha said, without enthusiasm.

"Is that all you have to say?" said her brother, offended.

"It was always your dream." Did she feel slightly relieved? Maybe. Relieved and isolated. She got up and left, and as she came out into the long hallway that led to the mezzanine, she remembered something Olav used to say: when you feel isolated, no place is lonelier than Rederhaugen.

19

I'M INCREDIBLY PROUD OF YOU

The phone rang. Sunlight shone into the office, pricking his eyelids. Sverre opened his eyes and reached out a hand for his mobile.

"Hello?" he said, in a crusty voice. He felt dizzy and befuddled after far too much alcohol and far too little sleep. Where was he? On the sofa, in his office. It had gone on late into the night, too many drinks and too many of Andrea's joints and whatever else they had consumed. After Sasha had left, the two of them had sat and talked into the early hours.

Mostly about his tour to Afghanistan and Andrea's many start-up ideas, but also about Sasha.

With her calm outward appearance and measured style, their sister went under most people's radars, but he and Andrea had always thought that beneath the surface lay a suppressed rage. It frightened them, as if she was chiselled from something different from themselves, as if she had dark forces hidden within her. She was like their father. And grandmother.

"Have you forgotten our appointment?" Olav was yelling down the phone at Sverre. "It was your suggestion!"

"Ah, yes."

"Seven-thirty by the boathouse, you said!"

Sverre brought his hand to his forehead, looked at the empty bottles and overflowing ashtrays littering the office, and discovered Andrea fast asleep in a wing-back chair. He had hung his jacket with impeccable care over his desk chair, as he always did, no matter how wrecked he was.

"I'm on my way," he mumbled, and hung up.

Barely conscious, he threw on some casual clothes and dashed out. It was a grey morning at Rederhaugen. The lawn had frozen overnight, the main house and tower were cloaked in dense morning fog. How many times had he walked along this path as a child? He had hated those walks. Hated Olav's "water habituation" exercises. Even all these years later the memories could be triggered just by walking barefoot on cold ground, let alone taking an ice bath. He loathed ice bathing, as the son of an alcoholic loathes the clinking of glasses.

Down by the boathouse, Olav was busy in the Grimsøy, rolling back the tarpaulin over the seats at the aft. On seeing his son, Olav pointed. "There's something wrong with the swim ladder. Can you fix it? Has to be done."

Sverre fetched some tools from the boathouse and secured the ladder.

Then they reversed the boat out.

There was still a hint of winter in the air, but the sun had begun to warm the fjord. Olav stood at the wheel, legs astride. There was something caricature-like about him when he was at the helm.

As children, Sverre and Sasha used to blush when their father, wearing a skipper's cap and chewing on his pipe, tried to engage with more seasoned sailors in their maritime lingo.

Sasha used to call him Terje Vigen, after the old sea dog in Ibsen's picturesque poem.

They had come out into the open sea and a Danish boat passed them on the horizon. Olav slowed down and threw out an anchor; it was reasonably shallow here. The bracing March air had cleared Sverre's head.

On one of the seats lay the Purdey rifle and a shotgun. For no apparent reason Olav loaded the shotgun and charged it. The boat rocked slightly. He handed Sverre the gun. "Let's see what you're made of."

His son looked at him suspiciously. "This is absurd."

"Can you hit that seagull up there?"

The bird was circling high in the wind, some thirty or forty metres above them.

"Of course. But why would I?"

"Come on. Let's see if that trigger's as silky as you say."

Sverre weighed the gun in his hands, placed its butt in the hollow of his shoulder. He took aim; of course he could hit the damned seagull.

"Hesitating, are we?" his father said behind him, laughing.

Sverre slowly lowered the shotgun, without firing. He imagined his father's face after an encounter with a rain of pellets. Sverre Falck, the patricide. He would never get away with a thing like that, not even if he tied his father to the anchor and let him sink into the depths.

Olav stood speechless, as though he could tell what Sverre was thinking.

Sverre emptied the weapon and returned it correctly to his father.

"It's against the law to shoot seagulls." He leaned against the railing.

"Who gives a fig?" said Olav.

"I'm going away for a while."

"Away?"

Sverre drew breath.

"I'm going to Afghanistan, with the Marine Hunters. They need a sniper in Kabul." He tried to keep a steady tone. "I've had an offer to go with them. And I'm going to accept."

"Well, I'll be damned," Olav exclaimed. "You did it in the end. You bloody well did it in the end, Sverre!"

His father smiled, shook his hand and slapped him on the shoulder. "That warrants a drink. And none of that Scots bog water! Something clean, crystal clear!" Despite it being breakfast time, he pulled out a bottle of frozen Beluga vodka from inside the cabin.

"A gift from Garry Kasparov, when he stopped by SAGA," his father said, raising a toast. They emptied their glasses in one. The vodka was surprisingly smooth and mild.

"You're a champion, you know that?" Olav said, refilling their glasses.

Sverre didn't answer.

"You just keep going, after all the punches you've taken. Remember the granite chin? The best boxers are those who can take the most beatings, that's what separates them from the journeymen. Life's about getting a beating but staying on your feet. You've got it, son, just like the Italian boxers. You're Jake LaMotta, damn it, you're Rocky Balboa, you're made of the *right stuff.*"

Sverre had almost forgotten what his father could be like when others hit the jackpot. Nobody could accuse him of being mean or petty: Olav loved it when people did well for themselves. He revelled in the success of others. Not just because it put him in a good light, but because successful people inspired each other, and because he could hold forth about his considerable experience of the joys and curses of success.

He *saw* you, thought Sverre, because he saw himself.

It was mediocrity, people's miseries and neuroses, he couldn't hack.

Olav gave him a hearty hug, and Sverre felt the power that was still there.

"I'm incredibly proud of you. You know that? But you must take care of yourself out in Afghanistan."

"*You* must take care of *your*self," said Sverre.

His father looked at him strangely and laughed. "You mean, remember to wear my life jacket on the fjord?"

Sverre shook his head. It was as if some outside force took over.

"Sasha's found out that you had Grandma declared incapacitated in 1970. She's going to use Vera's story to depose you and seize control of SAGA," he said.

His father straightened up and stared out over the glittering fjord. The seagulls circled over them; a few sailing boats and the Nesodden ferry crossed ahead of them. Olav revealed nothing of what he was thinking, but Sverre could see that his jaw was working, that the blood was pounding hard in his temples.

"Something's happened to Sasha," Sverre said. "She's changed."

"No," said Olav. "Alexandra has become what she always was. She's become like me."

What did he mean by that? Sverre knocked back the rest of his vodka.

"I appreciate your loyalty, Sverre," said his father, pointing towards the estate, which stood low on the horizon. "It will be rewarded."

20

A GRAVEYARD FOR
GRAVESTONES

Sasha was late, and almost broke into a run. She shivered in the icy breeze that was sweeping through Frogner Park from the portal on Kirkeveien and up the wide walkway towards Vigeland's grand Monolith.

She had gone through John Berg's articles. The main traces of him online were his freelance reports from the Middle East and Afghanistan, generally written between 2005 and 2010, as well as a few magazine interviews, including one with Hans Falck in Beirut. Grudgingly, she had to admit it wasn't bad. It made sense that he'd landed the job of writing Hans's biography.

The evening after her confrontations with Mads and then her two siblings, Sasha had sent Berg an email. In his reply he had asked a question that aroused her interest: had Vera Lind ever talked about how she had come to know Hans Falck so well? This had apparently happened in the winter of 1970, when she was working on a book while staying on the Falck estate in Bergen.

Yes, she had to talk to Berg. She might just get something out of it herself. And he had stressed that their conversation would be off the record.

John Berg stood leaning against the granite wall that separated the park from the monument. He was wearing a thin puffa jacket and carrying a small bag just as he had said he would be. Sasha had a clear image of what writers looked like, and he definitely did not coincide with it.

As she drew closer, she registered, despite the blustery wind and the woollen hat pulled down low over his brow, his dark features and playful green eyes.

"You must be Vera Lind?" he said.

She stopped and stared at him. "Pardon me?"

He put his hand over his mouth and smiled.

"Ah, did I say *Vera*? Oh lord, how insensitive can you be? Freudian slip. I'm sorry."

"No worries, I've never had that compliment from anyone under eighty before," she said, shaking her head with a smile.

"Thank you for coming," Berg said. "I'm Johnny."

Johnny? No one was called Johnny nowadays, and certainly no writers.

She nodded. He waited, as though hoping she would start the conversation.

"I was sceptical about talking to you at first," she said, as they wandered slowly towards the fountain at the foot of the Monolith.

"Why's that?"

"I just don't like journalists." Sasha shrugged her shoulders. "They always try to dig the dirt on my family."

"Couldn't agree more. But, Alexandra—"

"Sasha, please," she interrupted.

He smiled. "A Russian name?"

"My great-grandfather was a Pomor businessman. The family never saw him again after he left my great-grandmother carrying his baby in Svolvær. There are rumours he got involved with a Georgian member of the

Politburo and was taken out during the Moscow trials. That was all Daddy managed to find out about him."

She fell quiet. Less than a minute, and she had already said more about the family to a stranger than ever before.

"Well then, Sashenka."

She felt herself blush. Nobody except Vera had ever called her that.

"Let's take a walk," he suggested. "Just background, no tape recorder, no quotes. I just want to understand more about who Hans is and where he comes from. OK?"

"Why did you want us to meet *here*?" she said at last.

"We used to come here on New Year's Eve as teenagers," said Johnny. "We tried to talk the classy Frogner girls into inviting us to their after-parties on Madserud Allé," he said, pointing at the massive villas to the left of the obelisk.

"And how did that go?"

He laughed.

"They treated us like noble savages. Then ditched us."

He spoke in an almost neutral Oslo accent, north Oslo, she guessed.

"And because of some twenty-year-old memories of those Frogner girls you wanted to meet me here?"

"Yes," said Johnny Berg, an earnest expression on his face. "Perhaps it's just me; but are we ever as unhappy and yet happy as we are at fourteen? We have no real past. We have only our dreams. Then we construct a life for ourselves, as they gradually wither away. When we die, our dreams are gone, and only the past remains."

Who on earth talked like that?

Nobody Sasha knew. "So where are you on this scale? Mostly dreams or past?"

"Past, I'm afraid. And you?"

She smiled. "Had you asked me some weeks ago, I'd have said the same. But I'm not so sure anymore."

Sasha immediately regretted, for the second time in minutes, the way he had drawn her out onto thin ice. To her relief, he didn't pick up on it.

"I thought we might go over and take a look at the graves in Vestre Cemetery," said Johnny. "Hans's grandfather is buried there."

They passed the Monolith and continued on into the graveyard. The snow was gone now, barring a few small, scattered heaps in the shadows.

Johnny Berg certainly didn't seem like old money, or even new. He was no social climber. His eyes had something soulful about them, alternating between playful and melancholic.

They came to the northernmost corner of the cemetery.

"All the World War II heroes are buried here," she said.

The most famous resistance fighters and political leaders were all to be found there.

Sasha guided him to a simple soapstone slab.

Thor Falck
Shipowner
3.11.1903 – 23.10.1940

"Why is he buried in Oslo?" asked Berg. "Wasn't he from Bergen?"

She cleared the ground a little around the stone. "Good question! Big Thor and his forbears did live in Bergen. And though they loved being scathing about Oslo, they dreamed of getting recognition in the capital. Thor wanted to be where it happened, even after his death."

She raised her eyebrows and met his gaze.

"And Big Thor, as you call him, is your grandfather too?"

She nodded.

"Yes, although the family tree is a bit complicated."

She hesitated. A rock was about to be lifted that should not be, but it related to Hans and she had agreed to speak about him.

"Grandfather's first marriage was to a painter. She gave him a son, Per," she said flatly.

"The shipping company went downhill as SAGA shot to the stars. And Per Falck lost his fortune?"

"Exactly."

"Might a desire to avenge his father have been Hans's driving force in life?"

"You men are all the same, aren't you?" she said, with a wry smile. "Everything you do is either to impress your fathers or avenge them."

Johnny Berg did not rise to her mild provocation. It had only been a few minutes, but she'd already got the impression that he had no interest in the macho dick-swinging that her brother, her father and Mads all indulged in.

"Vengeance, then."

She nodded. "Hans became a self-elected member of the proletariat – and the communist party. No one talked with a broader working-class accent than him; he toured the Bergen pubs wearing dungarees and workers' shirts to seduce women. You'd have to talk to Daddy about all that, though. I wasn't born."

"Everyone I talk to mentions his way with women," said Berg. "I saw it close up in the Middle East too."

"Yes, he has a thing for Arab women."

"What makes him so attractive?"

"I'll tell you. He makes it seem like the world outside doesn't exist, and that the only thing he cares about is listening to what you have to say."

Johnny Berg had something of the same. "And he can get you to dream. When you talk to Hans, you believe anything's possible. That you can save the world."

They left the cemetery and headed south along Skøyenveien, a quiet road lined with Swiss-style villas. She recounted a few stories about Hans's numerous love interests, from the young Marxist politician to the TV news anchor.

"But there must be a downside to all this?" said Johnny.

"He's amazing with strangers and distant relatives. There are no limits to his empathy, except when it comes to family. The closer you get, the colder and more crass he becomes. I'd love to know what his daughter Marte really thinks of him. It's hard to imagine a more absent father."

Johnny Berg stopped outside an old dark-brown villa and pointed. "D'you know why this house is famous?"

"No, I don't."

"The shipowner who lived here was suspected of smuggling spirits in the late seventies. When the police searched the house, they found a secret room. A massive store of weapons and equipment, enough for a hundred men, together with sophisticated communications equipment and an antenna that could be raised through the chimney like on a submarine. It belonged to Norway's secret army, Stay Behind. Have you heard of it?"

"I run a post-war history archive," she replied, annoyed at what she took to be mansplaining. "Of course I've heard of Stay Behind."

"OK." Johnny grinned. "Hans told me something interesting about your grandmother, by the way."

Sasha turned away to hide her curiosity. "Oh?"

"Vera stayed in Bergen in the winter of 1970, when Hans was still at high school," said Johnny. "That's how they got to know each other, the young A-grade radical student and his eccentric step-grandmother, who was, Hans says, working on a manuscript. Then, one day in April, Hans's room was searched without warning by the secret police."

That was when *The Sea Cemetery* was seized, she thought, feeling her pulse race with a mix of unease and excitement.

"Hans noticed that the police didn't give a toss about his anti-Vietnam War leaflets. The search was just for show. What they actually wanted was to go through the Falck shipping company's private archive, which was housed on the estate."

Was there a link between Vera's manuscript and the archive? Sasha was suddenly reminded of her conversation with the PhD intern.

"But how is this relevant to Hans's biography?" she said.

"Vera, your grandmother, was important to Hans," Berg said seriously. "He came away from his conversations with her that winter with a different perspective, one that became central to his life: always take the side of the little people against the powerful. Never stop dreaming of a better world."

"Grandma stopped dreaming," she said quietly. "And writing."

They had wandered back into the cemetery. Johnny pointed towards a low building in the middle.

"Have you ever been to the graveyard for gravestones?"

"What?"

"Come on," he said.

His style might seem irritatingly rehearsed at times, like those pseudoscientific dating experts you came across occasionally, but there was something genuine, almost boyish about him that she liked. They turned onto another path. Sasha had so many questions, she found it difficult to gather her thoughts.

"So, who's going to publish Hans's biography?"

"Grieg Forlag, of course. I've brought the contract if you want to see it."

"I believe you." She laughed indulgently. "You should talk to Johan Grieg. He's always got lots of great stories and he's known Hans a lifetime."

She hesitated. Weighing the possibilities, for and against. No, she mustn't tell him anything about the manuscript. Johnny Berg was Hans's man, and it might lead him to Vera's will. It was too big a risk.

"There are so many unanswered questions about Grandma," she said. "If Grieg mentions her, especially in relation to what she was doing in 1970, feel free to call."

They had reached an area behind the low building where the tombstones lay strewn on the ground, higgledy-piggledy. They sat down on a bench on a little hill. Berg opened his bag, took out a thermos and handed her a collapsible silicone cup, then cut a slice of cold sausage with his pocketknife and offered it to her on the tip of the blade. She noticed some red dotted scars on the side of his hand.

The tea was sugary and warming. Johnny had the air of a well-seasoned traveller, with little to prove. And there was a simplicity to his hospitality, a quality she valued.

"This is where you end up when you don't pay your fees: in the graveyard of discarded gravestones," said Berg, a chill shadow passing across his green eyes. "But that's not something you Falcks would know anything about."

21

BETWEEN FRIENDS

Olav closed the blinds and turned off the lights in his office before heading down for dinner. Darkness was settling over Rederhaugen, first in the forest and the avenues of trees, then over the lawns and finally on the main house.

The intimate dining room, furnished in the style of the national romantic movement, with rustic wooden furniture painted with flowers and scrolls in the tradition of *rosemaling*, was on the first floor with a view over the auditorium to the west. It was often used for smaller gatherings, whether dinner parties or secret reconciliatory meetings. It was here, for example, that Israeli and Palestinian representatives had dined with Norwegian peace brokers in an early phase of the Oslo process.

Olav was rarely fearful, but what Sverre had said about Alexandra's intrigues had reminded him of the fear he always carried in his heart. He feared his daughter as he had feared his mother. They felt ungovernable, beyond his control.

Olav had felt lonelier since his mother's death than he had for years, but it was not entirely true – as his children often claimed – that he had only acquaintances and no friends. In recent years, Martens Magnus had become a confidant. After Olav had supported him through a break-up the year before, Martens had sent him a personal card, addressed *To my dear friend, Olav,* and he had felt unusually touched.

Yes, their relationship was of mutual benefit, that was for sure, but it was also a friendship.

When he was young, Olav had always sought the company of men older than himself. About halfway through life this had changed, and it was to younger men that he turned. He felt only contempt for his peers – for their ailments, their bodies, their stagnant approach in a world in constant flux.

Martens Magnus was standing before the open log fire in the adjoining room, with a drink in his hand, inspecting a national romantic painting over the mantel.

"Olav!" he said in greeting.

"Martens!" Olav embraced him warmly.

Martens was no longer so young. Now in his late forties, his face had deep furrows after all the years he had spent outdoors, first in northern Norway, then in the desert in Afghanistan, hunting down terrorists with the special forces. At the time there was talk of Martens as a chief of defence in waiting, but he had a calculating air about him that led many people to view him with mistrust. Perhaps he was better suited to working behind the scenes. He had gone on to lead the special forces cell in the Ministry of Defence. And to collaborate with Olav and SAGA as and when.

"Shall we sit? Dinner's ready. Prepared by my youngest."

Andrea brought in a velvety duck terrine with a delicious fragrance of cloves and fennel.

"Great starter," exclaimed Martens. "Do you have plans to become a chef, Andrea?"

"When I take over Rederhaugen, it'll be a boutique hotel with a three-star Michelin restaurant. I hope you don't mind me taking a few pictures. It looks so beautiful in here with the log fire."

Olav raised his eyebrows at the officer as his daughter held up her phone to the handsome coat of arms on the grand stone mantel.

Photography is the lazy man's art form, he thought, as she left for the kitchen below; even a beginner can strike gold.

"Take good care of that one," said Martens. "You might not see it now, but she's got real potential. When I was an instructor, people like her were the most inspiring to work with. The ones who had multiple talents but lacked direction."

"Andrea's good at everything," sighed Olav. "Except being good. She can't manage that."

Martens drained his wine, a bargain Beaujolais chosen by Andrea, then set the glass slowly aside and put a snus pouch under his top lip.

"You look tired, Olav," he said. "You should get yourself a woman."

Olav shook his head.

"No, my friend. I've got enough on my plate with all the women in this family already. Both the living and the dead."

He had, he confided, woken up in the small hours every day since Vera's death. And this had only worsened after Alexandra had started digging in the past. He left out the fact that she was trying to force him to step down. It made him feel strangely ashamed.

"You've never explained why her manuscript was so dangerous," said Martens, pouring more wine for them.

"That's catalogued under *family*."

"Olav," said Martens, looking at him sternly. "If I'm to help you, I need to understand the context." He crossed his powerful arms. "It'll stay between friends."

"Thor, my father," Olav began slowly, "was the director of the Hanseatic Steamship Company in Bergen when the war broke out. He was among the first to organise any resistance against the Germans along the coast. Without him, there would have been no Shetland bus and no radio transmitters in western Norway. He died in the ferry disaster in October 1940, the accident I survived as an infant, and was posthumously awarded the War Cross."

"I've heard of worse skeletons in the cupboard," said MM.

"But Father was also a shipowner and a businessman, caught in an impossible dilemma, between his own convictions and the occupying authorities. After the war, the history books were, as you know, pretty black and white, and my father's more – how should I put it? – problematic activities were airbrushed out. Until my mother decided, twenty-five years later, to write a book about it. And yes, he may have had to enter into certain agreements with the German authorities, but who are we to judge the dead?"

Olav drank more wine, trying to swallow his discomfort at having said so much.

"And now Sasha's looking for the manuscript? How did she get wind of it?"

"Initially I thought Mother had confided in her," said Olav. "But who knows? I'm leaning towards the idea that it was somebody at the publishing house. Mother's old editor, or even Johan Grieg himself."

"Grieg is a pompous old fool," said Martens.

Olav glanced at him with irritation. "Well might you say, but he knows about certain things that happened in 1970, things that point right back here."

"Isn't he on his last legs?"

"Yes, thank God," said Olav. "Perhaps nature will do the job, in this case."

Andrea brought in the main course, *boknafisk* fried in garlic butter, with lardons, a minted pea purée and carrots cooked in butter with cumin and honey.

They ate in silence.

"I'm afraid I've got more bad news," Martens said, wiping the corner of his mouth with a linen napkin decorated with the Falck coat of arms.

Olav felt his heart sink.

"What now?"

Martens cleared his throat. "It's Johnny Berg."

"Yes, I heard he was back in Norway," said Olav, doing his best to seem unruffled. "I don't suppose I need to remind you whose idea it was to use him."

"We'd never have got Fellah otherwise," replied Martens. "With everything that might have led to. Blood in the streets of Oslo, growing hatred between immigrants and the ethnic Norwegian population, vigilantism and more radicalisation. A situation spiralling out of control. Taking out Fellah was the best thing that could have happened. For the world, and for *multicultural* Norway."

Olav sat in thought for a moment. "I was always sceptical about using Berg, with his anti-authoritarian tendencies."

"He's like most exceptional people," retorted Martens. "Their strengths are also their weaknesses, and vice versa. Berg said yes because we could exert pressure on him. The problem is we didn't lift a finger to get him out when he was taken. Had we done so, we could have convinced him to keep—"

"Oh, that hindsight of yours!" Olav said, annoyed. "My impression was that he was out of the picture. Instead, he comes home and then gets released. Who's behind it all? Smells like HK from a long way off."

"It wasn't him," said Martens. "Hans Falck got Johnny out of Kurdistan."

"You *what*?" said Olav, in a voice that revealed he was genuinely shocked.

"It's quite logical. They knew each other from the Middle East. Berg interviewed him in Lebanon years ago. Two of a kind, if you ask me."

"Does Hans know what Berg did out there?"

Martens shook his head slowly. "I'm not sure. He's got pretty good contacts in the region, but I doubt it."

"How many people knew about the mission?"

"Berg, myself, the American volunteer he was on assignment with – who was killed – and a Norwegian Kurdish volunteer in Iraq, who acted as mediator."

"Who was the Norwegian Kurd?"

"Mike something or other. A soldier who left his unit and joined the Peshmerga in the fight against IS. A bit of a celebrity, uses Instagram to tell the world when he's fighting the terrorists."

"Damned social media," Olav mumbled irritably. Who in the world had let this kind of thing go online? It contravened everything he believed about war and strategy. The openness of social media made him feel old.

"I checked," Martens said, pointing to his mobile. "NordicSNIPER, his account, has been quiet for a while now.

I talked to some contacts down there. He's presumed dead. An artillery strike by IS two weeks ago."

"Even terrorists have their uses," Olav said thoughtfully. "But I want to be a hundred per cent certain. Are we sure that none of this, under any circumstances, can be traced back to SAGA?"

Contrary to what his friends and enemies believed, Olav preferred to exercise caution where possible. There had clearly been a high level of risk surrounding this assignment, but various layers had been put between the operator and SAGA, intended to make the whole thing watertight.

Martens Magnus nodded. "We've got it under control."

Olav had let SAGA work alongside the authorities and the intelligence services from the beginning. It would have been easier if he'd limited himself to conventional capitalism and to the pompous do-gooding associated with most foundations, but he'd have been horribly depressed. SAGA and the Rederhaugen estate had been a part of Stay Behind during the Cold War because it was in the nation's interests to be prepared in the event of a communist invasion. And when hundreds of young Norwegians went abroad to serve a terrorist crypto state like IS, it was in the national interest to eliminate them before they did harm to Norway. Hence his and MM's own brainchild: SB 2.0. Olav was convinced he was right, regardless of the political climate.

Here in the dining room, over a glass of wine, as Martens sat lost in thought across the table, his own historic mission shone brighter than ever: to defend Norway, by whatever means necessary. It might sound grandiose and pretentious. But it was his true calling.

Andrea came in with dessert, a creamy soufflé made from an old, dried-out Christmas loaf that wafted the warm aroma of raisins and cardamon, which in his current world-weary state almost brought tears to his eyes.

"Oh, by the way," he said, lightening the mood, "Sverre seems very motivated for the mission in Afghanistan. Thanks for getting him a foot in the door."

"Well, it was your idea, Olav." Martens smiled and raised his glass. "To Sverre. And to our friendship."

"Hmm." Olav cleared his throat, slightly embarrassed.

"Daddy?" Andrea stood in the doorway, wearing her black hoodie. "I'm off now."

"Andrea, come here, my dear," said Olav.

"What is it?" she said, blushing.

"You can be whatever you want to be," he said, hugging her hard. "Whatever you want."

She left the room. Sasha's betrayal had reminded him of how fond he was of his youngest daughter. Fortunately, she didn't suffer the same curse as Vera and Alexandra.

"One last thing." Martens seemed suddenly uneasy. "It seems that Grieg Forlag has signed a contract for Hans Falck's biography."

"A biography of Hans?" chuckled Olav. "Then we must lift the family ban on talking to journalists. I might even want to tell the author a few stories about Hans myself."

"I'm not sure that would be wise," Martens said seriously. "Hans's biographer, whose research will involve talking to various members of your family, is Johnny Berg."

22

YOU ARE A FALCK

Sasha had started to train daily, taking long runs along the fjord and finishing with a series of exercises aimed at strengthening her core. Any husband should have been worried at such a sudden change in his wife, but Mads displayed no reaction. His indifference provoked her.

The more she thought about how Mads and her siblings had taken her father's side, the angrier she became. She had always been accused of finding it hard to let things go, and this was no trifling matter, it went to the heart of the family's understanding of itself. Grandma had been wronged, and nobody dared countenance it. They were cowards.

She had gone to the Litteraturhuset to hear Hans Falck give a talk on "War and Feminism in the Middle East". In an auditorium so packed and oversubscribed that his lecture had to be transmitted on screens all around the centre, he described the situation in Kurdistan and the fight against IS.

The atmosphere was electric. Naturally no one else from the family was there. Olav would rather have joined the foreign fighters than sit and watch Hans Falck get a standing ovation for his "superlative humanitarian heroism", as the director of the Litteraturhuset described it.

The audience was duly moved and shaken by what Hans said. About the teenage girls who had been abducted and sold as sex slaves to wealthy Gulf Arabs in the slave markets of Mosul, and then managed to escape.

"And these women," said Hans, "who have lived through atrocities we can barely conceive of, now form the vanguard of the fight against terrorism, against barbarism. It is they who are fighting for their own and for other women's freedom in the region. Heroism is not a strong enough word to describe the actions of these female soldiers, nor does it encapsulate the respect I feel for them. One of them begged me: 'We need help! The world needs to know!'"

Despite the dramatic content of Hans's lecture, Sasha drifted into her own thoughts. It seemed increasingly clear to her that the events of spring 1970 would shed light on where exactly Vera's manuscript had gone. Grandma had been declared incapacitated, that much was certain, and she knew her father would wriggle his way out of any allegations if she failed to secure hard evidence. Until then, confrontation would have to wait.

Sasha had scoured the auditorium for Johnny Berg all evening, but he was nowhere to be seen. When the lecture was over and Hans stood in the foyer, surrounded by TV cameras, reporters and admirers, she pushed her way towards him.

"Sasha," he said, placing his hands on hers and looking into her eyes without a care for anyone else. "You look amazing. How lovely of you to come."

She praised his lecture and asked: "Can we have a chat?"

"Absolutely," he said disarmingly. "I'm off to dinner now with the Griegs, father and son, but I'll be at Rederhaugen tomorrow for the board meeting. What's it about?"

A group of journalists hovered around him impatiently.

"I want to talk about Vera," Sasha whispered.

A shadow of doubt crossed Hans's tanned face before the confident smile returned. "Vera Lind? An inexhaustible subject, Sasha dear. We'll return to it after the board meeting."

Returning from her run, Sasha took a quick shower, got dressed and went out into the living room. She looked at the clock over the kitchen door in the lodge. The board meeting was due to start in half an hour.

"We really must decide on our holiday soon," Mads said, staring into the Mac.

Sasha heard the girls arguing upstairs over an iPad.

"I suppose," she replied, leaning reluctantly over her husband's shoulder. His payment details were up on the page.

"Why does it say Mads Falck on your credit card?"

When they had got married six years ago, Mads had taken her surname. It was he who had insisted on a church wedding. Sasha would have preferred a rather less solemn event, at a foreign embassy, for example. But that had been out of the question. Mads had given his old mother as an excuse. She read the weekly magazines and followed royal weddings with the same devotion as others watched the World Cup; she'd die if they were married on a rainy Tuesday in Paris.

In his wedding speech, Mads had said it was out of love that he would take Falck-Johansen as his surname, at which a rebellious sixteen-year-old Andrea had immediately got up from her seat at one of the long tables and shouted: "Was it out of love you swapped the *t* for a *d* in Mads too?"

She hadn't said so at the time, but Sasha felt he was crossing an intimate boundary with that name change.

A year ago, she had noticed that the hyphen between the two surnames had been discreetly dropped, making his name Mads Falck Johansen. And now the Johansen had disappeared entirely.

"It doesn't mean anything," he said. "What matters is that we get some time to relax. We need it. Both of us."

He smiled. She did not.

On their first date Mads had taken her to his childhood home, a short train ride out of the capital, a drab little suburban town. Sasha had never set foot in such a place before, and he knew how to use it to his advantage. He pointed to a window at the top floor of a grey four-storey block. "That was my bedroom window," he said. "I stood at it every day, looking out at the shopping centre, planning how to get away from here."

Perhaps she should have read the signs then, but instead she kissed him behind the shopping mall, under the extractor fan of a fast-food shop, amid the warm smell of chip fat and ketchup, which she still associated with his stubble and tongue.

"I've found a place in Provence that you'll love," he said. "I'm booking it now."

"With nouveau-riche Saudis and duck-faced Eurotrash?"

"Not at all. A splendid property, in Brantes, in a village near Mont Ventoux. It belongs to a famous French chanteuse. It looks great. Not even a grocery store in the village. Nothing, just a bookstore and a market on Thursdays. Very bijou. Isn't that what you like?"

She cast a half-hearted glance at the pictures and shrugged.

"Looks OK."

Sasha went out into the kitchen in search of something to eat before going out. She heard the quiet tapping of the keyboard come to a halt.

"Is something the matter, Sasha?" Mads called out.

"How do you mean?"

"You've been a bit off lately," he said, appearing in the doorway. "Ever since Vera died. Like you've got tunnel vision. As though we, the people who live here, don't mean anything to you anymore."

"Your name is Falck now," Sasha said.

"Don't tell me it's about *that*?"

"It is," she said, glaring at him. "You're part of the family. And I'm fed up with the way we sweep secrets under the carpet."

"I just don't want the family to fall apart. When I talked to Olav, he was very clear that a death can unleash—"

"Have you been talking to Daddy behind my back?"

Sasha had to force herself not to yell.

His gaze flickered. "Not about that, of course. But I talk to your father all the time."

Mads put his arms round her waist. It felt clumsy and out of place. She pushed him away, and he sat back down sheepishly.

"Well, anyway. Let's book our trip. We can pay Martens' daughter to come as a babysitter. Then you can work as much as you want from there."

"Just book it. The house looks lovely," she said.

He smiled with relief and went back into the living room to enter his card details.

"Done. We're going to Provence!"

"But I shan't be joining you."

Mads looked at her, dumbfounded. "What are you talk-ing about?"

Sasha took her coat from the stand. "You want to go to Provence, the kids have a babysitter, I want to stay at home. Everything's perfect, right?"

"Fuck!" he said.

"The board meeting's about to start. I've got to go."

Sasha put on her coat, closed the door and breathed out in relief. It was freezing cold. Large, heavy snowflakes were forming a white blanket over Rederhaugen, they settled on her woollen coat and hair and melted against her fore-head. Spring was capricious. She lit a cigarette. Johnny Berg smoked too, she remembered. He didn't look like a smoker. She liked that anomaly. It was probably a habit left over from long days in the field as a journalist. She pictured him in a smoky expat bar in Beirut or Kabul. War reporters always smoked.

Why hadn't he contacted her?

23

PASSIVE HELP TO DIE

"I want to welcome you," Olav said, "to this extraordinary board meeting. Our first since Mother's tragic death."

Siri Greve sat at the other end of the table. She was acting as both speaker and chair.

"Where is Grieg?" asked Sasha.

Olav glanced suspiciously over at his daughter. It was one thing that she had disregarded his warnings not to enter Vera's dark labyrinth. But to conspire behind his back to have him removed . . . Even worse was the thought that a certain John Omar Berg was waiting in the long grass, to help stitch all this together. Had they already talked?

"Johan Grieg is indisposed," Siri said. "He has, as we all know, certain health issues. But he hasn't passed on any instructions."

That was some good news, at least, Olav thought. As far as he could tell, Grieg had kept his promise. He had not said a word.

"The main purpose of today's meeting is to orientate you all on the situation surrounding the transfer of the estate, specifically Mother's will, and the consequences this will have for the business," said Olav. "But first, I want to reassure everyone that our plans for the SAGA Arctic Challenge are on track. We're going to host the best conference ever seen in Norway. And not only that, we'll finally put our family's painful history with the Hurti-gruten disaster to rest. Sverre, could you elaborate?"

"Well," said Sverre, hesitantly, "Ralph Rafaelsen is no longer taking any calls. And his assistant just sent me an email saying he can't put his Exosuit at our disposal after all."

"Why not?"

"You'd have to ask him. But I don't think he enjoyed our last meeting. A lack of respect, his assistant implied."

Olav stared at his son for a moment. "Rafaelsen is a pathetic drama queen. You'll get this nonsense sorted, Sverre."

He turned and nodded at Siri.

"So, to Vera Lind's death," the lawyer began. "The situation with her will remains unchanged. All we know is that she picked it up on the day she died. And, as you're probably aware, it hasn't surfaced."

All eyes were fixed on her.

"In practical terms this means, should we declare there to be no will, that Vera's only son Olav will be her sole heir, and that her estate, including the properties at Hordnes, the Hunting Lodge and Rederhaugen, will be transferred to him."

"I demand a postponement," said Hans Falck.

"Hans Falck wishes to speak," Siri said dryly.

Olav tried to read his nephew's face. Had he underestimated him? It would not be the first time. He had never really taken Hans seriously before he became a renowned humanitarian doctor. He regretted that now. They could have worked together. Hans could have brought something to SAGA that it lacked. But it was too late now.

"The day before Vera Lind committed suicide," Hans said, "I received a phone call from her—"

"We've already heard this story of yours," Olav interrupted. "Although, last time you said it was *two* days before."

"Listen, Olav," Hans said calmly. "*You* may have heard it, but what about everyone else?"

The others looked at him questioningly, which he clearly took as an invitation to continue.

"During that call, verifiable in my phone log with a duration of 9 minutes and 34 seconds, Vera asked me to go to Rederhaugen immediately. She wanted to inform me of changes to her will. What this fully entailed, she only hinted at, although it was clear to me that she wanted to return to us the ownership of Hordnes. But before I could get to Rederhaugen, I was informed that she had died."

"What will you come up with next, Hans?" asked Olav. "That we pushed Mother over High Cliff to stop you getting a share of the inheritance? Take off your tinfoil hat, you paranoid clown."

"I can't be sure what Vera was going to say," Hans said, completely unaffected. "My only request on behalf of my branch of the family is that the decision be postponed. That's surely not unreasonable."

Andrea had been leaning back, rocking in her chair. She now took the floor.

"Hang on! None of us had anything to do with Grandma over the last few years. Not you, Daddy, not you, Hans. Not Siri or Martens. Not Sverre. Nor me."

Martens had been right at dinner: Andrea had a gift for cutting through the noise.

"There's only one person sitting at this table who can possibly comment on what Grandma really wanted. So instead of listening to some tiresome quarrel between

Daddy and Hans, on behalf of the rest of us, I want to hear if you have something interesting to say about all this, Sasha."

Sasha shuffled the papers in front of her, before straightening up. "I have the greatest respect for the views on both sides," she said diplomatically. "But from my conversations with Grandma I agree with Hans that it would be premature to assume that she didn't intend to leave a will. I say we need more time."

"Alexandra . . ." Olav objected, but his daughter was not for turning.

"I don't want Grandma's death to turn into some degrading fight between the two sides of the family. My suggestion is that this discussion be postponed until the entire Bergen branch can be present. Then I suggest a family council. Without external lawyers. I'm sure Grandma would have preferred that too."

"I'm not so sure about that," muttered Olav, but the others nodded. He was outnumbered.

"A family council it is then," he said resignedly. "But don't come to me if it all ends in scandal. Let's close the meeting and have lunch."

Lunch comprised a silky pumpkin soup served with croutons and melted Roquefort, followed by lamb fricassee with boiled potatoes, accompanied by a bottle of Château Margaux 2005, brought up from the cellar. The lamb was so tender it fell off the bone, and the rich tomato sauce with mushrooms and silver onions had a delicious aroma of rosemary. Only Andrea could have sprinkled such fairy dust on these tired old recipes.

Olav sat silently in his chair, the only one with armrests, at the centre of the long side of the table, as was the tradition among the upper classes. Lowlier Norwegians might have assumed he should sit at the head of the table, where he could exert proper control. Right now he felt his power slipping away from him, and that was intolerable.

Sasha avoided catching his eye all through lunch. But now Olav saw an opportunity to turn on the charm and reassert himself. "These Burgundy and Bordeaux wines are really something else. Alexandra, my dear, perhaps you could help me bring a few more bottles up from the cellar?"

It was a command, not a question, and she got up with visible reluctance. They walked down the hallway to the rose tower and down the winding staircase to the floor below. From there a creaking staircase led down to the wine cellar. The air smelled raw and damp. The bulb buzzed and flickered before coming on, a pale-yellow glow that cast heavy shadows.

Olav lifted a bottle of brandy up to the light, opened it and took a swig straight from the bottle. The fiery taste of fermented grapes leaped down his throat. He passed the bottle to his daughter.

"Aren't we supposed to be fetching more wine?" she said.

"I want to tell you something, Alexandra. Something I've never told anyone," said Olav quietly in the semi-darkness. "Things got difficult between Mother and me precisely because of her manuscripts. Your grandmother put her own needs before the family's."

"The war ended long ago, Daddy. All the contemporary witnesses are gone."

Olav weighed the brandy bottle in his hand and looked at his daughter's face, half hidden in the shadows.

"What could be so dangerous that you had to strip Vera of her legal capacity?" said Sasha.

So Alexandra knew about the Guardianship Order? A fan hummed steadily in the laundry room beyond.

"Why didn't you ever tell me about this?" she continued. "Why do I, an archivist, know fuck all about what's hiding away in the archives?"

"I doubt you can imagine," he said slowly, "what it's like when the person who should, by any natural law, take care of you, is in fact the one who needs protection. There's something fundamentally anachronistic about your investigation. You're looking at the people of the past through your own eyes."

"You're trying to talk your way out of—"

He interrupted her.

"Let me continue. The statutes of the Guardianship Act state clearly that an appointed guardian – that was me – has a duty of confidentiality that also applies after the order is withdrawn. I had the law on my side."

"I actually read the law recently," Sasha said. "It states clearly that the duty of confidentiality does not apply to their children or grandchildren."

There was so much he wanted to say, about Vera and her manuscript, about Johnny Berg and SAGA, but for once he was unable to formulate his thoughts in any meaningful way. He gazed at his daughter for a long time in the dark, his mother's features, that blend of something so utterly familiar, the closest thing he knew, and simultaneously so alien.

"Who knows about this?" Sasha asked. "The Greve family? Johan Grieg? He never answers his phone."

Olav could see his daughter was not giving up. He must visit Grieg as soon as possible.

"Johan is ill," he said. "But you can try to talk to him."

It was dark and snowing heavily as Johnny hurried across a busy Kristian IVs Gate and sought refuge under the awnings of the Hotel Bristol. He walked briskly up the red carpet leading to the ornate lobby with its golden arches held up by heavy Moorish pillars.

HK was sitting in his usual spot, in a little alcove to the left of the bar, sipping a glass of white wine with studied leisureliness.

"Best table in the Library Bar," he said. "Both the Grieg family and I have the secret number to book it. Will you have one?"

"I'm driving," Johnny replied. "You said it was urgent."

"First tell me how you are," said HK, who obviously intended to keep him on tenterhooks a while longer.

"I go running every day, and I've cut down to one cigarette in the evening," Johnny replied. "I took a walk in the park with Sasha Falck. We passed Big Thor's grave, Meyer's Stay Behind villa and the gravestones' graveyard."

"Excellent," said HK. "You took her on a little tour through modern Norwegian history. What were your impressions?"

"She seemed smart and a bit lonely," Johnny said. "But that's probably to be expected when you're unlucky enough to be an intelligent person born into a family of billionaires. She's sent me several emails since, none of which I've answered."

HK chuckled. "Better still. Oldest trick in the book."

"Why did you want to meet?"

"Last time we met, I mentioned that I was involved in the investigation of Thor Falck's widow, Vera Lind, in 1970. And you told me you'd visited Grieg Forlag."

He took a document out of his briefcase, his eyes sweeping over a room filled with West End wives, waiters and a pianist playing lounge jazz.

Johnny leaned across the table to see.

HK raised an index finger. "Steady now, Johnny. Sensitive documents have, as you know, a nasty habit of disappearing from archives. Don't ask me how it came into my possession, but you have before you the name of the secret police's source in the case against Vera Lind. And from what I can tell, it seems that this person had a bad conscience."

He raised an eyebrow teasingly. "Do what you want with it. Perhaps you'll manage a visit? The source is alive, though in poor health, so I'd act quickly."

Johan Grieg's villa was easy enough to find. Johnny turned into a driveway between two tall dark spruce trees. The gravel crunched under his tyres. He stopped the car, jumped out and walked towards the entrance. The heaps of snow were still piled high out here. Beyond the sharp silhouette of the brown-stained house he glimpsed the lights of the city centre.

He paused for a moment before ringing the bell.

Nobody came to open up and the windows were dark. But he was pretty sure Grieg was in. The question was whether or not he was alone.

"Who is it?" said a voice from behind the door.

"Johnny Berg. Hans Falck's biographer . . ."

The door opened a crack, and the publisher's pale, confused face poked out.

"How about you let me in? I'll explain everything."

Hesitantly, the old publisher opened the door. Dressed in a soiled cardigan and baggy suit trousers, he seemed very old. He walked unsteadily down a hallway lined with framed photographs of himself with authors and other cultural figures. Johnny stopped at a photograph taken in the Mirror Room of the Grand Hotel. A young Grieg with Vera Lind. He went closer. The picture was dated December 1969.

"You had a seat on the SAGA board in the early years?" Johnny asked.

"I did indeed. That's how I came to know the family so well. Although it went further back than that really. My father was close friends with Thor Falck, and Olav and I spent a lot of time together at Rederhaugen when we were young. We ran around in the underground tunnels there, it was a paradise. Parents weren't as worried about what their children got up to as they are now."

"So wasn't it rather . . . incestuous for Vera Lind to publish her novels with Grieg?"

He laughed. "What's publishing if not incestuous? Everyone knows everyone. Besides, I can assure you that Vera's novels satisfied the strict standards the house maintained. She was brilliant. Today we'd have sold her books abroad and to television channels for enormous sums. Anyway, when my father retired in the late sixties and I took over, it was only natural that I be offered a seat on the board."

He showed Johnny into the living room, dominated by a panoramic window that looked out over a darkened garden. Johnny noticed a faint smell of excrement and vomit, and a trolley piled with cardboard cups and medicines. On the table was more medication and a cortisone syringe.

"My home help is coming soon," Grieg said. "So, we don't have all the time in the world."

"Did you know Hans when you joined the board?"

"Not until a few years later. I remember him as a brilliant and arrogant youth, convinced he was right about everything. Well, pretty much how he is now."

Grieg chuckled and cleared his throat.

"Hans talked a lot with Vera when she was working on her manuscript in 1970," said Johnny.

The publisher's face took on the look of someone who knows he is being lured onto thin ice. "Is that so?"

"Vera wrote the first draft of *The Sea Cemetery* on the old family estate in Bergen."

A shadow crossed Grieg's face. "If you say so. I can't possibly recall all the details of an author's comings and goings from that far back."

"You say that Vera Lind was a brilliant writer. Isn't it odd then that *The Sea Cemetery* was never published? Hans Falck thought so at least."

Grieg took a glass of water from the trolley next to his armchair and brought it to his lips, his hand shaking. He collected himself.

"Not really. Vera wasn't a historian. She was a novelist. This book was an entirely different enterprise. It was about real people, it made claims that needed verifying. We could perhaps have released it as a novel. But then again, novels were more open to accusations of libel back then – you may remember the lawsuits against Agnar Mykle and Jens Bjørneboe. But that wasn't what Vera wanted anyway. This was personal. She said she wanted to change history. So, I'm afraid she bit off more than she could chew. And, anyway, what does Hans know?"

"So you couldn't publish it?"

"Not as it stood. It was an editorial decision."

"An editorial decision?" said Johnny. "Strange then that the secret police were involved."

Grieg tilted his head to one side. "What are you talking about?"

"I have a letter here addressed to the head of the security service. It refers to *The Sea Cemetery*. And yes, you're mentioned in it."

"That could well be a fake, young man."

"Sure," said Johnny. "Although it came from a reliable source, and it's so detailed that I think we ought to go through it."

The publisher did not answer, but his lower lip trembled slightly.

Johnny began to read. "'The aforementioned Grieg is well acquainted with the author Vera Margrethe Lind and her residence Rederhaugen, and has known the suspect since childhood, when he often played there. He also knows the tunnel system that runs under the property in detail.' You disagree?"

"Certainly I knew Rederhaugen. I've told you that."

Johnny read on. "'During a preliminary meeting at the Library Bar, Hotel Bristol on April 14, 1970, it emerged that Fru Lind has threatened to reveal in book form details pertaining to Stay Behind and Occupation Preparedness.'"

"Enough," said the old man.

"No, there's more." Johnny smiled and cleared his throat almost theatrically. "'Against this background, a full investigation of the author was launched on April 15 in connection with the unpublished manuscript of *The Sea Cemetery*. Following a ruling by the public prosecutor, the manuscript was seized at the premises of Grieg Forlag, Sehesteds gate 2, Oslo, on April 26, 1970.'"

"I don't want to hear any more."

Johnny got up and walked across the living room to the trolley.

"You must see that this is relevant to any biography of Hans."

"Not at all. This is Vera's story, not Hans's."

"I presented my ideas on how the biography should be structured at your offices the other day," Johnny continued confidently. "Everyone was in total agreement that the meeting in Bergen between Vera and Hans during the winter of 1970, when Vera talked to the young high school student about the most important values in life—"

Here Grieg managed a scornful laugh. "And what might they be?"

"That every moral person, whether they be a writer or doctor, has a duty to fight for ordinary people against the rich and powerful. Honesty is vital and the truth is never dangerous. Say what you will about Hans Falck, but it's easy to see how important these values have been for him."

"I have every respect for Hans. What is it you want?"

"To make a deal. You tell me what happened in 1970, and I'll consider burying it."

"It's true," said Grieg slowly, "that I spoke with the secret police on occasion. And yes, it had come to my attention that Vera was working on a potentially sensitive manuscript. And I shared that with my contact."

"So much for free speech," Johnny said.

"Times were different then!" Anger seemed to give Grieg renewed energy, but he was interrupted by a coughing fit. "The war heroes were still alive. An anonymous man rang me at the office. He told me that the manuscript had to be destroyed. He said they would search Vera's estates too, to make sure there were no copies left."

"And what did you do?"

"I smuggled it out." Grieg smiled. "And gave it to Vera."

Johnny read, " 'The publisher Johan Grieg is a strong advocate of the freedom of speech, and has reported to his handler, Officer Tofte, that he now has a guilty conscience at having informed on one of his own authors. It is recommended, therefore, that his work as an informant with the security service be terminated with immediate effect.' "

"I've loathed myself for forty-five years for what they did to Vera," Grieg said, gazing out the window.

"And what better way to make amends than to produce the manuscript and guarantee that it will be published this time?"

"Let's say, hypothetically, that I have this manuscript," said Grieg. "Why would I give the only extant copy to you?"

"There are two answers to that," Johnny said. "The first is that it would hardly look good for the publishing house if it came out in the press that the legendary Johan Grieg was an informer who squealed on his own authors to the secret police. I hardly think Peder would be impressed."

"An informer?" Grieg snorted. "Threats don't touch a dying man."

Johnny looked at the old publisher for a long time. "I think you actually wanted the best for Vera Lind. But you were a coward. You were afraid of the Falck family, especially Olav. The real reason that you're going to give it to me is that we want the same thing. We want the truth to come out, no matter what Olav says."

"It's possible we could meet halfway," said Grieg. However frail he might seem, he had clearly lost none of his horse-trading instincts.

"*The Sea Cemetery* is in two parts. The controversial and injurious allegations made against certain named persons, in particular Thor Falck, can be confirmed by documents held in the Hanseatic Steamship Company's private archive in Bergen. I'd be willing to give you the first part – in return for your total discretion about this security service story, naturally."

Johnny was unhappy that Grieg was dictating the terms.

"You will visit the archive in Bergen," Grieg continued. "In it you'll find evidence to prove that Vera was telling the truth. Without that, her claims are worthless, I'm afraid. If you can show me this evidence, I'll consider it a sign of your good faith. Then, and only then, may you read the rest. And let's be clear, the first part is nothing on its own. To go public with this, you'll need both."

He got up and tottered across the floor with the help of a walking frame, opened a safe that was bricked into the wall, and returned with a brown envelope.

"This is *The Sea Cemetery*," he said.

He handed Johnny the envelope containing a wad of pages.

"Take good care of Part Two," said Johnny.

"You can be sure of that," Grieg said. "Should any-thing happen to me, the manuscript is ready for publication. Please, leave now. My carer will be here any minute."

A car swung out of the gates of Grieg's property as Olav arrived. He rang the bell; no answer. It was years since he had been here.

The door was unlocked.

"Felicia?"

Grieg's croaky voice issued from the living room.

"Who's Felicia?" Olav asked as he stepped inside. "A new mistress?"

"Olav!" Grieg said, taken aback, before adding rather feebly, "No, such things aren't of interest to me any longer. Felicia's my carer. From the Philippines."

Olav felt his impatience bubbling up.

"We need to talk, Johan."

"Well, go ahead, Olav. Talk. You've always been so good at it."

Olav leaned on the edge of a sofa. Seeing Grieg's phys-ical decline elicited a certain malicious pleasure in him. He took a seat opposite the old man.

"Johan's curse! Isn't that what you say in the Grieg family? That's why you took the money from Stay Behind, wasn't it? The publishing house was facing a crisis, you had no choice. You were busy being the man about town instead of keeping control of the finances."

"I was a patriot and anti-communist, damn it," said Grieg. He had regained his composure. "Just like you."

"I understood why you did what you did," said Olav. "And it was the right thing to do. That manuscript could not be allowed to see the light of day."

The publisher reached for his glass of water; his trembling had increased. Olav decided to take a chance.

"Was it you who visited Mother and took the manuscript on the day she died?"

"What are you talking about?"

Grieg leaned forward in an attempt to get up, but as he did so his legs gave way, and he crashed into the trolley and lay sprawled and helpless on the floor.

Pill bottles scattered in all directions, along with a cortisone syringe, a mobile phone and an A4 envelope.

Grieg was lying in convulsions on the floor. "The syringe," he gasped. "Stick the cortisone in me. Call . . . you must call . . . an ambulance."

Olav stood calmly a few metres away, his arms crossed.

"Where's Mother's manuscript? Her 'testament'?"

Grieg retched.

"Have you heard . . . of an . . . Addisonian crisis . . . I'm dying, damn it," he whispered.

"Where is it?"

The publisher slowly turned his head, and they made eye contact.

"I beg you, Olav . . . Stick the bloody syringe in . . . and I'll explain everything."

"For the last time, where is it?"

Lying in a foetal position, Grieg pointed a shaky finger towards the padded envelope on the floor. Olav picked it up. It was open at one end. He took out the wad of paper and leafed through it. It was surprisingly short. "This isn't the whole manuscript," he said.

A grotesque smile appeared on Grieg's pale, distorted face. It was as though he had found renewed strength. "You think you can control everything, Olav. But this time you're too late."

Olav wavered for a moment. Then headed for the door.

"There was a young man here just now."

At that moment the publisher's phone rang. Olav stopped, took a few steps back. The phone moved across the floor like a beetle on its back.

On the display it read: *Alexandra Falck*.

Sasha walked across the half-empty lobby of Oslo Central Station. Grieg may not have responded, but she had received a text from Berg. From Johnny. From Johnny Berg. Mads and the girls would leave for France tomorrow, and her days would be filled back to back with work and nothing more. Just the thought of it excited her. Might the task of finding Vera's manuscript lead to other places? Maybe SAGA and Rederhaugen needed a woman at the helm.

The clock near the departures board showed half past ten. She passed Burger King and the ticket machines on the left and hurried up the escalator.

Johnny was sitting in the pub, a generic watering hole of the type found at most stations. He had chosen a table beneath a framed Wayne Rooney shirt.

He waved at the bartender, who immediately came over with a beer.

She noticed that Johnny had a suitcase with him. Where was he going?

"I've got something I think you'd like to read."

"What might that be?"

He pulled a large envelope out of a bag.

"I went to see Johan Grieg. He gave me this."

He opened the envelope and laid the typescript before her.

Astounded, Sasha found herself staring blankly at the wall of football memorabilia. How had he succeeded in getting hold of this when she had failed?

"Thank you," she said, still trying to collect herself. "I'll read it tonight and contact you tomorrow to discuss what to do next." She was aware how prissy she sounded. "But I can guarantee that I'll keep this confidential and reward your—"

With teasing eyes, he shook his head. "You can't believe that's how this is going to play out, surely?"

"This concerns *my* family."

"What you have before you," he said, tapping his finger on the cover sheet, "is not the complete manuscript. Grieg is no fool. This is only the first part. Which already contains what he called 'injurious allegations made against certain named persons'. Vera believed her allegations could be verified by letters and documents held in the private archive of the Hanseatic Steamship Company in Bergen."

That archive was on the old Falck property. She understood now why Vera had gone to Bergen to write the manuscript. She had been looking for ammunition.

"We made a deal," Johnny continued. "It's simple. If I can find the documents on which the manuscript's claims are based, then I'll get the second part from Grieg."

He took two tickets out of his pocket. "The train leaves in fifteen minutes. We'll read the manuscript on the train. You have your own sleeping compartment."

"We?" she said, looking at him strangely.

It was madness to get on a train with a stranger, just as it was madness to discuss family secrets with strangers.

"You know what I missed most when I worked in the Middle East? Having someone to work alongside. Writing's a lonely business. We'll work together on this."

"I'm in," she said.

THE SEA CEMETERY

BY

VERA LIND

PART ONE

Bergen

Let me tell you about the sinking of a ship.

All ships are built on dry land, even those that end their journey in the graveyard of the sea, encrusted with shells and starfish, surrounded by colourful deep-sea fish and luminous marine organisms that swim in through the portholes, consuming the remains of those who went down with it. They're welded together by shipbuilders, before being moored by the quayside, their pennants fluttering in the light inland breeze, while expectant passengers come aboard and lean against the rails.

They are unaware of their fate, naturally, that's true for us all. There is sorrow in the air, there is joy; mostly the former, for there is more pain than pleasure in the world.

In all the years since I was last at sea, I have written many books, but never about the disaster, never about what happened. It lay hidden, like a corpse in a well. Until I realised that the way to keep the dead alive was to tell their story.

Starting with the marine investigation held by the Salten District Court in the Masonic Lodge in Bodø on the day after the shipwreck, October 24, 1940, a great many lies have been told, even under oath, about what happened when the Hurtigruten DS *Prinsesse Ragnhild* sank off the coast of Landegode island. Among the few who have investigated her demise, there has been a consensus that she was sunk by a British mine. But that is not the truth of it. The *Prinsesse Ragnhild* was blown up from within, for reasons I hope will become apparent in this story.

Life may have begun in the sea, but every story about the sea begins on land. This story begins south of Bergen, on a magnificent hilly country estate on the north side of the Fana Fjord, where I lived with my newborn son Olav, an army of servants and my husband Thor, whenever he was in town.

It was a grey Saturday in October 1940. Norway was under German occupation, and I was late, as usual. Thor would complain that I could never be on time for anything, and as it was true, it always made me angry. This time, I couldn't find my identity papers and when I finally realised they were in Thor's safe, I cursed. What was the code again? Damn, I'd forgotten. No, it was his eldest son's birthday backwards, as was the family tradition. I got the butler to open Thor's office, and dashed in. What was Per's date of birth again? He wasn't my son. Thirty-five the year, ten the month, and twelve the day? I turned the dial, and to my great relief the safe door swung open. I grabbed my papers and dashed out of the house and down to the lower terrace, where one of the stable lads loaded my suitcase into the waiting taxi.

Our nanny had already been driven into town with little Olav; Thor was coming straight from a meeting nearby.

"The Hurtigruten quay?" The driver scrutinised me in his mirror.

I nodded uneasily, trembling as I powdered my nose. I was about to head north for the first time since travelling the other way. I was going back home. No, that sounded wrong, because when had I left four years earlier, after finishing middle school, I had sworn never to return.

But that was not why I was uneasy now. I had been working that year as a secretary at the Harbour Master's Office in Bergen. Thor was the shipping director of the Hanseatic Steamship Company and had reluctantly got me the job. Bergen was an important port on the west coast of Norway, and information about shipping traffic was vital to the intelligence services that watched from the shadows.

They had come to me two days earlier, as I made my way through the rain to the train station. I write *they* because the man who appeared in an alleyway not far from the office was anonymous. Lifting his hat, he asked: "Which ships will leave the Festning quay and Skoltegrunn quay today?"

"What do you mean?" I replied.

"Just answer, Fru Lind." His resolute, authoritarian tone made me hesitate.

"A German flotilla with six *Räumboote*," I replied. "All with a displacement tonnage of between 110 and 160 and a range of 1,100 nautical miles, armed with C/30 guns, on a mine clearance sweep north towards Stadt. In addition to the Norwegian ships *P. G. Halvorsen*, *Vela* and *Hovda*, and the Danish ship *Juliane*."

"Tell me, Fru Lind, were you born with such a good memory?"

I shook my head. "It's something you have to train up. Like lung capacity or muscle strength. And it's different for everyone: a chess player remembers opening moves, but not necessarily other things. One secretary at the office always forgets her mother's birthday. I remember shipping schedules."

We followed Teatergaten to the junction where it met Håkonsgaten. My nervousness had begun to fade, when he said: "It's come to our attention that on Saturday you're going north on the *Prinsesse Ragnhild*."

I felt watched, intruded upon. "How . . .?"

"The *Prinsesse* has an excellent music lounge in first class," he continued. "There's a Chesterfield sofa along the shipside wall, clearly visible from the entrance, surrounded by chairs, under a portrait photograph of Queen Maud and Prince Olav. Be there on the first evening of your journey, at nineteen-thirty hours precisely. A man will invite you to dance. You will then receive further instructions."

I felt my throat and chest tighten. "I'm travelling with my husband and my baby. What if I refuse?"

The man with the hat laughed and shook his head. "You won't. You see, we've heard that there are certain complications in your marriage and that you've behaved in a dissolute and immoral manner on several occasions. If you don't do as we say, it's possible that a relevant judicial authority will have to assess whether you're fit to take care of your son. The music lounge, Saturday at nineteen-thirty hours," he said, lifting his hat, as I stood there nauseous and trembling.

The taxi was turning into the docks now. We drove past the crates of herring and barrels of cod liver oil at the open fish market, past the fishing and pleasure boats bobbing in the oily water near the quay, while I cast uneasy glances into the shadows between the warehouses.

The Hurtigruten ferry was moored at the furthest pier, below the Bergenhus fortress. I opened the car door before the driver had time to do so, grabbed my suitcase and dashed out to board the ship.

I struggled to catch my breath. I was still in bad shape after giving birth. Ahead of me, I saw the words PRINSESSE RAGNHILD painted in large letters. Black steam oozed out of the gently sloping funnel midship, creeping over the lifeboat davits and the poop deck, and settling like a carpet of smoke across the bay, before dispersing over the sea's choppy surface.

Along the ship's rail passengers stood waiting for departure. Fine ladies, sleek businessmen . . . and German soldiers. My gaze was caught by a man standing near the gangway, with a black patch over one eye, like a pirate. His one Cyclops eye watched me without wavering. It made me uncomfortable. I looked away and hurried on. A quay officer threw a rope up to a sailor on deck. What if I missed the boat my child was aboard?

In fact, the passenger hatch was already closed, and the gangplank was about to be raised, but I argued my way on by telling one of the sailors that I had worked as a maid on the sister ship, *Queen Maud*, when I sailed south four years earlier. As he let me past, he whispered that they were having a party in the panty-alley later, and I was invited.

I stepped onto the teak deck. The surface felt soft under the soles of my shoes, almost like a forest path. I joined the queue at the ticket window midship. All around me were businessmen hustling to upgrade to first class, shabbily dressed fishermen and awkward scholarly types looking to get full board.

Astern I caught sight of Jorunn's stocky figure, a blanketed bundle in the crook of her arm, and one hand on the flagpole. I shoved through a cluster of passengers before sprinting the last few metres and, with relief, reclaimed my little Olav.

But the minute he was in my arms, he started to howl.

"I've been lookin' all over for you," said Jorunn. "I was certain you'd missed it." She pursed her lips. "You've a habit o' being late, Vera."

It didn't help that Olav refused to stop bawling until Jorunn took a bottle from her bag and lifted it to his gaping mouth.

"I had something important to do before I left."

She placed her hands on her broad hips. "Tell me, what's more important than being on time for the boat that's carrying your baby son?"

A short, stocky fishwife with a rather dour expression, Jorunn came from one of the islands in the far north of the county. As a young woman she had raised bairns of her own, probably with more chapel discipline than love. After losing her husband at sea, she had moved to town and worked as a nanny for upper-class families. Which was how she had ended up with the Falcks, first as Per's nursemaid, and now as Olav's nanny.

Her inquisitive, coffee-bean eyes saw right through me. She never had a bad word to say about other wealthy folk. The fact that they were rich and she was poor was the natural order of things. But in me she saw a social climber, a woman of her own class who hid her accent and wore lace frocks bought on Falck credit.

"Have a rest," I said. "I'll look after Olav."

Jorunn leaned on the ship's rail and gazed out thoughtfully. "What is it really ails your ma?"

"Tuberculosis," I said quickly. "It's got worse."

"We must hope she gets t' see little Olav."

"Yes." I squeezed her large, puffy hand. "Thank you for your help, Jorunn. Where's Mr Falck?"

"Shipowner's cabin, I reckon."

I stayed there on the rear deck as the ship sailed out of the fjord. Olav nestled his little head, with its kitten-soft hair, against my winter coat.

The thought of what lay ahead made me shudder, but I knew this was my one chance. I had to get away, from Thor, from the chicken-hearted collaboration of his shipping company, from the suffocating wealth of the Falck estate.

It was early Saturday morning. In less than two days we would steam into Trondheim. It was there I would meet him. We had not seen each other since the summer camp the year before, but we had exchanged frequent letters. My hands trembled against the rail. How would things turn out? The pistons beat faster, and the ship gained speed, until the city beneath the mountains vanished. The wake spread out after us like a white bridal veil on the grey-blue sea.

If things went to plan, we would be free. But what was freedom really worth when our country was occupied?

Bergen–Florø

All these many years later, I still remember the salt-laden breeze that whipped my cheeks and merged with the sooty smoke from the boilers in the ship's belly.

Thirty years have passed. In this rainy winter of 1970, . I have returned to the estate in Bergen. But for short visits, I have barely spent any time here since I moved to Rederhaugen with Olav shortly after the war. Bergen holds too many memories. My excuse is that I need *inspiration* and *quiet to work*: the two things writers cite when they visit their lovers or just want time to themselves. But who is there to care? I have no husband, and I am nothing but a hindrance to Olav at Rederhaugen.

I am sitting on the top floor of the old *stabbur*-like annex that houses the Falck shipping company's private archive. I have a good view from the window here, looking down over the roofs of the estate and beyond to the dark, rain-heavy fjord.

The archive downstairs covers all four walls, from floor to ceiling, of a windowless room. I have barely begun to take it in.

But my memories carry me back in time, such are the workings of the human brain, so that I am there on the ship in 1940, on the deck outside the ticket office, waiting for the purser, who will lead me to the shipowner's cabin.

Having worked four years earlier on the *Dronning Maud*, the *Prinsesse*'s sister ship, also built by the Nordenfjeldske Steamship Company, I knew what was under the promenade deck. Far ahead, at one end of the orlop deck, lay the servants' quarters, where the maids slept, as well as the galley gang. One level up were the crew – youngsters, deck boys, greasers, engine boys, those without any gold stripes on their arms – and, at the very front, where the ship's bow narrowed, the bosun's cabin.

Towards the back, almost directly under the lounges in third class, was the engine room, where you might see the odd coalman or engineman stick his head out the door. As a rule, though, they kept to themselves.

Midship, where I would be sleeping, the wages and ranks were more elevated. Above me, next to the command bridge itself, was the captain's cabin, and those of the first and second mates, the pilot and telegraph operator. But the heart of the ship was the ticket office. The mate on duty there was receptionist, doctor, policeman and friend-in-need all rolled into one.

The purser raised his hand in the air. "Fru Falck?"

He guided me to the staircase by the dining room that took us up to the lounges in first class, beneath the command bridge in the wheelhouse. But at the top of the stairs, instead of turning right, we turned left, until the purser stopped by a lacquered mahogany hatch.

The cabin inside was furnished with a wide bed next to the midship bulkhead, a small desk, a washbasin and a leather corner-sofa under a porthole with a view over the deck. The room smelled of aftershave, cigarettes and schnapps. Thor was standing there, stock-still, gazing out of the window. He was elegantly turned out as ever, in a dark pinstripe suit, loosened tie and handcrafted shoes. Slowly he turned.

"You can go," Thor said to the purser. "I want to talk to my wife." Giving me a cool peck on the cheek, he said, "Vera, my dearest."

"You haven't seen Olav since just after he was born," I said, using the informal "du" in addressing him, as I handed him his son.

At the start of our marriage, Thor had demanded that I address him with the formal "De" rather than "du". There was talk of its being traditional among the upper classes on the Continent, especially France, where spouses addressed each other as "vous" and not "tu". I refused to call my husband "De", it went against everything I'd grown up with, every value I held dear. I told Thor something I had read in a book by George Orwell: when the anarchists took power in Barcelona in the Spanish Civil War, they banished the formal forms of address, just as they swapped top hats and suits for berets and dungarees. Thor still found me irresistible back then, and he laughed indulgently, stroked my hair and smiled. "Vera, Vera, my precious darling. Then you and I shall be 'dus'."

He glanced down at his son now, holding him at arm's length. "He's grown," was his only comment before he handed him back.

His suitcase lay open by the bed and in the open wardrobe behind me hung three suits, an extra pair of formal shoes and some winter boots. Thor returned to gazing out of the porthole.

"I feel so guilty about Mother," I said. "I'm terrified she might die before we get there."

Thor made an awkward effort to stroke my back.

We were only two years married, but we might as well have been on "De" terms again, we lived such separate lives. Almost twice my age, Thor was a third-generation shipowner, a director of the Hanseatic Steamship Company, the jewel in the crown of the Falck shipping empire.

The company had an extensive fleet, both at home and abroad, and Thor had worked very closely since the invasion with his competitors in the Nordenfjeldske Steamship Company, with which the Hanseatic had close ties, and which owned many of the ships on the Hurtigruten line, among them the *Prinsesse*.

This put Thor in a unique strategic position few Norwegians could compete with at the time. Before planes and lorries took over, the shipping lanes along Norway's long coastline were the chief means of transport for people and goods. For centuries the famous jekte-captains had transported dried fish, cod liver oil and caviar from the north to the south, and returned with grain and other goods that were scarce in the north. The Hurtigruten ferries were a vital lifeline between the fishing grounds in northern Norway and the important trading centres in the west.

Strategic control of the coast was no less important now, with several hundred thousand German soldiers on Norwegian soil. The Germans were keen to build defences and reinforce the northern front in case the non-aggression pact with the Soviet Union was broken.

"Vera," Thor said, sitting on the bed and speaking in a gentler tone. "Come here, my darling."

Carefully, so as not to wake Olav up, I pushed his basket across the cabin floor and under the washbasin and sat beside Thor. Not only was he fifteen years older than me and from a completely different world, he belonged to another era, an era when men were expected to be corpulent and wear bow ties, morning coats and lorgnettes.

But there was something about him I liked. His predictability. In contrast to my nerves and mood swings. If he had, against all likelihood, read a book by Virginia Woolf, Sigmund Freud or some other sensitive modern mind, their neuroses would probably have seemed as foreign to him as the family vendettas in the old sagas seemed to me. Thor never went around biting his nails about things. The German occupation and the discouraging news from the Western Front were not evidence for him that Judgement Day was nigh.

The Nazis are, without a doubt, vulgar oafs, he could say over his morning coffee at Hordnes. *Although I think the newspapers have blown these alleged persecutions of Jews out of proportion.*

But right now, he was gently stroking my lower back. I felt his large hand move slowly sideways and downwards.

"Vera, I know how hard things are for you. What with your mother being so ill. And the baby being such a handful."

"I've been so lonely," I said softly. "You should spend more time at home."

He avoided my eyes and shook his head irritably. "Property doesn't pay for itself, you know. The life you lead doesn't come for free."

I wrenched myself free. "If this is about money, I can sleep on the floor in the hold."

He put his powerful arm about my shoulder. "Don't be silly, you'll sleep here, with me. The circumstances of our trip could of course have been better. But we're going north, Vera. Past some of the most beautiful landscapes in the world."

He stroked the nape of my neck with one finger. "I love you, my darling."

He kissed me on the throat and ran his lips down over my breastbone, until he met my brassiere, and then traced its lacy edges. I closed my eyes. With one hand he explored the inside of my thighs. I opened my eyes again and stared around the room.

"No," I whispered.

His lips brushed my ear. "Why not?"

Annoyed and embarrassed, he rolled away from me.

We lay there staring in opposite directions. The ship's pistons pounded, and through the walls we heard distant voices, laughter, excited chatter.

Just then Olav started crying in his basket. I lifted him up and rocked him in my arms, gently kissed the soft spot on the top of his head, inhaled the sweet, slightly nauseating smell of his soft hair. I guided his gaping bird-mouth to my breast, and he sucked with the helpless infant's indefinable strength.

"I've been thinking," Thor began, as little Olav suckled contentedly.

Fathers, according to him, had nothing to offer a boy before he was old enough to develop manly virtues. One day, Olav and his half-brother Per, a sickly and lacklustre boy of five from Thor's first marriage, would take over his businesses. His sole job as a father was to prepare them for that. Until then, others could steer that particular ship.

"Why don't you get a wet nurse?" he continued. "There's no need for you to feed him yourself."

A heavy, sweet smell was rising from Olav's nappy, and I laid him on a blanket on the bed to deal with it.

"And as for changing him, surely you'd rather not."

"I like doing it myself," I said. "Had it been up to me, we wouldn't even have had a nanny."

Caring nothing for bairns himself and growing up with a host of wet nurses, nannies and governesses, this was beyond his ken. He had no idea who I was, where I came from, how we had to batten down our houses with ropes against the winter storms or battle our way to the barn to feed the animals in gale-force winds. How could this man, who had never done a day's graft, understand our joy when the house was scrubbed clean on a Saturday? Had the womenfolk in my village been asked if they needed a nanny to give them time for their artistic pursuits, they would have shaken their heads in disbelief.

"I think you'd like the freedom it would give you."

I had looked after other people's bairns from a young age, so why would I not look after my own? I loved my little lad. Loved him even more than I could have imagined as I wandered about Hordnes, waiting for his arrival, during that long, dark spring and the first months of summer. He was born in July.

Reality took on a different hue after the birth, like the moment between wakefulness and dream-sleep that sometimes follows you beyond the dawn. My body was no longer the same, torn apart, but radiating vitality. My perspective changed. Little things gained in magnitude – vomit on a collar, the baby smiling up at me on the changing table. So too did the timeless questions, the scope of the starry sky and the endless cycles of the generations.

But I found it impossible to cope with the war, German soldiers in the streets, the news that the Wehrmacht was rolling through Europe like ink across a page.

Thor was away from Bergen when Olav was born, but a couple of weeks later he came to town to see his son. One rainy August day he sent a telegram out to the Fana estate, asking that I come to the Falck shipping company's headquarters with the boy.

When I arrived, he was sitting in his office with a doctor. He kissed me coldly on the cheek before nodding to the doctor, who took the baby and laid him on a blanket, then gave him sugar water and took a sample of blood from his heel, provoking a howl.

"What are you doing?" I asked, though it had begun to dawn on me.

"Just a formality," said Thor.

"What d'you think I am?" I said, angrily.

"There's no cause to be anxious," he said, shrugging. The silence was suffocating, almost audible. It was still raining outside.

Eventually the doctor returned.

"It's AB positive," he said, with relief in his voice. "Science has moved on by leaps and bounds, but given your blood types, we can confirm with absolute confidence that you are the child's biological parents."

The significance of a moment is rarely apparent to us until later, but I know now that this was when I made my decision. I had to get away, from Thor, from Bergen, from everything that had become mine without really being mine.

"I'm not happy about Jorunn and Olav sleeping several decks beneath us," I said after a short pause. "What if something happens?"

"There's nothing to worry about," he replied. "The Hurtigruten line hasn't seen a single accident since the occupation. And the *Prinsesse* has an echo sounder. Besides," he continued, "we have an engagement with Admiral Carax, the German Navy commander responsible for the west coast of Norway. He and his wife will dine with us. Tomorrow, I believe."

I wanted to confront Thor about his blatant collaborating, but given that I now found myself under the resistance movement's banner, to do so could work against its aims. Then again, it might arouse his suspicion if I just smiled and played along with it, since he was well aware of my views on the matter. I steered a middle course.

"Mightn't it be seen as a provocation to be wining and dining a German admiral?"

He sighed. "In your subversive circles, perhaps, where people live on air and love. But I have jobs to consider."

I shrugged.

"By the way," he said, getting up to leave, "the captain asked for your company at dinner tonight."

"I'd like very much to meet him," I replied politely.

Thor closed the cabin door after him. Olav let out a whimper in his basket but fell straight back to sleep. I went over to the washbasin and stared at my own reflection. I resisted the urge to cry. There was always something to look forward to. In two days, we would arrive in Trondheim, and in another two days my life as I knew it would be over and something new would begin.

I changed my dress and headed for the first-class dining room, which was almost directly beneath our cabin. Out in the stairwell I caught sight of the one-eyed German officer again. It felt as if he was watching me. I could see now that his eyepatch was in reality dark brown and held in place by a dark strip of elastic that went diagonally across his forehead.

I was greeted by the smell of freshly caught cod as I walked in. Thor was sitting next to a short gentleman in his fifties with wavy blond hair, a piercing gaze and four stripes on his jacket sleeves.

"Captain Brækhus," said Thor, formally, "meet my wife, Vera."

We were served poached cod and boiled potatoes with grated carrots and a nutty parsley butter, *real* butter, which the chefs carried in on a large silver dish, the fish fillets trembling to the ship's rhythm. The situation was vastly different here out on the water, explained Captain Brækhus, in contrast to the towns, where food shortages were proving a real problem. "The sea is an inexhaustible pantry," he said.

I ate slowly, consciously savouring the fish's delicate flavour and flaky texture, the sweetness of the vegetables, the satisfying butter with its chopped parsley.

"Our coastline stretches such a distance, the highway of the sea! But tell me, is this the young lady's first trip on the Hurtigruten line?"

I shook my head.

"I come from the north," I replied. "I signed up on the *Dronning Maud* as a maid when I finished high school and decided to go south. We girls slept in the servants' alleyway under the mast house. The 'panty-alley', they called it."

Thor was noticeably riled, but Captain Brækhus seemed to be thoroughly enjoying himself.

"Ah, the *Dronning Maud*, our sister ship!" he exclaimed enthusiastically. "But I can assure you, my dear Fru Falck, our facilities here on the *Prinsesse* are on another level."

"My wife is exempt from such duties now," Thor said, stroking my back. I shivered when he touched me.

"A maid from the *Dronning Maud*!" said Captain Brækhus smiling. "That's a solid woman you've married, Director Falck."

"Yes, you can be sure!" Thor laughed uncomfortably.

"So, what do you do with yourself when you're not working at the Harbour Master's Office?" asked the captain, turning back to me.

"I write," I said seriously.

Brækhus nodded earnestly. "So, what do you write about?"

My writing was still no more than a distant ambition. There was a vast chasm between my dreams and the staccato passages I put on paper. But I was already good at bluffing.

"Well," I began, "I grew up by the sea. Life originated in the sea, yet there is scarcely anything we fear more than water. I've always been fascinated by shipwrecks . . ."

"Vera, darling . . ." said Thor, looking at me sternly. "That's hardly an appropriate topic here."

The captain smiled. "On the contrary, this is all very exciting."

"I've always admired the maritime code of honour," I said, looking deep into his eyes.

"What in particular are you thinking of?"

"That the captain is the last to leave a sinking ship."

"Yes, quite right," agreed Brækhus. He did not know that days later he would face this very predicament, as described in the marine accident investigation report:

The ship rose and then went straight down. The captain witnessed people clinging to the rails as the ship disappeared. He reports further that he was pulled down into the depths and took in a great deal of water. When he resurfaced, the ship was nowhere to be seen, but he saw vast quantities of flotsam and could hear many people around him.

But what did Captain Brækhus, or any of us who sat there that day in the first-class dining room, know of the future?

It was coming up to seven-thirty. I left the dining room and went into the stairwell, with its thick red-check carpet and mirrors on the walls. The ship was rocking gently as we approached land. The pistons pounded louder, and we slowed; the ship would soon anchor at Florø. I could hear excited voices from the lounges on the decks above. I gripped the cold brass banister and climbed the stairs.

The second mate swaggered past, lifting his cap to me before his back disappeared from the mezzanine mirrors.

Two drunken travelling salesmen whistled as they passed me.

Up on the landing, I followed the arc of the stairwell to a narrow door that led into the cloakroom, lit by unsteady, flickering candlelight. I followed the hum of voices, through the swing doors, with arched windows and Norse carvings in mahogany, into the music lounge.

Through the windows, I glimpsed the dim contours of land – with the wartime ban on lighting we had all developed the night vision of cats. The ship manoeuvred sideways to dock and I could hear the loud commands of the sailors and men on the quayside, and the sound of the loading crane being prepared.

I was the first guest in the lounge, which made me feel uneasy; I wanted to disappear into a crowd, not stand out. The only other guests were Queen Maud and little Prince Olav, who gazed down from a photograph between two blacked-out portholes on the hull-side of the room.

I waited. Lit a cigarette, powdered my nose. The music lounge was modest in size: a long Chesterfield sofa, groups of comfortable matching armchairs and low tables, a black piano near the exit, and a small dance floor in the middle.

At last, the swing doors opened, and two German offi-cers strode in, their hats tucked jauntily under their arms, one balancing a tray full of crystal glasses. They nodded amiably in my direction. I exhaled through my nose and slowly stubbed out my cigarette, avoiding their gaze.

Their uniforms bore the skull and crossbones emblem. They were SS men. I lit another cigarette, even though I knew it would make me nauseous. My lacy bodice tightened round my midriff.

Can humans smell fear, like dogs?

I was sweating and shivering all at once.

The evening's pianist made her entrance in a sage-green evening gown. Her black hair was held up in a tight knot, accentuating her slightly sticky-out ears and large nose. She was attractive in the way a weary Parisian chanteuse might be. She sat down and tested out the piano, and I sat watching her fingers flit elegantly over the keys.

I looked up at the clock. Seven forty-five. The lounge was suddenly filling up with German officers and civilian passengers. Why had the man in the hat told me to come to this precise place? It was a trap. My mind raced like a hamster in a wheel. I was lost. The meeting was bait only I could have been naive enough to take.

The SS officers raised their glasses and glanced in my direction as they made a toast.

Where was the man who was going to ask me to dance?

"Help me, Queen Maud!" I whispered, looking up at the picture of the queen.

To my right, sat two men and a woman. The woman was roughly my age, her hair in the style of the film stars of the day, a sharp parting through water-combed hair. Elegant to the extreme. She leaned over to me and with studied theatricality asked for a light; I handed her my lighter. Judging from the way she rolled her Rs, she came from Sunnmøre.

"Are you here alone?"

I nodded.

"Join us, if you want."

"Later perhaps."

The hum of the engines grew louder.

I was impatient for the ship to leave harbour; out at sea, I thought, we were safe. At that moment a figure appeared in the doorway. In the dim light I could make out a scar etched diagonally across his face.

He looked me up and down but said nothing. Then his gaze took in the lounge, lighting on the Norwegians, the pianist and the Germans. He gave the woman beside me a friendly nod, then sat in a leather chair opposite me.

"You're going north?" he asked.

"My mother is seriously ill," I said. "Tuberculosis."

"I'm sorry to hear that. Where are you heading?"

"Lofoten."

"The birthplace of the Hurtigruten line." His voice blended in with the music and the low hum of chatter. "I've always felt very at home in the north. You're more open-minded up there. Jens Hagemann, by the way."

I gave him my name, but we didn't shake hands. "Hurtigruten is from Vesterålen," I said.

The pianist was singing Bing Crosby's "How deep is the ocean, how high is the sky".

Hagemann placed a cigarette case on the table. He pushed it discreetly over to my side. Its smooth surface was broken only by an enamelled engraving of a ring of rope, with the letters N and F above it, and D and S beneath.

"It looks from a distance as though it were made of silver, right? Take a cigarette, I'll treat you."

He leaned across the table to light it.

"But it's actually a base alpaca alloy of copper, zinc and nickel," he continued, examining it. "A glittering surface hides all manner of things. Nothing is as it seems. It's extremely resistant to corrosion in water and it never rusts."

He scoured the room with his eyes.

"It's yours from now on. Carry it in your inside pocket."

He stared at the alpaca case, then at me.

"A dance?"

We got up, and he led me out on the dance floor.

"Before I do as you say, I want some guarantees," I said.

"I'm not sure what you mean."

"Guarantees that you know people who can help me cross the border."

Hagemann whispered in my ear as we danced. "Your husband is going to hold meetings with the German authorities here on this ferry. Have you heard of Admiral Carax?"

"My husband is a patriot," I whispered. "I won't spy on him."

"Otto Carax is the admiral in command of Norway's west coast. He's going to suggest that the shipping companies your husband speaks for work more closely with the German authorities."

I felt my pulse quicken but said nothing.

"When the ship docks in Trondheim in two days' time, on Monday, go to the door of the Palm Garden at the Hotel Britannia. At eleven o'clock, precisely, a man will ask you for a cigarette. You will take out the case and offer it to him."

"Thank you for the dance," I said.

Jens Hagemann led me courteously back to my seat, and without another word slipped out of the lounge.

I took the case and opened it. The row of cigarettes was held in place with a piece of elastic. One of them was a couple of millimetres shorter than the rest, and very slightly off-white. Fear mingled with pride. Surely this was what I had always dreamed of? To do something for my country?

What were the voices outside?

I pricked up my ears.

They were getting louder.

Moments later a powerful light flooded through the swing doors. For a split second the entire lounge was illuminated. We all squinted around the room, confused, like guests in a dance hall when the lights are switched on, and all the flaws they have hidden come into view.

The swing doors slammed open, and the Germans stormed in.

Florø–Måløy

There were at least ten soldiers, all armed, followed by two men in grey coats bearing the insignia of the secret police.

Everything had happened so fast that nobody had managed to move a muscle.

The candles on the tables went out, all but one, which stood there flickering.

With the soldiers came nervous commands that rang through the lounges, the slamming of doors and the barking and snarling of German shepherd dogs on tight leashes.

"Everyone stay where you are!" the Gestapo officer bellowed. He wore a white shirt and tie, and an elegant double-breasted jacket with gold buttons and wide lapels. The close-fitting uniform emphasised his tall, athletic figure. He had an angular face and prominent cheekbones.

The SS men got up and greeted them, and the German naval officers stood to attention.

The soldiers pointed their torches and rifles at us.

The cigarette case in front of me on the table gleamed in the harsh light. Had Hagemann tricked me? For a second I was paralysed with fear. Of course, it was a trap. To think I could be so naive!

"Norwegians in the corner on the right," said the Gestapo commandant, a tall, blond man standing straight-backed with his chin held high. The officer issued further orders in a clipped, correct manner.

The pianist cursed the intruders loudly and was immediately dragged into our corner by two soldiers. Besides me, the woman from Sunnmøre and her two gentleman companions, there were very few Norwegians. We stood squeezed between two chairs and a table.

Queen Maud stared down at us from the wall.

The last candle went out with a sputter, and the smoke rose and settled over the lounge.

"My name is Kriminaldirektor Müller," said the Gestapo commandant. "And yours?"

He nodded in the direction of the young woman from Sunnmøre.

"Betsy Flisdal."

"Place of work and reason for travel?"

"I worked as a clerk at a fish-filleting factory in Ålesund. I'm on my way to Bodø to start a new job at a ladies' outfitters."

Müller inspected her ticket and identity papers.

"You're travelling third class, Miss. How do you come to be in this first-class lounge?"

"None of your business!" Betsy replied angrily.

Unruffled by her provocation, Müller gave her a scornful look but said nothing. Her companions explained haltingly that they were currently without permanent work, and made a living helping out on fishing boats, which was why they were on their way to Måløy.

Then it was my turn.

"Vera Lind," I said, in a barely audible voice. "Secretary at the Bergen Harbour Master's Office. I'm travelling from Bergen with my husband, my son and our nanny." My voice regained some calm. It felt like a plausible explanation. "We're going to Stamsund to visit my tubercular mother."

"I see," he said. "And do you have papers to confirm the purpose of your journey?"

A trickle of sweat ran down my back. I hoped he could not see how nervous I was.

"Unfortunately," I said, "it all happened too quickly. My mother is at death's door. But I do have my birth certificate here. It proves that I was born in Lofoten and live in Bergen."

I handed it over. He barely glanced at it. "That is a necessary journey. We have understanding for your family's situation. Just remember your papers next time."

Müller turned and walked slowly across the small dance floor. He inspected our table. The crystal glasses were half full; the ice cubes had melted into the spirits. Then he reached for the cigarette case, held it up and squinted at it. "Who owns this?"

We stood in silence like a church congregation.

If ever I needed divine intervention, it was now. Queen Maud, I thought, help me.

In the end I broke the silence. "It's mine."

"I forgot my cigarettes," Müller said in an almost cheery tone that scared me even more. "Have you got one to spare?"

I nodded and held my breath.

The officer opened the case. The room was so quiet that I could hear the little click as the lid was flipped. Almost feminine in his movements, he ran his fingers over the row of cigarettes. I closed my eyes and pictured a prison cell.

He took out a cigarette.

If he inspected the case more closely, I was done for.

Kriminaldirektor Müller studied it for a final time, shut it carefully and put it back where he had found it.

"Thank you, Fru Falck."

Relief trickled through me.

Müller lit his cigarette.

"However," he continued, before I had time to digest my relief, "it is your work at the Harbour Master's Office that is the subject of our investigation."

My heart leaped into my throat again. How did he know?

"You must therefore come with us."

"What do you mean?"

"You heard me perfectly well."

I was about to step forward when the swing doors opened again.

It was Thor, together with the purser, dressed in a suit and holding his hat in the crook of his arm.

"What's going on here?" he said with authority.

"We're conducting an investigation into possible insurrectionists and resistance fighters," said Müller, almost submissively. The Germans had respect for people of rank.

"You are, of course, within your rights to do so under the new regulations," said Thor, pedantic as always. He took a few steps towards me.

"But the woman you are addressing is my wife."

Müller shifted uneasily.

"Have they treated you well, my dear?" Thor asked in a soft voice.

I nodded and looked down at the floor. Thor turned to the Gestapo man.

"Unless you have any concrete evidence against my wife, you have no right to harass her."

"She works at the Harbour Master's Office," Müller said.

"My wife is both dedicated and loyal in her work," said Thor.

The Gestapo commandant conferred with his assistant in a whisper. Then he politely nodded to Thor. With his soldiers in tow, he marched out. As he reached the doorway, he stopped and turned. "Thank you for the cigarette."

Måløy

That night the ship was docked in Måløy harbour. Thor lay snoring beside me, while I lay wide awake.

I first met Thor in the early summer of '38, at the preview of his wife's exhibition, on the same estate where I sit writing this now, more than thirty years later.

Harriet Constance Mohn was from one of Bergen's richest families and grew up on Kalfaret. To the city's upper-class matchmakers, a Falck–Mohn alliance sounded perfect. Both families had money, or "assets", as they preferred to say. Thor came with a substantial marriage portion in the form of the Falck shipping company's large fleet, while Harriet brought with her the artistic aspirations so prevalent among women in elevated circles. Unfortunately, for all involved, it soon became clear that she lacked both talent and skill.

I knew nothing of this, of course, on the day I turned up at a grand mansion in Fana, south of Bergen, far out in the countryside back then. I'd been sent by my employers to Hordnes because one of their regular maids had reported in sick. The estate, I was told beforehand, had been built at the turn of the century by the eccentric shipping magnate, Theodor Falck. I had cleaned and waited at table for many wealthy folk in Bergen in my two years of living there, trying to earn enough to complete my education at the *gymnasium*. But nothing I had seen could compete with this place.

Over the front gate, a carved falcon with outstretched wings perched above the motto *Familia Ante Omnia*. A steep path led down to a large courtyard, framed by tall, well-kept hedges, which I later learned served as an exercise arena for the Lipizzaner horses that the Falcks kept in the stables to the left of the entrance. I stepped into a conservatory, then into a living room the size of a ballroom. This was where the exhibition was to take place. With a couple of other girls, I carried trays of champagne, lobster and caviar in for the guests – mostly rich, bedizened wives who looked through us, and their husbands, who stared at our white blouses. Thor was hurrying back and forth between his guests and the kitchens, looking decidedly tense as he instructed us to top up their glasses before he declared the exhibition open.

There was just one problem. Word had it that the artist was suffering from one of her bouts of fatigue. Harriet Mohn-Falck had taken to her bed up on the third floor and locked the door behind her. So we filled the guests' glasses, while Thor Falck valiantly stood up to speak. The star of the show, he told his guests, was indisposed that evening, but the private view would of course continue as planned. A restless buzz swept through the room, interspersed with malicious titters. It was still possible, Thor added some- what desperately, to secure a watercolour should one desire.

On my return through the back corridor to the kitchen, I saw him standing there shaking his head. He seemed upset.

"Are you alright, sir?" I said carefully.

"Of all the ungrateful, spoiled women," he muttered in his nasal Bergen accent. "Here we all are, for a bunch of watercolours nobody gives a damn about, and she can't even be bothered to show up."

I went over to him and stood near the wall. "I know how it feels, sir."

He glowered at me. "What do you mean?"

"My ma was ill and bedridden all throughout my childhood."

"A waitress!" he said. "And you presume to talk to me about something so private?"

"I'm sorry, sir. You just seemed so sad."

He was almost twice my age then, in his mid-thirties. He wasn't handsome, but there was a softness to him, a vulnerability in his eyes. Little did I know it, but my words had plunged a lance through his stoic outer armour.

"I'm probably just a little disheartened," he said, in a friendlier tone. "My wife lies in a darkened room all day long. She can't seem to manage anything."

"Artists are often oversensitive."

"My wife is *not* an artist." He spat out the words. "She's a spoiled housewife who paints the occasional watercolour."

Thor Falck paused, then knocked back a glass of cham- pagne in one. "But why am I making an idiot of myself in front of a complete stranger?"

"Sometimes we need to let off steam."

Thor nodded, reluctantly, thoughtfully.

He straightened up. "Tell me, how did things turn out with your mother?"

"Not too good," I replied. "She's getting worse. Though I've not seen her for years now."

"You left her?" His eyes lit up with something resembling hope, though he tried to hide it.

I smiled. "We only live once, don't we?"

To cut a long and complicated story short: Thor left too. There was no romance in the usual sense. Not for me, at least. I was an eighteen-year-old serving girl from outer Lofoten who had nursed her sick mother in a draughty old house on Yttersia.

What choice did I have when the great shipping magnate Thor Falck invited me soon afterwards to go for a ride on his Lipizzaner horses?

We may appear free. But we are subject to forces beyond our control. Naturally I turned up blushing to the agreed location beyond the grounds, at a respectable distance from his wife's studio. Thor was waiting with two saddled horses under a large, moss-covered ash tree. I bobbed politely, he kissed me on both cheeks. We rode out beside the fjord, over fields and through the forest, on paths at the water's edge and along cart roads with the sun on our backs. Thor at a confident trot, back held straight like a Russian cavalryman, and I lagging behind with as much grace as a sack of potatoes. I laughed in the right places, of course, held his gaze rather too long, and when we tethered the horses and moved out onto a secluded rock in a secluded bay far from the estate, I let my clothes fall, revealed my sex and winked at him as I walked out into the water.

"What are you waiting for?"

He did not wait long. With eyes filled with desire and his member hidden behind one hand, he stumbled out of his clothes and ran after me into the water. I had acquired certain skills by then, thanks to a secret affair with a married actor at Den Nationale Scene who occasionally invited me up to his attic apartment in Nordnes. When we came up shivering after our romantic dip, I bent down and took his member in my mouth. It tasted of sex and salt water. He stared at me in rapture.

Afterwards I lay on my side on the warm rock with my head in my hands, my eyes searching his.

"I'll never be your mistress, you know that?"

He grew unsettled. "What do you mean?"

"If you want to do this again, you must get a divorce." Thor would probably deny that things went so fast; it did after all take an entire summer. But, regardless, he stood up to all the gossip mongering in the city's elite circles and filed a scandalous divorce against Harriet. Credit where it's due.

Naturally her family were furious at his adultery, especially with an impoverished eighteen-year-old girl from the morally dubious north. Only after negotiations between their legal team and Thor's razor-sharp lawyer, August Greve, did they reach an agreement of sorts. Thor was a tough negotiator, and all Harriet received was a modest allowance so she could continue her painting. Granted, the boy would be raised by his mother, with Thor as his financial benefactor and guarantor. But this suited Thor perfectly. Besides, his son would also inherit a large share of the Falck shipping company, which would be released to him as soon as he came of age.

Thus began an entirely new life. I learned the rules of dress and proper table manners, I learned whom to address with the formal "De" and who should be ignored. I attended the theatre and dined with consuls, businessmen, politicians and other shipping magnates. We travelled by steamship to London and went by train on the Night Ferry from there to Paris. Places I had only known from books rose before my eyes. My childhood dreams had come true, my life had become a novel of the kind I had devoured in my youth. And all the time I told myself, as Thor moaned over me in hotel rooms and pressed his rough tongue into my mouth, that as long he continued to desire me, I had won. I could do as I pleased.

But it wasn't that simple. In wealthy circles, women who took paid work were scorned. You were free to paint watercolours or write short stories, so long as you behaved like a respectable wife otherwise. I wanted to study. I wanted to take in all the knowledge of the world. And I wanted to work.

Thor was completely dismissive of the idea. Why would I settle for a poorly paid job when I could look after the estate in his absence? It was pointless, to his mind. He suggested I hire an academic as a personal tutor instead of "loafing about with agitators and *Mot Dag* readers". But that was exactly what I wanted. I turned nineteen that spring. I had graduated from the gymnasium, taking my examinations in secret.

I began to defy Thor. Whenever he was away, which was often, I went into town to attend lectures in economics or to listen to Arnulf Øverland and the German refugees in the Student Society and take a beer in the evening. I joined the Workers' Youth League. In 1939 I went to their summer camp in Sunndalsøra, and what happened there is part of why I sit here writing this today.

Ålesund–Molde

I had lied to Thor. Not only was our marriage a sham, I was *not* going north to see my mother. She was long dead of the tuberculosis that had plagued her for years. My travel plans were just one of my many fictions, not unlike the stories I wrote when I was bored at Hordnes.

I spent much of the second day of our journey walking restlessly around the ship rocking Olav in my arms. We were travelling at a good speed north. The coastal strip of low green islets and reefs was gradually replaced with alpine mountains, jagged like fools' caps and axe blades, and breakers that turned white as they crashed against colourless rock. Stadt and Hustadvika were areas that every experienced skipper feared, with good reason. Here the treacherous shipping lanes were barely wider than a river, and underwater reefs came into view as unnatural ripples on the sea's surface.

News of my mother's death came by telegram, sent by Dr Schultz and put in my hands at Hordnes one September day in 1938: *Dear Vera, It is with sadness that I must inform . . .* I knew immediately what was coming next and I ran down to the fjord and screamed until I had no more tears left.

I cried over Ma's wretched end and the fact I had failed her by coming south. Life had been a struggle for her ever since that Russian got her with child one night in Svolvær, only to disappear on his Pomor ship. Ma was poor and suffered with her health, but she raised me as best she could. She rented a room from a local boathouse owner in a fishing village on Yttersia called Å. She worked all she could and made us salted pollack or cod six days a week, with the occasional Sunday lunch of fishcakes, barley soup and one prune each.

I was eleven when Ma fell ill. She could lie the whole night coughing, the air in her room growing heavy from her consumptive breath. I sometimes found blood-caked handkerchiefs that she had hidden. Where she would once have got up to care for the animals or help with whatever needed doing, now she lay in bed exhausted and ordered me about.

I often skipped school for her sake. We needed the money. There were limits to how long we could live on other people's goodwill. I scrubbed floors, split fish heads and knitted clothes, even though everything in me baulked at such work, and if I had strength left, I'd lie down of an evening and read by the flickering light of the oil lamp.

Books were my only escape. They allowed me to travel, to leave the village, to travel up the coast to the hospital in Gravdal – the furthest I had been – and across the fjord, far from the dark winters, from the mountains and sea, and from all the folk who called me a Rusky whore-sprog.

The world I had come from sank into the sea when I went south as a sixteen-year-old, and after Ma's death there was nothing left for me there. But I had an aunt in Sulitjelma, to whom I had always been close. And it was she, my Aunt Gerd, who was crucial to my plans now. When the *Prinsesse* called at Bodø, I was going to sneak off the ship unseen with little Olav and head to Sulitjelma with a valid travel permit.

Thor believed we were going to visit my mother further north and would not discover my absence until I was far-away in Vestfjord.

With so much happening on the ship that first day, *he* had slipped to the back of my mind. Since our meeting that summer, the memory of him had animated my entire reality. He was in everything I did, every song I heard, it was *him* and not Thor who touched me in bed at night. Perhaps he was just one of the fantasies that had always given meaning to my life. Perhaps the fairy tale would fall apart on meeting with reality. Perhaps. Tomorrow I would find out. The mere thought made my head spin.

Thor was in meetings for most of the day. Now and then we'd hear a blast of the ship's horn, and the ferry would slow and come into dock. In Ålesund goods were unloaded from the hold with a huge crane. Crates of cabbages, potatoes and milk, lumber and car wheels, and horses that poked their confused heads out from under tarpaulins. The quay seethed with activity, the first mate and shipwright stood bent over the cargo map, a sailor fastened the girder and guided the boom in the right direction. By the ship's bell a young apprentice sailor sat trying to polish spots of verdigris off the brass.

I had returned little Olav to his nanny. Down by the ticket office I bumped into Betsy Flisdal, the woman I'd seen in the lounge the previous evening. She looked less glamorous in the cold light of day. She was bent shouldered and hollow chested, her skin was grubby under her make-up, and her eyes darted about as though she were tracking a fly.

"Hello again. That were a right to-do yesterday," she said. "Where d'you know Jens from?"

"Here and there." I shrugged, hoping she didn't know too much, which could spell trouble. "I've met him in Bergen once or twice, but I can't say I know him well. And you?"

"We worked together in the old days," Betsy said, with a knowing smile. "Shall we go up on deck?"

As we stood leaning over the ship's rail, she said pensively, "I didn't want to talk about these things where folk could hear."

"Oh?" I said, hesitantly.

"We used to cross the North Sea a lot, if you get me."

"Not exactly," I replied. She didn't strike me as too smart.

"To meet a liquor smuggler in Shetland."

Jens Hagemann had had the furrowed, world-weary look of a liquor smuggler and I wasn't the least surprised that Betsy had been involved in such an enterprise. She was certainly the type.

"Why smuggling? Surely the liquor ban was repealed years ago?"

"There's plenty folk that still want smuggled spirits," Betsy said, smiling with discoloured teeth. "We've been over lots of times, even since the Germans came. The coastline is long, it isn't difficult to . . ."

Her face suddenly grew more serious.

"What's the matter?" I asked, staring down at the water below.

"Except this summer," she said, quietly. "At the beginning of July, July sixth; I know that 'cos it were the day after Ma's birthday."

"What are you talking about?"

"We were going to cross the North Sea like usual. We went to Bremanger. We were going to meet a Shetland boat there, the fishing smack *Irma*. But we were met by the bloody Germans instead."

"How many German boats were there?"

"Three. They surrounded us out at sea. And they took my fiancé. I've not seen him since."

I had been at work on July sixth. I had complete overview of the coastal traffic that day. There had been no German boats near Bremanger. I cast my mind back. *Irma*. She had lain at the quayside in Bergen that day.

So Betsy Flisdal was lying.

But why? What did she want?

I laid a sympathetic hand on her shoulder. "I'm sure you'll see your fiancé again soon. But I really must go back to my little boy now. I'll see you around."

As soon as I was inside, I stopped. Looking through the porthole, I saw Betsy head decisively to the aft, along the ship's rail on the starboard side of the galley deck.

I took the stairs up to the promenade deck and continued in the same direction as her, past the poop, until I reached the stairs that led down to the flagpole on the stern. Here I stopped. There were very few people about; most passengers had gone ashore to stretch their legs. I leaned my face into the wind, trying to listen.

Then I heard her voice. "Shall we walk on? Reckon we need to discuss a few things."

A male voice growled an indistinct reply.

Hearing their footsteps disappear, I crept down after them. They headed deeper into the ship, past the staircase that led up to the lounges, past the main deck, and as far down as passengers could go. Where were they going? I followed them at a good distance, then heard their steps echo from further down.

The staircase only went as far as the second deck. They hadn't spotted me. I waited on the mezzanine until I could no longer hear their voices. Only then did I venture out into the wide corridor. A few metres away, towards the engine room, I heard a door slam shut. I followed the sound. The walls were hot to the touch. I slipped into a short, narrow passageway lined with cupboards full of equipment. On one was marked: *Provisions Room. No unauthorised access.*

I put my ear to the door, then gently tried to push it open.

It was shut.

Although I have barely set foot on a boat since 1940, these images from the *Prinsesse* come clearly to me as I sit here at Hordnes writing this. My memory is very much intact, but memories are not damning evidence.

Each day I take long walks. The Falck estate here in Fana has fallen into disrepair in the thirty or so years that have passed since its glory days. The ornamental shrubs are obscured by tall weeds, the stables have not been painted in years. Per now runs the shipping company. I see him each morning from the attic window, a stooped figure crossing the courtyard. I know he is going into town to negotiate more loan guarantees for the Falck fleet, his face pale and drawn from all the terrible news. A crisis in shipping means a crisis for the Falck shipping company, that much I know, and Per lacks the strength to solve these problems.

I don't think he knows what he's let himself in for, by allowing me to stay here and giving me access to the archive. But that's his affair. I am not here as a novelist, I have a more serious task: the Hanseatic Steamship Company's archive holds documents that can confirm that my story is true and not a work of fiction.

Our dinner party with Admiral Otto Carax and his wife on the evening of our second day on the *Prinsesse Ragnhild* plays a central role here. The Caraxes had reserved a private alcove for the occasion in the first-class dining room, right under the music and smoking lounges on the foredeck. I was wearing a blue floral dress I had bought in Paris. Thor cast an approving look at me as we strolled in.

Admiral Carax was no vulgar Brownshirt; he was a very correct and somewhat pretentious aristocrat of the old school, with wavy blond hair and a watchful, slightly arrogant gaze. His wife, who was around forty, surveyed me critically and ventured a few remarks on the "marvellous" Norwegian composer Geirr Tveitt and the national romantic painters, which died a death the minute Thor cleared his throat.

"A toast, dear friends. The admiral and I may have our differences when it comes to the occupation, but we are in absolute agreement on the most important thing: that the wheels of the country must not stop, that jobs must be preserved, and that people must live in peace and prosperity."

We all raised our glasses. Admiral Carax shot a glance in my direction, which his wife instantly picked up on. She glared furiously at him and then at me. For my own part, I was busy reflecting on the absurdity of it all; that I was sitting here on a Hurtigruten ferry having supper with a German admiral.

Thor and the admiral got down to business, while we ladies were expected to chat about other things. I had nothing to say. Thor's world of modest, subservient women was not mine.

Eventually he noticed how bored I was. He turned to me.

"Vera darling, Admiral Carax has been looking for somewhere to live, a property that could function both as a residence and for gatherings of an official nature. He, and not least his beautiful wife, are very selective in their tastes. It's a question I think the ladies' half of the table might be more qualified to discuss than shipping."

I understood now why I had been invited.

"I've enormous respect for the Norwegian proclivity for moderation," Carax said, sipping his fine wine. "But if it was up to me, your countrymen would have built more residences of a decent size. But you have a beautiful home south of Bergen." He leaned over the table and smiled.

"You're thinking about our residence in Hordnes?" said Thor, uneasily.

The German smiled again. "Absolutely."

I could clearly see that Thor was made uncomfortable by the German's quiet, friendly insistence. "No, Hordnes isn't available to rent. Not even to good friends," he said.

"It isn't?" Carax said.

"But the family has a property just outside Oslo," said Thor. "It's called Rederhaugen. It's fallen into disrepair in recent years, but it's larger and more valuable than the Bergen estate. What do you think, Vera darling?"

I knew that Rederhaugen had been built by Theodor Falck in or around 1900, and we had stayed there a few times when we were in Oslo, but I'd never felt any connection to the place. No one in the Falck family did at this time.

"It's a beautiful location," I said, looking at each person around the table in turn. "But they say it's haunted."

"Haunted!" exclaimed the admiral, before bursting into laughter. "You have quite an imagination, Frau Falck!"

His wife seemed a little troubled by what I had said, but Thor followed up. "I'm sure the admiral can handle a few ghosts, just as he masters any other challenge that comes his way."

"I think so too," said the admiral, leaning back in his chair with a look of triumph. "We'll come back to the practicalities, of course, but it's possible that certain underground improvements will need to be made on the estate."

"For what reason?" asked Thor.

"Well, the damned British haven't capitulated yet, and who knows . . . They might be foolish enough to send planes over Norway."

"They've enough to do defending themselves," Thor said.

"True," said the admiral, winking. "But we like to be prepared."

We raised our glasses to cooperation and to Rederhaugen.

It is winter and the rain is falling soundlessly over the Fana Fjord as I look out of the window. I have gone through the Hanseatic Steamship Company's correspondence for 1940. One letter in particular catches my attention. The date and the names.

From Dir. Thor Falck,
The Hanseatic Steamship Company
To Admiral Otto Carax

It is dated 21.10.1940. The day on which the *Prinsesse Ragnhild* docked in Trondheim.

It says:

With reference to the transfer of German troops.

Following our meeting in Trondheim on October 21st, the following has been agreed upon between Hauptabt Volkswirtschaft and the Hanseatic Steamship Company:

The German authorities may, when required, requisition the company's Hurtigruten ferries for the transport of German troops in 3rd class. Payment to be made according to current passenger rates, with special rates for the shipping of cargo, particularly where this includes flammable or explosive materials.

I make a note and return it to the file.

Thor was awarded the War Cross with Sword posthumously for his actions during the war, and I accepted it. Did they know about this? Did they know that alongside his supposed resistance work, he and his company earned millions from the transport of enemy troops all around the country?

I hurried down to the orlop deck and knocked on the door to the cabin where Jorunn was looking after little Olav. The more I thought about the meeting with the admiral, the more upset I grew. What should I do? Should I sound a warning?

Olav's nanny stuck a confused, denture-less face out of the cabin when I knocked. It was clear she had already gone to bed.

"Vera?" she said.

"May I?" I said, nodding into the darkened cabin.

"Olav's asleep," she whispered.

"No matter." I stepped forward, and she moved reluctantly aside.

Through the gloom I saw Olav's peaceful little face in his basket on the floor. The sight of him filled me with unconditional love, but also unease about what lay ahead. I climbed into the slanting top bunk and took off my shoes.

"Tomorrow," I began.

Jorunn cast a slightly anxious glance up at me. "What about it?"

"Thor will be in meetings all day," I said. "I need you to take care of Olav."

"I see," she said hesitantly.

"But," I continued, looking deep into her eyes, "I don't want you to say anything about it to Thor."

She looked at me. "You're not happy, Vera, are you?"

I was touched by her sudden show of concern, but a single word could not convey my feelings at that moment. I was both happy and unhappy. Shaking with excitement and fear.

Tomorrow it would happen.

"Can I sleep down here tonight?" I asked.

Kristiansund–Trondheim

His name was Wilhelm.

W. for War, W. for Weltschmerz, W. for Wilhelm. What his real name was, I had no idea. All the dissident Germans at the camp operated under aliases for their own security.

The Workers' Youth League 1939 summer event took place in Sunndalsøra. Before setting off, I had my first big quarrel with Thor. Earlier that summer I had succeeded in getting an article published in one of the city's news-papers. For the most part Thor allowed me to do as I pleased. He wasn't even bothered that I was part of a radical organisation like the League. It was an expression of my "youthful delusions", he said patronisingly. My assertions in this article, however, were too much to swallow. "War is imminent, and with such crises comes Socialism's radical redistribution of the means of production," I wrote, and with members of the Falck family choking on their morning coffee at my gloomy utterances and radical language, he put his foot down.

I would not be attending any *socialist* camp.

"You're not my father!" I screamed, so it reverberated through the balustrades.

"Perhaps that's the problem," he replied coldly.

My voice was shrill with rage. "What do you mean by that?"

"You've always lacked a father figure, Vera."

I pointed my index finger at his chest. His chicken heart. "You will never say that again. Never. And the summer camp is social *democratic*."

If the article created problems for me in the Falck family, it gave me higher status in the Workers' Youth League. I had always written, and it soon became clear that I had a talent for the witty formulations and personal attacks that added spice to a newspaper polemic. Social democrats, or at least those not among the intellectual circles in the capital, lacked such skills. They were good-hearted, down-to-earth folk who genuinely sought to make the world less hellish for the oppressed. But write, they could not. Their articles were as dry as accountants' reports, unreadable.

I was only nineteen, but already I understood that politics and even reality were not something one just documented.

They were something you manipulated. And recast in your own image.

An author was essentially a magician, a seducer, an illusionist. I was not yet the finished article perhaps, but I caricatured the enemy and conjured dreams of a new future. I was a dreamer. I always had been. Were dreams not the essence of all forms of socialism, and of life itself for that matter? Dreams of a happy life, of a future as free people, in which paid work and the pursuit of profit were secondary to joy and happiness, where people could love who they wanted, where the expectations heaped upon women were replaced by the freedom to do what they wanted, to create art or bathe naked in the full moon.

But I was also a naive and rather ignorant young girl, and I was brought down to earth that summer. Both red and Norwegian flags flew over the camp at Tangen, down on Øra. Our delegation from Bergen was larger than ever. True, two comrades had fallen in the Battle for the Ebro at the end of the previous winter. But this had only made us more certain in our beliefs: fascism was a plague that must be defeated by any means necessary.

The white tents spread across Øra like a small city. From where ours were pitched we could watch with awe as Einar Gerhardsen, a tall, lean and very serious figure, stood bare-chested with foam on his face, taking his morning shave.

There were bigger tents too, used for dining and the most important lectures, when they were not held in the open air. Although we heard leading lights like Gerhardsen and Trygve Bratteli, it was the social democrat German refugees who made the strongest impression. You only had to hear them speak for a moment to see the difference. Their faces were often older, furrowed, pensive, their eyes filled with the refugee's dispossessed longing and burning desire to return. Many of them had become scarily good at Norwegian, and their well-formulated and precise lectures all spoke of the tragedy that had befallen their country.

The informal leader of these German exiles was a man who called himself Willy Brandt, who had lived in Norway for some years. His voice was deep and resonant, his demeanour calm and confident, his arguments logical and incisive, and all in a language he had learned in adulthood.

We were spellbound.

It was during his lecture, in which he conjured in barely an hour the gloomy situation Europe's social democrats faced in their struggle with fascism, that another man appeared and took a seat at the back. Unlike Brandt and the other Germans, he had something distinctly nonchalant about him that instantly captured our interest. He was almost sprawled in his chair, in loose corduroy trousers and a crumpled linen shirt, with a hat under his arm. But when he stood up after the lecture and asked Brandt a question, he was a different man.

I don't remember the exact wording of his question, but he asked what strategy radical Germans should use against National Socialism. There ensued a heated debate between the two countrymen, because the linen-shirted chap was of the opinion that Brandt's approach was doing more harm than good.

My own naivety was thoroughly exposed in that same discussion. After their exchange, I raised my hand and gave a wholehearted defence of the Soviet model, a society with no private property or capitalist exploitation, a society of new socialist human beings. Here my speech grew more emotional, as I suddenly pictured my father, standing behind me, weather-beaten, a scythe over his shoulder. My contribution was applauded by many of the young Norwegians in the League, among whom the Soviet Union was still revered.

Willy Brandt took up my claims one by one: yes, he had allowed himself to be seduced by the Soviets himself once. But the whole country was a Potemkin village, he said, looking at me gravely.

"A Potemkin what?" I gawped.

Grigori Potemkin, he explained, erected fake settlements when Catherine the Great visited the Crimea in 1787, to convince her that progress was being made. They gave a picture of how reality should be, not how it was.

Potemkin village: Brandt clearly meant it negatively, but I liked the phrase.

In this *ideal society* of mine, Brandt continued sternly, millions died of starvation, or were forcibly deported or executed on the least suspicion. Moreover, the rigid Marxist division between the bourgeoisie and workers had the consequence of driving moderate sections of the middle classes straight into the arms of the fascists, when what we needed more than ever was a united front. Dreamers like myself were pure and simple at heart, but incapable of grasping the fundamentally chaotic nature of politics.

I must have made an impression nonetheless, for that night, as I sat outside the tent I was sharing, reading under a kerosene lamp, the man in the linen shirt appeared in the twilight. Most of the others were busy round the campfire, and he stood watching me from the shadows before he stepped forward.

"What are you reading?" Like Brandt he spoke excellent Norwegian, with a polished German accent.

"*Sinners in the Summer Sun*. It's Norwegian. I don't suppose you know it."

He took the book. "It came out in German before the takeover. *Sünder am Meer*. I read it in German and then in Norwegian. It's easier to read novels you already know. I enjoyed reading it in Norwegian. The boys are called Fredrik and Erik, yes?"

"You mustn't forget the girls," I said.

"Everyone's so naive," he said. "They believe in a new type of person who'll create a better world. Without war, without oppression, where people can cultivate love."

"And you don't?" I gave him what I thought was a teasing look, but he was deadly serious when he answered.

"We believed that too," he said sadly. "But love and fellowship do not defeat Nazism."

"I'm Vera," I said, holding out my hand. "What's your name?"

"Wilhelm," he replied, calmly. Even though he could not have been much older than me, I was struck by his calm. It rubbed off on me. He had an open, trusting face and a gaze that held my attention.

"You mentioned the Soviet Union," he said, rather stiffly and politely, causing me to wonder if he found it difficult speaking in his second tongue. "Why is it important to you?"

Nobody had ever asked me so directly before. I had buried that side of myself for years. Thor knew nothing of it; that part of my life buried in Nordland. Far away I heard the excited voices of the other campers. I stared into the ground.

"I'd prefer not to talk about it," I whispered.

He nodded and peered out into the darkness.

We sat like that for a long time.

"But thank you for asking."

He got up and disappeared into the shadows between the tents.

I looked for him all the next day. There was swimming at Tippen, and in the afternoon our local team thrashed the bigwigs from the Workers' Youth League in a football match. Men like Trygve Bratteli and Brandt were certainly better at talking than kicking a ball. Wilhelm was nowhere to be seen, which only increased the air of mystery surrounding him. There was a dance that evening, and I was approached by one local leader after another, but I spent the entire time looking over my shoulder until I went back to my tent early and drifted into a confused doze in my sleeping bag. I have no idea how long I'd slept when I heard a voice through my dreams.

"Vera?" it whispered.

I looked about the tent. My companions were asleep. The dance was long over. A man's silhouette appeared at the opening, backlit by the moon, his features obscured.

Wilhelm.

"A walk in the moonlight?" he continued. "Bring a sweater and good shoes."

Too dazed to be either nervous or excited, I quickly pulled on some trousers and laced up my shoes. We walked out across the dewy grass and crept soundlessly away from the camp. The sky was high and star-strewn, the mountains dark.

"Look over there," he said, pointing at two men's bicycles leaning against a pine tree. I sat on one, though I had to stretch my legs to reach the ground. We cycled through

Øra, him first, me close behind. Except for a grey cat that streaked across our path, the streets were empty. The road out of town was wet with dew, and I had to take the corners slowly so as not to lose control.

After we'd crossed the river, the uphill slopes began. My bike had only one gear. While Wilhelm cycled up with the greatest ease, I had to stand and shift my weight from leg to leg to keep moving. It was heavy going. We followed the fjord out, then headed up the mountainside. After an eternity, the road ended.

Darkness still enveloped us. The nights had started to lengthen after the summer solstice.

He hopped off his bike effortlessly.

"You might have told me we were entering the Olympics!" I said breathlessly.

"You were great, Vera."

A well-trodden path, visible even in the gloom beneath the trees, took us deep into a birch forest. He led the way. The trail climbed abruptly. Soon the trees and vegetation were replaced by rocks and stones. Suddenly my bicycle almost skidded on a smooth boulder, and he was instantly there, grabbing my wrist and holding it with a vice-like grip. Our eyes met. Then we separated and walked on, without saying much.

Only when we reached the plateau, did I see that it had started to get light. In the distance, behind us, I could make out the clusters of houses and tents down at Sunndalsøra, and in the other direction the fjord winding its way between the mountains towards the sea, a thousand metres below.

We sat on a narrow ledge near the top. Wilhelm fished out a mutton sausage, which he sliced with a knife.

"We have mountains in Germany too," he said. "But the sea doesn't reach into the valleys."

"You should see Lofoten," I said. "It's as if the water's risen around the Matterhorn and the mountains surrounding it."

"Is that where you're from? You seem to have a northern accent."

"Can you really hear a difference?" I laughed.

He nodded. "Why don't we go to Lofoten?"

I smiled. "My life is down south now."

Wilhelm gnawed on a bit of sausage. "How so?"

I cannot say why, but I began telling him my story. It all tumbled out. About my childhood home on Yttersia where the sun never set or never rose. And the dark basement room that Ma rented from the boathouse owner in a village called Å.

The last letter of the Norwegian alphabet.

The end of the world.

I told him the story that Ma had told me. How in the summer of 1919 she was working in the little general store in Svolvær to earn enough money to start teacher training, and how one beautiful warm evening she went to a dance with a friend.

A Russian Pomor ship was moored in the harbour, and her sailors on shore leave drank kvass and vodka as they played the accordion and danced folk dances. Ma's friend went home soon after the dance, but Ma stayed behind with a stranger with dark eyebrows and red glints in his hair. His name was Dimitri. He talked about Russia, of cities with churches with gilded domes, and towns that were so cold they lit fires under their cars at night so they could be started the following day. He talked of splendid houses with servants who served wine and black bread with caviar and silver dishes of roast beef that dripped with fat, of how they would get married in a magnificent church with the light falling in through blue stained-glass windows, and how he would never leave her.

That night I was conceived. And when Ma woke up the next day, Dimitri and the Pomor ship were gone.

"And he never came back?"

"When I was old enough to understand," I continued, "Ma took me out to the boathouse and showed me a Lofoten sea chest that she had packed, as the fishwives did for their husbands, in case he ever did. It made me sad at first, Ma's wishful thinking from which nothing would ever come. But I began to see it as a sign: we must always be ready to travel. As soon as I finished middle school, I left. I packed all my things in that Lofoten chest and vowed never to go back.

"But I can't believe I'm telling you this," I exclaimed. "I've never told anyone before. Now it's your turn."

Calmly he began to speak.

It was a complicated story about factionalism in the German Social Democratic Party between socialists and social democrats, with a long list of names I didn't know. Willy Brandt had abandoned theoretical, intellectual socialism and joined the Socialist Workers Party. Everything else in the united front against fascism, Wilhelm said, was subordinate. But whereas most other Germans in Norway were stateless and on Germany's wanted list, with Brandt only able to return in 1936 disguised as a Norwegian student, Wilhelm's situation was very different.

He came to Norway as a teenager and got involved in the strongly anti-Nazi exile community through some

Norwegian student friends. His parents worked for the German delegation in Oslo and were largely apolitical. He had a clean record, and when he returned to Germany in the autumn of '38, there was no way out of military service.

"So, are you in the German military?" I asked.

He hesitated before answering.

"There are many ways to resist, Vera. I have mine. And you must find yours."

The first rays of sunlight tinted the mountains around us as we sat there on our ledge. Writing this, more than thirty years later in the attic room overlooking the Fana Fjord, I can still feel the rock beneath me, the heather tickling my ankles, the sun's warmth on my bare forearms and the taste of the salty mutton sausage. I still see his open, boyish face, the slanting eyes and sensitive mouth, the dark blond hair, and the khaki shirt, sweaty and crumpled from the ride up. And I still wish that I had, that fabulous summer of 1939, up in the mountains between Sunndalsøra and Øksendal, on that clear July morning, put my hand over his and whispered, "Come on, let's go, you and I, today."

But that's how it is with all the things we ought to have said or done, the people we could have loved, the books we might have written: the chronicle of all that could have been is endless.

The rain came that same evening, turning the camp into a mud bath. Wilhelm was gone. Two days later I returned to Bergen. That autumn Thor got me pregnant. The war came. Olav was born, like a light that shines through a narrow opening into a deep mineshaft.

Trondheim

I slept fitfully that night, and when I woke up in Jorunn's cabin, I spied Munkholmen through the porthole. We were on our way into Trondheim. I was too nervous and excited to eat any breakfast. It was going to happen today. I was going to see Wilhelm for the first time since the summer camp.

I stood on the promenade deck with Jorunn and little Olav as we docked, the hull meeting the quay with a thud. Thor came up behind us, immaculately dressed in a brown tailored suit and bowler hat.

"The ship won't be leaving until tonight," he said.

We didn't answer. Olav whimpered in my arms.

"I've got a string of meetings," he went on. "Well into the evening."

This was precisely what I had hoped for, and the joy of having it confirmed and the expectation of what the day might hold made me take his arm.

"I'd have so loved to see the city *with* you, but that'll have to wait until next time."

He smiled contentedly at my flattery. "So, what are the *ladies* doing today?"

"I'm told there are some smart clothes shops down in Nybyen," I said. "And we're thinking of taking tea and a family day room at the Hotel Britannia. Aren't we, Jorunn?"

Olav's nanny nodded glumly. We moved towards the gangplank; there were a good many other passengers getting off.

"Good luck with all your meetings," I said, and in the commotion I gave him a kiss when we came ashore, in front of the shelter at the Hurtigruten terminal.

"See you tonight," he said, smiling and vanishing into the crowd.

"You lied to him," Jorunn said when he was gone. "Your own husband. It isn't right."

I sighed.

"I wish I could tell him the truth. But sometimes the truth comes at too high a price. If Thor asks what we've done today, you must say that we were at the Britannia. You understand?"

She did not reply, but dropped her gaze.

"Is there somebody else?" she asked finally.

"Yes," I replied. "There's somebody else."

Jorunn took Olav and carried him off.

The copper spire of Nidaros Cathedral stood like a scalpel against the iron-grey sky. It was one of those autumn days that never gets quite light, when daylight appears only as a brief interlude in the eternal darkness.

In the hours before I was to meet him, I wandered around the city aimlessly. My heart beat like a thousand galloping Lipizzaners. I had often dreamed of him. In my dreams he would drive into the courtyard in front of the house at Hordnes and say gallantly, "Hop in, Vera," and we would race through the countryside with the sun behind us. Sometimes he'd carry me on his strong shoulders across the border into Sweden. But who was this man? A German refugee at a Workers' Youth League summer camp. What did I really know about him?

Seen from the entrance, the western facade of the cathedral looked like a sheer, unclimbable mountain wall. Under the Gothic arches on the lower level, and the rows of saints, cherubim and gargoyles that surrounded Christ and the rose window above, stood a group of German officers smoking.

I no longer feared them. I walked straight into the cathedral.

Its grandeur took my breath away. A wide aisle cut through the rows of pews, leading to an illuminated altar at the other end. On either side were the massive arcade walls, the triforia above them supporting the pointed arches that held up the ceiling, formed like the bow of an enormous ship. There was the cool smell of granite walls and still air, with a hint of incense and hot wax from the flickering candles.

The place was all but deserted. I slipped out of sight and followed the shadowy arcade down to where it widened out into the transept.

The clock struck twelve; he was nowhere to be seen.

Towards the middle, the cathedral opened out on both sides to form a cross. I sat down near a pillar to the left of the aisle. I put my head back and stared up at the vaulted ceiling. The air was heavy and cold, as in a cave.

I was suddenly filled with anxiety. It might be better for everyone if nothing happened. If he did not come. But it was too late to back out now. I leaned on the pew in front of me and bowed my head as if in prayer.

The first thing I noticed was the sound of footsteps, clacking hard against the stone floor. Then I saw the shoes, tight-fitting, polished to a shine. My gaze slid up a dark-blue trouser leg, with sharply pressed creases. I instinctively started to shake.

A hand was placed on the backrest behind me and I heard him whisper my name.

I could not reply.

"Have you lost the ability to talk, Vera? That's not how I remember you."

"Tell me it's not true," I muttered. "Tell me you're not a German officer. That you weren't at the camp as an infiltrator."

"I can't deny that I'm wearing the uniform, Vera."

Everything stood still. I felt dizzy.

"That doesn't mean I'm a Nazi. You Norwegians weren't the first people to sound the warning about Nazism, put it that way. You've got to believe me. Even though I can't tell you everything. I'm sure you have your secrets too. We all have."

I smiled. "You win. I have a son, of three months."

"You see. And there are many anti-Nazis in the armed forces," he said. "More than you Norwegians think."

"The Nazis have conquered Europe with the world's strongest army," I interjected. "France, the Netherlands, Denmark, Norway. And the fascists are in control in the south. Even if what you say is true, what can a few resistance fighters do?"

A bunch of gangly choirboys in dark gowns crossed the stone floor. They were younger than me, but stared at us with grim faces like monks.

A portly churchwarden walked with heavy steps down the aisle.

"We mustn't be seen together. Come on," I whispered. "This way."

We crept silently behind the pillars until we reached the font near the altar, richly decorated and raised on a pedestal. The silver crucifix lit up the green-tinted ashlar stone, and high above us Christ hung on his cross.

We followed a passage behind the altar until we reached a well.

Wilhelm leaned over the edge, as if he was nervous of talking directly about his feelings. "Every German Catholic knows about this holy well. This is where Saint Olav was first buried. Miracles occurred when pilgrims drank the water."

Maybe Wilhelm was a believer. He had arranged to meet here, after all.

"Yes, of course," I replied, not without a hint of sarcasm. "And Olav's nails went on growing after his death."

"That's actually quite logical," Wilhelm said. "When a person dies, they lose the moisture in their skin. It contracts, making the nails *seem* longer. The Olav myth is a quirk of nature. Nothing more."

"But what's the difference between a truth and a myth?" I asked.

"What do you mean?"

"Right now, you are standing in Norway's holiest place. *Cor Norvegiae.*"

He smiled.

"Norway's heart. That name has a ring to it."

"After his death Saint Olav was laid in the coffin. Nobody knows where he is now, and that's almost irrelevant, when the myth has given meaning to so many people."

We continued under the colonnade. At one end of the transept was a room that at first glance looked like a little chapel within the cathedral: a choir, an altar and rows of pews divided by an aisle.

We were so close that I could feel the warmth of his breath on my face.

"Since our last meeting, I've been kept awake with regret," I whispered.

"About what?"

"That we didn't run off together."

He looked down. "We barely know each other."

"I'm married to a man I can't bear. You're in an army you hate. We haven't got much to lose."

"You have a son."

"I've taken Olav into account. We'll leave and cross the border. I have contacts. But you must promise me one thing," I whispered.

"What?"

"That you're honest."

His gaze did not waver.

"Because if you're not, I'll forget everything. You do understand? I'll forget the cathedral, forget the ship, and forget you."

"I have a ticket for the *Prinsesse Ragnhild*. Meet me on the bridge wing when it has left harbour," he said.

I went out into the nave and gazed up at the rose window.

The stained glass filtered the light. Ruby-red centre, yellow flames against a blue background. And angels blowing the trumpets of judgment.

The rose window warned of doomsday.

PART III

DANGEROUS CONTACTS

24

FINSE 1222

The Bergen train switched tracks, quaking and howling as it went through a tunnel. Sasha lay on the narrow bunk, sleepless, unable to get her grandmother's voice out of her head. They had read the manuscript aloud to one another, taking each chapter by turn as the train rattled westwards and up through Hallingdal, until they were finished and Johnny Berg packed the pages away in his bag.

She was biased, of course, but she could not get the story out of her head. Nor *his* voice. Johnny had read the section set in Sunndalsøra, taking his time when he saw the shock on her face when Wilhelm appeared.

Who was this man? Had Grandma fallen in love with a German while she was married – unhappily, that was clear – to Big Thor? Sasha would have remembered if her grandmother had mentioned it. But she never had. Grandma had never breathed a word about Wilhelm. When the manuscript came to a close in the cathedral, Sasha had felt the intangible feelings that a church interior can inspire, a sense of the infinity of history and the tragedy that lay waiting. She wondered if Wilhelm had gone down in the shipwreck.

The train passed Ustaoset.

Sasha felt surprisingly awake. She got dressed and went out into the narrow corridor that led towards the back of the train. It was night, a deep black outside, but she could vaguely make out that the forests had been replaced by bare rocks and plateaus. Some military service recruits in uniform were dozing in a four-seat compartment, a man of her own age sat engrossed in a novel, a rare sight that made her both happy and sad. Two girls about the same age as her daughters slept in a sprawled embrace.

Johnny was sleeping against the window, his breath steady, mouth half open, with the bag containing the manuscript as a pillow. He had insisted on making do with a seat. He always slept like a baby, he said, no matter what.

The train pitched to one side. She stood in the gangway looking at him. His dark features seemed even more pronounced in the twilight. Suddenly he opened his eyes and stared at her.

"Keeping an eye on me, are you?" he said in a hoarse voice.

She blushed, hoping it was not visible in the darkness.

"I thought you were asleep."

"I always sleep with one eye open," he whispered with a dazed smile. "Old field trick."

Old field trick. Sasha had met enough elderly veterans to know this was the sort of expression military men tended to throw around, but it was unusual for a journalist.

"How about a walk?" she said.

They went together between rows of seats, through darkened carriages lit only by the occasional reading lamp or the dim reflection from an unblinded window, rocking, legs wide apart as if on a ship in rough seas, until they finally reached the narrow corridor where the sleeping compartments were located.

Sasha stopped and put her palms up against the cold window. Outside, the snow gently lit a magnificent panorama of white snow-covered water under a starry ice-blue sky. And far away rose the silhouette of the Hardanger Glacier. The train slowed and rolled into Finse.

"I need a ciggy," said Sasha.

They went out onto the snowy platform.

The air was arctic cold. It was still midwinter up here. She could barely make out the frost-covered sign that read HOTEL FINSE 1222. She was suddenly reminded of Mads's postcard, just before Vera's death, and everything changed. A few tourists unloaded their heavy kiteboarding and skiing equipment onto the platform and carried it towards the old hotel that stood out against the frozen landscape.

"Vera writes about some powerful stuff," Johnny said. "Must really be quite special for you to read it."

Sasha nodded. "I feel in a way that I'm getting to know Grandma for the first time. But even though I might know her better, there are so many things I can't understand."

"Like how she hated her husband?"

"For example, though I always sensed that whenever Big Thor came up. But the idea that her mother died two years before the journey. For as long as I remember, the family story has been that Vera went north to say goodbye to her. What happened during the war? All I know is she went over to Sweden in 1944. Daddy was too small to remember it. Those years are a blank."

Johnny took a deep drag on his cigarette. "Are you sure you want to go on with this?"

"What do you mean?"

"It's your family, not mine."

"Everyone that was alive back then is gone. If there was ever a time this could come into the open, it's now. I'm more certain of that now than before I read the manuscript."

"We'd better not miss the train, then," he said, flicking his half-smoked cigarette into a snowdrift, just in time to offer her a hand before the doors closed and the train slipped calmly out of the station.

They stood facing each other in the gangway.

"What did Johan Grieg say about the archive in Bergen?" Sasha asked.

"That without the correspondence between Thor Falck and the German authorities, Vera's story is nothing more than a draft of a novel. We need to find the contract with Admiral Carax."

"I've been thinking about Wilhelm's identity," she said excitedly. "I can call the Workers' Youth League archive and ask for the names of any exiled Germans who attended the Sunndalsøra camp. Or try the Bundesarkiv in Koblenz and ask for a list of names of German Navy personnel in Bergen."

He hesitated. "Perhaps."

"You seem . . . how shall I put it? A bit reticent," she said, as the train hurtled into a tunnel.

He looked at her and bit his lower lip before answering. "I can see how important this is to you, Sasha, but I'm writing Hans's story. Vera Lind has only a bit part in that, a fascinating one, but she's not the main character in my story."

"So why are you here?" she asked.

"Because all your family's secrets are of interest to me," Johnny said, looking at her steadily.

She looked down. "What has that got to do with Hans?"

"I recognise myself in the outsiders of the Falck family," he said. "Putting work before family, sacrificing their nearest and dearest for something greater. It's tragic, in a way. But relatable too. You understand?"

"Is that what you've done?"

Johnny smiled, an almost doleful smile. "If I start on that we'll be in Bergen before I get halfway. Shouldn't we get some sleep?"

"Where's *The Sea Cemetery* now?" Sasha asked. "The manuscript itself, I mean."

"I've got it here," he said, pointing to the bag on his shoulder.

"Could I perhaps . . . take a look at it tonight?"

He smiled at her through the darkness. He stood for a while like that, his body moving in rhythm with the train. Eventually he put down the bag, opened the zip and took it out.

"Of course you can." He handed her the envelope. "But make sure you get some sleep, Sashenka. I think you need it."

He turned and headed back along the carriage. Sasha stood watching him go. In theory she could throw the manuscript out the window, the words would dissolve in the wet snow, and everything would be as before. There was something intense about Johnny, yet detached. Here she was, having dropped everything to join him on the night train to Bergen. Other journalists would not have been able to hide their voyeuristic delight at finding skeletons in the Falck closet. Sasha had lived long enough with Mads to know the allure that power and wealth held. But Johnny seemed oblivious. Though she could not help but notice his

interrogative gaze, which seemed to observe her every gesture and physical detail, from the manicured nails to the
floral lace on her blouse, and then see through it all, right
into her, without being particularly impressed by what he
observed there.

Who did he believe himself to be? Who was he?

25

WE HAVE RAISED OURSELVES
TO BE LIKE GODS

Spring came to Rederhaugen overnight, as abruptly as a scenery change onstage. The last snow melted, and the colourless winter landscape was replaced by the buzz of a new season. The forest filled with ants and insects, the edelweiss flowered, blackbirds and robins burst into song. As streamlets trickled over stony beds down to the water's edge, the frozen odourless winter gave way to pollen and the sharp scent of pine needles.

The warm föhn wind caressed Sverre's face as he jogged towards the gates of the estate. He had woken early. The sun was still low over the fjord. He was in better shape than in fifteen years. He felt proud and strong. He saw his father driving towards him along the avenue. Sverre waved and upped his pace and moments later the car passed out of sight.

Names meant nothing in the armed forces. Your family pedigree did not lie on your shoulders like a yoke there. In the military he stood on his own terms.

From the front gate he continued on the rugged pathway along the fjord. Although he liked to listen to leadership podcasts as he ran, or to history podcasts about past empires, great battles and daring military gambits, today he was too full of energy to concentrate on anything like that. It was as though he had come straight to the lowlands from high altitude training in the Himalayas.

An hour later, exhausted and satisfied, he ran back into the main house and was about to go into the locker room to change and do some lengths in the pool, when he heard his little sister behind him.

"Sverre," said Andrea. "Have you seen the glazier?"

"Glazier?"

"For the tower. Someone's coming to fix the rose window today."

"Can't say I have," he replied. "A lot on my mind."

His little sister leaned against the stone wall. "When are you leaving?"

Sverre shrugged with casual confidence. "Orientation starts next week, so we'll probably leave a few weeks after that."

Andrea looked at him thoughtfully. "I don't want you to go."

Sverre put a hand on her shoulder. "I know foreign assignments are as tough for the people we leave back at home."

His little sister turned and shook her head. "It's not us I'm talking about. It's just not good for you."

"Of course it's good for me. It's a unique opportunity."

His sister opened the outer door a crack and lit a cigarette. "Last time you came back from Afghanistan, you had that dead look in your eyes. Like a monk who's been meditating non-stop for ten years in a Bhutan monastery. You weren't made for war, Sverre."

He had that nagging feeling inside that always came when he was confronted with unpleasant truths. He had often wondered how the man who participated in meetings with top businessmen and leading politicians was the same one who lay in bed tormented by dark thoughts and insomnia.

"You're entitled to your opinion," he said, cheerily. "But it was the armed forces who asked me."

Andrea looked as if she wanted to say something else.

"That was the only time in my life that I've been happy, Andrea. I wouldn't have traded Afghanistan for anything."

And it was true, he would *not* have traded it. And it wasn't just the sense of adventure or the camaraderie, but the IED wires at the roadside, the flash of light before the vehicle was thrown up by the explosion, the smell of cordite and diesel, even the Taliban shooting at them from up in the mountains. He would not have changed any of it. Civilians did not understand, and they never would.

"A husband who betrays his wife may be happy while he's doing it," Andrea replied. "It doesn't mean he should."

"I *am* going," Sverre said, closing the subject.

Sasha's daughters came running down the stairs, deep in some game or other.

"Margot! Camilla!" Andrea cried, flinging her arms open. The two little girls rushed up to her, casting frightened looks at Sverre, who had never had his younger sister's way with children.

"We're going to France today," said the girls in chorus, beside themselves with excitement. "With Daddy."

"Isn't Mummy coming?" Andrea asked.

Camilla looked as if she was about to cry. "Mummy's never home nowadays."

"She's *working*. Don't you understand anything?" Margot said sharply, glaring at her sister. Sverre had always liked Margot, who was nearly eight now. She was a little nerd, with glasses and knowledge that far surpassed that of her sister or other children her own age.

"Why does she have to work now, when it's Easter soon?" Camilla said.

"Mummy's trying to find out why Great-Grandma Vera was so cross with Gramps. It's a very important job," Margot said in her most grown-up voice.

"Yes," said Andrea, with a smile. "Mummy's trying to find all the *ghosts* in the family." She loved making up stories for her nieces.

"Ghosts?" said Camilla, anxiously.

Margot looked up at her. "Can you tell us a ghost story, Auntie Andrea?"

"OK," she said, kneeling before them and lowering her voice. "I'll tell you a story, but first you must promise to be very quiet as we go up the rose tower. Or we might wake the evil spirits. Is that understood?"

The girls nodded, their eyes growing bigger. Followed by her nieces and Sverre, Andrea led the way up the winding staircase, past Sverre's office on the first floor and Olav's on the next, and then two more floors up, where the stairwell was darker.

"Grandma used to bring me here when I was little," said Andrea, with a teasing smile. "We need someone to be the evil spirit. How about Sverre?"

Sverre bared his teeth, made devil horns with his fingers, and howled: "Owoooah!"

The girls screamed excitedly: "Evil Sverre! Evil Sverre!"

The stairs narrowed and creaked underfoot. The treetops came into view through the turret windows, blurred behind the white mesh. Andrea perched on the top step.

"Once upon a time, back when your great-grandfather, Big Thor, was alive," she said, lighting a match, "there was a nanny called Jorunn. She came to Rederhaugen to look after a little boy called Per. Her fisherman husband had been taken by the autumn storms and vanished into the sea. Jorunn was strict but fair. She was kind to Per, but whenever he was bad, out came the cane. Per was a bit of a weakling who cried into her skirts when the bigger boys teased him. Then Big Thor had another little boy with Great-Grandma Vera. Olav was big and strong from the moment he was born. And it was only natural that Jorunn should be his nanny too. But one day Jorunn went on the Hurtigruten ferry with baby Olav and his mummy, Great-Grandma Vera. And down into the waves went poor Jorunn—"

"Andrea!" interjected Sverre.

"Behind you is the rose window," Andrea continued, ignoring him. "If you look through the ruby-red window in the middle you'll see angels among the yellow flames on the background of blue. The end is nigh."

Camilla held her little hands over her face.

"I know all about rose windows," Margot said. "I read that you get them in churches. But Rederhaugen isn't a church. Why do we have a rose window here?"

"Because we've committed a crime against the church's most important law," Andrea said gravely. "We have turned our backs on Jesus as our saviour and raised ourselves to be like gods. That is prideful and arrogant, and for that sin we must be punished."

"I don't believe in God," Margot said, as she and her sister swung on the banisters of the winding staircase.

They heard footsteps coming up and moments later Mads's head appeared.

"Margot, Camilla! There you are! We need to get going, or we'll miss the plane!"

"Bye-bye, Auntie Andrea and Evil Sverre," called the little girls, as they ran down the stairs.

When their footsteps had faded Andrea squinted out of the window, and said: "Why do you let Daddy bully you?"

"What do you mean?"

"You know what I mean. Sasha's always been the apple of his eye – until now at least." Andrea laughed. "I don't give a toss on my account. But he treats you like shit. And let's be honest, you don't handle it very well."

Sverre sat on the sill of the arrow slit opposite the rose window. He sighed heavily. He liked confiding in his little sister, but not when she started analysing him.

"I'll be off soon anyway," he said defiantly. "Father is Father. He'll have to do his own thing."

Andrea shook her head slowly. "You're so naive."

He swallowed and glared at her disdainfully. "Naive?"

"You think I didn't see that sly bloodsucker Martens Magnus come over to you? I noticed because I saw him here at Rederhaugen a few days before and then a few days after. He and Daddy had dinner. They thought I wasn't listening, but they were talking about you, Sverre."

"Me?" he said, feeling the contents of his stomach rise into his throat like water in a flooded basement.

"About how you needed a challenge, and how a trip to Afghanistan with the Marine Hunters could be good for your *character*. Daddy was the one pushing for it. MM only agreed to it at the end. Reluctantly."

"That can't be right," said Sverre, noticing how his voice faltered. From the punch his sister had landed to his guts.

No. From Olav's scheming, which left him hanging on the ropes.

His father's voice rang in his head:

You're a survivor, Sverre. A boxer with a granite chin.

He had been looking forward to going on this mission precisely because it was the one place where Olav's words meant nothing. "But they talked with my old troop commander, he was the one who recommended me . . ."

"I heard them say that," Andrea said, shaking her head. "Daddy's got very long tentacles, brother dear. But that's just one of the many reasons you shouldn't go to Afghanistan. I have a feeling that something's about to happen round here, that this ship has sprung a leak, if you catch my meaning."

She disappeared down the stairs. Sverre leaned against the rugged stone wall. As he did so, he noticed he was crying.

26

THE FALCK PONY CLUB!

It had been years since Sasha had visited Hordnes, and there was no doubt the place had seen better days. But the Fana Fjord was as enchanting as ever as its sparkling surface came into view through the trees. The rain had stopped, and the spring sunshine warmed the morning air.

They stopped at a narrow junction surrounded by overhanging evergreens and maple trees. The road was barred by a large rust-coloured gate. Johnny stopped the rental car and Sasha jumped out to let them in.

"Have you met Hans's family?" she asked.

"Not yet," Johnny replied. "But he's talked a lot about them, especially his daughter."

"He worships Marte," said Sasha. "He never mentions his sons or his new girlfriend, a locum he met in the A&E department and got pregnant. This must be his third litter."

"Hans talks about her with warmth," Johnny said, giving her a sidelong glance. "You and your Oslo crowd oughtn't to be so quick to condemn him."

It was said in a playful tone, but he had a unique ability to make her uneasy with his comments. The road that wound down to the sea was in desperate need of levelling and re-gravelling, with potholes and wheel tracks so deep that any ordinary car would have got stuck. On a field to their left stood what appeared to be the remnants of a tractor, and behind that a barn with boarded-up windows.

The driveway ended in a fountain, as at Rederhaugen, but this one was dry, and the rearing horses were flecked with rust and dirt.

"You read about the Lipizzaners," Sasha said, pointing towards a dilapidated stable with a pastel-coloured sign that read: FALCK PONY CLUB! SHETLAND PONIES FOR HIRE: RECOMMENDED AGE 3–6 YRS.

"This estate put Rederhaugen in the shade back in the thirties. Now look. Falck Pony Club indeed! How low can you sink?"

She stepped in a pile of horse manure as she got out of the car, and muttered an expletive. "The Bergenites are like a bunch of drunken French aristocrats," she grumbled. "The ones who live in lavish castles but sit shivering in front of the fireplace."

"Can't say I feel sorry for them," Johnny said, lighting a cigarette. "Why not just sell this dump and move into a three-bed terrace?"

"A terraced house?" She rolled her eyes. "Besides, the estate is actually owned by Vera. Or *was*. Hans and his family rent it at well below market price. And it's not so easy to sell an estate like this. No wonder they're obsessed with the will."

Like Rederhaugen, Hordnes was built on a peninsula, albeit smaller and hillier, dominated by a main house on elevated ground. It was bathed in sunlight now. A massive, rapeseed-yellow Swiss villa on three floors, it had blue window frames with peeling paint, an impressive entrance with steps leading up to it, an overhanging balcony on the floor above, and a pointed gable at the top.

Marte and another woman sat on the steps, each breastfeeding an infant.

"Sasha!" Marte exclaimed, getting up with her child on her arm, and giving her cousin a continental kiss on both cheeks. "Lovely of you to come. You look better than ever!"

Sasha had to admit, to her annoyance, that pregnancy number three had not diminished Marte in the slightest. The poncho and the dress beneath it were stained with breast milk, but that only heightened her free-spirited, hippy air. She was tall and elegant, with an aristocratic nose and large, quick eyes. She was a force of nature.

Marte turned to the other woman on the steps, about the same age, but with dark circles under her eyes. "Dad's out, I'm afraid. But this is Synne . . ." She paused. "How best to explain? Dad's girlfriend, my stepmother."

Synne nodded politely, while trying to rock her baby to sleep.

"And *this* is my new half-brother," said Marte, smiling at Sasha and Johnny as she stroked the other baby's hair. "Say hello to little Per."

Sasha smiled and gave the boy's cheek a gentle squeeze, then turned to Johnny.

"Johnny, this is Marte. Marte this is Johnny Berg," she said.

"Oh, my God!" Marte's face lit up. "You're the guy who's writing Dad's biography?"

She shook his hand, holding it a little too long. Men buzzed round Marte like wasps round a honey jar, they always had. Even though Marte was younger, Sasha had always looked up to her. She had the same nonchalant, give-a-fuck attitude as Andrea, but where there was something asexual about her little sister, Marte Harriet Falck was the embodiment of raw, erotic sensuality.

"Stay for supper. I'm sure Dad would love that," Marte continued, pointing towards the sea. "He usually catches us something on the fjord."

"As long it doesn't get too noisy," said Synne. "Per can't sleep then."

Marte raised her eyebrows and sent Sasha a despairing look. "There's nothing better for a child than to fall asleep to the sound of laughter and loud voices around the table."

She smiled at Johnny. "So, Johnny, what exactly are you planning to write about Dad? We should talk."

"Sure. Anytime. But I'm working with written sources right now."

"Oh?" Marte threw back her dark-blonde hair and bounced her baby on her hip.

"Anything to do with the Falck shipping company, its relationship to your father and the inheritance," Johnny said cautiously. "Vera Lind stayed here in the winter of 1970, which was, as I understand it, how she and your father really got to know each other. It seems there's some stuff in the old archive."

Sasha watched Marte's expression change from sceptical curiosity to eager attention as Johnny talked. How much did she know about the last conversation between Hans and Vera?

"I haven't been in the archive for years," said Marte. "It's just collecting dust. You'll probably find Hitler's diaries in there if you look hard enough, it's pretty wide-ranging."

"Could you take us there?" Sasha asked.

Marte led them up the slope to an outhouse resembling a traditional *stabbur* between the old stables and main house.

"Synne is *such* a drama queen!" she grumbled as they went.

She unlocked the door, and as a waft of dust and stale air rushed towards them, stood with her arm outstretched towards the entrance.

They gazed about them. The room was chaotic; it looked as though nobody had cleaned there in years. The shelves were filled with unmarked files of the same colour, and the floor was covered with large cardboard boxes, making it difficult to move.

"Enjoy!" said Marte.

Sasha watched her round the corner and return to the house.

"Beautiful, isn't she?" she said, closing the door.

"Not bad. Tries a bit hard, though," Johnny replied. Sasha felt a hint of malicious satisfaction.

She took a file marked "1896–1898" down from a shelf. It was filled with orders, accounts and yellowing correspondence. "DHS Correspondence, Head Office, January–March 1896. If it's all organised like this, it won't be too difficult," she said. "We just need to find the correspondence for 1940, or, more precisely, from October of that year. That's where any written agreements between Big Thor and Admiral Carax would be."

"Mm," Johnny said, stroking his chin.

They divided the task between them and started work. Johnny concentrated on the boxes on the floor, while Sasha tried to find a system to the files. It did not prove easy. Only the first two decades' worth – between 1896 and 1918 – had the year written on their spines. After this the archive became more labyrinthine. The correspondence was still sorted by quarter – January–March,

April–June, July–September, and so on – but she had to take random samples from each to determine the year. The files covered every subject under the sun, from the building of ships and delivery problems, to the creation of a scholarship for "specially gifted children" in partnership with Bergen's charitable foundation, Den Gode Hensight.

She looked over at Johnny. He was working systematically through the boxes, wearing big headphones. Why was he so invested in all this? There was a military quality about him, in his physicality and how he scanned a room, yet there was something else that was at odds with what she knew of her father's and brother's officer friends. Was he a graduate from the elite Russiskkurs perhaps? No, there was something streetwise and almost playful about him that she did not associate with the people she knew from there. The intelligence services? She would find the right opportunity to ask.

"Johnny?"

Sasha had worked her way through metres of shelving, the kind of monotonous task in which she was well practised.

"Yes?" He lifted one headphone from his ear.

"Have you found any correspondence from 1940?"

He shook his head. "1941–1945 is here," he said. "We'll just have to keep looking."

She had only one more wall of files to look through. Starting from the top and going from left to right, she took out every single file, checking the year to which the correspondence belonged. 1929. 1937. 1931.

She found the files containing the entries for 1940 in the very bottom corner. At once the lethargy she had begun to feel was blown away. DHS. FOURTH QUARTER: 1940 OCTOBER–DECEMBER.

"Johnny!" she yelled.

He pulled off his headphones. "What?"

"I think we've found it."

Johnny came over.

"It's what we're looking for. Look. It starts here. October 1, 1940 – the same month as the ferry disaster."

She thought of the letter in the manuscript from Dir. Thor Falck to Admiral Otto Carax, dated 21.10.1940, "With reference to the transfer of German troops".

"Well, well! Look who we have here!" said a cheery voice behind them.

They both jumped and turned towards the door. Hans Falck's furrowed brow was bronzed by the desert sun from his latest stay in the Middle East.

"Alexandra Falck and John Omar Berg," he said. "A stunning couple if I may say. Have you sent your social democrat turned right-winger packing, Sasha?"

She sighed.

"He's on holiday with the girls in Provence."

Hans grinned. "When you start taking separate holidays, believe me, your marriage is essentially over."

"Yes, wrecked marriages are among your areas of expertise," she replied. "Along with field anaesthesia and the Kurdish struggle for independence."

He glanced about the room. "So, what are you two looking for?"

She had thought a lot on the journey over the mountains about what her answer to this question should be. "I'm going to give a talk about Grandma's life and literary works for the SAGA Arctic Challenge, so I'm trying to map out that fateful trip on the *Prinsesse Ragnhild*. And you're rather familiar with Johnny's work, I take it."

"Never seen him before in my life," Hans joked. "But from my time in the Middle East, I've heard it whispered that he's not to be trusted. Has either of you found anything of interest?"

Sasha glanced at Johnny. "Maybe. In fact, we could do with an hour more."

"I won't hear of it!" exclaimed Hans. "There's a freshly caught cod waiting in the main house. You can carry on tomorrow. Nobody's been in these archives since 1970, and if you hadn't come, they'd probably have remained untouched for another forty-five years."

27

THEY ARE ALL DEAD

Johnny ambled down to the main house. The pieces had fallen into place just as he had hoped: Grieg handing over the manuscript, Sasha taking the bait, the story with its compromising material about the Falcks. And that was just the beginning, he was sure.

The interior of the house was, to put it mildly, a giant hotchpotch, like a city where periods of grandeur and decline form layers in the architecture. The Falcks' rich maritime history was manifest in the dark watercolours of schooners in heavy gilded frames that hung against floral wallpaper, above handsome fireplaces or once-valuable pieces of antique furniture; the family's fall, financial and otherwise, in the draughty rooms with their peeling wallpaper and threadbare carpets. The living-room floor was strewn with toys, the walls lined with wonky IKEA bookcases, crammed to bursting with magic-realist novels in paperback. In the kitchen the counter was covered with half-chopped carrots and herbs, surveyed from the windowsill by greying busts of Lenin and Karl Marx.

"I'm putting Per to bed now," Synne said.

In a gentle haze of nappy odour, Hans kissed the boy good night, and then kissed his girlfriend on the top of the head before turning to Sasha and Johnny.

"Thirty-five years of being father to one baby or another!" he said, throwing out his arms. "Thirty-five years. Can you imagine?"

"Sounds like self-inflicted torture," Sasha said.

"It's brilliant to have you here, Sasha, really it is," he continued, with a hand on her shoulder.

A tall, powerful figure with jet-black hair in a ponytail that fell over a tracksuit top appeared and gave Marte a kiss. "You know Sasha. This is Johnny," she said. "Meet Ivan, my husband. He's an installation artist – he has his studio here."

Ivan nodded but said nothing.

"But tell us, Dad," said Marte, leaning on the kitchen counter with a glass of wine in her hand. "How did you and Johnny meet?"

"In Beirut," Hans said, giving Johnny a manly pat on the back. "It didn't take me long to see that this boy was made for something greater than journalism. The other journalists sat for the most part in their hotel lobbies, but Johnny was out in the field. There was one of those blasted Israeli invasions. South Beirut was bombed to pieces. A humanitarian crisis of epic proportions."

"Weren't you scared?" Marte asked, looking at Johnny.

"Of course I was scared," he said politely. "You shouldn't listen to people who say they're not. But these conflicts seem more frightening from a distance than when you're there."

Marte smiled. "You sound just like Dad."

"How was Kurdistan?" Johnny said, turning to Hans.

"Worse than ever, of course. I remember we had a visit once from some Norwegian MPs to the occupied territories in Palestine. 'It can't carry on like this,' they said when they saw how the Palestinians were being treated. They clearly knew nothing about how the region works, because it's been like that for sixty years. But it's bloody awful in the Kurdish areas now. The jihadists are gaining ground and the West is standing on the sidelines, so the brave Kurds are the only ones holding out against a Turkey-backed caliphate from Damascus to Basra. They bombed a maternity unit with artillery. We got the children to safety, thank God."

Hans smiled wearily. "Well, enough about that. How about we eat?"

They filed through to the dining room, lit by dusty crystal chandeliers, and took their seats around the long mahogany table.

Marte and Hans carried in dishes of poached cod, boiled potatoes and warm parsley butter, and poured cheap Chilean red wine into generous water glasses. Marte's husband sat silently at one end of the table.

Marte, who was clearly assuming the role of hostess, started by boasting about Ivan's forthcoming exhibition at the Bergen Kunsthall, but was interrupted by Hans clearing his throat at the other end of the table.

"First of all, I've got some bad news. I've just been informed that Johan Grieg has died. A man that many of us around this table knew one way or another."

"Johan, dead?" said Sasha.

"Adrenal insufficiency," Hans continued. "He's been ill for a long time and last night he had an attack. Poor bastard. Couldn't find his syringe."

Johnny glanced over at Sasha. Her jaw had dropped.

"To Johan," Hans said, raising his glass. "A good friend, and a formidable husband and publisher. A long and good life."

"To Johan," mumbled everyone around the table.

They ate on in silence.

"Superb fish, Dad," Marte said. The others nodded, and Hans immediately held forth on the subject of net fishing, and the tricks he had picked up in Lofoten as a young, radical doctor up north in the seventies.

"Vera was from around there," Hans said, looking at Sasha. "Although she had a complicated relationship with the place. I don't suppose you and Olav have been up there much?"

Johnny noticed Sasha shift uncomfortably in her chair.

"Did you meet . . ." She hesitated before continuing. "Did you meet many people up there who knew Grandma?"

"Fewer than you'd have thought," Hans said. "Life was hard, people died young or moved away. The settlements on Yttersia were abandoned after the war."

"Somebody must surely have remembered her?"

Hans poured more wine. "Have you heard of Dr Schultz?"

Met by silence, Hans continued. "Schultz was a pioneer and a man with a calling. A legendary district doctor who left the radical cultural milieu of Oslo that he grew up in to help fishermen and ordinary folk in the north. He was a role model for me and countless radical physicians of my generation."

"How did he know Vera?"

"He cared for her at the hospital in Gravdal when she had polio as a girl."

"Grandma had drop foot the rest of her life," Sasha said. Johnny could see she was moved. "But she was good at hiding it."

"Doctor Schultz and his wife, a teacher, realised early on that your grandmother was uniquely gifted. They took her under their wing, provided her with books and insisted she finish middle school, even when her mother was against it. They helped her travel south. And they took care of her later too, when she came to Lofoten after the ferry disaster."

Johnny could feel Sasha's curiosity from across the table.

"Did Vera live with them during the war?"

"For periods, I think. But I've told Olav all this on several occasions, and he's never shown any interest."

"I'm interested," Sasha said. "I want to tell her story at the conference."

"Ah," Hans nodded. "So that's why you're going through the archives here?"

Before Sasha could answer, a voice yelled through the draughty house: "Hans!"

Synne had left the table to put the baby to bed. Now she was leaning over the banister of the steep staircase, with the baby in her arms and her face just visible through the dining room door. She looked irritated. "Per's not sleeping. And it's your turn."

"Let the boy cry and come and have a glass of wine with us, darling," shouted Hans.

Synne did not let herself be charmed. "I'm breastfeeding!"

"And you know as well as I that the Norwegian breastfeeding council is made up of priests and moralists. A glass of wine will do you and the baby nothing but good!"

A door upstairs was slammed hard.

"Can't you teach her some tricks, Marte?" Hans sighed. "You had everything under control from the moment yours were born."

Marte tossed her hair and seemed to bristle with self-satisfaction. She was clearly accustomed to being the centre of attention, used to men's praise and adulation. But it was the quiet strength of a woman like Sasha that fascinated Johnny.

Hans went grudgingly upstairs.

Marte poured herself more wine and took a sip. She turned to Sasha. "Did you destroy Vera's will?"

There was silence around the table, interrupted only by the scraping of cutlery on plates and a soft patter on the windowpane; it had started to rain again. Then:

"What are you talking about?"

"Dad told me that Vera wrote a manuscript here on the estate in 1970," Marte said. "It was seized and destroyed."

"Since you obviously know more than me," Sasha replied sharply, "I'd be grateful if you had some tips about where the will might be. Because I have no idea."

"Your side of the family comes out of it rather badly," continued Marte. "Dad hates conflict, and he wouldn't for the world want to create a bad atmosphere while you're here. But the fact is that Vera gave him concrete promises before she" – here Marte made air-quote marks – "took her own life."

Sasha's face went pale.

"This is beyond any decency," she said with suppressed anger. "What are you trying to say? I was the one who found Grandma. The police have investigated her death."

"Vera promised Dad that this property would be transferred back to us," Marte replied. "Along with a large sum of money. But there was more, which couldn't be discussed over the phone."

"Johnny?" It was Hans Falck whispering hoarsely from the stairs. "Come up here. Now that I've got the baby to sleep, I want to show you something."

The staircase walls were decked with Toulouse-Lautrec prints, a shelf filled with well-thumbed crime novels and a large watercolour of DS *Prinsesse Ragnhild*.

Johnny stopped by a chest of drawers on the landing, its surface crammed with framed photographs with dignitaries and community leaders from home and abroad, along with a couple of Arab honorary professorships and plaques. It was like a pantheon of Hans Falck's friends: Arab, Kurdish and Afghan leaders.

"They're dead now, most of them," whispered Hans. "Heroes don't grow old, not out there."

"These pictures really take me back," Johnny said quietly.

"What's the first thing you think of?"

"The smells," said Johnny. "Cumin, cedar, diesel, grilled lamb."

"You see this woman?"

Hans stopped at a picture and pointed. A young man in a khaki shirt and a scarf over his head, presumably Hans himself, with a panorama of olive groves behind him. And a young woman in a black, tight-fitting singlet, carrying a Kalashnikov. The face was maybe too sharply defined to be conventionally beautiful, but Johnny could not take his gaze from the melancholy, burning eyes.

"She's the first thing I think of," Hans said softly.

"Who is she?"

"Mouna Khouri. A Palestinian refugee from a Christian family who fled to Lebanon in 1948, central in the militant organisations. A force of nature, killed by the Phalangists in Beirut during the massacres in the Sabra and Shatila camps."

"The woman you tried to bring out?"

"It was impossible. Yet I've asked myself for over thirty years if I could have done more to save her."

"Hans, you've saved more lives than most."

"I expect you're right," he said thoughtfully.

Johnny looked at him. "What did you want to talk to me about?"

"What have you discovered since last time?"

"I was with Johan Grieg just before he died," said Johnny. "He gave me the first part of *The Sea Cemetery*."

Hans stared straight ahead, not meeting Johnny's gaze. "The manuscript from 1970? Well, I'll be damned."

"It was Grieg who squealed to the secret services in 1970," Johnny continued. "I was passed a document that proves it. I used it to pressure Grieg into giving me the first part. I let Sasha read it with me. We've come here to verify the claims it makes."

"Excellent work, Berg. I knew you were the man for the job. Let Olav and his descendants saw off the branch they're sitting on."

"The manuscript describes the first part of the *Prinsesse Ragnhild*'s voyage from Bergen to Trondheim. It contains some concrete accusations against Thor Falck, which are apparently backed up by a letter in the Hanseatic Steamship Company's archive. That's what we're here to find."

"Take all the time you need," said Hans.

"It's still unclear to me what Lind's manuscript has to do with the inheritance settlement, let alone with Olav abandoning me in a prison cell."

Hans hesitated. "OK. Last thing first. When I was there last week, I met a Norwegian guy in the Kurdish militia, a sniper."

"Mike aka NordicSNIPER," said Johnny. "I met him once. Wasn't he killed at the front?"

"He's not dead," Hans said softly. "I saw him at a hospital north of Mosul. But he's fucking furious with the Norwegian authorities, who he believes stabbed him in the back. He says he acted as a middleman between the intelligence service and a Norwegian operator who was going to carry out an assignment inside the caliphate a year ago."

"Oh?" said Johnny. He felt his heart pound.

"The Norwegian operator was taken, and when Mike reported it, he was told that the guy was actually a jihadist, and that he himself was suspected of helping a terrorist. It's you we're talking about here, Johnny."

"And where's Mike now?"

"Back with his Peshmerga unit at the front, I presume. You're not thinking of going down there yourself, Johnny? Remember, I've given you the job of digging up Vera Lind's will."

The smell of the Middle East beckoned.

"Listen carefully, Hans," Johnny replied quietly. "I've found out more about this affair than anyone else in fifty years. In *The Sea Cemetery* Vera describes a meeting on the *Prinsesse Ragnhild* with a German admiral, with whom Big Thor enters into an agreement. But wartime collaboration is one thing. This was the start of something much more enduring. The Germans built tunnels and bomb shelters on the Rederhaugen estate during the war that were used later for a Stay Behind weapons depot. In 1970 Vera Lind writes a manuscript which is seized for reasons of national security. I don't know the details, but there has to be a link between SAGA and the Stay Behind network. Last year I was on an assignment for SAGA, without even knowing it. In other words, the relationship between the foundation and the secret services still exists. If you really want to get to Olav, you should cheer me on when I go to Kurdistan. Because both these stories point back to Rederhaugen. To Olav."

"OK," said Hans. "Just be careful."

28

SOMEBODY REMOVED THESE DOCUMENTS

Sasha had slept with her mobile on silent and woke up to a string of missed calls and voicemails from Olav. His messages were brief, as always, but he "urged her strongly" to call "in regard to this so-called biographer, Johnny Berg". She knew that her father would give her the usual lecture about the Falcks never talking to journalists, and what a waste of space this biographer was. Johnny had also left several messages, but they could wait.

She got dressed and went downstairs. Hans was already in the kitchen with a simple breakfast on the table. The door to the dining room stood ajar. Nobody had bothered to clear the dinner table from the night before. The grease marks on the half-empty wine glasses showed up in the morning light. A black cat was gnawing at the leftover fish in the baking dish.

"Sleep well?" he asked, breezily.

She nodded.

"Olav's been trying to call me," he said.

"He can wait," Sasha said, stirring milk into her coffee. She had no appetite.

Sasha was bursting with questions about Hans's telephone conversation with Grandma, but decided they could wait too.

"Is Johnny up?"

Hans poured some orange juice from a carton and poked about restlessly in the kitchen. "He got up early today."

Sasha felt a slight unease. They were working together, he had said. She didn't want him starting without her. "He's already in the archive?"

Hans hesitated. "Johnny had to leave."

She was knocked sideways. "What do you mean?"

"He asked me to send his apologies for not telling you in advance. But you know how it is, things happen fast in the Middle East. One of the most important leaders in the Kurdish Communist Party, a man I've known a lifetime, agreed to an interview at short notice."

"Wait a minute," Sasha said, rubbing the sleep out of her eyes. "Are you saying Johnny's gone to Kurdistan?"

Hans nodded.

"Morning flight via Frankfurt. Berg is my biographer. Vera's story may be exciting, but she only has a supporting role in my life."

Sasha got up and went to the window. The fjord sparkled. Something felt very wrong here. She had dropped everything she was doing, on Johnny's request. She had been so happy when they had read and discussed the manuscript together, no matter how compromising its contents. Now she felt cheated. I must take back control, she thought.

"I have a suggestion," she said, staring at Hans. "That you and Johnny Berg end your collaboration on this biography project as of now."

Hans leaned back on his chair and smiled, his hands behind his head. "A bold proposition, Sasha. What about freedom of speech? I thought you took after your

Grandma, with her quest for the truth. Now you sound more like your father."

"I thought you communists were critical of 'bourgeois' concepts like freedom of speech."

Hans laughed, rather patronisingly. "These days I probably see myself more as a free socialist."

"I didn't say that you should abandon the book, I said you should end your collaboration," Sasha said. "I want to use Berg myself, to find out the truth about Vera. I'll pay him through SAGA. I think we should be able to outbid any advance from Grieg Forlag."

"A smart idea," said Hans. "But I'm not sure Johnny's all that motivated by money. Olav doesn't believe such people exist, but I thought perhaps you were different."

There was silence for a few seconds.

"You know Johnny from Lebanon?" Sasha said finally.

Hans laughed. "Look, Johnny is a talented young guy, and they don't grow on trees. You read the interview he did with me in Beirut?"

"Do you know what Johnny's been up to for the last few years?" Sasha asked. "Most of his articles are five to ten years old."

"From my understanding he's had a tough time of it," said Hans. "Working like that takes its toll, I've seen it countless times. War is a powerful stimulant, perhaps the strongest there is. Reporters are particularly vulnerable. Being so isolated, without any professional guidance, lots of them come to grief. He was pretty down when I found him."

"What do you mean, *found* him?"

Sasha was increasingly getting the sense that the wool had been pulled over her eyes.

"Johnny was imprisoned in Kurdistan last year," Hans said calmly. "I don't know the exact details, but the Kurds were worried about Western foreign fighters, with good reason, so it might have been based on a misunderstanding. There are quite a few Western journalists sitting in jails in the Middle East with dubious charges laid against them."

Had Johnny sat in a Kurdish prison?

"There aren't many Norwegians with better contacts than me in the region," Hans continued. "The truth is I was contacted, on the quiet, by a friend in the secret services."

"Who?"

"Someone who'd probably prefer to remain nameless. He asked me to use my contacts to get Johnny out on humanitarian grounds."

Sasha looked out over the fjord. The rain had eased, but a layer of fog hung low over the water.

"We live in Norway," she said, "not some banana republic where the authorities don't help citizens in a sticky situation unless some radical doctor intervenes."

She sat back down at the table, and Hans put a hand over hers. "The fact that Norway's a good country doesn't mean that dirty games don't go on here too. The *official* Norway doesn't like stories that challenge its untarnished self-image. That tell of our involvement in foreign operations. Or challenge the perfect image of our wartime resistance heroes, as your grandmother was set on doing. You're an archivist, Sasha. You dig about in facts from the past. Are you ready to deal with the consequences of digging about in your own family history?"

Sasha straightened up in her chair. "Yes, I am. You were living here in 1970 when Vera was writing her manuscript, right?"

315

For the first time in their conversation that morning Hans seemed rattled by something she'd said. Without answering, he cleared the breakfast table and started to stack the plates in the dishwasher.

"That's right," he said at last.

She got up from her chair and looked straight into his face. "What really happened, Hans?"

"Investigating archives is your specialty, Sasha. Maybe it's best you work it out yourself. The answers should be there," he said, pointing towards the building that housed the archive. "And if not, that might be an answer in itself."

The damp west-coast air hit her as she left the house. What had Hans meant by that? The grass squelched. She headed along the overgrown path, wet reeds whipping against her trouser legs.

She opened the HSC correspondence file for the first quarter of 1940. She wanted to start at the beginning of the year, wanting to get some context. What, for example, did Thor Falck and the other directors in the Hanseatic Steamship Company understand about how things were building up in Europe? Very little, basically. Life and business seemed to go on as usual.

After the invasion in the spring of 1940, Thor Falck had engaged in a hectic round of meetings with the German authorities, usually with innocuously named "committees" or "departments" that drew minimal attention to themselves. Not that such activity could be viewed as illegal or especially unethical. A shipping director had to adapt to the new system, whatever it was. In mid-August, the deputy director took the most important meetings. That was a couple of weeks after Olav's birth. "Director Falck was granted three days' family leave."

Eventually, Sasha got to the fourth quarter, beginning October 1. The correspondence was extensive and rigorously filed by date. Sasha tried to get a grasp of all the details; an endless list of technicalities about ships and tonnage, which meant nothing to her: *P.G. Halvorsen*, *Vela*, *Hovda*, *Juliane*. The Norwegian ship SS *Tindefjell* left from Tolbods quay; the Norwegian ships *Finse* and *Taiwan*, together with the German ship SS *Kattegatt*, left from the Laksevågs workshop and Dokken. And so on.

Then she discovered something peculiar. While there were several entries for every day of the month until Friday, October 18, there was nothing from October 19, when the ferry had left Bergen, to October 24, where it was recorded: "Yesterday DS *Prinsesse Ragnhild* sank off the coast of Landegode. Many feared dead. Director Falck among those missing."

She checked Vera's manuscript again. The dates did indeed match those now missing from the file. There was nothing to substantiate the claims in Vera's manuscript, not one word about the agreement between Thor Falck and Admiral Carax. Sasha got up and walked across the room. The very room in which Grandma had written *The Sea Cemetery*, that winter all those years ago, before the manuscript had been seized.

She thought about what Hans had said about Norway's untarnished self-image and the grey areas during the war. Someone had removed all evidence of Big Thor's misdeeds, the way inexpedient people are airbrushed from historical photographs. But who? And why? Had they read the manuscript and known what to look for?

She would pursue this, wherever it took her. And she would find the last part of Grandma's manuscript.

29

RUSSIAN OVER THE RADIO

Kurdistan, Northern Iraq

Johnny was sitting in the passenger seat of the taxi, an old Toyota with a taped-up side window and a chassis that scraped the ground whenever there was a bump in the road. The jihadists had set fire to the oil wells, and thick black smoke and a heavy, acrid smell filled the air.

The burning of oil wells was a bad sign. It was obviously done to reduce visibility for the Allied bombers. When IS set fire to its own income source, it meant something big was brewing.

The driver stank of old sweat and passed his time listening to Islamic Nasheed songs on the old radio on the dashboard. Shortly after they had passed a road sign that read MOSUL 29 KM, the driver's old Nokia rang. Johnny could hear that he was speaking Kurdish and could pick out a few words.

"Foreigner . . . journalist . . . yes, we're on our way."

The disquiet he had felt from the moment he had landed in the Kurdish capital grew stronger now. Although the Kurds were among the caliphate's greatest enemies, there were many who supported it. Not that the taxi driver would even have to agree with it ideologically, he could just be some poor bastard with a family to take care of. A foreign journalist was a valuable commodity. Several of those who had their throats cut on live TV were reporters.

Johnny leaned forward in his seat and pretended to scratch his right ankle while checking that his knife was in place. Bought on the black market the day before, it was a handy little black-blade KA-BAR combat knife from the US Marines, with a brown ridged handle. Where it had come from, he had no idea. The Americans had supplied the Iraqis with large quantities of equipment, which the jihadists had then stolen. The knife had presumably been taken as war booty when the Kurds stormed forward.

The flat desert landscape broadened out. The driver slowed down. Johnny cast a sidelong glance at him. Up ahead was a manned roadblock. If, as he expected, it was an IS checkpoint – and that would be clear when they got close enough – he would have to ram the knife into the throat of the man at his side and wrench the steering wheel round. Would it work? The driver would have no time to react, but would Johnny manage to get away?

He didn't know.

There were only a few cars on the road in front of them, and the queue for the checkpoint was moving fast. The soldiers were wearing American uniforms, which could be bad news. In a shock offensive the year before, the terrorists had overpowered the US-equipped Iraqi forces, taken their equipment and given them a choice: join us, or accompany us to the ravine where the mass executions are taking place.

"*Sahafi*," Johnny said to the bearded soldiers. "I'm a journalist."

A guard took his papers and disappeared. Johnny drummed the dashboard impatiently. It had all gone faster than he'd dared hope. When Hans had mentioned the story about Mike, he had known straight away. He had to go. The Middle East was what he knew best, not Norwegian history. No matter how traumatic his memories of the prison, the key to what had happened lay here.

He had flown from Bergen to Frankfurt, and from there to the Kurdish capital. Before landing in Erbil, he was worried that his name might have been compromised somehow. The American interrogator who had led the waterboarding was the only man who had managed to extract his real name. But everything had gone smoothly.

He had passed through customs quickly and gone to a guesthouse on the outskirts of the city, in the ancient Christian suburb of Ankawa, an area he knew from the old days. It was still possible to get alcohol there, besides which he wanted to avoid the five-star hotels, which were generally awash with Western journalists and aid workers.

He had messaged NordicSNIPER on Instagram, and during that first night in the hotel room, Mike rang him on an encrypted line. Things had changed, Mike said. The front was under growing pressure. They were on high alert. General Kovle, a former Kurdish assassin who headed the unit, had cancelled all leave. The only way they could meet, he said, was if Johnny came out to him.

"I think I know what happened to you," the Norwegian said. "But let's not discuss it over the phone."

Travelling in war zones involves a lot of waiting. And it was no different now. After an eternity, the checkpoint guard returned. The sun hung low in the sky. The warmth of the day was about to be replaced by the cold inland dark. The nights were still chilly here.

"Out, journalist," the guard ordered, indicating that Johnny should stand, legs apart, hands up against a brick wall.

"Journalist, you said?" He fished Johnny's knife out from his trouser leg. "Front . . . closed . . . for *sahafi.*"

Johnny stared into the peeling render on the wall. He had always had a good nose for who could be trusted. These men were not jihadists. Yet the area was closed to the press. He decided to take a chance.

"*Mukhabarat,*" he said in Arabic, before switching to English with a strong American accent. "I'm with the intelligence services. We're working to locate Western foreign fighters."

Whistling, he mimed the landing of a mortar shell.

"Ah!" The guard's face lit up. "You will . . . kill . . . Daesh terrorists . . . boom! Welcome to the Kurdish Peshmerga front, my friend!"

It was dark as they drove into the village to which Mike had directed him. After Johnny had said the word *mukhabarat,* his driver had shown him respect.

The low sand-coloured brick houses took on a blue-grey tint in the twilight, their silhouettes interposed with minarets and church spires. Christians and Muslims had lived side by side here before the barbarians came. That was no longer true. The thought made him sad. The Middle East always made him feel sad and energetic at the same time. The taxi driver honked his horn, and a couple of soldiers came out. Johnny paid him and nodded. The car disappeared.

It was eerily quiet. Some stray dogs barked in a back alley. Johnny carried his light backpack into the guardhouse, which turned out to be a private villa abandoned by Christian Assyrians the year before. A group of Kurdish soldiers sat on the floor playing cards, while others watched what was presumably a Turkish soap opera on a small screen. Everyone seemed calm. On the wall hung a picture of General Kovle.

"I have an appointment with Mike," he said.

A German Kurd who spoke English explained that Mike was at an outpost a mile away and offered him a lift. "Things might get pretty hot tonight," the Kurd warned, as they bumped along a dirt road.

"You don't seem to be on very high alert here," Johnny said.

"Listen, my friend. We know Daesh. We hear them over the radio every night. We know when they attack. It is not kicking off right now. But tonight, perhaps."

He pointed to a darkened building. "You find Mike there."

Even in the dark of night Johnny could see that this must once have been a church. He talked his way past some young soldiers standing guard and entered a room with a high ceiling. He found a winding staircase near the choir and went up a floor.

Mike was sitting by the wall. In the faint glare of his mobile, Johnny could see he had short, dark hair and a well-trimmed beard that framed his round face. Along the walls there were stacks of paperback novels in Norwegian, by Jan Guillou, Jon Michelet and Ken Follett, together with recoilless launchers and hand grenades.

"You found your way," he said, in the refined dialect of eastern Norway. "What a day to arrive on. It's been calm for a long time now. I just got back from hospital. I don't usually come up here, but tonight I think it was probably wise."

Johnny had no idea what he had expected, but this man seemed measured and mild-mannered. A sniper rifle was mounted in a sandbag position at the centre of the room, its barrel pointed towards a narrow slit-window.

"That Barrett rifle has saved me many times over," Mike said. "Didn't really have enough money for it, but thanks to crowdfunding I got it. Worth its weight in gold."

He was interrupted by the crackling of the radio, in French. Johnny did not understand it all, but there was a lot about "Kurdish dogs".

"It's the enemy. Daesh. Volunteers who speak various languages. Arabic, of course, Russian, French. They listen to our radio communications, and we listen to theirs. I wish I could speak French so I could tell them to belt up."

"I might be able to help you there," Johnny said. "Try *Ta gueulle, Mohamed, nique ta mère.*"

Mike smiled wryly. "Say again?"

After Johnny had corrected his pronunciation Mike went for it, and the channel instantly exploded with French expletives.

Johnny noticed that he felt relaxed with Mike. Just as Norwegians always recognised each other abroad, he could always tell when a person had killed.

They comprised a nation of murderers, and Mike was most definitely a citizen.

"Frenchmen," laughed Mike. "I'm never worried when it's them. But when we hear Russian, we know there's trouble ahead. The Russians are easily the best soldiers in IS. Sometimes we get French intelligence and special forces coming out to the front. We never eat as well as then – *vin rouge* and ratatouille all round."

Johnny remembered HK telling him the same thing and found himself wondering what his old boss would say if he knew he had come back to Kurdistan. No doubt he'd smile into his beard.

"French intelligence are here to map the whereabouts of French foreign fighters, so they can kill as many as possible. There's a fucking ton of them in the caliphate, and if they get back to France, all hell will break loose."

When Mike got up and went to the window, Johnny noticed he was limping.

"It was Hans Falck who treated you, wasn't it?"

"Lucky he was around," Mike said dryly. "Otherwise, my leg would have been a goner."

"Hans told me about your meeting," Johnny said. "But there are a few things I don't understand."

Mike had served in the sniper squad and been on several tours in Afghanistan. But the caliphate's advance on his parents' homeland had changed everything. Sitting by to watch the massacres play out wasn't an option.

He had terminated his contract and packed his bags. Through a German Kurd he knew, he had ended up in General Kovle's unit. There was a military flavour to the way Mike told his story – concise as a telegram, without adjectives or exclamation marks.

Mike had signed up for the intelligence services in Norway during a period of leave from the front, but heard nothing. Time passed.

"Next thing, I get a message from an old colleague in the sniper squad. He uses a military code, so I know who he is."

"Who was it?" Johnny asked.

"A man called Sverre Falck."

"Sverre Falck?" Johnny's eyes widened.

Mike nodded.

"I felt sorry for the guy when he was in the squad. The other men laughed at him, called him a daddy's boy, billionaire's son, they all said he was only there because his father had put a word in for him. A skilled sniper, to be fair, but otherwise hopeless. Weak psyche. Fell apart after a few skirmishes in Afghanistan, ended up spending more time with the field chaplain than with the guys."

Mike continued. "Anyway, Sverre Falck was a different man when he came and met me. Way too smartly dressed for Kurdistan. Said he was from some humanitarian organisation, but it reeked of intelligence from a mile off. He had ten thousand dollars in cash, the first half. I didn't want any money, but he insisted, so I accepted it on condition I could buy some stuff for the boys here. The rest would come later if I did as he asked. That is, procure a handgun and place it together with five thousand dollars—"

"In a vault in Kurdistan International Bank," said Johnny, completing his sentence. "That was where I picked up the equipment."

Mike nodded. "Falck was working for the Norwegian intelligence services."

"No," Johnny replied. "Sverre Falck came on behalf of SAGA. This operation would never have got political approval in Norway, so it wasn't the intelligence services who were behind it. It was a private assignment, without our knowing it."

"We were both used and left in the shit."

"Sverre Falck is the key here," said Johnny. "Nobody will ever believe us if he doesn't tell it like it was. But if he does, we can expose SAGA. I should be getting back."

"Reckon it's going to be a hard night, mate," Mike said.

Just then the radio crackled again.

This time the voice spoke Russian.

30

IT STOPS NOW, YOU SICK
BASTARD

On his return to Rederhaugen after a punishing three-day ski trip, Sverre had made up his mind. He would still go to Afghanistan, even though it was Olav who had secured him his ticket. Nobody knew except Martens Magnus. His father would be forgotten the instant the sirens went off and he could show what he was made of.

Four days earlier he had taken a long train journey high up into the mountains. Then he had proceeded to ski back alone, raging and hungry, through the wind and snow. In the evenings when he checked in at the hiker refuge huts, he went moodily to bed without giving a thought to all the athletic single girls with men in their sights.

Not that he was unattractive. And when a billionaire's son hung up his storm lamp, all sorts of creatures were guaranteed to come flying. But Sverre had no desire to bed gold diggers, however beautiful, not even in protective gear.

The women he wanted did not want him.

He had not had a proper relationship since Afghanistan. Truth was, he had barely had any before, either, but back then his bachelor existence had just been an amusing detail. "Sverre's waiting to find the *one*," his father had said. Nowadays he said nothing, just quietly expressed his contempt for those who did not reproduce, and thereby failed to continue the family line.

Maybe it was all down to Afghanistan. He had felt happier there, his life seemed to have more meaning and purpose, before the wave he was riding crashed over him after his homecoming. He had become distant, tormented by insomnia and inexplicable bouts of rage, none of which helped when he ventured onto the dating market.

You don't really see me, said one.

OK.

I know you fought for our country, said another, *why won't you fight for me?*

Just fuck off.

It was not altogether true that his father treated him badly. When Sverre had come home from Kurdistan after his meeting with Mike last year, Olav had briefly changed his attitude.

Sverre had known Mike for almost ten years. The Norwegian Kurd had kept a low profile in the sniper squad. The boys were shocked when they heard he had joined up with the Peshmerga and was documenting the fight on Instagram.

All the forces whispered about Mike. The officers were furious. Sverre's old comrades who still worked on the inside said you could get in trouble with the service and military police just by leaving positive comments on his posts. But to most of the guys, Mike was a Norwegian hero who stepped up to the plate when the politicians and defence leaders were too cowardly to do it themselves.

The courier job had been simple enough. It was Martens Magnus who had set it up. It had involved the delivery of a large sum of cash and two meetings: one with a Kurdish organisation and one with Mike. He had then returned home. The mission itself was never mentioned, but it was obvious his father was proud of him, asking him to represent the family at dinners to which he would never have invited him previously.

It did not last long. That summer Olav went back to his usual modus operandi of constant criticism. Blowing hot and cold, cold and hot.

Sverre was sitting up on Knatten now, Rederhaugen's highest point.

To the right he saw his father's villa, and at the bottom of the driveway the gatekeeper's lodge. He had always wanted to live there himself, but when his sister started a family before him, it was given to her, while Sverre had to content himself with an apartment on Gimle Terrasse. Rising before him was the main house with the rose tower, and on the left the swaying treetops of the forest around Vera's cottage, before the landscape ended in the precipice overlooking the sea.

There was rustling in the bushes below, dry branches snapped and a figure came into view.

"You wanted to see me," said Siri Greve. She was, as always, immaculately turned out, a MILF or a cougar as the websites he frequented termed it, although today her ankle boots had been exchanged for a clean pair of Nikes.

Sverre threw a pine cone in the air.

"Can I trust you not to go to my father with this?"

She laughed. "If you knew how many secrets I *don't* tell your father."

"I want to sell my shares," he said, without hesitation.

She looked at him disapprovingly. "Your shares in what?"

"The SAGA Group. There's no future for me here. No, I'll reframe that, there's nothing I want here. I want to start again."

"Was it Olav's Afghanistan plot that brought this on?"

So she knew about it too.

Fuck.

"It's not just that," he ventured.

"OK," said Siri. She sat down next to Sverre, brushing the bark and pine needles from her expensive coat. "Then it's presumably because Olav has treated you the way he treats everyone, like a subject or servant."

He could not remember hearing her criticise his father before.

"Olav has his good points, of course, and history will remember him as one of the great builders of our post-war society. But he's an old man, and the older he gets, the more he has to camouflage his weaknesses by criticising others. Vera's death hasn't helped. My question is whether you have what it would take to challenge him."

Sverre was taken aback.

"Have what it would take?" he repeated.

"Don't be naive. You know that Olav demands absolute loyalty. From me, from the board, and particularly from his children. That's what Sasha's always handled so much better than you. But now even she seems to have started to look to the future. If you try to sell, even within the family, it's a declaration of war. Do you have what it takes to stand up to your father?"

"What if you've been sent to lure me into a trap?" he said. Perhaps Olav had foreseen this and instructed Siri to keep him in check.

"Now you're being paranoid, Sverre," Siri said firmly.

He needed to breathe calmly now, just like when he was pulling the trigger to hit a Taliban soldier at a thousand metres.

"There was a guy called Skavik in the sniper team in Afghanistan," he said. "Nobody could do more bench presses than him, nobody ran faster in the 3,000 metres, nobody scored higher on the practice range or boasted more about the women they'd slept with back home. He used to tease the life out of a guy called Johansen. But the first time we came under fire in a *wadi*, a dry riverbed, Skavik was so terrified he lay there in a foetal position. He had to be carried back to our vehicle by Johansen. Next day he was sent home. After that he was just Scaredy-vik." Sverre leaned back and looked at her. "Nobody knows who's got what it takes."

"Spare me the moral fables," said Siri. "You want to sell. Well, there's a clause attached to your shares. Only family members can buy them, and then at half-price, precisely to avoid the kind of sale you're proposing. Olav has always been unwilling to let anyone in the family sell. Far better, in his opinion, to have them bound hand and foot on the inside. The Bergen branch has wanted out for years, they're desperate for money, but Olav has never been willing to buy. Perhaps they'll think again. It's just possible that they could find a way to buy you out, rather than selling their own shares."

"I can call Marte," Sverre said.

"Yes, do that," said Siri, raising an eyebrow. She got up, brushing off her clothes. "Call Marte Falck."

Did she know all about *them* too, he wondered when she was gone and he was alone again on Knatten.

When he felt resentful about his miserable bachelor existence, he often blamed Marte Falck.

He had never loved anyone as much as he loved Marte. He had loved her since they were children, running naked through the sprinklers at Rederhaugen or Hordnes or up at the summer farm. It had been so innocent, so beautiful, memories with the colour palette of old Polaroids. He was eight and she was six. Marte winked at Sverre and dragged him into a thicket, kissed him and guided his trembling hand onto her smooth crotch, and a quiver went through him, like when he rubbed himself against the pole on the climbing frame.

They were eventually discovered. Olav was so angry that he threatened to send Sverre to a British boarding school; Hans Falck took it more calmly. "Children's sexuality can be very powerful," Sverre overheard him say one night when he could not get to sleep.

It might have ended there, as an embarrassing childhood memory, were it not for an incident years later. One morning Sverre woke up in the blue room, which so many Nobel Peace Prize winners had slept in, with a pounding headache and blank memory, after a binge with the younger members of the extended family. Across the bed from him sat Marte, naked.

He realised instantly, of course, that this was beyond the pale. But the flesh cares nothing for morality, and the thought of being taken by Marte Falck filled the young Sverre with wild, uncontrollable desire.

Sleeping with Marte became an annual tradition, one he would spend the entire year looking forward to. Why did she continue with it? Maybe because of the transgressive thrill of fucking a cousin behind the toilet hut outside the summer cabin or some other similarly squalid place? Maybe she just had an insatiable sex drive?

He had never dared suppose that *he* might be the driving factor. Like all men with big egos and low self-esteem, he found it impossible to imagine that anyone might actually love him.

This tradition had continued until Ivan, the installation artist, appeared on the scene. One clear Easter evening outside the summer farm at Ustaoset he had pulled Sverre aside and said quietly, with an ice-cold Putin look:

"I know what you're doing. It stops now, you sick bastard."

And it did. Sadly. But once you've been taken by Marte Falck, you never forget it. The dream of her lay dormant, like an animal hibernating, or a virus in hiding.

31

BLOOD AND EARTH

Front line, Northern Iraq

The attack was preceded by an *Allahu Akbar!* over the radio followed by high-trajectory fire from Daesh's mortars. First, a faint rumble from the other side of the front line, followed by a low hissing sound like a New Year's sky-rocket, and finally the explosion itself, some distance away. The floor shook a little. Mike limped over to the church window and scanned the surrounding area through his night-vision binoculars.

"It's going to be a full-on attack," he said seriously. "They're zeroing in with the mortars."

Johnny came up alongside Mike, who passed him the binoculars. At first he saw only a no man's land of ditches, earth ramparts and barbed wire. Then, as he trained the binoculars upwards, he saw it.

On the other side, some five hundred metres away, rows of white pickups and other vehicles painted with black flags were standing ready to attack.

There was another hiss and bang, considerably closer than the last. Paperbacks and cutlery spilled onto the floor. Mike walked calmly over and fetched the Barrett rifle.

"There are men coming through no man's land," said Johnny, who had spotted dark silhouettes moving towards them. The mortars had got his adrenaline pumping. "Looks like a recon patrol."

Mike settled in behind a sandbag with the rifle at his shoulder. Johnny looked on through the binoculars.

Mike fired a single shot towards the back of the patrol. It was impossible to see any detail through the grainy-green binocular lens, but one man fell instantly, and the other jihadists flung themselves to the ground. Mike shot two of them in quick succession as they tried to get up. The last two ran hell for leather back to where they had come from.

"Good shooting," said Johnny.

"They'll think twice now before trying again," Mike said.

The smell of gunpowder tore into Johnny's nose.

Another rumbling sound rang out from the enemy lines.

Then, from the left, there was a terrible blast. Both men were tossed around the room, and when Johnny regained consciousness, he saw that one of the walls of the tower had been ripped apart. His ears were ringing.

"We've got to get out of here!" Mike shouted, getting up, grabbing his rifle and some grenades, and taking the binoculars from Johnny and hanging them round his neck. "Bring whatever kit you can carry!"

Johnny followed him with the recoilless rifle over one shoulder and an American M-16 on the other. The stairs were covered with broken stone from the collapsed wall and several of the steps had disappeared. The sky was filled with tracers, humming drones and artillery shells. Part of the building had been set alight.

"They're moving in," Mike roared. "Run like fuck!"

They sprinted across the church grounds between some small cypress trees just as another mortar landed with a massive explosion behind them. The tower in which they had been sitting moments earlier was blown away. Kurdish guards were running in all directions, yelling and screaming.

Instead of heading away from the front line and towards the village, Mike ran towards it, making for a sandbank that marked the edge of no man's land.

They threw themselves down behind the rampart. Daesh had also started firing at their positions with shoulder-fired missile launchers. Behind them, a car went up in flames. The sky lit up with tracers.

"We're safer here," Mike shouted. "They'd rather shoot too far than too close with RPGs. They won't hit us."

"Until they attack with infantry," Johnny said.

One of the terrorists' drones veered off course and landed a hundred metres behind them. Two young Peshmerga soldiers rushed towards it. Mike roared at them, "DON'T touch the fucking drone!"

It was too late. A delay-action bomb went off, flinging the two young boys into the air.

"Shit," said Mike. "Never go near a downed drone. Are you ready to shoot, Johnny?" he added. "We've got to stop them crossing the front line. We've got to hold our position."

"Ready," said Johnny.

Everything had gone so fast. There had been no time to feel fear. Only now did he notice that his hands were shaking and his teeth chattering. Yet again, he had made the wrong choice. He should never have come.

He checked that the automatic rifle was loaded and crawled along the sandbank until he came to a little gap with a clear view of no man's land. Carefully he raised his head. Just then a volley of shots came at him, whipping up the earth mere metres away.

"They've seen us!" He crawled back down and shouted to Mike, "Can you give me cover?"

Mike nodded. Crouching low he ran from the sandbank and threw himself behind a bush twenty metres away.

Johnny fired three shots in quick succession, but he was unable to see whether he had hit anyone. He raised his head again.

The jihadists must have been scared off, as there was no return fire.

Johnny tried to get a better overview of the front line. On the ramparts either side of him, more Peshmerga soldiers were defending their positions. It was hard to say in the dark exactly how far it was to the enemy lines – five hundred metres perhaps. The terrain before them sloped gently, before it was cut through by a long, dark trench. This was a security measure. The terrorists could cross it on foot, but not with large vehicles.

Suddenly he saw a flicker of movement in his viewfinder. Small trees moving in the breeze perhaps? No. Out of the darkness came ten to fifteen enemy soldiers heading slowly for the Kurdish positions.

Mike had clearly seen the same thing and passed on his observations. Moments later the sky was lit up with a flare.

"Fire!" Mike yelled.

Johnny rolled over and tried to do what he had done so often before. It had been a long time, but it came automatically. Rifle into shoulder, finger curled around the cold trigger, quick, controlled breaths, the light recoil.

He fired two shots; a jihadist fell to the ground.

Two more – the same result. Then came a round of sniper shots from Mike's position.

The flare went out as abruptly as an electric light being switched off.

The problem was that the Daesh fighters were in the majority. For every terrorist he and Mike took out, there were three more. Some with simple automatic weapons, others with heavier machine guns or missiles, which they aimed from the pickups. Slowly, metre by metre, they were cutting through the defences. Besides which, Johnny had been stupid enough to bring only three magazines, so he had to save on ammo.

They noticed that, because they lacked enough fire in the air, Daesh were driving several large vehicles down towards the ditch. Johnny reached behind his back for the recoilless rifle. It was essential to take care when aiming it, since on firing it released a flame behind the launch tube. Could he risk it? He had not been near anything like it since training years ago, and never in combat. Whatever the case, he needed Mike, it took two men to operate it.

He ran over to Mike. "I'm almost out of ammo. But I've got the Carl Gustav. Can you work it?"

Mike shrugged. "I can try."

They stretched themselves out on either side of the gun. Mike aimed it, Johnny took a rocket and loaded it into the launch tube.

"Ready!"

There was a roar, and the truck parked on the opposite side of the ditch went up in flames.

"Well done," Johnny said.

Mike looked out. "Fuck me, they've got pi-troops," he said quietly, scouring the area through his binoculars.

Daesh had engineering troops who built bridges and blasted out roads for their suicide vehicles.

What Johnny saw now beggared belief. Down in the ditch, sheltered from the bullets, a stream of people ran back and forth before vanishing under cover. Another explosion followed.

"They're making way for the bulldozer," Mike said.

"Bulldozer?"

"It's their worst weapon. If it comes this way, we're toast."

A bulldozer flying the black flag was moving towards them. It was reinforced with armour plating and steel bars, and whereas the other vehicles drove at top speed, the bulldozer seemed to be taking its time as it descended calmly towards the ditch.

The position to the left of Johnny and Mike peppered it with machine-gun fire, with as little effect as welding sparks against a wall. It rolled into the ditch. Then its huge claw came into view as it climbed steadily towards them.

"Reload!" yelled Mike. Johnny slid a second rocket into the chamber and covered his ears. The missile hit the armour plating and exploded. No effect. The vehicle was still coming straight at them. How far away was it? Two hundred metres?

"What do we do now?" said Johnny, hearing the terror in his own voice. "Pull back?"

"We're the Peshmerga. Those who face death," Mike said.

The bulldozer continued to grind towards them. Like a monster in a movie that looks dumbly at all the arrows flying towards it. If it managed to get this far, the whole area would be turned into a crater.

Two hundred metres. The vehicle juddered as it drove through no man's land. A fence was mowed down, a landmine exploded, all without doing any major damage.

A hundred metres. Johnny could now see the front of the bulldozer clearly. Its windows were clad with steel plates, with just a narrow slit for vision.

Then two Apache helicopters came into view amid the grenades and tracers in the smoke-filled sky. They fired rockets at the suicide bulldozer and cleared the enemy positions. Daesh soldiers were sent running in all directions. High in the sky, drones showered the terrorist vehicles with hellfire missiles. Johnny sprang away from no man's land, driven by forces outside himself. A massive explosion flung him into the air. And everything went black.

Birdsong, somewhere in the distance. Johnny was lying with his face half buried in the hard sand. He moved his head gingerly. The horizon in the east had begun to glow red. His adrenaline was ebbing out; it was like walking home from a party when your alcohol levels are dropping. A terrible fatigue washed over him. Mike came out from his hiding place, wild-eyed, his black beard now grey and tawny with dust and dirt. Everybody stumbled about as though they'd been beaten to a pulp.

General Kovle, the commander-in-chief of the Peshmerga unit, drove towards them at high speed, leaping from his Land Cruiser, with dark glasses and a cigarette in the corner of his mouth. He stood on top of the ramparts and surveyed the area, then shouted an order in Kurdish.

"He says we must clear up no man's land," Mike translated.

The general headed towards them.

"Great job!" He nodded to Mike, who thanked him.

"We don't usually accept foreigners in our unit," he said to Johnny. "But you seem to know what you're doing. You're welcome to join us if you want."

All across the plateau, smoke rose steadily from the enemy's vehicles, now burnt-out wrecks. The stench of diesel, excrement and burnt flesh tore into Johnny's nose, and he pulled up his neck gaiter. Overhead, carrion birds were already circling.

Dead IS fighters lay flung about, some with bloodied entrance wounds to the head or upper body, some blown apart by the suicide vests they had managed to trigger. Others, who looked totally untouched, had probably been knocked unconscious by the blast pressure from bombs and rockets. They were dead, he was alive. And right now, that was all that mattered.

Some of the Kurds dragged the fallen jihadists back towards their lines by the hair, then as they searched their uniforms, held up their grey, waxen faces and took selfies with them, grinning.

Behind the smoking wreck of a car, they found a jihadist who was still alive and conscious, despite his blood-soaked shirt. Johnny could see, even from some distance, that the wounded jihadist was a handsome man, with large, round eyes and jet-black hair that hung over his shoulders. He could have been Abu Fellah's little brother. A couple of Peshmerga soldiers went over to him to empty his magazines of ammo, followed by the general.

"He needs medical treatment," said the general, bending over the soldier. "You hear that?" he continued in Arabic to the man on the ground. "We treat our enemies like human beings. That's the difference between you and us."

With his last drop of strength, the Daesh soldier lifted his upper body and spat in the general's face.

General Kovle put his aviator glasses in his pocket and calmly wiped his cheek with his sleeve. Then he pulled out his pistol and quickly fired six shots into the prisoner's head. The last thing Johnny observed as he turned to walk away was how rapidly the body fluids soaked into the ground, making an alloy of blood and earth.

32

YOU WERE RIGHT

Sasha followed the path through the Blindern campus and crossed the cobbled square towards the university library.

It was four days since Johnny had gone off to Kurdistan. She had returned home from Bergen, but she was avoiding both her father and siblings. Mads and the girls were still in France. Which was good, since she needed to be alone. She checked her phone. Still nothing from Johnny. It was warm for the time of year, and students were lounging about on the front steps and around the fountain.

With Johnny Berg gone and no sign of the letter from Thor Falck to Admiral Carax, Sasha had to change tack. There was another mystery in *The Sea Cemetery*. How exactly did Wilhelm fit into the larger historic picture? Was he involved with the resistance movement within the German armed forces?

This was Sindre Tollefsen's area of expertise, and Sasha's former intern was now sitting at one of the café tables in the library foyer, with a thermos brought from home. He greeted her with a measured, rather anxious nod. Sasha sat down opposite him and folded her hands.

"Thanks for seeing me," she said, getting straight to it. "I expressed myself in a rather unfortunate manner when we last talked."

The academic nodded but said nothing, scrutinising her as if to determine her intentions.

"As you no doubt know," Sasha continued, "a lot has happened since that conversation."

"My condolences," he said flatly.

She mumbled her thanks and asked what he was doing with his time now.

"Not much," he said with a hint of bitterness. "I work a bit as a supply teacher at a private school, and I'm hoping to get my place back on the doctoral programme this autumn."

There was an air of impotence about him, mixed with the academic envy she had often observed in SAGA's interns. But stupid he was not. And occasionally, historians like him could be in possession of detailed information on a complex subject, the final piece of a puzzle.

"It's about your doctoral research project," said Sasha. "I have a few questions."

"The last time you questioned me about that you sounded like someone from the Inquisition," Tollefsen said. "How do I know you won't steal my research?"

Sasha was prepared for that. "From a formal point of view, I had every reason to terminate your contract," she said. "You were going far beyond the remit of your research."

He was about to protest, but she raised her voice to discourage him. "I have, however, concluded that you were right. I think there *is* a connection between your research and Vera."

Tollefsen looked surprised. "If you say so."

"Do you have evidence that members of the German resistance were active here in Norway during the autumn of 1940?" Sasha asked.

"The problem with the Wehrmacht anti-Nazi movement," began Tollefsen, "is that it has gone largely unrecognised, even among historians and experts. People have heard of the Weisse Rose students, and the officers' conspiracy against Hitler in 1944, but they've no idea that there was massive opposition within the German armed forces. And yes, of course, in Norway too. The Nazi regime had several hundred thousand men on our territory during the war. Research tells us that soldiers are like the rest of the population: a minority become sadistic and zealous, the majority do pretty much what they're ordered, and another minority – often about twenty per cent – actively resist. Don't forget that many German soldiers in the Wehrmacht and Kriegsmarine were sympathetic towards social democracy and communism."

The researcher poured himself some coffee from his thermos. Sasha felt a pang of guilt. "Can I get you something?"

"This'll do me," he said. "For a long time I was fumbling in the dark. A source told me that Norway's future prime minister, Trygve Bratteli, met in secret with an old social democrat friend who was serving with the Wehrmacht here. It seems they'd met previously at a summer camp in Sunndalsøra in 1939, which the future German chancellor Willy Brandt also attended, along with many oppositional Germans."

"Really?" said Sasha. This fitted exactly with Vera's description. Could this be Wilhelm? "And what have you discovered?"

"Well, I went through the Labour Movement's archives with a fine-toothed comb. But they'd had the foresight to get rid of any relevant documents before the occupation, making it impossible to find evidence of any such links."

"That would make it difficult, yes," Sasha muttered.

"But the two men about whom I'm writing in my doctoral thesis, German naval officers Karl Neipel and Peter Ewinger, were stationed in Norway in August 1940."

This was clearly Tollefsen's baby; he hardly drew breath as he talked. "These two officers worked in the city shipyard under the Marine Command. In 1944 they came into contact with a Norwegian intelligence agent who had got wind of the fact that they were anti-Nazis. They provided him with the coordinates of German convoys and ships, which he passed on so the Allies could target them. Whether they were active in the resistance as early as 1940, I don't know. But it's possible."

Again, this story chimed with Vera's manuscript. Tollefsen had a childlike glow in his eyes now.

"During a wider investigation of Norway's military resistance organisation, Milorg, the German secret police became aware of certain oppositional Germans. Around that time, the Norwegian agent was arrested. One day in February 1945 he was driven to the provisional military court outside the city. He feared it was all over, but it turned out he had been called to give evidence against the two German naval officers. They were led in. Karl Neipel had a limp, having been injured during an escape attempt. The judge explained the charges that were being brought against them and what the punishment for high treason would be if they were found guilty. The two men knew, of course, what awaited them. They were sentenced to death seven times over, execution by hanging. Then they were led out. Neipel spat in the face of the executioner. Both men refused to wear hoods when they were hanged in the afternoon sun on Odderøya."

"A powerful story," Sasha admitted, trying to hide her disappointment.

"I'm not finished yet," Tollefsen said. "At first, I had only the Norwegian agent's word for what had happened. But when I accessed the German archives and went through the records of the military court, which still exists, I came across something rather interesting. It revealed that these two Germans belonged to an unnamed resistance group that was active in Norway throughout the occupation. Another officer whose name was Hoffmann, but who went by 'Cyclops', was suspected of sinking a Hurtigruten ferry off Bodø in 1940."

Cyclops. Sasha had not forgotten the descriptions of him in the manuscript. Had he sunk the *Prinsesse Ragnhild*? Vera had hinted at this, yet it broke with the usual strategies of the Norwegian resistance movement, which was still a rather ad hoc organisation at the time.

She leaned forward. "Well, I've read the marine accident report from Salten District Court. Sabotage of this nature was unusual in Norway, for fear that civilian lives might be lost; that's deep-rooted in our national mentality."

"Exactly, but it wasn't the Norwegians who did it. Imagine you're an anti-Nazi German in the autumn of 1940. Germany is securing victory on all fronts. You have very little to lose. The German resistance tried to kill Hitler as early as 1938. They weren't so concerned about the loss of civilian lives. Besides, the Hurtigruten ferry was a legitimate military target; most of the passengers were German soldiers. With a few exceptions. Your father, grandfather and grandmother among then."

Sasha sat up straight. "Did the name Wilhelm crop up at all? He was on the *Prinsesse* when it went down. I don't have his surname, but I know that he lived in Norway before the war."

"Probably a false name," said Tollefsen. "Germans in Norway generally used aliases. Willy Brandt travelled around Germany as Gunnar Gaasland, the name of a close friend of his. But no, it doesn't ring any bells."

"Do you have anything to support the idea of sabotage?"

"Well, that's the problem," said Tollefsen, leaning back. "Not a lot's been done on the ferry disaster. A handful of shipping nerds and hobby historians are interested, and they've dug out a few testimonies that support it. There's a chap up in Lofoten called Bjørn Carlsen who knows all about it. I'm sure he'd be happy for you to ring him. Whether his evidence would hold up in a serious doctoral disputation is another matter. The *Ragnhild*'s secrets are buried deep, three hundred metres under the sea to be precise, beyond the range of any wreck divers."

Sasha leaned across the table and placed a hand on the researcher's shoulder. "This has been very useful, Sindre. Give me a week, and I'll see if I can help you – with your doctorate."

They parted and Sasha left the café. Still no message from Johnny. It was clear to her that she faced a string of secrets dating back to the war, many of which Vera had described in her manuscript. And they were drawing her north, to Lofoten, where Vera had grown up, to a shipwreck on the seabed.

33

GOD SAVE THE KING, BRO

The law firm Rana & Andenæs had its offices on the ground floor of a dilapidated apartment building in Grønland in the East End of Oslo, next door to an "underground" mosque from which there emerged a regular stream of serious-looking robed men with long beards.

In the days that followed the battle at the Mosul front, Johnny remained in a state of utter fatigue. He said good-bye to Mike, travelled back to Erbil and took the first flight out of Kurdistan. He had a host of messages and missed calls from both Sasha and Hans Falck. But the inheritance dispute seemed unimportant after everything that had happened. I'm doing this for myself, he thought, not for Hans, or for anyone else. He fell into a deep, dreamless sleep on the flight back, and one of the first things he did on arrival was to pay a visit to Rana & Andenæs.

Jan I. Rana was also Mike's lawyer, and the Kurd had recorded a witness statement concerning the events that had led to Johnny's arrest in Kurdistan, in case anything happened to him at the front.

Rana welcomed Johnny in the doorway with outstretched arms.

"Johnny Omar! Long time, no see! Good to see you, bro." He tapped himself on the cheek, indicating Johnny's cuts. "Took a beating, eh?"

"Got mugged by some fucking delinquents down by the river," Johnny said. "They blamed child poverty and overcrowded housing. Probably your clients."

Rana laughed. "Doesn't help having as many swords on your War Cross as Shetlands Larsen when twelve-year-old Abdulrahim rolls up with his switchblade because the local council reduced his youth club's opening hours."

"Andenæs? Your partner?" said Johnny, pointing at a sign.

"I know what you're thinking. Grønland, right? Why are we operating here in the ghetto, and not in Frogner or Tjuvholmen?" He pointed in the direction of the mosque with his thumb. "Put it this way: sometimes the guys there need a lawyer. When they've strayed down to Syria, for example."

Jan I. Rana was short and overweight, with a childlike face and a suit and tie that made him look like a boy at his confirmation party. In fact, he was probably Johnny's own age. His eyes twinkled. He was quick up top.

He led Johnny through reception, manned by a white legal secretary – of course he had white secretaries – and into a simple meeting room dominated by a veneer table with rounded corners. On the wall was a large portrait of the king in full regalia.

"Point is, Johnny, the name Andenæs sounds good. You've no idea how many law professors are called Andenæs. With a ligature of course – always with a ligature. It's like every fucking Andenæs born in Norway in the last fifty years felt the need to become a lawyer. I considered Klaveness, another good lawyer name, but Andenæs sounds more Norwegian. It speaks of ten generations of old money, gardens with compost heaps, summer cabins with outside toilets and cross-country skiing in Marka. Everything Norwegians love and we immigrants don't have."

"Can you name your firm anything you like – legally, I mean?"

"No, but I've got that side sorted," said Rana, with a grin. "My secretary, my partner, is called Andenæs. I got her from the law college. Found out they had an Andenæs and said she could be my partner if I could use her name. How many law students get offered instant partnerships, eh, Johnny? But her name was worth it."

Mia Andenæs could not be much older than twenty. She brought in some coffee and pastries, to which Rana helped himself greedily.

Johnny took an envelope out of his pocket and pushed it over the veneer table.

"What's that?" asked Rana.

"It's from Mike."

"Mike, aka NordicSNIPER? Mike who loves the smell of dead jihadist in the morning? I've got a man-crush on that guy, Johnny. He's a one-man, private pest control service. So long as he doesn't kill *all* my other clients with that sniper rifle of his."

"It's a sworn witness statement, in case something happens to him," said Johnny, tapping the envelope with his finger. "He presented it to me personally."

Astonished, Rana looked up at Johnny. "Ah, now I understand where those scratches came from. You've been to the Middle East? Fuck me, it was you who gave IS a beating."

He picked up his mobile and opened Mike's Instagram account. Between the blurred images of dead jihadists was a picture of a man, his face also blurred, with a bare chest, his head wrapped in a grey keffiyeh. The three scars across his chest were clearly visible. Shit, he had no recollection of this moment. *A little morning exercise with a comrade from the north,* Mike had written.

"I've been thinking about your case," Rana continued.

"Right. Any ideas?"

"The intelligence services are afraid of only one thing," Rana said. "Openness. It scares the life out of them. They're terrified of the press. You need to tell me everything that happened, Johnny. We need to get your story out there. I know people, the best journalists – they'd give their right hand to tell this story. I'll back you legally. Tell your story, Johnny, and the public will be your safety net."

Johnny hated the press. They all did – everyone like him, everyone he knew.

"The hero who sacrificed everything so we Norwegians can sleep safely in our beds. The man who was wrongfully imprisoned as a terrorist and spent almost a year in hell!" Rana intoned. "Be honest, Johnny, and you'll get massive sympathy. Sure, there'll probably be some debate about secret operators who take the law into their own hands, and all that. But the public will love you. And it won't just be sympathy. When people understand who you really are and what you've done, they can't go saying you're sick or come up with ridiculous claims that you're a jihadist. And if they can't do that, your ex won't have any grounds to keep you away from your daughter. You'll get your parental rights back."

"Listen, Jan," said Johnny. "The fact that you've not heard from me in ages doesn't mean I've got anything against your plan. Not exactly. But I can't go to the press right now."

"Why?"

"Because I don't have enough evidence. For you it's a win-win. If I get vindicated, you win. If I get hung out to dry and dragged before the courts for violation of the Security Act, you still win, as a lawyer in a high-profile case. That's the difference between us. Twenty-one years in jail for espionage and murder for me is a victory for you. The case I'm building is this: secret, private actors are carrying out extrajudicial executions of Norwegian citizens. That's why I went to the front to talk to Mike."

Rana nodded. "Smart."

"I know exactly what happened to me," Johnny said. "I know how these people operate. They used Mike to get to me. But if we're going to expose them, we have to pull in the whole chain. And I know how, and where it'll lead us."

"Where?"

"I don't intend to tell you until I've got better evidence."

"You're a hard nut to crack, John Omar Berg," Rana said with a smile. He got up. "By the way, a woman called. Fuck, I could smell money the minute she opened her mouth, and sure enough, it was Alexandra Falck. Wondered if I had any news about a 'certain client' of mine – 'a chap called Berg'."

He laughed. Johnny felt his heart skip a beat.

"Are you blushing, bro? Still selling dope and swimming naked with the posh girls like we did in the old days?"

"I've stopped with the dope," Johnny said.

"I did a bit of checking on the question of withdrawing a War Cross," said Rana. He pointed to the picture on the wall. "It's the King-in-Council who revokes it, but in practice that means the government."

"Well, the king's an OK bloke," said Johnny, laughing.

Rana smiled. "Exactly! Nobody loves the king more than us foreigners. Norwegians don't understand that. They think we just sit in front of cable TV watching mad mullahs who want to sneak sharia law into Norway. And yes, those people exist, nobody denies that. But I tell you: nobody loves the king, or a 17th May parade, more than us immigrants. Norwegian flags and old heads of state with inherited titles – foreigners *get* it . . . they understand it."

Johnny nodded.

"Norwegians don't understand how bloody happy we are in this country. And that's exactly what you're going to communicate when you eventually do go to the press, Johnny."

"What?"

"God save the king, bro."

34

SENSED-PRESENCE EFFECT

She spent an age at the mirror making it seem like she hadn't thought about her appearance. In the end she decided on a collarless red blouse that she had bought in a vintage shop in Paris. She put on some eyeliner, then with a sigh, wiped it all off again and went out.

It was a light and unusually warm spring evening. The air buzzed with insects and the burble of small streams released by the new season. A low sun gilded the green leaves. Sasha pulled off her jacket and draped it over her arm; she didn't feel cold even with turned-up sleeves.

Johnny had texted her, apologising for his silence and suggesting they meet up. Rederhaugen, she had replied. Where's that, he asked. Where I live, she said. Could he find his way there? What was she up to? Searching the archives, she said to herself as she walked towards the gates to let him in. The trail led to northern Norway, to Vera's past, to the wreck at the bottom of the sea.

She found him waiting for her, leaning on a pillar.

"Sasha," he said, embracing her.

He had a different look in his eyes, more inward-looking, it reminded her of Sverre when he'd come home from Afghanistan. She noticed his scratches but said nothing, just led him in through the gates and up the driveway.

"You've got some explaining to do," she said after a while.

"What do you want to know?"

"You just disappeared. Back to Kurdistan, of all places."

"I had some interviews to do."

She interrupted him. "Interviews . . . Sure you weren't locked up in jail for espionage?"

"Did Hans tell you that?"

"It's irrelevant who told me. You know a lot about my family, but you've said nothing about yourself."

They followed the driveway to the fountain. On the hilltop to the right stood the rose tower, swathed in golden afternoon sunlight.

"That's because I haven't been honest with you," he said.

"Oh?" She noticed a twinge of unease.

"You do understand I wish you all harm, Sasha?"

"Us *all*. Who do you mean?"

"SAGA, the Falck family, your business interests." He shrugged. "Don't take it personally. I'm talking about the one per cent, no, the one per mille, in Norway and beyond. I think it's unjust that some have so much" – he pointed over the glinting treetops towards the main house – "while so many have so little."

"It's ours," she said. People like him would never understand that her ancestors were not decadent aristocrats, but daredevils and visionary business folk, who had, at huge personal risk, built companies and created jobs. "What's your alternative, a collective farm?"

"I remember the first time I came out to a place like this," Johnny said. "You know, when you're thirteen or fourteen and starting to realise that the world's bigger than just the neighbourhood you grew up in. I was still living with my foster mum in Bjølsen. My friends and I used to deal a bit around Frogner, and one day we were invited back by some of the local posh girls who wanted to buy some hash. We ended up in this awesome pool, even though Abu, my friend, couldn't swim. When a girl collapsed and the others called the police, they came to take us in."

"Were you caught?"

"No." He smiled. "I was never caught. I was too fast."

She unlocked the side entrance and showed him into the library.

"This is where I work," she said.

Johnny stepped into the room and stared up at the ceiling of the atrium. "Quite a place," he said. It was the first time he had seemed impressed by anything she had shown him.

Up until now she had failed to assert herself. She had felt like a nervous little girl in his presence. It was time to take control.

"I've not been quite honest with you either," she said, looking straight into his green eyes. "There's a reason for my particular interest in Vera's manuscript."

"It holds the key to your inheritance dispute with Hans and the Bergen side of the family," Johnny said. "That's pretty obvious."

"It's more complicated than that," she said. "I've an offer to make you. I'll tell you everything, but first you have to give me a guarantee."

Johnny smiled warily. "A guarantee?"

"That you'll take a break from working on the book about Hans."

He drew breath to say something, but she continued.

"All the threads in this story lead to Nordland. That's where Grandma came from, where she stayed during the war and where the shipwreck lies. I talked to an expert in the field. Like Vera in her manuscript, he maintains that the ship didn't hit a mine, but was blown up from within. If we could dive down and find the hole in the hull, we could prove that she was telling the truth, and that the official version is a lie."

Johnny shook his head. "The *Prinsesse Ragnhild* lies three hundred metres under the sea. And 'we' are going down there? Good luck with that, Sasha. There are more living American presidents than people who've gone to that depth and come back alive."

"I know that. But the thing is we have access to specialist equipment. That's the advantage of being a Falck. Or we had. My brother arranged to borrow an atmospheric diving suit from a salmon farming tycoon up there, Ralph Rafaelsen. Although Daddy seems to have offended him somehow."

"Lofoten, Vesterålen," Johnny said. "I'm known up there. Or *was*. You want me to dive?"

She fixed him with her gaze. "I'd buy you out, of course, remunerate you on a project basis with funds from SAGA."

Johnny burst out laughing.

"How much do you want?" she said seriously.

"Hazard pay, that's for sure. For diving three hundred metres down in an atmospheric diving suit."

It was early evening when they left. The air was still mild. As they walked across the damp, claggy lawn towards the music pavilion down by the sea, she told him about the two anti-Nazi Germans who were executed towards the end of the war.

"Now *that*'s heroism," Johnny said.

"Absolutely."

"Not to speak ill of the Norwegian resistance guys – they took risks, they were brave – but they were only doing what was expected of them: defending their country. They had the people's backing. But these Germans committed treason for their ideals."

"Would you have chosen to do that?"

"I don't know," he said. "I'd like to think so, but we don't really know till we're put to the test."

She tilted her head so her hair fell on one shoulder. "You remind me of Hans," she laughed. "Do you think you could have done what he did?"

"What do you mean?"

The twilight was creeping up like the tide. They were suddenly bathed in darkness.

"Putting Middle Eastern assignments before your family?"

"It's not what I wanted," he said, "but that's how it turned out. I wasn't a good father. And being imprisoned in Kurdistan for a year didn't help my case."

She stood in silence for a moment.

Without knowing why, she had assumed he was childless, and she was surprised by her own reaction.

"Hang on," she said. "You have a child you didn't see for nearly a year?"

Johnny nodded.

"How did you survive?"

He shrugged.

"Have you ever heard of the sensed-presence effect? It's common among polar explorers and sailors – people who don't see their families for months on end. It's the brain's way of helping us deal with loneliness. People we love come to us. Not as a vague memory, but as a felt presence.

My daughter came to me every evening when I was down there. She would sit on the edge of the bed and dangle her legs, her knees grubby and grazed from playing outside all summer. I combed and plaited her hair, then brushed her teeth and read to her. After that I sang her nursery rhymes. It helped."

Sasha pictured the scene, then turned.

"Would you like to see the rest of the house?"

They headed back and went in through the sunken door to the rose tower, which housed Olav's office. The alarm was biometric, and turned itself off when she said her name into a receiver on the wall. Johnny stood gazing at the emergency evacuation floor plan of the house.

"So what's it like working so closely with your father?" he asked.

She hesitated. "Daddy's OK. Though all his talk of moving with the times is a facade; deep down, he's just another conservative patriarch who thinks the world was better when women weren't allowed to compete in the Holmenkollen Relay. He's obsessed with preserving the Falck traditions. Opens the safe every morning to look at Big Thor's War Cross. His desk goes back to Theo Falck's time; he boasts that the code to the safe, his fountain pens, his wine, are the same as when Big Thor was around."

"And you spent a lifetime finding a man like your father."

"No. Or perhaps yes, in a way. I *thought* he was like Daddy. But he isn't. What about the mother of your child?"

"Not like my mother, at least. Though who knows, I never knew her. You remind me of my ex, though. Smart, sophisticated, intellectual, a bit snobby, forthright, a couple of weight classes out of my league."

"I think you do pretty well, Johnny Berg."

He seemed unnerved by her compliment. They went down the staircase, Johnny two steps ahead, until they reached the basement and the entrance to the changing rooms. She decided to take a chance.

"D'you fancy a swim?" She pointed. "You'll find some trunks in the men's dressing room. I'll see you in the pool on the other side in five."

He seemed to think for a second, then nodded and disappeared through the other door. Sasha changed quickly into a cream-coloured bikini that hung there, and examined herself under the strong light over the mirror. Goosebumps pricked her arms. The red in her hair was stronger in the light. She tied it up in a tight knot at her neck.

He was taking so long she began to wonder whether he had got cold feet and left. She was already in the pool, swimming lengths, when she saw him walking over the heated tiles, wearing a pair of her brother's trunks. She stopped and leaned on the edge with her arms spread. Johnny was skinnier than she had expected. Three diagonal scars across his bronze-coloured chest. Where had they come from? He dived in and swam calmly towards her.

"Nice pool," he said, looking around as he smiled. "It's almost like being a fourteen-year-old dope dealer again, visiting one of the posh girls."

"What happened in Kurdistan? I can feel it in your voice. You're different."

"It was unreal," he said. "War is unreal. IS attacked the base I was staying on."

"Did you kill anyone?"

"Yes. Or they'd have killed me."

They both stood with the water up to their necks, just centimetres apart. She still had one option for retreat.

"I can't solve this on my own," she whispered. They were so close now that she could see the shape of the water droplets on his cheek. "You want to come to Nordland with me? You and me."

"Can you prove I can trust you?"

"Yes," she said, and kissed him. A dimmer light tinted the walls violet. The surface of the water swayed gently.

Then she closed her eyes briefly, pulled away, hoisted herself up onto the edge of the pool, crossed the heated tiles without looking back and went into the changing room, where she tore off her bikini and took a long shower, letting it get gradually colder until she finally stood, teeth chattering, under an icy stream.

35

REPUTATION IS ALL THAT'S LEFT OF US WHEN WE DIE

The skiing season lasted longer north of Marka. While the temperature at Rederhaugen was in excess of twenty degrees due to the warm föhn winds, and Oslo's outside cafés spilled over with patrons dizzy with the joys of spring, there was still plenty of snow just an hour's drive out of the city. Perfect for an Easter ski trip.

Olav had spent the last few days at Martens Magnus's log cabin in Mylla. He had no desire to travel further, not now. He would usually have stayed at the Hunting Lodge in Geilo with his family. But the ground was crumbling away beneath his feet.

Recently he had been thinking about Johan Grieg, remembering how his old friend had lain in spasms on the parquet that night. At the viewing of the coffin up in Grieg's villa, Olav had given a eulogy in which he described him as "the most life-affirming publisher in the second half of the twentieth century, whose work in the name of freedom of speech and of the press will be writ large when future historians revisit our nation's history in the era of oil and prosperity".

It was late afternoon. The days were getting longer. Martens and he had been out cross-country skiing for some hours. The officer had an impressive diagonal stride, and Olav struggled to keep up as they headed across the slopes on the south side of Mylla, over the Fugle Marshes and up towards their destination, the abandoned Bislingen mountain lodge.

"The Formo trail," said Martens, grinning over his shoulder at Olav, who was a few strides behind as they neared the top. "Named after Ivar Formo. Olympic gold medallist, Innsbruck, 1976. This was his regular route."

"Yes, Ivar fell through the ice here some years ago," Olav said grimly. "Damn tragedy."

Martens stopped in front of the building and leaned over his ski poles, waiting for Olav to catch his breath.

"You think too much about death."

"It's hard to think of anything else in a place like this," Olav said, waving his ski pole towards the building.

The once grand mountain lodge was in a sorry state. The outer walls were flaking, the doors boarded up with sheets of ply, and spruce trees were growing through the broken windows. The sight of decay had always terrified him.

Martens planted his skis in a snowdrift and walked over to the picture windows of the common room on the ground floor. He stepped in over the window ledge.

"This was once Nordmarka's pride and joy," he said, shaking his head. "I used to take the ski bus up here when I wanted a quiet Sunday ski with the sun on my face. And now?"

The rooms had been stripped by thieves and wrecked by local hooligans.

"You know, Martens," Olav said thoughtfully, as they peered into the smashed-up kitchen, "I wake up from a nightmare sometimes in which Rederhaugen looks like this place, with nothing left of the building but a shell, and all the windows boarded up."

Martens looked over at him. "What do you think those dreams are saying?"

"That everything we have, and what we are, will disappear one day. We can work as hard as we like, we can cling to our wealth, but eventually something will come along and pull the ground out from under us. Our own mistakes, or something beyond our control."

"Death represents the ultimate loss of control," said Martens.

"You *talk* too much about death," Olav mumbled.

The dilapidated building had imposed a sense of gloom, and they went back out. The air was fresh with the crisp smell of the mountains, but it was sunny and warm. They sat on a slope looking out towards the gentle hills that stretched southwards as far as they could see.

Martens passed Olav an orange and offered him his hip flask.

"You, my friend, must take back control," he said.

"That's more easily said than done. Sverre and Alexandra don't want to know me, and we've got a blasted family conference in a couple of days with the Bergen crew."

"Let's just take one thing at a time," Martens said, in a professorial tone. "The family conference will be a doddle, you'll see."

"What do you mean?"

"Be honest now, Olav," said Martens. "You're worried that Vera might have bequeathed the property in Bergen to Hans. Give it away! Get rid of the damn thing. Get it in black and white that the will hasn't surfaced and that the agreement you're all entering into is legally binding."

"Give away Hordnes?" cried Olav. "It's a magnificent property that they've been renting for peanuts, and now it

looks like it's been overrun by a tribe of bloody gypsies."
He pointed backwards with his thumb. "Won't be long
before it's like the Bislingen lodge."

"Shall we head back? It's getting dark."

Just then Olav heard his phone ringing in the pocket of
his ski association anorak. It was in a mitten, and only
after much fumbling did he manage to fish it out.

"Olav Falck."

"Johnny here," said the voice. "Johnny Berg."

Johnny was walking slowly along the road towards Rederhaugen, past the villas with their Teslas parked outside
and the high hedges intended to screen them from view.
He was on his way to meet Sasha, but before that there
was something he had to do.

"Berg, yes . . ." said Olav Falck at the other end of the
phone, slowly, as though playing for time. "This is a surprise, I must say. I heard you'd been released. Yes,
what goes on in the armed forces is no damn business of
mine, of course, but I hope you get back into the service
in some capacity. Norway's a small country – we need
good people. And you were one of the best, maybe *the*
best."

"Thank you. But that's not why I'm calling. I want to
meet."

"You want to meet?" Olav sounded hesitant. "It's presumably about . . ." He searched for the words. "Hans's
book project? Well, yes, I could probably supply the odd
word about our dear Hans. We go back a long way, and
the branches of our family are forever intertwined. In fact,
I was thinking of ringing you myself."

"Right, yes," Johnny said. "I'd love to have a chat about Hans. But that isn't actually what I'm calling about either. We almost met when I visited your old friend Johan Grieg a while back. He certainly looked frail, but I didn't think it would happen so soon. I don't know if it's tragic when anybody that ill and old passes away, but it's sad nonetheless. Grieg gave me the first part of your mother's manuscript and promised to give me the rest as soon as I'd found something in the private archives in Bergen. But it wasn't to be, of course. Grieg's gone . . . and with him the manuscript."

"A fanciful speculation, Berg." Falck sounded angry and impatient. "What do you want?"

Johnny was nearing the gates of Rederhaugen.

"The reason I took the job of writing Hans's biography was, of course, to get a better understanding of how you treat people who try to tell the truth about your activities. Your mother was put under a Guardianship Order, I was abandoned in the Middle East as a jihadist. But you can't hide all this forever. One day the truth will come out."

Olav Falck waited a long time before answering, so long that Johnny wondered if the line had gone dead.

"Look, I decided early on that a traditional career in shipping like that of my father and the men on my father's side did not appeal to me. Money always runs out. A few generations who don't share your hunger, and it's gone. I wanted to build something lasting. What is reputation worth, Johnny Berg? I have no belief in the afterlife. To me, reputation is all that's left of us when we die."

"You're ducking the issue," Johnny said, noticing that his mobile was getting sweaty against his ear. "But listen carefully. I may be willing to give the manuscript back to the family. In return for a favour."

"Oh?" Olav's tone was sceptical, but more amenable.

"I've been declared unfit for service, and the meaningless accusations that I was a traitor and jihadist present me with problems on a private level that I'd rather do without. I want it all annulled."

"People overestimate me, you might say it's one of my talents," said Falck. "But I can't override the security services or the medical corps and the chief physician."

"What a pity. Then we have nothing more to discuss."

"Wait," Olav muttered. "I may be able to make a phone call or two."

"Good," Johnny said, and hung up.

He passed through the gates of Rederhaugen and continued towards the main house. It was Sasha who had, the previous evening, inadvertently given him the final details he needed to carry out his plan.

The area around the entrance to the rose tower looked like any other construction site now, surrounded by a galvanised steel fence with a NO ACCESS sign. He jumped over.

In the twilight he could make out the shapes of cement mixers and containers full of planks and neat piles of scrap metal. He lifted the netting at the bottom of the scaffolding and crept under it. It was darker in here. The smell of paint and building materials hit him. He started to climb the ladder. As he reached the first platform he tripped on a forgotten bottle. It spun to the edge and fell to the ground with what seemed to him like an enormous crash.

Shit. He stopped. Listened. A dog barked in the distance, and the steady drone of an outboard motor drifted up from the fjord below. Otherwise, nothing. He continued on, but stopped at the rose window. Shining his torch at it, he noticed that the ruby-red pane in the middle was badly broken. He tested the rest of the window and frame; they were reasonably firm.

He continued climbing to the top platform where he swung himself over a crenel. His eyes were accustomed to the dark now. He stopped for a moment, awed by the magnificent view. He could see the whole of Rederhaugen – the symmetry of the walkways, the dark patches of forest, the auditorium, the long, straight avenue of linden trees, the clifftop that plunged vertically into the grey-blue night sea. And in the distance, a rim of glittering city lights.

The door had been taken off during the work, and he opened the temporary plywood hatch that had been put in its place. He was inside the tower now. The winding staircase led back to the rose window, and then one more floor down. This was it. The place he had seen on the floor plan. The carpenters had knocked through the old wooden wall in the middle of the room. Peering into the darkness, Johnny bent down and found the grille on the ventilation shaft. It was easy to shift. He lifted it off and placed it gently to one side. Then he wriggled into the shaft. It was as narrow as the torpedo tube of a submarine. He had to press his arms and legs hard against the walls so as not to come crashing down. It was hard work. He breathed heavily and moved slowly downwards.

A metre below he could see light. He felt around him. The walls were more porous here, the original ceiling in the corridor must have been lowered. Carefully, Johnny positioned his feet on each side of the vent grille and lifted it up.

From here he was able to drop down onto a Persian carpet that absorbed his fall. He rolled over and got up.

The alarm panel by the door to Olav's office beeped ominously. He took out his mobile, held it to the speaker and played the recording.

"Olav Falck."

It went quiet. Johnny stood motionless.

"Alarm deactivated," said the mechanical female voice at last.

He took a deep breath and used a slip card to open the door.

The office was more up to date and less ostentatious than he had expected. An antique desk dominated one part of the room, but the artworks were modern. The safe was set into the wall behind the desk, flanked by two shelves.

If Olav had the same code for the safe as Big Thor, that could mean one of two things: that Olav was still using Thor's eldest child's – so Per Falck's – birthday backwards. But that was unlikely. Tradition *and* modernity – change to preserve – was Olav's mantra. This meant he was likely to have kept to the same principle. It had to be Sverre Falck's birthday backwards. He had checked it out. February 9, 1980.

80–02–09. Johnny turned the dial.

The safe opened with a click. Carefully Johnny opened the heavy door.

He knelt down. The safe had three shelves. He found a little red case and opened it carefully. It contained a plain cross with the Norwegian Lion embossed in the middle, fastened to a flag ribbon by a little gilded wreath, like a key ring. And across the red, white and blue ribbon: a sword.

Thor Falck's medal.

Johnny held the War Cross with Sword in his open palm, overcome by the memories it brought back from his own life: the generals, the king, the ceremonial uniform, tight around his waist. It all felt so long ago, even though it was not.

Johnny came to again. Remembered he was in a stranger's office. He laid the medal down gently, closed the case and put it back in the safe.

The manuscript was on the shelf below, in a brown envelope marked Grieg Forlag, identical to the one that Johan Grieg had given him that night. Johnny weighed it in his hands; it seemed less bulky than Part One. He removed it carefully from the safe and laid the other in its place. He resisted the temptation to leave a message for Olav Falck.

As Johnny hoisted himself back up through the hatch and left the way he had come, he had the unpleasant feeling of being cheated. It was too light.

When a thing seems too good to be true, he thought, it generally is.

Sasha finished her glass of wine and walked through the lodge, past the oak table and antique bureau, as light on her feet as a hare in the snow. The curtains fluttered gently. She sat on the windowsill and lit a cigarette. I have Part 2 of *The Sea Cemetery*, his text read. Coming over now.

During their last luncheon, Vera had placed her liver-spotted hands over Sasha's and asked how things were, whether she was happy in love.

"I have lots of love in my life."

"And Mads?"

She hesitated. "There's love between us. Not of the romantic kind maybe. I'm too old to blush and get palpitations."

"Fiddlesticks. How old are you now? Thirty-three?"

Sasha nodded. She was thirty-four.

"Trust me," Vera had said. "If anything, you're too young. It's not over. It's now it begins."

As ever there was some truth in her pointed observations. It isn't true that adult passion is a pale echo of youthful feelings, Sasha reflected. It might be more powerful. She saw him now in every room, he sat beside her at the table, he sat alongside her on the windowsill, smoking a cigarette.

Sasha checked her phone: no new text from JB, which he was saved as. As she stubbed out her cigarette she heard footsteps outside, on the other side of the house. Her heart skipped a beat; she felt a heat spread through her body.

She heard a knock at the door. She leaped up from the windowsill, cast a quick glance over the kitchen and living room; they were clean, if not exactly tidy. She ran downstairs, tousled her hair in the mirror and checked her make-up.

"Coming, Johnny," she said.

There was another knock.

She opened the front door.

It was Olav. "Am I interrupting, Alexandra?"

"Goodness no. Come on in, Daddy," she said, hurriedly.

Without bothering to take off his shoes, he walked in and paced about the living room as though he were looking for something unknown even to himself.

"A glass of wine," he said. "Got some open?"

"Come through to the kitchen."

He leaned against the counter as she poured him a glass.

"Once, back in the sixties," he said, "Vera came to me and old Grieg because she was thinking of changing publishers. Gyldendal publishing house was standing in the wings with a new vision and a hefty pile of cash. Vera was upset that her books weren't selling better, despite their popularity. Most authors live in a perpetual state of dissatisfaction. But changing publishers, old Grieg told her firmly, is like getting a divorce. It might be justifiable under some circumstances, but on the whole it just creates a new set of problems without solving the old ones. Because they rarely stem from the other party, they begin and end with you. And old Grieg knew what he was talking about."

"Why are you telling me this?"

"You've been to Bergen," Olav said calmly.

She took a cigarette from her bag and lit it almost defiantly.

"Don't smoke," he said.

"I went to Bergen to search the archives of the Hanseatic Steamship Company for correspondence from the war," she said, blowing out smoke through her nostrils. "Not that I found anything of interest. I assume the relevant documents vanished shortly after the seizure of Grandma's manuscript. And why? Because they showed that Big Thor wasn't a war hero, but a war profiteer."

"Look around you, Alexandra," said Olav, going to the window. "Do you really think something like Rederhaugen comes without some personal sacrifice?"

"Sacrifice! Lies, more like. Who knows how many bones lie buried beneath us here."

He shook his head.

"Don't be naive. Who are we to judge? Father had to make choices that you and I should be grateful we've never had to make. How to preserve a family business and jobs along the coast when a foreign power has occupied your country? How to do it in a way that safeguards your patriotism and love for the Fatherland? Say what you like, but Father did it with bravura."

"Was it to safeguard his reputation that you removed parts of the archive?"

Olav ignored her question.

"Have you got a cigarette?" he asked.

"Really?" she said, raising an eyebrow and handing him the pack. He held the cigarette ineptly between his index and middle finger as he lit it.

"Most people have no idea about this period in history," he said, taking a drag on his cigarette. "How former enemies came together after the war in the fight against communism. In 1949 a delegation of German admirals came to Norway to brief our officers on all the artillery positions and fortifications they had built during the war. They were *here* too."

He pointed out over the lawn.

"Over the next few years weapons depots were established across the country."

"Stay Behind," said Sasha. "I know *that* story."

"Then I presume you also know that it was Mother who permitted them to come here," he said, coughing. "She approved the plans for Occupation Preparedness at Rederhaugen."

Sasha felt uneasy. She had been prepared for more lies and obfuscation, not straight-talking.

"But then in 1970, for some unfathomable reason, she decided to disclose it all. Can you imagine what the consequences would have been, Alexandra dear? It would have been catastrophic. Occupation Preparedness, which wasn't uncovered until almost a decade later, would have been set back years. It was about the security of the kingdom. But that wasn't all. It may seem to you that SAGA is cast in granite. But that wasn't the case in 1970. I was young. SAGA was new. Per Falck was still running his lamentable shipping company from Bergen. If we hadn't put a stop to it, I dare say we wouldn't be sitting here today. We'd have lost everything, Alexandra."

"Stay Behind is no longer a state secret," she said. "I've decided to get to the bottom of Grandma's story, even if that means uncovering some discomforting truths – for SAGA, for us."

"Get to the bottom . . ." Her father sighed heavily.

"There are so many so-called truths that have never been questioned," she went on.

"Your point being?"

Sasha stared at her father. "You've always said that the *Prinsesse Ragnhild* struck a British mine. But what if it wasn't like that at all?"

She saw Olav's lower lip start to tremble, then he slammed his fist into the table, causing his glass to fall over and wine to flow across the table.

"It struck a British mine! The conclusions of the marine accident investigation were unequivocal!" he yelled.

"Why are you so angry? It doesn't bloody matter *why* a Hurtigruten ferry sank seventy-five years ago, surely?"

"Yes, it does," said Olav. "And you're naive enough to believe this is all about history and freedom of speech. What you overlook is that our opponents will use this as a way to destroy us."

"Our opponents?" She almost had to smile. "You think everything's a boxing match."

He nodded.

"I'm thinking of John Omar Berg."

She jumped when he pronounced the name.

"You know absolutely nothing about him, Alexandra. He was a foster kid, a charming petty criminal and squatter from Oslo whom the armed forces got on the right track. They gave him the best civilian and military education. Part of some viability study. Berg became their most important operator – he was involved in everything: Afghanistan, Iraq, Lebanon, Russia, who knows what else. He became a legend. Few men could have borne the pressure he was under."

"What pressure?"

Olav ignored her and continued. "We should take better care of those who sacrifice the most. Poor John Omar Berg. Things were bound to go wrong. He began to hate the country that had given him everything. It was the usual story: PTSD, marital breakdown, a child custody case. He started flirting with extreme Islamism. He went to Islamic State as a foreign fighter. He was arrested in no man's land at the front line, after visiting Norwegian jihadists. And now he's back."

"Johnny almost sacrificed his life in a fight against IS in Kurdistan just last week," she replied. "Do you think a jihadist foreign fighter would have done that?"

"I think you know very little about what a man like him does on foreign soil, Alexandra."

"Well, I know this at least," she said, opening her Instagram account and going to NordicSNIPER. "Here's Johnny Berg with the Kurdish Peshmerga, after a battle against IS."

Olav put on his reading glasses and looked briefly at the screen. "The picture's blurred. Am I to suppose you recognise this man with the bare chest?"

"Yes," said Sasha, blushing a little. "I do."

"There's something you need to know about people like him," said her father sternly. "They're trained manipulators. Their job is to get people to talk, by any means necessary. Emotional blackmail, straight from the dark arts of psychology. They'll do anything to achieve their goals, even if it involves a personal liaison."

"*A personal liaison*. What kind of language is that?"

Olav did not answer. Then he said: "Johnny Berg is a dangerous man, extremely dangerous. He's out to destroy SAGA, and he'll do whatever it takes to bring it down. Why, we can only speculate. Even if it means presenting himself as Hans Falck's biographer. You surely didn't believe he was actually writing the damned thing?"

Sasha suddenly felt uneasy.

"He's got a contract with the publisher. And I *know* he was jailed in Kurdistan. In contrast to you, he's always told me the truth."

"That contract isn't worth the paper it's written on. Journalistic cover is frequently used in his circles to get closer to the target. It's Berg's specialty, his signature move. He comes up with a good excuse to make contact. A bit of off-the-record gossip about Hans. Who could resist?"

Tick-tock. Sasha looked at him with growing horror.

"Then," continued Olav, "he mentions in passing that during his research into Hans he's come across something interesting about Vera in 1970, perhaps you can assist him? And a woman who adored her grandma, who's a bit tired of her husband and needs a new project in her life, is the perfect victim when such a charismatic chap rolls up. Who can resist a little adventure? Naturally she accepts the offer."

She gasped. Tick-tock, tick-tock.

"They go to Bergen together. But Johnny Berg is too smart to push his attentions. No, he uses psychology's oldest trick. He feigns a lack of interest. Are you blushing? So, we find ourselves in the unique situation where our archivist, Alexandra Falck – loyalty itself, who's never once breathed a word to outsiders about internal affairs – is now the one being pushy, begging Johnny Berg, with whom she has of course fallen in love, for his help in destroying the family business, the family itself."

Olav smiled.

"I don't know, my dear Alexandra, I'm just a tyrannical old fraud whose time is up, but might that bear some resemblance to what happened?"

An hour later Johnny sauntered from the main house to the gatekeeper's lodge clutching the stolen envelope. He was bursting with adrenaline after his raid on Olav's office.

The gates were closed. He knocked gently on the entrance door.

"Sasha?"

Silence. She should be in now, and he had only ever known her to be punctual.

The door swung open. In the darkened hallway he saw only her silhouette, and the dog at her side. Ears back, growling and baring its teeth.

Something was wrong. Very wrong.

"Sasha?"

"You lied," she said, without meeting his gaze.

"What are you talking about?"

"Is it part of your training to feign surprise when your victims confront you with your lies?"

"You've got it all wrong."

"You're not writing Hans's fucking biography. You're out to destroy my family, and God knows what else. Was it Hans who put you up to it, or somebody else?"

Johnny took out Grieg's envelope. "Here's the second part of *The Sea Cemetery*. Now we can find the answers about Vera's—"

"Jazz is my guard dog. If you try anything, he'll go for you."

Jazz snarled menacingly.

"You can leave," she said. "Do whatever you like with the manuscript. I never want to see you again."

He stood rooted to the spot.

"Just tell me *one* thing," Sasha said, her voice brittle with rage. "Was all this just part your *mission*?"

He said nothing. He felt her pain, he had been there himself.

"You told me to leave," he said.

"Answer me, then you can leave."

"It was all a lie," he said, meeting her gaze. "Just remember one thing. The way your grandmother was silenced – they did the same to me. But perhaps you'll prioritise family loyalty over the truth of what happened. I may not have a family, but I could understand that."

"Just go."

"I'll find out if your grandmother was telling the truth," he said. "And yes, it may have started as a lie, but it became something else."

Johnny turned and left. He walked through forests and along dark fields until he came to the train station. He took the airport express, bought a ticket to Nordland, and still he could not get the thought out of his head. The rich and powerful write history, and anyone who muddies the waters must be punished. Sasha Falck could try to get away from this, but she was running in circles.

History is a hamster wheel. History repeats itself.

Johnny started to read.

THE SEA CEMETERY

PART TWO

Trondheim–Bessaker

Down on the Hurtigruten pier I noticed a change in mood. It was as if the war had come to the ship. A column of German trucks had driven up alongside her, and soldiers were loading equipment aboard. A strong smell of diesel from the idling engines lay warm on the fresh sea breeze. Everywhere an excited hum of German voices.

I slipped in between the vehicles, the winches and the big, tarpaulin-covered trucks. The whole pier was abuzz with soldiers wearing brown mountain boots, loose field trousers and brown anoraks, each with a trekking pole. They did not look like any Germans I had seen before. They had rugged, bearded faces, and a flower, an edelweiss, sewn onto their hats and sleeves.

"It's the Alpine Hunters," a boy said, craning for a better view.

"Alpine whats?" asked his companion, a cocky little lad wearing a chequered grey sixpence cap.

"They say they're the best fighters. They're going up to strengthen the northern front."

"They've got a ton o' weapons, that's for sure," said the second boy, pointing at the sealed wooden weapons crates and shiny metallic ammunition boxes being lifted onto the ship, along with provisions and motorcycles with sidecars.

I went back on board and caught sight of Wilhelm dressed in his Kriegsmarine coat. He was in the crowd outside the ticket office, with the one-eyed German.

The ship slipped slowly away from land into the night. Alpine Hunters were swarming everywhere. So, these were the men Thor and his shipping company were earning their money from.

I hurried to the shipowner's cabin. Luckily Thor was not there. I put on some make-up, but looking in the mirror again, I changed my mind and wiped everything off with a paper napkin. Wilhelm wanted to meet me out on deck. Under the bridge, he had said. I wrapped a scarf round my neck and went out.

The air was mild. The temperature had risen by several degrees over the last few hours and the wind had dropped. It was dark now, and I was met by a wall of fog; the shore-line was obscured from view. The rhythm of the pistons indicated that the ship had slowed down due to the poor visibility.

Wilhelm appeared through the fog. He was in civvies now, dressed like a Norwegian, with an Islender sweater and a knitted hat.

"Come on," he whispered, leading me onto the outer deck and past the dining room. The heavy iron hatch to the foredeck was closed, Wilhelm had to lean back and yank it up to open it. I slipped through it. He closed it behind us and pointed upwards, silently mouthing, *the bridge wing.*

"Follow me," he whispered.

Under cover of the thick fog, we crept past the tarpaulin-clad loading hatch, past the mast house, all the way to the stern. We stopped. I turned round. I could just make out the command bridge before us. It was only then I noticed that Wilhelm had seized my wrist, and for a moment we stood like that before I pulled my hand away.

There was silence.

"D'you know what that is?" I said softly, pointing at a little deckhouse. A mast rose into the fog.

"You're the one with local knowledge."

"They lock the drunks in there. The crew below were often kept awake nights by some rowdy sailor or other."

I kicked a bollard gently.

We sat against the wall in front of the mast house. It was out of sight from the command bridge, even on a clear day.

"Have you noticed how low the hull is in the water?" I asked.

"There are hundreds of soldiers on board," he said seriously. "They're reinforcing the northern front."

"Who's the man with the eyepatch?" I asked.

He smiled in the fog. "Dieter? He works with me in the Kriegsmarine."

"I don't like the way he stares at me."

"He's a good man," Wilhelm said earnestly. "A man you can trust. One of the few."

I stared thoughtfully across the dark water's surface.

"Are you beginning to trust me yet?" he said.

"I prefer people who break laws and rules to those who don't."

Our voices had got louder. We were getting over-confident, we should have known better. There was a noise. We both froze. Someone opened the door to the mast house on the starboard side, a few metres away.

"Hello?" A voice rang out into the fog.

My thoughts raced. We had to do something. There, next to our feet, a chain lay coiled up in a box. Quick as a flash I seized it and flung it towards the flagpole to divert attention. As it clattered loudly onto the deck below, I grabbed Wilhelm's hand. A figure emerged, looking for the source of the noise. We crept behind the mast house, headed for the door on the other side and rushed down the narrow staircase.

We were confronted at the bottom by the sailor who had invited me to the party, hands on hips and a startled look on his face. I froze. Wilhelm seemed not to have any ready excuses either.

"Was that you at the stern? The foredeck is strictly off limits to passengers."

Clutching at straws, I smiled at the sailor, a pimply lad, who had to be younger than me. "You asked me to the party in the panty-alley, remember? We were just taking a shortcut."

The sailor stood deathly still for a moment, before his face broke into a grin.

"Ah, it was you who worked on the *Maud*?"

"That's right." I've got him now, I thought triumphantly.

"The *panty-alley*?" said Wilhelm.

"Where the maids live," I said. "The girls who work on board."

The sailor and Wilhelm nodded in greeting.

The ladder was steep, and we followed him down into the bowels of the ship, to the panty-alley. Through a half-open door, I saw two waitresses sitting on the edge of a bed, swigging liquor from tin cups. And from the crew mess, at the front near the bow, came the sound of shouting, singing and clapping, and the stink of alcohol, roll-ups, heavy perfume and sweat. The sailor opened the door, revealing a small room crammed with crew members.

"This is Vera," said the sailor. "With her sweetheart."

"I don't believe it! Vera Lind!" shouted a voice. It was one of the maids who had worked with me on *Queen Maud*. "Our Vera could drink the engine lads under the table, I can tell you!"

The stoker and chefs whistled and cheered. The maids whooped.

Everyone was laughing, the mood was sky-high. I was handed a cup of moonshine. I knocked it back in one. It burned my mouth and made me writhe. I instantly felt better. We toasted. I leaned against Wilhelm, he smelled of after-shave and tobacco, he stroked my hair gently. I leaned closer. The waitress from the *Queen Maud* passed me another cup. The machinists cheered and stamped on the floor.

"A superb party," said Wilhelm.

"What did you say?" asked the young sailor.

"Superb party."

Sailor Fagerheim turned to the others. "A *superb* party, he says!" He laughed. "Where are you from?"

"Let's go, Wilhelm," I whispered.

"I asked where your fella is from," the sailor repeated. "Is he a German?"

The conversation stopped. All eyes were upon us.

"Come here," I said. Fagerheim took a step towards me. "Do y' know what I used t' do with big-mouthed sailors like you?"

I took a firm grip of his crown jewels with one hand and twisted till I could feel his balls and penis shrink like a snail into their shell. Fagerheim had a tortured expression on his face.

"Come into the daylight afore you accuse folk o' things you know nowt about."

I pushed him away. The cheers were so loud that I thought the hull would explode. I thanked the others for our drinks, hugged the maids and hurried out with Wilhelm. We went up the stairs we had come down, and followed the passage aft till we were out of the crew cabin area. I bumped into the corridor wall several times as the ship rolled. From the engine room came the regular chug of the pistons, and the stairway rang with loud, slightly drunken voices. Finally, we found ourselves outside the door to the cabin where Olav was sleeping.

Wilhelm stood leaning into the wall panel.

"Thank you," he said.

"You're too nice," I replied, kissing him.

Bessaker–Rørvik

The next morning I was woken by an ear-splitting blast of the ship's horn. I opened my eyes, confused. Jorunn lay snoring heavily beside me. I sat on the edge of the bunk. I had barely slept, and felt dizzy and nauseous, as if I was still drunk. From Olav's cradle came the soft sound of breathing and the occasional whimper. Quickly and quietly, like a cat, I washed myself, got dressed and went out into the corridor. The stairwell was empty. I glanced over my shoulder. An out-of-breath passenger was dragging a heavy leather suitcase after him. A clock showed half past six. It was still dark outside.

I went up on deck. We had entered Follahavet, an area known by coastguards as the sea's graveyard, where the winds blew hard and thousands of treacherous, razor-sharp reefs lay hidden beneath the waves. I breathed in the coastal air as though it were pure oxygen and I had just surfaced. The landscape was bathed in grey light. A magnificent canvas of islands, of smooth skerries, of blue and white rolling seas opened up before me. Foaming waves crashed steadily against the black shoreline. A seagull sailed on the wind, then swooped down into the water.

It felt good to be alone. I sat down on a bench. Suddenly, towards the aft of the ship, I glimpsed the figure of a man approaching me. He came closer. A shudder went down my spine. It was the German with the eyepatch. Dieter. Wasn't that his name?

Without saying anything, he sat a few metres away. I stared straight ahead. From the corner of my eye, I could make out a spar buoy and lighthouse on the distant horizon.

"You worked on a Hurtigruten ferry before the war?" he said in German.

It struck me that I had only ever spoken Norwegian with the Germans before, not just with Wilhelm, but also with the Gestapo officers who had carried out the raid in the music lounge. I could speak German, not perfectly, but we'd learned it at school, and I'd always had an aptitude for languages.

"I don't usually spend time discussing my past jobs with strangers," I replied.

"I'm more curious about whether it's possible to get into the cargo hold from the passenger corridor on the lower deck," he said. "Perhaps you could show me."

I turned to him and stared straight into a leather patch on one side and an inquisitorial eye on the other.

I went cold. Who did he work for?

"I don't work on this ship," I replied nervously. "You'll have to ask the first mate."

"Ah," he sighed. "That would just cause alarm."

He got up, raising his officer's hat. "Tell me if you change your mind, Frau Falck."

I went on sitting there for a good while. There was a peculiar atmosphere on board, as though everybody was skulking around, watching each other. I tried to go aft, but was stopped in my tracks by some German military police, who informed me that the dining room in third class was reserved for the Alpine Hunters. There was clearly big money in transporting German troops north.

Back in the first-class dining room, I met Thor. "You were already gone when I woke up," he said, in an ominously mild tone. "Did you get up early?"

"I ended up sleeping in the nanny's cabin with Olav. I'm less relaxed about being parted from him than I expected."

I looked around. "The ship's overcrowded, the hull's lying very low in the water. I'm worried something could happen."

He lifted the little porcelain cup to his lips, but a sudden roll of the waves spilled scalding hot coffee substitute over his hand and shirt lapels. "What sort of thing is that to say?"

"The entire aft deck has been blocked off for the German Alpine Hunters. And I saw how much weaponry and ammunition came aboard in Trondheim."

The colour drained from his face, and he shook his head vigorously.

"Have you done this so the shipping companies will make even bigger profits?" I continued softly.

A hitherto suppressed rage was unleashed.

"Do you think a ticket for a Hurtigruten ferry, much less for the shipowner's cabin, can be bought with the monthly earnings of a port authority secretary? Last time I checked, it was one hundred and forty-five kroner."

"I've barely seen you since our baby was born. And you think some bloody cabin will make up for it!"

I laid the steaming teabag on my teaspoon and wound the thin string around it. Outside, the white waves rolled past.

"I've been working, damn it!" Thor bellowed. "Day in and day out, so you and the boy can thrive."

He regained his composure, but his hands trembled slightly.

"I don't want to hear about money," I said.

"We're married. I've never even so much as looked at another woman. I've sworn absolute fidelity. Tried to do my best, for us, for you, for our little boy. I've given you everything. Do you have any idea how much you've been given?"

My thoughts were elsewhere now. He could say whatever he liked, it would mean nothing to me.

"And if that weren't enough," he continued, "should anything happen to me, you'll inherit a significant share of my property holdings. It's all in my will, from last year. But if you continue like this, we might have to review the finer details."

"I'm frightened, Thor," I whispered.

In an instant his expression softened.

"Do you want to tell me why?" he said, reaching out to stroke my arm.

"It's difficult," I sobbed, so quietly as to be almost inaudible.

Lies are most effective when planted alongside truths, that much I knew. I cleared my throat. "On the day before we left," I began, in another tone, my more refined Bergen dialect returning, "I was walking home from the Harbour Master's Office. As I turned a corner, a man came over to me. Quite out of the blue. He said they had me under surveillance. That they would take Olav away if I didn't do what they said. If I didn't deliver a cigarette containing a microfilm to a man in the music lounge."

"You should have told me, Vera."

"I was warned not to. So, I met the man. And long story short, I smuggled the microfilm into Trondheim. I was so frightened, Thor."

He grimaced.

"Well, well," he replied. "I appreciate your honesty. Now there's something I need to share with you."

He took out a photograph. The man in the picture had no eyepatch when it was taken, but there was no doubt: it was Dieter.

"The company has been informed by reliable intelligence sources that this man is trying to infiltrate and break our Norwegian resistance networks. His expertise is in shipping, and what makes him particularly dangerous is that he speaks impeccable Norwegian, having lived here for years. If you come into contact with this man, Vera, you must, whatever the circumstances, tell me."

Rørvik–Brønnøysund

I stood watching as the engines went into reverse and the great ship slipped elegantly in towards the pier. Ropes were cast over the bollards, as easily as Laplanders lassoing their reindeer. My story had won me a little time with Thor, but it would not keep me afloat for long.

What Thor had told me could be true. Doubtless he was trying to put a shine on his own reputation and play down the fact that he was making money out of the occupation, but that didn't mean he was lying. And if Dieter was a provocateur who was trying to get closer to Thor through me, what did that make Wilhelm? Were they in league? It could not be ruled out. I felt nauseous. Few feelings are worse than that of being hoodwinked. Had everything been staged? The thought of it made me dizzy. Was Wilhelm already working for German intelligence when we met at the summer camp?

I went onto the lower outer deck. Why had Dieter expressed such interest in this place? The hatch was open this time. I put my ear to the steel. Nobody there. I quickly descended the ladder, opened the door to the provisions room and peered inside. Had any unauthorised persons found their way in here?

As I stood there thinking, I heard sounds from the hatch above. I slipped soundlessly into the room, gently closing the door after me, and looked around for somewhere to hide. In the far corner stood some milk churns and a pile of fish crates. I crouched behind them. I would have no chance if there was a thorough search. I just had to hope they wouldn't come in here. In the rush of adrenaline I hadn't noticed how cold the room was. Footsteps descended the steep ladder. I tried to work out whether they belonged to two people or one.

"This is the safest place on board," said a voice. It was Thor. "Vera says that even the walls on this ship have ears, and she's right."

"What's down here?" a woman's voice asked.

My heart skipped a beat.

It was Betsy Flisdal.

I was paralysed. I no longer felt the cold.

"How can we be sure no one's listening?"

"Pull yourself together," said Thor.

The iron door rattled.

"It's stuck," said Thor.

The door of the cold room creaked open. A narrow shaft of light crept in. He's going to see me now, I thought. I held my breath. A drip on the floor.

Plop, plop, plop.

In a quiet voice, just loud enough for me to hear, Betsy described the evening in the music lounge. How she had noticed me, "an attractive but very young lady". And how I had danced with a man with a diagonal scar.

"Jens Hagemann. That much we know."

I shuddered. Thor knew his name.

"It was dark in the music lounge," said Betsy, "so although I tried to follow what was happening, I'm not sure. I think Hagemann handed her something. And then the Gestapo stormed in."

"The thing is this," said Thor. "My contacts in the German police have long suspected leaks and illicit activities from elements in the Kriegsmarine. Ships inexplicably sunk by British planes after leaving port. A great many lives lost, primarily German, but also Norwegian. Cargo worth hundreds of thousands of kroner. And with that, the shipping company's profits and Norwegian jobs."

"But surely there'd be more to do if the shipyards had to build new ships?" said Betsy.

She really was an idiot.

Thor ignored her and continued: "When I talked to people at the Reich Commissariat in Oslo last week, the message was clear: these pointless acts of provocation must end. And the majority of Norwegian shipowners agree. Germany will win this war by a good margin."

He went on: "The thing is, there are two men on board who are part of a resistance cell within the Kriegsmarine."

I pricked up my ears.

"One of them goes by the cover name Wilhelm Frahm and the other is Dieter Hartz, recognisable by a patch over his right eye."

I shuddered at what he was saying. It was pure evil. Not only was Thor collaborating financially with the Germans, but to protect his privileges he was also spreading life-threatening lies about real resistance fighters.

"The provisions room isn't a place to hang about in," said Betsy. "What happens now?"

"Listen carefully," Thor replied. "Are there any Germans on board whom you know?"

"No." She hesitated. "But there's the military police with the Alpine Hunter Battalion."

"They have no authority on the ship."

"I know the chief of police in Sandnessjøen," said Betsy. "We worked together on earlier investigations."

Thor paused before answering. "Good. We arrive at Sandnessjøen at half past ten tonight. Go ashore and warn the police, they'll make sure that the two Kriegsmarine officers are met by a proper welcoming committee in Bodø tomorrow morning. Just don't do anything daft before we get to Sandnessjøen."

"No," Betsy replied. "But I need money."

Thor sighed irritably and there was a rustling of what had to be banknotes.

"Ta," she mumbled. "What'll happen to your wife?"

"That's my affair," Thor said. "But she's no longer my wife. She'll probably be charged with resistance activities. For which the penalties are severe."

"Harsh words."

Their footsteps disappeared back up the ladder and the sound of the ship's pistons took over again. I stayed crouching there for a while. Something in me wanted to stay forever, until my body temperature fell, and I lost consciousness and disappeared into eternity. I had heard it was quite pleasant to freeze to death. And I was living on borrowed time anyway. I got up, my joints cracking from the cold. The countdown had begun. According to the ship's schedule I had less than ten hours before my fate would be sealed in Sandnessjøen.

I got up and crept out.

Betsy must not leave the ship in Sandnessjøen. But how could I stop her?

Brønnøysund–Sandnessjøen

Yesterday I took the train from Bergen, and I am back now in Rederhaugen as I write these words. I found what I needed in the archives there in the west. It is April, and as the snows melt and summer warmth advances, my story glides onwards like a steamship in calm waters.

As I write, I wonder what sort of reception my words will receive, how the Norwegian public will react. All authors do this, of course. While we fantasise about fame, we also fear being dragged naked across the public square by the critics, though what we usually get is as simple as a benevolent shrug, followed by oblivion.

The situation here is different. There will be no lukewarm reactions. What will Thor's descendants say, or Olav?

Now in 1970, nearly thirty years later, it is a barely disguised truth that those who committed economic treason were given far lighter sentences than other collaborators, if they were punished at all. They were not directly involved like Vidkun Quisling's men, who fought alongside the German invaders, or torturers with blood on their hands. They just "tried to keep the wheels turning", to quote the words of a certain influential defence attorney. Big capital is not just a good way to spread risk, it also fragments responsibility across directors and boards, between parent companies and subcontractors. Who should be punished for the Hanseatic Steamship Company's cooperation? They simply did what any good capitalist would have done.

But what makes the situation more poignant is that Thor was awarded the War Cross with Sword posthumously in 1949, on the recommendation of August Greve, the family lawyer, "for having organised, at great personal risk, the resistance along the coast during the early stages in 1940".

I had no choice but to accept the award on his behalf, although I left the ceremony early, shortly after King Haakon, with the excuse of feeling unwell. I locked the medal in the wall safe at Rederhaugen and never took it out again. As Olav got older, however, he grew increasingly interested in the whole thing, and my hints fell on deaf ears.

But the real reason for my story being so incendiary is yet to come. Because crimes committed during a war do not fade away; they cast long shadows into peacetime.

It was already dark when we headed out of the harbour in Brønnøysund. The wild and hilly Helgeland coast, which had seemed so beautiful when I had travelled an eternity ago in the opposite direction, now appeared like a jaded theatre backdrop. Back then the ship had been brightly lit and inviting like a casino, now the night was black.

It had begun to sleet. Sleet occurs at around zero degrees, which is when the temperature becomes dangerous. It's at that point we freeze to death.

I took refuge in the cafeteria near the stern in third class, where Thor would never go. I sat there fiddling with a pepper pot on my table. In less than five hours Betsy would go ashore and alert the police. Then we'd be done for.

A voice behind me.

"Vera?" said the waitress.

"Thanks for the party," I said.

"I have a letter," she said, giving a little bob and disappearing before I could reply.

I looked around me then cut the letter open. *Meet me in Cabin 31. W.* That was all. I tore the small note into tiny pieces and hurried down to the main deck, where Cabin 31 was. Wilhelm opened the door. I slipped in and kissed him as soon as he closed it. It was a simple cabin: two beds crossing over each other to save space, a lacquered desk beneath a little porthole. But it was a cabin. I sat down on the lower bunk.

"A colleague was held up," he said. "With the ship so overcrowded, I'm pleased to have a cabin at all."

A shadow crossed his face when he saw my expression of panic. "What's the matter, Vera?"

As calmly as I could, I repeated what I had heard in the provisions room.

"We've got to do something about Betsy. Time's running out."

The ship rocked. Outside, in the corridor, I heard voices speaking in my old dialect, albeit with the sing-song and bantering tone of the people of Brønnøysund, an odd mix of Trøndersk and northern Norwegian. Wilhelm looked at me with both tenderness and disquiet. In that moment it was just the two of us, before the gravity of the situation rushed over me. We had come out onto the stretch of open sea towards Sandnessjøen.

We would be there in a few hours.

"You know her," he said thoughtfully. "What motivates her?"

"She's driven by one thing only: money. Ideology is beyond her."

"I have money. Not much, but something. Two hundred kroner. What's that? A month's salary?"

"We can never outbid Thor," I said despairingly.

Wilhelm sat with his face buried in his hands. "Do we have a choice?"

"There is another possibility," I mumbled, not that I was completely convinced myself. "Stay here."

Betsy was not in any of the first-class lounges. Perhaps she had sought refuge in a cabin before we went into harbour. I began searching the ship. I headed aft on the galley deck until I was stopped by the military police and could go no further. I went upstairs and out onto the empty promenade deck, past the engine house where the larger lifeboats were lined up against the rails, and then around the cabin house on the poop.

There she stood. An icy wind blew through my clothes. Over the transom a pennant fluttered.

"Ah Betsy, I've found you at last!"

"Vera . . .?"

"Remember you told me how your husband was taken?" I said. "July the sixth, wasn't it? You were going to meet a Shetland boat, but met the Germans instead?"

She still suspected nothing. "That's right."

"It's just that I was working at the Harbour Master's Office that day," I continued. "And because I've got a good memory, when it comes to my job at least, I know every detail of the boat traffic that day. It was at Bremanger, wasn't it? There were no German boats in the vicinity that day. They were further south, near Osterøy. You lied, Betsy. Like you've lied about everything else."

Stunned, Betsy leaned on the rail. Our eyes were accustomed to the dark. Over her shoulder I could see the wake of the ship.

"You're a grass, Betsy," I continued, my voice oddly calm. "Who informs on patriots for money. And now you're going to inform on me in Sandnessjøen. I hope you'll get a decent wage for that. But I have another proposal."

"Help! Help!" cried Betsy. "A woman from the resistance is trying to threaten me!"

I grabbed her by the collar, but she slipped from my grasp and fell, tumbling towards the hatch.

I flung myself after her and landed on her leg. She screamed in pain, kicking out frantically. A blow to my chest took the air out of me, but rolling to one side, I elbowed her in the belly. A wave crashed over the ship, covering us in spray. Confused, I got up. As did Betsy. We stopped to catch our breath. Then I punched her in the face. It was not my best aim, but she fell howling back towards the rail. Then I kicked her hard in the shin.

"Feckin' bitch!" she screamed, as I squeezed my fingers round her neck. "Help!"

She managed to wrench herself free and rammed me up against the rail. The freezing cold steel dug into my back and my head and upper torso hung outside the rail.

I thought of the propellers churning below. Just a few centimetres more and I would go overboard, down into the icy sea. She was surprisingly strong. With all the strength I had, I clenched my stomach muscles to keep balance.

"Die!" screamed Betsy.

Years later, as I write this, I can still see her face, steely eyed and tight lipped, feel the sleet and see the turbulent water around the stern. In a last desperate move, I freed my arms, twisted my body out of her grip, crouched down under the ship's rail, and flung her over it and into the water.

With the din of the propellers churning the water, I did not hear her break the surface. I stared around. Nobody had seen. For a moment I stood and looked back over the stern, but she was lost in the wake that flung itself out behind the ship.

Sandnessjøen–Bodø

I stood in the doorway. I was shaking. My clothes were dripping wet, my jacket was ripped. Terrified, Wilhelm got up from the bed. Without saying anything he took me in his arms. I cried. He said nothing. It was best that way. It was what I needed. For a long time we stood like that in the cramped cabin as the sea rocked us from side to side.

"Betsy Flisdal won't be notifying the police," I said finally.

"Do you want to tell me about it?" he asked.

"No," I replied.

"It'll be alright."

That was probably as good a response as any.

He found a bottle of brandy and handed it to me. I took a swig and sat next to him on the bunk, resting a trembling right hand on his thigh.

"She was just a girl," I said. "An idiotic, naive girl, yes. But she wasn't evil."

"It's alright," Wilhelm comforted me.

"It isn't bloody alright!"

I sobbed as I paced about in the tiny cabin, throwing punches at the bunks and cupboards. He grabbed me resolutely and forced me down onto the mattress.

"This is war," he said.

"What would you know about taking a life?" I sniffed. "You're just a sailor."

And again, I saw Betsy's sprawled body falling over the rail and screaming into the water below.

"Sometimes it's right to take a life," he said.

"Easily said in theory, but it's different in practice."

"How do you think it feels to fight against fascists in your own country, who have the support of almost the entire population?"

"Are there many people opposed to the regime?"

"More than you'd think. Even among those wearing uniform. But I'm only telling you this because the choices we have to make are often very hard. If not impossible. Just like the one you made today."

I whispered, "What kind of choices?"

"Should we report the movements of German ships so the British can bomb them? To you they're the ships of an occupying power. But to me that can mean, in absolute terms, condemning hundreds of my own countrymen to death;

good people, ordinary people with a wife back home and children they love."

He took a swig of brandy. "So, I know a lot about such choices."

He sat in silence.

"How can you justify it to yourself?" I asked.

"Because I hold some ideals higher than others. I believe the fight against Nazism is so vital that any, absolutely any means, must be used to crush it. Even if it means taking civilian lives."

I let this sink in.

Wilhelm was a traitor.

And it was this that made him a hero. After all, weren't most of those fighting against Nazism in Norway simply defending their own country? The German social democrats dared to commit treason because they were fighting for a higher ideal.

Was that not as close as one got to a definition of heroism?

"There's just one thing," he said with a worried frown, grabbing me hard by the wrist. "I'm getting off at Bodø. And so must you and your son."

"Why?"

"If I tell you, it's on condition that you tell nobody else, no matter how dreadful it might seem. You understand?"

I swallowed and nodded.

"Dieter," he continued, "belongs to the same network as me in the Kriegsmarine."

"Cyclops?"

"Call him what you want. He's going to put a fuse in the cargo room, fixed to a simple ignition mechanism. It'll start a fire. The ship, as you know, is loaded with weapons and ammunition. It'll have the same effect as a massive bomb."

"My God," I muttered, thinking of the crew, the captain, the waitresses, the machinists. "There are hundreds of Norwegians on board."

"And hundreds of Alpine Hunters," he replied, a sudden coldness about his mouth. "Wars are ultimately decided by individual soldiers. A soldier who falls asleep on his watch can bring down the whole house of cards. If the Alpine Hunters don't arrive to reinforce the north, the war will be one step closer to being won."

Putting my elbow on the bunk, I rested my head in my hands.

"So, tell me *your* plan," he said.

"Thor thinks we're going to visit my dying mother. She died over two years ago. I got the news after she was buried. But that was the story I told him so I could come north. The ferry stops for an hour in Bodø. I have friends who can get us through the checkpoints. We'll be in Sulitjelma before Thor's suspicions are aroused."

His eyes widened. "Sul-i-tjel-ma, nice word."

"I've got relatives there, it's near the border. An aunt and a cousin. It's not far from there into Sweden. And there the struggle can begin."

Wilhelm took off his dog tag and weighed it in his hand. "Well, I can't travel with my name around my neck."

The porthole's steel cover was held open by a chain hooked onto the ceiling. He released it, and hidden in the ceiling, behind the cover, was a ventilation duct. I took out the cigarette case, he laid the dog tag in it, and together we put it in the duct.

It was the two of us now. I kissed Wilhelm. He held me in his strong hands, pulled off my coat and lacy dress and loosened my bra, while I tore off his uniform, until our clothes lay strewn across the floor. The ship rocked back and forth, and the pistons beat, drowning out the sounds from the aft.

It was just gone midnight, October 23, 1940, and perhaps we knew in that moment that there was only one way from here – northwards, past Nesna and Indre Kvarøy and Grønnøy and Ørnes to Bodø and on to Lofoten, and from there, into the depths.

Bodø–Stamsund

Sleet was falling as DS *Prinsesse Ragnhild* called into Bodø on the morning of October 23, sleet carried on an icy, blustery wind. The foamy white sea undulated like snow-drifts on a plain, as the ship rolled in on the waves towards the quayside.

I stood for a moment at the rail, alone on deck in the foul weather. Bodø had been bombed that spring, and naked chimney stacks shot up against the sky over the sad ruins of the town. I was dissolving inside. Still giddy from the night's secret liaison with Wilhelm, still trembling at the sight of Betsy Flisdal disappearing into the dark waters. Terrified by what had happened, and what would happen next.

The plan I had shared with Wilhelm in the small hours was simple in theory. Thor would be standing near the exit, on the lookout for the police. It was vital that he should believe that Olav and I were still on board. I needed to slip past him unseen. Thor was not the most observant man, so I knew that a blanket wrapped around me would make me almost invisible to him. But it would be harder to leave the ship anonymously and get lost in the crowd if I was carrying Olav. That was for Wilhelm to do. Nobody would dare challenge him in his German uniform.

I would leave the shipowner's cabin unlatched, so he could go in and take Olav, who would be having his morning nap. We would meet behind the fish hall in town and from there the three of us would head for Sulitjelma.

I hurried down to the galley deck. The gangplank scraped against the quay, and the hull thudded against rubber tyres as we docked. The terminal forecourt was teeming with people, many obviously eager to cross the fjord to Lofoten. Children in bobble hats were skittering about. Two sailors were helping a lady, unsteady on her feet, to shore. I got off the boat without being seen, shoved my way through the crowd and followed the road, turning the corner on the right, past a red-painted warehouse, until I saw the fish hall on the other side of the street.

I was filled with the expectation of seeing him, and of being reunited with little Olav. But it was not Wilhelm I found waiting there.

"Out to stretch your legs in this weather?" said Thor, holding on to his hat. In the other hand he held little Olav's basket.

My heart skipped a beat. What had happened? Thor glanced calmly and confidently down at his watch.

"We don't have all the time in the world, Vera. How about we get back to the *Prinsesse*?"

I had to come up with something. "Listen, Thor," I said seriously, with my back to the wind. "We're in grave danger. They say someone's planning to blow up the ship."

He laughed condescendingly. "Blow up the ship! I doubt that, Vera."

"We can't go aboard!" I shouted. "Not you, not me, and certainly not Olav!"

Thor grabbed me by the shoulder. "Enough now. I'm sick of the lies you've been serving me. You'll come with me right away. Now!"

Amid the scrabble at the dock I saw one-eyed Dieter leave the ship and melt into the crowd. What could I do? I went back with Thor.

Shortly afterwards DS *Prinsesse Ragnhild* set out from the quay. It was half past ten in the morning, Thursday, October 23.

I get up from my desk. It is evening, a cool spring evening. I am sitting alone at High Cliff when I hear footsteps behind the cottage.

Someone knocks, then opens the door without waiting and walks in. Standing in the pale light from the window is Olav. My boy is almost thirty years old now. He has grown tall and strong. His gaze is ambitious, his smile charismatic. He has more of his father in him than of me. In recent years he has been working for the intelligence services.

"Mother," he says, standing there.

"Olav?"

We are both on our own side of the room, saying nothing, as though waiting for the other to make a wrong move. His self-control unnerves me a little. But on closer observation, I notice an almost imperceptible tremble in his lower lip.

"A drink?" I go into the kitchenette, fetch a bottle of beer, open it and put it on the table before he has time to answer.

"I know what you're writing about," he says.

"No," I say coolly, though when I clench my fists at his words I can feel that my palms are wet. "You have no idea."

"I've come to ask you to stop."

"You've not read a word of what I've written."

"You just wrote. Night and day, you wrote," he says with a mildly reproachful look, just like when he was a boy. "And every winter you went away, for months on end, and when you were here, you were never *really* here, but with some lover or in your own world."

"That's not true," I say.

"All I wanted when I was small was to impress you," he says quietly. "For you to show you loved me, because you did in a way, but you never said so. Until I realised that deep down you were an egotist, and that you put yourself above anyone else. Maybe you were damaged, by your mother who was so ill, and your father whom you never met . . ."

"Stop," I say, with a gesture of my hand.

"Why have you never said anything about Father?"

"Because I express myself better in writing. It's all here," I say, pointing to the typewriter.

"I beg you to stop this now," says Olav. "For the family. If you don't do as I say, I can no longer protect you."

"It's about the tunnels and Occupation Preparedness," I say.

He nods curtly. "Are you aware of what publishing something like this will mean? For our country and for us?"

"A country that has to resort to illegal means to defend itself isn't worth defending," I say.

408

"What I don't understand is how a story from 1940 can tell us anything about Stay Behind. It started well after the war."

I shake my head. "It started *during* the war. It started with the agreement Thor made with Admiral Carax about the transport of German troops and equipment. This means that his shipping company profited financially from doing business with the Nazis."

He is about to protest, but I raise my hand to silence him.

"Eventually Admiral Carax became commander-in-chief of the Northern Fleet and moved into Rederhaugen, where he built the tunnels and bunkers. But he wasn't a torturer or concentration camp commandant of the type brought before the courts after the war. The minute the Nazi regime fell he slipped imperceptibly into the German military. Meanwhile, you and I moved here, you grew into a skinny, studious schoolboy, but one day when you were small we received a rather grand visit at Rederhaugen. A convoy of cars swung into the driveway. Out jumped a bevy of senior officers, bureaucrats and politicians, among them Admiral Carax."

"Carax came back?" says Olav.

"He did," I reply. "He had been working as a NATO adviser on questions regarding the northern flank, drawing on his considerable experience with Soviet military strategies in the Barents region. Together with some of the officers, both Norwegian and German, as well as several politicians, he disappeared down into the derelict tunnels and bunkers under Rederhaugen. They didn't resurface until late that evening, when they brought me security clearance documents that I had to read and sign. As the owner of the property, I placed all the underground rooms at their disposal for Occupation Preparedness. For the security of the nation. My duty of confidentiality was absolute and for life. I did as they said, and the following year construction workers came to Rederhaugen to begin restoring and upgrading the tunnels.

"So, there you have the link between the war and the present," I say. "The present, you know more about."

My son prowls round the room.

"You can't publish a book about this."

"Can I say something, Olav?" I look at him for a long time. "Show me what's hidden down there. What's so damned secret."

"Mother, I can't. You know that."

"Show me."

Olav laughs despairingly and flings out his arms. "You want to see? Alright, Mother dearest. You can bloody well see it."

Only now do I notice that he has a cylinder with him. He opens a plastic lid at one end and takes out a rolled-up map and spreads it across the table. It is marked *Geheime: Organisation Todt.* Our eyes meet.

"To you these tunnels have never been anything but a fevered, literary fantasy, have they? But this is not some Gothic romance set in an English country manor. They were built by German engineers as bomb shelters during the war. Some of them are marked on the floor plans, others are not. They're still in use, so perhaps you understand now what's at stake."

There is a trapdoor in the hallway between the living room and bedroom that leads down to the woodshed and potato cellar. Olav lifts it with a ring, and we descend the steep staircase into the cellar. I have a torch in my hand. Olav pushes aside a shelf and stands in front of a cupboard. Pressing his hands against a certain point in the ceiling, he stamps on the floor.

I hear the sound of a mechanism, and a second later the wall divides to create an opening the size of a door.

I stand open-mouthed.

"Come on," says Olav. I follow him for fifty metres through a cylindrical passage with white-painted walls until we reach an iron door marked HIGH VOLTAGE: DANGER. Olav enters a code and eases the heavy hatch aside.

The room is dark, some fifty metres square. In the torch-light I see that the walls are covered with shelves, in front of them neat rows of weapons.

"This," says Olav, weighing a large gun expertly in his hand, "is a German MG-34. Next to it are recoilless rifles, while this beast is an MG-3 machine gun, and here you have Mausers, Schmeissers, communication equipment and hand grenades."

I am lost for words.

"This radio transmitter," Olav continues with almost childlike enthusiasm, "has an antenna that can go up through a pipe, like a periscope, and then be lowered again. And do you know why we have all this, Mother?"

"This isn't the way to do it," I mutter. "Norway has defence forces, we have intelligence services, under the control of parliament."

Olav stares at me, eyes smouldering. "This is our fallback, should all else fail. There are military secrets that can't be entrusted to elected officials and others who go by the book. They rest in private hands. If you write about this, it will all be put in jeopardy. Occupation Preparedness will be set back by ten years. And just as importantly: it'll all be over for Rederhaugen and the businesses we've established here."

"This began with the German admiral Thor met on the *Prinsesse Ragnhild* the day before the disaster," I answer. "The public has a right to know what's been going on."

Olav leans against one of the shelves. "No," he says. "Certain things should not be talked about."

"I'm going to publish," I say.

"Then you are making a choice," says my son, "between the family's interests and your own ego. If you publish, you are no longer a member of this family."

Olav is not a man to make empty threats.

"You think you know all there is to know," I say. "In reality you have no idea."

The *Prinsesse Ragnhild* has entered the turbulent waters of the harbour basin. In his rage, Thor has stormed off with Olav, leaving me alone and distraught on the deck. I can bear it no longer. I need to find my boy. Where has Thor taken my little Olav?

I must find him. First, I rush to the shipowner's cabin.

I put my ear to the door. Not a sound, neither footsteps nor the cries of a baby. My God! They're not there. I run through the ship and down to the nanny's cabin. It is empty. No sign of her or Olav.

Where to look? The ship is big, but not that big. I run back up towards the cloakroom area, then sweep through the half-full, U-shaped smoking lounge under the command bridge and the empty music lounge. Of course, they are not there. I shove aside some locals and rush out onto the promenade deck on the starboard side. I'm blinded by the light. The icy wind tears at my clothes, but I feel hot, fear is hot. It's almost empty out here, a few Germans are leaning over the rail, further along some newly arrived passengers stand about with their hands in their pockets. I pass the lifeboats, heading for the aft house on the poop deck. There I catch sight of a baby. Almost tear it from the arms of the woman holding it before I realise it isn't Olav, my Olav. I descend the aft staircase in two leaps.

Where can he be?

German military police watch in wide-eyed surprise as I push through the crew mess in third class. Olav isn't there. Of course he isn't. But nothing is as you would expect now. The ticket office lies midship. The coxswain greets me amiably, but his face fills with concern when he sees the look on my face.

"Fru Falck! What's the matter?"

"My son," I answer desperately. "I can't find him."

He takes a deep breath. "He's gone? That's dreadful news. But I'm sure it'll be down to some misunderstanding."

"Misunderstanding?" I yell. "He's gone! Sound the alarm!"

"The last time I saw your son he was with a nursemaid. Have you found her?"

"No. Do you know where she is?"

"I saw her with your husband. Yes, it must have been shortly after the ship left Bodø."

"You must sound the alarm!"

"Listen, Fru Falck. I understand how frightening this must be for you. But your son is obviously with his nanny or your husband. You must realise that raising the alarm would only cause disquiet on the ship."

Half crazed I start hammering on doors. "Olav! Thor! Jorunn! Are you in there? We've got to talk." Cabins 1, 3, 5, 7, 9 and 11, but apart from one annoyed soldier and northerner, nobody opens any of the doors to the cramped third-class cabins. Back again, on the starboard side, 10, 8, 6, 4, 2. They're not there, of course. I go over to first class. The ship's postman gives me a strange look. The heat from the engine room radiates into the narrow passageway.

I am still hammering on doors when I hear a voice behind me.

"Vera!"

Wilhelm is dripping wet. "Where were you?" I say, my voice filled with desperation.

"Thor took your little boy before I could get there. He saw me. I think he's got wind that something's going on between us. I've been looking for the fuse. To disarm it."

"And?"

He looks at me with resignation. "I'm sorry. It's over."

I squeeze his hand and we run in opposite directions. The explosion that follows is so powerful it knocks the air out of me, compressing my chest with such force my ribs crush my heart.

PART IV

KONG OLAVS VEI, LOFOTEN

36

THE SHACK

Ramsund, Northern Norway

Johnny woke up when the plane tilted to one side and the pilot announced they were landing.

Below him the water's smooth surface sparkled in the sun, and in the distance the snow-capped peaks of Lofoten rose out of the sea. The sky was higher, the mountains steeper than any place he knew. The fjords wound their way deep into the landscape until they ended in turqouise shallows and chalk-white beaches. Lofoten was a mountain range encircled by sea, its valleys and plains filled with water, with only the peaks reaching up above the surface. It was like flying over Europe after the sea had risen three thousand metres, leaving only the Alps visible, like looking down on the world after Noah's flood. A wide, shiny fjord, silver-coloured and foil-smooth, divided the archipelago from the mainland. Somewhere down there, three hundred metres deep, lay the wreck of DS *Prinsesse Ragnhild*.

Sasha had taken her father's side and Johnny was making the journey she had proposed. She could pretend to be different, but when the chips were down, Vera Lind's story would always lose out to the interests of her father and the Falck family. And any evidence of wartime collaboration in the archive was long gone. He had nothing.

Or . . .?

He had not initially understood why it was so important to dive down to the shipwreck to establish whether the blast had come from an underwater mine, or from within the ship, from an explosion. But after reading Vera's last chapters, it made perfect sense. Thanks to the deal struck by Thor Falck on behalf of the Hanseatic Steamship Company and its competitors, the ferry had been packed to the gunwales with German weapons and ammunition. Who had blown up DS *Prinsesse Ragnhild*? If Vera was telling the truth, a German resistance member named Dieter was behind it. But who was ultimately responsible?

It was Thor Falck himself. It was he who had led the negotiations with the German authorities.

The plane landed on Evenes. It had clouded over. The cold, damp air hit him. After picking up his rental car he swung out onto Europavei 10. Last time he was here, it had been called Kong Olavs Vei. A far more appropriate name, he thought.

He drove the short distance out to Ramsund. Johnny had been there many years ago, when he had passed the basic selection tests for the Marine Hunters. Among the armed forces, Ramsund was a mythical place, and he remembered his disappointment when he had first arrived here, one icy winter's day all those years ago. Cadets always imagined a high-tech, state-of-the-art facility. What they found was a godforsaken village of cheap military housing, and a ring-fenced docking facility with administrative buildings, baggage halls and barracks.

That was, of course, the point. Ramsund was where you toughened up. The main focus of his training up here, in the first phases at least, was how to operate underwater.

Everyone must become *water competent*. For untrained civilians the open sea, and especially the Arctic Ocean, was a source of fear, associated with storms and shipping disasters. People were afraid of it, and not without reason. With the Marine Hunters you learned to love it; the icy water you bathed in every morning, the torpedo tubes you crawled through, the pool into which you were lowered with your hands tied behind your back and a blindfold over your eyes. It was an alternative life, all-consuming in the moment, but eventually pushed aside in your mind until it was a distant memory, like any other.

The base was exactly as he remembered it. Thoughts of the training and the relentless grind conjured the sensation of a sodden uniform against his skin. A RIB engine roared on the fjord. He turned off the main road into a little cul-de-sac.

If Ramsund was mythical, it was largely down to the Shack, the Marine Hunters' recreation centre, modestly housed in an old private residence. Johnny looked at his watch. He was early.

He knocked, and eventually a young guy with a well-groomed beard and a bull neck like a hockey player opened the door a crack and looked him up and down sceptically.

"Group 44," said Johnny. "I have an appointment with Einar Grotle."

The man stood in the doorway for a second saying nothing, then nodded curtly and stepped aside. Johnny went in.

On the floor were a bucket and mop; he was probably a cadet who had to do the cleaning. The Shack had a clear hierarchy.

Johnny turned right into the bar, which also served as a museum covering all the unit's former operations: Kosovo in 1999, Tora Bora in 2002, Helmand Province in 2005–6 and others. Sitting at the far end of the bar was a man of about his own age, who nodded in greeting.

Johnny got himself a beer, took a seat along from him and played with a beer mat as he drank.

"Veteran?" said the man. Quiet music played in the background, an old Tom Waits record.

"Kind of," Johnny said.

He stared at the pictures of fallen comrades. The two men's eyes did not meet.

"Kind of?"

"Wasn't here long. Sent back south."

"*Injured*, were you?" said the man patronisingly. "That's generally the reason guys don't go the distance. Hard time mentally?"

"Changed departments," Johnny said. "Desk work for me."

HK had drilled it into them during their training: if anyone asks for more information, you work in the logistics office. They'll stop asking then.

The man laughed.

"At least you're honest," he said. "Most guys who come here, journalists, for example, feel the need to brag about themselves."

The man had a West Oslo accent, with its characteristic nasal tone.

"I'm not a Marine Hunter either," he continued, a smile appearing at the corners of his mouth.

"No?"

"Served as a sniper. A number of tours in Afghanistan. Got pretty hairy down there in Faryab, 2009, 2010."

Johnny nodded. "I can imagine."

The guy was looking at him, as though wondering something.

"Didn't I meet you down there?"

Might well have, thought Johnny. Although they generally operated undercover, they did occasionally come upon other soldiers.

"Me, in Afghanistan?" Johnny laughed. "Not a chance. We might have met at Gardermoen when we were delivering equipment to you guys before you flew off to your next mission. Like I said, I worked in logistics. Amateurs focus on strategy, professionals focus on logistics, you know."

"My mistake." The man smiled. "My father always said the same thing. But anyway, we're setting up a squadron for an operation in Kabul right now. Monitoring Afghan special forces, they're proving to be pretty good. Had a lot of practice, put it that way."

Bullneck was mopping the floor but seemed to be hovering around them, listening in.

"I'm Sverre Falck, by the way," said the man at the bar, stretching his hand out to Johnny.

Johnny had to smile.

"What's the joke?" Sverre asked, suddenly insecure.

"It's a small world. I'm working on Hans Falck's biography. I'm Johnny, by the way. Johnny Berg."

Bullneck glowered at Johnny and put his mop in the bucket. A bunch of other guys streamed into the bar, younger, clearly new recruits. They might have been him a decade ago.

"Did you say Johnny Berg?" Bullneck said loudly, swaggering towards him. "I know who you are. We've heard all about you up here. Sling your hook, Jihadi John. You've no business coming here."

Johnny looked around, first at Sverre Falck's confused face, then at Bullneck, who was squaring up to him with his tattooed arms crossed. The newcomers were moving in behind him now. Johnny tried to think fast. When the shit hit the fan, you had to confront the problem quickly with whatever means were at hand. A heavy beer glass might do the trick. But these men would have had similar training, if not better. Furthermore, they were ten years younger and in better shape. And what would the consequences be, if, outnumbered as he was, he decked this man?

No, it was impossible.

Slowly Johnny reached out for the bottle. "I'll just drink up and head off."

Bullneck placed a hand on his forearm.

"You shameless bastard."

Johnny did not answer. This was no joke.

"You join up with IS, then you think you can come in here and have a cosy little chat. You should have been made fucking stateless."

"What do you want?" Johnny asked.

"Just this," said Bullneck, dragging Johnny down from his stool in one motion, before flinging him onto his stomach halfway over the bar, winding him. *Whatever happens in the Shack stays in the Shack,* Johnny thought as he gasped for air. Bullneck grabbed him by the collar and threw him across the floor. He felt a boot slam into his diaphragm, winding him again, and another kick in his side, like an electric shock.

"They should have stripped you of your War Cross!" Bullneck growled.

"Remember the two swords," Johnny groaned, getting to his knees. "You'll never earn those."

"You being funny?"

Bullneck lifted Johnny up against the wall.

"What the hell's going on here?"

Einar Grotle pushed through the crowd. Johnny freed himself from Bullneck's grasp.

"Last time I checked, jihadists didn't have access to the Shack," Bullneck said.

The other guys nodded. He was obviously their silver-back and informal leader. Grotle lifted the brawny cadet off his feet as if he were a little boy. Johnny had forgotten how strong he was.

"Berg has done more for Norway than you'll ever dream of, laddie," he said. "I want the ladies' toilets sparkling clean for inspection in half an hour. Understood?"

The man slunk out into the hallway.

"Sorry about that, Johnny. Ignorance abounds, as you know. Shall we talk somewhere more private?"

37

JOHNNY'S NO FUCKING TRAITOR

Mads and the girls came back from Provence the day before the family council.

After her father's tirade, and then telling Johnny Berg to go to hell, Sasha was left with the shame of being duped. What Berg had done or not done in the Middle East was of little importance. Everybody had secrets. What was intolerable was how she had let herself be moved around like a chess piece on a board. It turned her stomach in knots. His laughter in Frogner Park, the train ride to Bergen, the kiss in the pool: had it all been an elaborate performance? The mere thought filled her with such intense discomfort that she could not retain the images in her head. Nor eradicate them, for that matter. She had been so naive – a dreamer, like Vera.

Mads was not a man to hold grudges. Like most husbands (judging by her friends' group chat) he avoided conflict, preferring to sweep problems under the carpet if it ensured peace at home. And if he had had any intention of quarrelling, they disappeared the instant she greeted him with a long, tearful embrace and a good dinner, then cuddled up to him in bed, whispering that she'd love to do *it* if it wasn't for her period. It had been so long he had lost track of her cycle.

They had come down to the beach below the house for a picnic. The girls disappeared behind some rocks, and Mads grabbed her and kissed her, a tender kiss. She felt happy at his expressions of care, the security he radiated.

"Now," said Mads, "let's eat." She unrolled the picnic blanket and laid out the food, while he fished out two cans of beer to have with it. Camilla, who had been given a new camera in France, insisted on taking a family snapshot of them all.

After lunch Sasha sat and studied the photo on the screen, while Mads went off with the girls for a swim. Maybe this was where happiness resided, in the everyday. That was what wise people always said.

"Did you find out anything about Vera's book?" Mads asked amiably as they ambled side by side along the shore a little later, while the girls flitted about in search of crabs and shells, happy to see their parents together for the first time in ages.

"I discovered a huge amount," Sasha said, with a shrug. "The problem is, it's impossible to trust anything she writes. She was a novelist. So I've decided to let it rest. It's probably better that way."

"Sounds sensible. It's the future that counts," he said.

She was lying to him with an ease that both surprised and frightened her. The truth was that she couldn't get Vera and Nordland out of her head. In spare moments she surfed the net for old fishing villages, hiking trails and museums in Lofoten. She opened Google Earth and revelled in the feeling of tumbling down from space to this remote place. Å, Vera's childhood village, surrounded by mountain peaks and the endless Atlantic, or the island of Landegode, near where the *Prinsesse* had gone down. It was as though forces beyond her drew her north.

Now and then, Johnny popped up in these fantasies, but then she would straighten up and tell herself to "stop it". She knew she had to go north, but she also knew there was no place for him in this story. I hate him, she thought.

And she did, in a way. The only problem was that he had the second part of the manuscript. She had to read it. She had to know what Vera had written. If only to put it behind her. No, the actual problem was that whenever a text or email popped up on her phone, before her logical brain could overcome her body's impulses, something in her hoped it was a message from JB.

Her pocket vibrated. She opened the email, feeling mild disappointment mingled with relief. It was from Bjørn Carlsen, a local historian from Moskenes, to whom she had written some days before: *Alexandra Falck: Many thanks for your inquiry. Come whenever you want. We're very hospitable in the north, especially when it comes to inquiries about our beloved Vera. I have an oral testimony that proves she's telling the truth, and that the* Prinsesse Ragnhild *was the victim of saboteurs on board.*

She put her phone back in her pocket, said goodbye to Mads and took the girls back to the main house, where she was going to meet her siblings. In the dining room, Olav stood contemplating a large painting. It was a portrait of his great-grandfather, Theodor Falck, sitting in a carved chair dressed in a morning coat, his forearms resting on the armrests.

Sasha stopped in the doorway behind her father, her attention likewise drawn to the portrait. The sunlight revealed the unevenness of the oil paint on the canvas. For a long time, her father stood there unmoving, with his back to her.

"Alexandra," he said. How he knew she was there was a mystery. "What would good old Theodor have said about our present predicament?"

"The dispute over the will?"

Olav nodded, turning slowly towards her. "Theo was a man of compromise, an outstanding diplomat, they say. Played an important, though quiet role in 1905, in the dissolution of our union with Sweden, and had the ability to make his opponents feel that they'd won, even when they'd been fobbed off with glass beads and trinkets."

The room fell silent.

"Come here, Alexandra," he said, opening his arms.

After his diatribe against Johnny Berg, Olav had said no more on the matter. Just the thought of discussing anything personal with him felt uncomfortable, like continuing an intimate conversation with some random acquaintance in whom you had for some incomprehensible reason confided. But yes, it happened on occasion.

"Theo and the men who followed him, including Father, were all diplomats in spirit," he said absently, before fixing his gaze on her. "But that being so, they still knew how to put their foot down. They could pull the trigger if somebody had to die. Hans and the others expect fireworks from me at this family council."

"Then you had better dig out Theodor Falck's diplomat suit," said Sasha.

He placed his hand on her arm. Her father had big, strong hands, despite never having done any physical work.

"No," he said.

"All in?"

"Absolutely," Olav said, breaking out in a smile. "All in. But you'll be our spokesperson against the Bergenites."

"You mean that?" Sasha took a deep breath.

"I do," said Olav. "Come up to the office and I'll explain everything you need to know."

She followed.

Coming down half an hour later, having memorised the talking points for the family council, she was utterly shaken by her father's brilliant ruthlessness. There was a reason he had built a billion-kroner concern while most people had empty current accounts at the end of the month.

But then again: Hans Falck had tried to trick them by unleashing Johnny Berg on the family like some kind of Trojan Horse, and for that he had to pay.

She went to the kitchen, where Andrea was busy cooking. Sverre was also back, sitting at a table drumming his fingers. He looked better after some time away from Rederhaugen and their father.

"Back from Nordland then?" Sasha said.

He nodded, sneaking a piece of toast with crushed tomato. "Weekend leave. Flew out early this morning."

Andrea poured them a glass of wine each. "Great you could both come."

Sasha and Sverre sent each other sidelong glances, astonished that Andrea had taken the initiative for once.

"Things got pretty heavy last time. But Sasha was right about one thing: we've got to stick together. I think it was smart to meet beforehand, so we're all on the same page."

Sasha almost had to smile – this was too little, too late – but she did not let her expression reveal her thoughts. It was a quality that separated her from her siblings, and she had learned there was power in it. Andrea was expressive and outgoing. And even if Sverre tried to be stoic, his feelings shone through like a child's.

"Absolutely," Sasha said, looking at her little sister. "And what do you think our approach should be?"

"Meet them halfway," said Andrea. "I get that they're pissed off. Everyone knows Daddy duped that idiot Per Falck back in the day. Can't he just give them a couple of hundred million? Then we're kind of quits. It's no more of a financial ask than anyone else giving a thousand kroner to a TV charity appeal."

"That just explains why Daddy's rich and you have to shop on credit," Sasha said.

"Fuck off," Andrea laughed. "You're not as smart as you think, Sasha. You don't have to be old money with zero cash flow in Bergen to know Grandma planned to leave heaps more to Hans and the rest of them. If we can offer them a deal that's so massively attractive they have no choice but to say yes, we can get them to stop looking for Vera's will."

Sasha had to admit that there was some logic in what her little sister was saying, but she didn't let it show. "Duly noted, Andrea. I'll pass that on to Daddy. What do you think, Sverre?"

He had been sitting in silence while his sisters talked.

"I wanted to talk to you both," he said anxiously. "I want to ask you if you'd be interested in buying my shares. Lock, stock and barrel."

The unexploded bomb had gone off. Sasha folded her hands under her chin. Andrea's jaw dropped.

"Sverre, what the fuck . . .?"

Sasha interrupted her with a hand gesture. "That *might* be of interest," she said, looking at her brother. "But can you tell us why?"

"Selling would give me the capital to start something of my own."

"It's not about that!" cried Andrea. "You're furious with Daddy because he conspired with Martens to send you to Afghanistan."

"I'm not following," said Sasha.

Without waiting for her brother's approval, Andrea told Sasha how she had discovered the plot.

"Is this true?" Sasha asked.

"More or less," Sverre admitted. "But I've talked to Siri Greve, and from a legal perspective there's no problem with selling shares within the family."

"You can't," said Sasha. "I won't allow it. We're family and we stand together. You're angry, and with good reason. But that's precisely when you should *avoid* making such decisions."

Her brother rose to his feet. "That's easy for you to say. Daddy has always treated you well. But I'm done with the lies and the power games. I thought perhaps you'd see things my way, after you started researching Grandma's past."

"Daddy's not the only liar in that story," said Sasha. "Vera—"

Sverre interrupted her. "I happened to bump into Hans's biographer in Ramsund. He's an ex-Marine Hunter."

For the first time during their conversation, Sasha was unable to hide the expression on her face. "You talked to *who*?"

"He said there are lots of unresolved issues surrounding the manuscript Grandma wrote in 1970. Documents that have disappeared from the archives . . ."

"I can say a fair bit about that," Sasha said. She was relieved that her brother was coming out with stuff she already knew about, and that it led the conversation away from Johnny Berg.

"It's true that there are a few gaps in the archive at Hordnes. But I've looked closely into Grandma's story. Like all good conspiracy theories, it's seductive at first glance. But on closer examination, the evidence falls apart."

Sverre ignored her. "I met Berg in the old days, in Afghanistan. I'm guessing he was involved in some pretty hairy operations out there."

He went on to describe their conversation, up to the point it was interrupted by the recruits who called Johnny a traitor and set about him, before he was rescued by an older operator and former colleague.

"He reaped what he sowed," said Sasha, still unable to say Johnny's name. "That man tried to undermine our family, under the pretext of writing Hans's biography."

Sverre shook his head.

"What you don't know is that Johnny Berg has a pretty good reason for being angry with Father. And he has massive support among the experienced Marine Hunters. After he'd gone, I sat and talked with some of the older guys. Do you know his story, Sasha?"

She was itching to hear it, yet she couldn't bear to. It was like someone offering to fill you in about your husband's mistress.

"We don't have time for this," she said.

"Yes, you do, sister dear," Sverre said confidently. "I can see it."

"Can we go for a walk?" said Sasha, looking at Andrea, who shrugged.

"Berg was always a special guy," Sverre continued, as they came out onto the lawn. "Nobody knows where he comes from. Somewhere in the Middle East probably. He was adopted by a family here. Bit of a handful, thrown out at sixteen, squatted with lowlifes in an old apartment block. Then for some reason he decided to become a Marine Hunter, and being so free-spirited and strong, he managed it. He was recruited by a secret section of the intelligence services."

Sasha had often thought her brother's problems were down to something a psychologist friend called "covert narcissism". He certainly had a high opinion of himself and was just as self-centred as megalomaniac narcissists like Olav and Hans, although he lacked their drive or audacity. "I could have been a Marine Hunter," he would whinge when he got drunk. It was typical of a closet narcissist, as was his tendency to either idolise people or denigrate them. And Johnny Berg was most definitely the type her brother idolised.

"The thing is," Sverre continued, when they got to the pavilion, "it was Martens Magnus who recruited Johnny Berg for the mission that ended in a jail cell in Kurdistan. That's interesting in itself, but what's really hard to stomach is that our own father lobbied the authorities to abandon him to his fate."

"How do you know that? Because some Marine Hunter or other spun you a yarn over a whisky?"

"I can't tell you," Sverre said, looking at her steadily. "But Johnny Berg *is* innocent. And I can well understand that someone who takes a job from Martens Magnus and then gets left to rot in some IS jail might not be best pleased with him up there."

He pointed up at the rose tower.

38

A TAX-FREE LUMP SUM

Sverre stood in the bright sunshine at the entrance to the main house, waiting to receive the Bergen delegation. Hans Falck came striding across the lawn together with his girlfriend, little Per in the baby carrier, and his three adult children.

Sverre still felt a sting in his chest whenever he saw Marte, who kissed him on both cheeks, her fragrance filling his nostrils.

"Lovely to see you, Sverre," she said, rather formally, probably because of the Russian she had in tow.

Ivan, who had one of their sons on his shoulders, greeted Sverre with an iron handshake and impassive expression. Andrea emerged from the house, walked straight up to Marte and kissed her demonstratively on the mouth.

"You look fucking amazing, Marte. Better than ever, honestly."

"Have a couple of kids, Andrea," Marte purred. "Contrary to popular belief, it makes us *more* attractive."

Hans's eldest son, Christian, was a boring stuffed-shirt and trekking fanatic of about Sverre's age, with a respectable wife and two healthy kids. His little brother Erik, also in his thirties, was by contrast a wastrel and dopehead with scared, bloodshot eyes, podgy and bloated from antidepressants. They were both the product of Hans's brief relationship with a news anchor in the eighties. Olav claimed to see "a lot of both Per and Harriet" in Erik Falck, who had, in his opinion, the "weak constitution" that afflicted certain parts of the "Bergen tribe", and had probably never recovered from Hans's absent parenting style.

"I hear you're off back to Afghanistan," Hans said, placing a hand on Sverre's shoulder.

"Yes, I've come straight from the orientation sessions."

Hans shook his head. "When will the politicians realise that occupying that country has never done anyone any good?"

"I'm a soldier, not a politician," Sverre answered. He always tried to avoid Hans's tirades.

"No," said Hans, staring hard at him. "You're an occupier. And I've seen what happens to occupiers down there. In 1985 when the mujahedin began firing at Soviet helicopters—"

"With Stinger missiles supplied by the US, who thought they were a solid ally in the fight against communism, when in reality they went on to found al-Qaeda," piped up Andrea, finishing his sentence. "You've told us this a hundred times over, Hans."

"Yes," Hans said. "And I'll repeat it until somebody actually listens."

"Shall we crack on with enjoying our inherited freedom and prosperity, huh?" Andrea looked at Hans. "We're the richest and freest people who ever lived!"

They went into the downstairs dining room, where oysters, foie gras and generous quantities of Pol Roger champagne were served. It was still warm, and the party spilled out onto the terrace. The children roamed about in the hallways and on the lawn. Sverre felt a tension behind the convivial mood. He excused himself and went to the toilet, and when he came out, he heard a voice behind him.

"Sverre?"

Marte. How beautiful she was. The golden blonde hair, darker at the roots, that fell over her shoulders in soft waves, the high cheekbones, the blue eyes and the dark, arched eyebrows. And the smell of her, the fragrance, exactly as it had always been. It ought to be illegal, he thought.

"You rang me," she said sternly. "How many times do I have to tell you not to ring me?"

"I was calling about Vera's legacy."

She stared at him with interest. "What about it?"

"Follow me," said Sverre. They went up the grand staircase in the entrance hall to the study on the first floor. Marte sat on a rococo chair, one leg crossed over the other. Sverre opened a cupboard and fumbled slightly as he selected an old whisky.

"I'll pass," Marte said dismissively. "Say what it was you wanted."

"The truth is, your side of the family are set to get nothing at all," he said. "Selling to outsiders is out of the question, you know that. We could, in theory, buy your shares and pay you some sort of compensation. But Olav doesn't want that. He wants to keep you on the inside."

"I know all this. You didn't bring me up here to say that," she said.

Sverre took a deep breath. "I've offered Sasha and Andrea my holding in SAGA. They don't want it. And since I'm off to Afghanistan, which makes one contemplate the bigger things in life, I thought I should see if your side of the family would be interested in buying my shares.

I'd be selling to direct descendants of Big Thor, which means the restrictions don't apply. If you can buy me out, they're yours."

Marte nodded towards the cabinet. "I need that drink."

He poured her a glass and sat down next to her.

"I'll ask around. We don't have any cash right now. You know that. But things might change, and then it could be of interest."

"How might things change?"

"When Vera's will surfaces."

Sverre tilted his head, listening to make sure nobody was outside. "The will *is* gone, as far as I know. But I'd want some kind of assurance."

"Continue."

"If something were to happen; if Father lost his grip, for example, and dropped out of the picture, I'd want to know I could buy back in, even if I'd sold."

Marte smiled at Sverre with a mixture of sympathy and pity.

"This is about your father."

"No, it's about lots of things."

"Like what?"

He looked at her despondently. He knew this moment was as wrong as could be for what he was about to say. But it tumbled out. "I just want you to be happy. I've always liked you, Marte."

"And I've always liked you, Sverre," she said, putting a hand on his shoulder. Her tone did nothing to lift his heart, quite the contrary. He watched her drain her whisky.

"Do you love him?" he asked.

"Was that why you dragged me up here?" Marte said, toying with the empty crystal glass. "Look, Sverre, it was never anything. And this thing that was never anything has long been over."

Marte leaned over him and kissed him lightly. Then she left, closing the door behind her.

Sverre sat motionless in the rose-carved *kubbestol* chair until her fragrance faded away. From the terrace below he could hear sociable chatter and the excited voices of the children. He rose and padded across the room, suddenly feeling as though he had the body of an old man. As though he had gone straight from being young and promising to old and frail, without the usual midlife phase of a busy career and kids. As though his unrequited desire for women and recognition was a chasm through which all his strength and energy was drained.

When he finally staggered downstairs, they were taking their seats at the table. Sasha had joined them, along with Mads and the girls. His brother-in-law was holding a desultory conversation with Christian Falck about trekking in Jotunheimen. Sverre acknowledged them glumly and walked on. Olav was nowhere to be seen. The long dining table was magnificently laid, with an elegant lace tablecloth, floral decorations, navy-blue china, sparkling silverware and tall antique candlesticks. A large candelabra glittered with crystals.

Sasha's dog Jazz was dozing under the table.

Suddenly the hum of voices stopped, and everyone's head turned towards the door. Olav was standing there, a rifle raised in the air. What the bloody hell is Father up to, thought Sverre.

A collective gasp went around the table.

"Dearest Bergen folk!" he said. "As we all know, ours is a proud lineage that represents the best of Norway – from its trading traditions along our lengthy coast to the administrative heritage of our capital city. This can sometimes lead to disagreement, but today is a time for reconciliation."

"With an old rifle?" said Hans.

"This gun here, a bespoke Purdey, was found, together with its ammunition, among Mother's effects at High Cliff." He looked at Hans. "It was used by my father and your grandfather, Big Thor, when he went out to British East Africa in 1935 to hunt antelope and zebra with a group of English aristocrats. Come here, Hans."

Hans rolled his eyes as he got up and went over to Olav.

"I'd originally planned to give it to Sverre, who is without question the family's best shot."

Everyone nodded towards Sverre, who looked round with a look of both pride and discomfort.

"On reflection, however, I realised that it had passed into the family at a time when Thor was married to his dear Harriet. With this in mind, and as a sign of our good will, I want to give it to you. The gunstock is as delicate as the inside of a woman's thigh . . ."

"Daddy!" Andrea objected. "The gun may date from 1935, but your choice of words doesn't have to!"

"Hmm." He ran his fingers over the stock. "Here we have the falcon emblem, with our family motto: *Familia Ante Omnia*. Family before all else."

He held it out with both hands.

Applause rippled around the room while waitresses in white blouses refilled the champagne glasses. Sverre wondered why his father had chosen to provoke the Bergen side so openly on the eve of the family council. None of them would be interested in some rifle. Some were even vegetarians, and if Hans had ever held a weapon, it was as a young radical in the Middle East, and it would have been aimed at people like his hosts at Rederhaugen here.

As if to underscore the theme of hunting and weapons, a red suckling pig was carried in. Sverre helped himself greedily, without having much of an appetite. He drank quickly and soon felt his thoughts slow and his speech begin to slur. His conversation with his tablemate, Christian Falck's boring and respectably pretty wife, quickly ran aground. Marte was sitting diagonally across from him. She was glowing, bathed in the attentions of his father and Hans, with whom she was chatting, while sending the occasional fuzzy but devoted look towards her husband.

Sverre drank more and started to sway, as though he were swimming in his own alcohol intake. His little sister noticed and dragged him into the toilet off the hallway, where she lined up two snowy tracks with her credit card.

"This is good stuff, Sverre. Particularly in your present state. Doctor's orders."

He snorted the powder through a banknote, felt his nasal passage go numb and his brain clear, and returned to the dining room, where he drank more. Cocaine was the ultimate jet fuel; you could drink on and on.

It was then that Hans got to his feet, clinked his glass and cleared his throat. "Well now. The job of concluding sacrificial ceremonies often falls to me," he said. "But the person we must thank, besides Olav and the fine colonialist weapon he has so generously bestowed upon us, is Andrea Falck, the guardian of taste and hedonism here at the family pile. Andrea, your charred suckling pig was as soft as butter . . ."

"A twenty-one-day-old baby!" exclaimed his son, Erik Falck. "That's what you're eating. If you'd seen the same films as—"

"We'll skip the YouTube lecture tonight, Erik," interrupted Hans patronisingly, before continuing his toast to Andrea. "On the night before a duel, one must eat well, an art our dear Falcks here in the east excel at.

"As some of you know," he went on, "I have reached an age where one looks back as much as forward. So I have decided, in collaboration with a promising young biographer, to open up about my life and everything I've been involved in, which over time amounts to quite a bit."

Here Sverre glanced over at Sasha, who was staring impassively at the white tablecloth. He noticed his glass needed refilling, but there was no sign of the waiting staff.

"My biography will not be a whitewash," Hans continued. "That much I can promise you. If it happened, it will be included, even if it shows me in a bad light. I understand my biographer has asked you to contribute. I hope you do. Honesty, I have always thought, and acknowledging human fallibility, trump any concern for family harmony."

He paused for breath and sipped his wine. "And so, I would like to say a few words about someone who will probably play a more important role in my biography than you might expect, and who is sadly no longer among us.

"Vera, dear Vera," he said in a lowered voice, as Olav shifted uneasily in his chair. "Vera played an influential role in most of our lives. Including mine. She was an inspiration to me when she spent a winter with us at Hordnes, writing her story about the Hurtigruten disaster before everything was taken from her."

Hans paused, and Sverre noticed that his father's face had gone grey.

"Taken. Everything taken from her," Hans went on. "Betrayed by the most powerful members of society, and by those who should have stood by her."

He stared at each of the Oslo Falcks in turn. "Vera never forgave you."

"We'll wait until tomorrow to continue," Olav said sharply. "There'll be time enough for your little stories then."

"No, let's not wait," Hans said. "Because I was the one who knew her. Throughout the years that followed, I visited Vera. First at Blakstad Hospital, then at High Cliff. I listened to what she had to say. To her stories, crazy as they sometimes were, about the ghosts from the shipwreck. About the nanny who disappeared in the disaster, and who now haunts the dark passages under Rederhaugen holding little Olav crying in her arms. She told you all these things too, but you refused to listen."

"I think it's time for dessert," said Olav, clapping his hands.

"Not quite," Hans said. "Two days before Vera died, she called me. I've not recounted the details before now, but she said that she wanted to transfer – return is probably the right word – the Hordnes estate to us. And she had sensitive information she couldn't give me over the phone that would shed new light on the question of inheritance. You may scoff, Olav, but it's precisely this question that my biographer will help me to answer."

He raised his index finger in the air like an old-fashioned public speaker. "Unless, that is, we can solve it during this *informal* family council."

Sverre drained his glass.

"You know something?" Olav said. "I agree with you, Hans." He loved to knock his opponents off balance with unexpected suggestions. "We'll drop tomorrow's meeting. We'll get this wretched council over with right now. Say what you want to say."

Sasha had felt growing discomfort as she watched the scene unfold. The disgrace of it all, from the idiotic Falck rifle that now stood by the dresser under the gilt-framed painting and Theodor Falck's commanding gaze to the way Hans had bared his soul without filter, humiliating himself in front of the extended family. It was all so pathetic, there had to be something behind it. She had barely sipped her wine, but her siblings were clearly the worse for wear, as were several of the Bergen household.

Hans's strategy must have been to expose secrets about his relationship with Vera to sow fear before the next day's meeting. He had misjudged Olav there. But was he telling the truth? Had he really been Vera's steadfast friend and support since 1970?

Olav leaned forward at the head of the table. Then he got up slowly and walked round to where Sasha sat, stopped and leaned towards her ear. She could smell his old man's scent. "Are you ready, Alexandra? Go for it!"

As so often when she spoke in public, Sasha's nerves evaporated the moment she got up. She had wondered beforehand if she'd need a script to remember the key points, but she recalled every word.

"You want to sell. I'll remind you first of what it says in SAGA's articles of association, which are, quite rightly, based on the will of our ancestor Thor Falck. Existing shareholders have a pre-emptive right to buy, at fifty per cent of the value. So, if we estimate the starting point for their sale price to be one hundred million, this sum will be halved. Furthermore, after the bankruptcy of the Falck shipping company, Vera entered into an agreement with Per Falck to buy the property on Fana and rent it back to him for a symbolic sum. It was clearly stipulated in the lease" – Sasha smiled now, as she noted that what she was about to say did not trouble her in the least – "that should you wish to sell your shareholding, then the lost rental income should be included in the calculation. We can estimate that this lost income amounts to – let's see what our accountant came up with – 52.8 million kroner over forty-four years, minus of course the token 5,000 kroner a month that you've paid, which amounts to 2.6 million in the same period. Which means, we stand at approximately zero point zero. This is how things will look if you sell. You're not entitled to anything. As a gesture of goodwill, however" – she smiled – "we would offer you each a tax-free lump sum of 50,000 kroner."

She had her gaze fixed on Marte and Hans as she said this. They said nothing.

"Fifty thousand kroner. Fuck." Erik Falck broke the silence.

Sasha sat back down, buried her nose in her wine glass, and leaned back with her eyes closed.

"Without having discussed this proposal with my family," replied Hans, "I have no reason to believe that we would be interested in it."

The Bergen Falcks nodded in the flickering light of the candelabra.

"I'd like to say something," said Marte Falck, flashing the same look at Sasha as she had when they were younger. The last thing Sasha wanted now was to have to contend with her wretched cousin.

"There's an offer on the table that changes *our* assessment of the situation," Marte said. "As we know, the SAGA Group is controlled through your ownership, Olav. Aside from my family's symbolic shares, each of your three children has their own. It now appears that Sverre wants to sell his holding."

"Sverre?" Olav said, scornfully. "He can't just wave a magic wand and sell to an outsider. Only a direct descendant of Big Thor. Have you forgotten the statutes?"

"Absolutely not," Marte replied, still confident. "I mean within the family, to us – pre-emptive rights and at a fifty per cent discount."

Olav sat with an elbow on the table, scratching his chin thoughtfully.

"And how do you plan to finance this acquisition?" said Sasha. "Even with my brother and the statutes on your side, it'll cost a great deal of money, discount or not. Money you don't have. I hardly think 50,000 kroner each will stretch to such an acquisition."

"It goes without saying that we won't be entering any agreement yet. We'll finance it with the assets we secure through Vera's will," Marte replied. "When it surfaces. And if it doesn't, your dishonesty is going to be exposed anyway. Dad told me his biographer is currently on his way to the Hurtigruten wreck off Bodø. You're going to lose, and you know it."

The mood was sombre, like an election party after a landslide defeat. People got up from the table. Sverre avoided his father's gaze and dashed back out to the toilet with Andrea.

Moments later Sasha heard a glass breaking and excitable voices in the hallway. She ran to the door and saw Sverre with his hands round Ivan's throat, jamming him up against the wall, and a screaming Marte trying to pull them apart.

Then Erik Falck came running up behind Sasha, waving the Purdey.

"No!" cried Andrea. "Stop him! He's going to shoot Sverre!"

From the side room, as though in slow motion, Sasha saw Jazz come bounding up, saw his gaping wolf-like jaws and lolling tongue as he got ready to pounce. Like a wild beast, he went for the throat, and in an instant Erik was on the stone floor, the rifle beside him, and Jazz standing over him, snarling viciously.

Erik Falck's eyes were filled with terror as he clutched at his bloodied neck.

"Get that crazy animal off of me!" he roared.

Olav barged his way through. "You'll all have to get a hotel for the night," he said, looking at Hans and Marte. Then, glowering with contempt: "And that goes for you too, Sverre."

When Sasha emerged into the fresh air, she had bought tickets north for the following day.

39

THE SEA IS A MYSTERY

"Let's get this straight," said Ralph Rafaelsen, staring out over the grey Atlantic through the picture window in his living room. "You want to use my Exosuit to dive down to the wreck of the *Prinsesse Ragnhild*?"

"And we'll need a boat with a proper winch," Grotle interjected. "You have the right model."

Rafaelsen was a tough, bullish man. The only way was to be equally bullish. Johnny moved towards him. "How soon can we leave?" he said.

Ralph did not answer directly, but nodded. "Follow me."

The living room was furnished with white sofas and chairs arranged in front of a screen so big they might have been in a cinema. Tropical rhythms issued from a surround system on low volume. Johnny and Grotle exchanged glances. A Filipina maid cleared the coffee table.

"You can go, Tri," Ralph said.

Their host wore tight denims, loafers and a T-shirt printed to look like an admiral's uniform, with medals and a red sash across the chest. Walking with a powerful spring in his step, he took them down a long corridor with Ola Enstad sculptures of frogmen hanging from the ceiling.

It was the profits from his aquafarming empire that had allowed Ralph Rafaelsen to buy Norway's only Exosuit and to build this property by the sea. The whole house had something surreal about it, Johnny thought, like a museum rather than a home. It was set in an exceptionally harsh, windswept location on the exposed side of Vesterålen, a couple of hours' drive from Ramsund, and the media had written about it extensively.

Ralph's father had been a major player in the fish processing industry by the standards of his time. He had brought an American beauty queen up north, hence their son's English name. That was before he was hit by the crisis in the nineties and lost his fortune. The wife disappeared with it, of course; in fact, there were rumours that Ralph's biological father was a district doctor, a known ladies' man who worked in Finnmark at the time. Rafaelsen had been obsessed with making things right after his dad ended his life at sea: maybe it was the whisky, maybe it was suicide, either way he was dead.

Because Ralph had fought all his life, he was the type who would bulldoze you if you showed weakness. But he had respect for special forces soldiers. He had dropped out at the end of the Marine Hunter recruitment process and had gone on to qualify as a clearance diver. He and Grotle went way back, which was probably why he had agreed to their visit.

He opened a door at the end of the white hallway and led them down a pathway of wide stone slabs until they reached a modern boathouse with a roof that sloped sharply to the ground on both sides. There was no snow down here, only a strong smell of seaweed and salt. Rafaelsen unlocked the door.

Oxygen tanks, wetsuits and other bits of kit hung on the walls. It smelled of rubber, it smelled of the past. It was years since Johnny had dived.

"I was going to be a diver," Rafaelsen said, staring out across the sea. "Before this pathetic business took over my life. The Exosuit's up there."

In the dim light the suit looked like a dead man on the gallows. From the ceiling hung a thick cable that disappeared into the neck of the human-shaped device, with its visor, oxygen tanks and grabber claws.

"I bought it for five million kroner," Rafaelsen said bullishly. "A bargain. The market price is at least double."

Johnny looked up in wonder.

"This brute is two metres tall, weighs two hundred and forty kilos and has eighteen moving parts in hard aluminium. The problems of deep-sea diving are eliminated for good! Decompression sickness and complicated oxygen mixtures are a thing of the past. The pressure inside is exactly the same as on the surface. You understand?"

Johnny nodded, overwhelmed.

"You're as safe as in a submarine," said Rafaelsen. "And at the same time, you can move your arms and legs. You can grab objects with the claw on each arm. You have a four-horsepower thruster propeller on your back, and a cable connecting you to the surface supplies a communication system, a camera and a rebreather with enough oxygen for fifty hours. That's how long you can stay on the seabed if things get bad."

"Grotle," said Johnny. "Can you show Ralph the pictures of the ship?"

Grotle took a laptop out of his bag and put it on a bench.

"This," he said, "is DS *Prinsesse Ragnhild* in the Vestfjorden."

Their host looked at it closely, nodding. He was clearly interested.

"When one of the armed forces' mini submarines found the shipwreck in 2000, it took some pictures."

This was their sales pitch for Rafaelsen. Johnny figured he must be bored up here. A flickering image appeared on the screen.

At the top of the picture it read: *Date: 02/29/00. Location: Vestfjorden. Time: 12:37:33. Depth: 289.32.* A dark, impenetrable sea. Johnny could just make out the silhouette of the hull. It looked grey in the light from the submarine. Then he saw the bow and poop deck, the portholes and smokestacks, the deck cabins and bridge wing.

Having read the manuscript, he now pictured the young Vera as she crossed the teak floor with desperate steps. It was here they had seen the flash from the explosion, felt the hammer blow that followed. It was here that they had run and yelled, survived or died.

"Three hundred metres," Grotle said slowly, looking at the two men in turn. "The seabed's just a white blank on old maps. Human beings know more about space. The sea hides a reality beyond anything we see on dry land. Did you know there are organisms in the deep that we can barely comprehend? That give off colourful, flashing lights that make Times Square seem dull. Octopuses with eight glowing arms, jellyfish that flash blue like a police car when they're attacked. The sea is a mystery – perhaps the greatest mystery of all."

Rafaelsen had sat quietly waiting while Grotle talked. Now he got up. "The *Prinsesse Ragnhild* is a protected wreck, a 'ship cemetery' in other words, under Norwegian law. This means that any diver who finds human remains has to maintain proper distance from the find. They mustn't be disturbed for any purpose other than to move the body to a cemetery or burial ground, something that can be ruled out in this case."

Johnny was prepared for this. "Then I expect you're also familiar with the Cultural Heritage Act, Section 14, which says divers should exercise due care and attention, but does not prohibit such dives. Admittedly, some well-known wrecks such as *Blücher* and *Tirpitz* are protected by the National Heritage Board because they suffered looting by hobby divers, but that won't apply to a shipwreck three hundred metres down."

"You could use underwater drones," said Rafaelsen.

Johnny shook his head. "Drones or mini submarines won't get to the hole in the hull. The bow is to the right of the picture. That means it's the port side we see here. And the explosion happened on the starboard side. We've got to get down there. And the only way to do that is with the Exosuit."

Ralph Rafaelsen observed them in turn. "That Olav Falck guy down at SAGA in Oslo – him and his son are nagging me about using the suit for some conference up here later this year. Why should I put it at your disposal?"

This was the moment Johnny had been waiting for. "I'm working on Hans Falck's biography."

"Hans Falck," said Rafaelsen solemnly. "Good man, a legend. Even if we are poles apart politically."

"His biography," Johnny continued, "is just a cover for what I'm really doing."

"Which is?"

"Did Olav Falck treat you properly?"

Rafaelsen frowned.

"It was Hans who told me to ask you. For years Olav has been throwing crumbs to Hans and his side of the family. We're diving down to the wreck to prove he's lying about the cause of the explosion, so Hans Falck can get his rightful share of the inheritance. Olav Falck is going to be made to suffer."

Johnny folded his arms and waited. Grotle said nothing. Rafaelsen paced back and forth across the floor of the boathouse. Then he smiled at Johnny mischievously.

"We'd best take a look at the fishing smack then. It's down by the pier. Sure as hell, we'll go down to the shipwreck."

40

AN EXPLOSION FROM WITHIN

Sasha left for Bodø next morning. From there she continued on a small plane out to Lofoten, where she rented a car.

She drove west, past red-painted fishermen's houses, fish-processing sheds, roadside kiosks and empty fish-drying racks silhouetted against the sea, then in the shadow of sheer snow-covered mountains, along rocky shores washed smooth by white frothy breakers, until the landscape finally opened out into flat valleys with green fields, tunnels and bridges. She stopped at Flakstad for a cigarette.

The air streams from the Atlantic were different out here: puddles got stretch marks in the wind. Johnny had still not responded to her texts.

As she approached Moskenes, it started to snow. At first it was just a few spatters on her windscreen, but soon it was so intense she had to slow down so as not to drive off the narrow bridge that finally took her into Reine. There, she parked the car and hurried through the snowstorm to the address she had been given. It was a traditional wooden fisherman's house, built partly on land and partly over the water on poles, surrounded by fishing boats. A sign on the door read REINE WAR MUSEUM.

Local historian Bjørn Carlsen, a small, bright-eyed seventy-year-old with grey hair fastened in a ponytail, looked like Willie Nelson, the country and western singer. He led her into his museum, clearly glad to be showing it off.

The room was filled with glass cabinets containing mannequins dressed in Norwegian, British, Soviet and German uniforms: Norwegian Milorg anoraks, British bomber jackets, Red Army winter camouflage uniforms, equipment from the Wehrmacht, Luftwaffe and Kriegsmarine, parade dress and Alpine Hunter uniforms. Interspersed among them were wartime relics, tableware, medals, ships' bells, weapons, recruitment posters, old newspapers and framed black-and-white photographs. Hanging from the ceiling was an array of stuffed ravens, gulls and sea eagles.

"Impressive collection," she said.

Carlsen stopped at a display of watercolours. "Who d'you think painted these?" he asked in his light, gravelly voice, and before she managed to open her mouth, he said: "By a certain A. Hitler, they are, from 1940."

"Goodness," Sasha said, with raised eyebrows.

"Came across them in Bavaria a few years ago when an old lady's flat was cleared by relatives. Art historians and so-called experts didn't believe me, of course, but I shut 'em up."

Sasha was suddenly filled with doubt about this trip north.

She didn't consult amateur doctors; why would she listen to an amateur historian?

She went into Carlsen's office, which was also overflowing with knick-knacks and treasures. This room had a certain maritime flavour, with model ships and plaster figures in captain's uniforms.

"Let's get straight to the *Prinsesse Ragnhild* disaster," Sasha said. "I've read the report from the marine accident investigation. It seems pretty clear that the ship struck a British mine in Vestfjord."

"Investigation report!" exclaimed Carlsen. "Fit only for kindling. You really believe that nonsense? It was put together during the occupation, in front of a Nazi court. Folk were terrified, paid lip service to the Germans."

"Maybe," said Sasha. "But what do you have that says otherwise?"

"Wait here." Carlsen said. He returned a few minutes later. "This here is an eyewitness – Knut Indergård, skipper o' the freighter MS *Batnfjord*."

"I remember that name from the report," Sasha said, after thinking for a moment.

"The first thing you need to know about Indergård," said Carlsen, "is that he and his crew were heroes. Even the report says it outright. I have it here: *They took around a hundred and forty survivors on board the* Batnfjord, *of whom seven died on the way to Bodø. Well over half of these were German soldiers.*

"One hundred and forty souls!" cried Carlsen. "One of the great deeds of the war. And it got no recognition. You won't read about Knut Indergård or MS *Batnfjord* in the history books. He didn't get any medals. But his heroism is beyond doubt. What's controversial, though, is what he said about the shipwreck after the war, when the Germans had gone and folk could talk freely."

He held a USB stick up to the light and inserted it into a computer. "This is an interview made with Indergård towards the end of his life, donated to the Association for Norwegian Shipping History in Kristiansund on Nordmøre, who have been kind enough to share with me."

A poor-quality audio file crackled into life, and a voice with a heavy Nordmøre accent, presumably the skipper, began talking.

"She were a boat o' one hundred and forty ton, bought from France in the last war. A very good ship, a solid machine. Never had any fuss wi' any of her parts in twenty years. We sailed the Norwegian coast, east and west, but mostly between Bergen, Trondheim and Finnmark. We were on our way from Trondheim to Havøysund. And before we left, we lay at anchor next to the *Prinsesse Ragnhild*."

Carlsen pressed pause. "*Batnfjord* and *Prinsesse Ragnhild* were moored next to each other in Trondheim and followed each other up the coast, all the way to the site of the accident."

"Go on," said Sasha. She could feel they were getting to the heart of it now.

He pressed play again, and the interviewer asked Indergård what he thought the cause of the accident might have been.

"I am in no doubt whatsoever. Though I may stand alone in that. There were an explosion from inside the ship. Or else her side would not have blown outwards. And if I may add t' that, Captain Brækhus were rescued, but both the first and second mates went down. I have visited Brækhus at home in Bergen several times, and we talked. First he said it could not be anything but a mine, and I were sure it were not, for a mine will damage the outside of a ship. The beams in the smoking lounge and the wood panels were all gone. Only the iron structure were left. And dead folk were flung about in there. That's what the folk on board said. Three times I visited Brækhus, and the second time he tells me he's heard that the Germans put ammunition in crates labelled as oranges by way of camouflage. But remember this too, I said, there were several hundred German soldiers on board, and they had hand grenades, ammunition, rifles. That were explosives enough."

"So why didn't he say this at the investigation?" asked Sasha, impatiently.

Carlsen pressed pause again.

"Wait, just listen to what he says," said Carlsen. "It seems he may have mentioned it in the Salten District Court."

The recording came on again, with Indergård's voice: "I tried to tell 'em at the hearing, but it were too risky for me. The Germans were there, they were in charge, and they wanted the hole in the ship to go in and not out."

Sasha got up and stared at the museum walls.

Carlsen might be an amateur, but the recording was credible. It confirmed everything that Vera had claimed. The ship had been blown up from inside, but the Germans hadn't wanted that to be made public.

"My father only just survived," she said. "Rescued from the waves, perhaps by Knut Indergård."

The other nodded. "Very possible. There was another boat there too, the *Gange-Rolf* from Sortland, but Indergård felt that her crew didna' do enough."

She could picture it clearly, anonymous, honest seafarers from Nordmøre pulling her grandmother and her father out of the ice-cold sea, the waves, the screaming, people clinging to planks and other flotsam. Without these men, the ancestral line would have been cut. No Daddy and no her.

Life was so random.

"There's sommat not right wi' the story o' Vera Lind," said Carlsen. "She isna' registered in any papers after the sinking. If it were not for her fame after the war, you might think she had gone down wi' the rest. She never returned to her home town after the war either. During the occupation we had to register ourselves all the time. We could hardly travel anywhere wi'out some stamp or other. But there's nowt on Vera Lind."

"She went to Sweden."

"That was three and a half years later."

"But where could she have been in the meantime?"

"You need to go to Bunessanda on Yttersia."

"Where she grew up?"

He nodded. "It's not far. There's not many folk left on Yttersia now. But there's an old lady still lives out there. Else, daughter o' Dr Schultz. A fine, upstanding man."

41

COME TO LANDEGODE
LIGHTHOUSE

The air was very different out on Yttersia, it was colder, and the wind was stronger.

Sasha walked along the snowy cart road that skirted the fjord, then climbed a hill and made her way down towards the open Atlantic, blue and endless. To her right, Helvetestinden stretched towards the sky.

She crossed the beach, covered with driftwood and garlands of seaweed, stepping across shallow streams of meltwater cutting their way through the white sand. There, to the left, on a small peninsula, was the house. Painted red, but for the white frames of its small windows, it had thick guy ropes tying the gutters to the ground, which spoke of how exposed to the elements it was out here. Sasha knocked on the door.

Nobody answered.

"Hello?" She knocked harder.

She took a tour around the house. Through a window at the front she glimpsed a silhouette. She waved and waited until the figure appeared again.

The window opened a chink. "This isn't a damn tourist centre!" shouted a woman's voice.

"Stop a moment!" called Sasha. "I've come to find out if you ever met a woman who lived here during the war. My grandmother, Vera Lind."

The older woman craned her neck out the window. "What did you say?"

Else Foss was in her mid-seventies, rosy-cheeked with short grey hair. Wearing a sceptical expression, she opened the front door for Sasha, who stepped inside. The house was neat, with simple 1950s furniture, lace cloths on the tables and a little kitchen with an old-fashioned radio, from which the good-natured hum of a morning chat show spilled into the living room. She obviously lived alone.

"I came to ask about Grandma," Sasha said.

Else offered her some freshly brewed coffee at the kitchen table. "You'll excuse the simple fare. I live in Bodø during the winter and I've only just got back."

"You were at Grandma's funeral," Sasha said. She remembered Else's face now. She had been talking to Hans and her father .

"But of course. Anything else would be unthinkable. I'd be lying if I said I never wondered if someone might come to see me one day."

Sasha nodded, already feeling warmth towards this woman.

Else got up and carried some plates over to the sink. "I just hoped it would be you and not your father."

"Why?" Sasha asked, though she could guess the answer.

The woman gazed at her sympathetically. "We're done with polite niceties, aren't we? I take it you're here because you're wondering what happened to your grandmother?"

"Yes," Sasha said. "I am."

Else poured more coffee and began.

Else had first met Vera Lind in the autumn of 1969, at a packed debate hosted by the Student Society in Oslo.

Vera was on the panel and Else was a twenty-four-year-old student. She remembered little of the meeting itself, but when the panellists were in the bar afterwards she had plucked up the courage to go over to Vera. She had never had any desire to stand out in a crowd, but she admired those who did, and was totally captivated by Vera's forthright personality. Else had given a polite bob and gone on to explain that she was the daughter of Gjertrud Schultz, a teacher, and Dr Schultz, the district doctor in Moskenes.

Vera had looked utterly stunned for a moment.

"I have your parents to thank for everything," she said, when she had recovered herself and embraced Else. "Absolutely everything."

The two women spent all evening talking. And in the end Vera told her about a manuscript she was struggling with.

"Another crime novel?"

"No," said Vera. "This is a true story. And there are lots of people who won't like it."

It was Vera of course who secured Else the job at Grieg Forlag. It was nothing glamorous, mainly routine and secretarial work, but Else could type fast and accurately, and was given more and more responsibility. They spent a lot of time together that autumn. When Else went home for Christmas, she brought with her a long handwritten letter from Vera to her parents. Else never found out what was in it, but one day between Christmas and New Year her father took her to Å.

"Father took me to the village where Vera had grown up in poverty, explaining that he hoped Norway had become a better society that gave its young people greater opportunities than in her day. She was so brilliant, he said. He had never met such a uniquely gifted child. But she was also damaged, he said, because of her mother's illness and the father she'd never met."

"Did your father say anything else?" Sasha asked, breathing deep to speak calmly.

"He said everyone looked up to Vera because she was so clever and fascinating. But one had to be careful. When Vera tells the truth, we think she's lying, and when she's lying, we all believe her. How can you know that, I asked him. Because Vera lived with us during the war, after the Hurtigruten disaster, he replied."

Sasha got up and went over to the window. She did not doubt a word that Else was saying, which was why it hurt so much. For here on Yttersia, with the endless sea outside the window, another story was emerging, completely different from the one her father had told, which she had obediently lapped up.

Sasha came back to the table. "And then the police raided the publishing house?"

Else nodded.

"Johan Grieg had been nervous for days," she said. "He probably realised something was brewing. Early that morning he took me aside and gave me Vera's manuscript. You're the fastest secretary I have, type this up as quickly as you can, he said. Then he gave me a hollowed-out copy of *The Count of Monte Cristo* and told me that his father had smuggled secret documents in that selfsame book during the war. And type I did, at breakneck speed. Later that day the police stormed in, and Grieg gave them the original manuscript, just as I put the newly typed manuscript in the hollowed-out book. I walked past them unnoticed."

The Count of Monte Cristo, thought Sasha. More than one generation had used that book to carry information.

"But Grieg said it was he who smuggled the manuscript out."

"I would never say a bad word about Johan Grieg, I was very lucky to work for him," Else answered politely. "But that is simply not true."

"Good God!" It tumbled out of Sasha.

Else smiled at her warmly.

"If I've learned one thing from working for important men, it's that they like to put themselves in the starring role. Anyway, Vera and I were both pretty paranoid after what had happened, and we were afraid that the police might come after us too. Where should we put the manuscript? It was Vera who came up with the idea of leaving it with the Oslo City Court, as a last will and testament. And in a way that's exactly what it was. An ingenious solution. Nobody else could remove it from there, by law. Even the police would have trouble getting hold of it. And should anything happen to Vera, if it went so far as someone taking her life, then her 'will', in the form of *The Sea Cemetery*, would be there."

Sasha thought of the second part, which Johnny Berg had waved at her when she shut the door in his face.

"So, the entire manuscript was left with the City Court?"

For the first time Else hesitated.

"No," she said. "Not the last chapter. The most revealing. She sent that to me."

"But wait," Sasha protested. "This sounds complicated. Why should she deposit the manuscript with the court and then send the last chapter to you?"

"It's not at all complicated," Else said calmly. "You've read the manuscript, haven't you? It's about Thor Falck's cooperation with the Germans and its consequences after the war. That was what Olav was so hell-bent on suppressing. But he never found out the real secret."

"But with respect," Sasha said, "you were peripheral in Grandma's life. Why would she share something with *you* that she didn't tell anyone else?"

"Because I was the only person who knew what had happened," Else replied. "I had just been too young to realise it."

Sasha did not know what to think. "Tell me what it says," she demanded.

Now Else smiled. "I saw you and Ruth Mendelsohn walk over to Vera's writing cottage after the funeral. We've never got on, Ruth and I. When I saw you leaving, I went in myself and left the epilogue in—"

"The hollowed-out copy of *Monte Cristo*!" said Sasha, bringing her hand to her forehead.

"Vera knew that anyone who could find this hiding place had to know about what happened in 1970. For anyone else, it was just one book among thousands. But if you knew her story, that was where you would look. I won't say any more now. We can talk when you've read it."

Sasha went outside. It was blustery, there was rain in the air, and the rocks were slippery. She could not keep Johnny out of this. With cold fingers she wrote a text:

Johnny. You must answer. I'm in Lofoten. I know there's a missing chapter. And I know where it is. Will you come back with me?

Truth be told, she didn't expect an answer, but her pocket vibrated at once. JB. It was the first time she had heard from him since that evening. She fumbled with her phone, a few drops of rain landed on the screen, she had to dry it on her sleeve before she managed to open his text.

Come to Landegode Lighthouse. I am going down to the wreck asap as I promised. See you there.

She stood a moment, trying to work out if there was some hidden meaning here, but there wasn't. He was asking her to come. And he was going to dive. She was about to text back that the dive could wait, but she knew it was a waste of time.

Instead, she went back inside. "I have to go to Landegode," she told Else. "A friend is going to dive down to the *Prinsesse Ragnhild*. To find out whether it was holed by a mine or from within."

"That's good," said Else. "But there's one thing that's not in the manuscript. And it's no small question: who Wilhelm really was."

"How do you mean?"

Else left the room and came back with a white cardboard cylinder. She opened it and laid the deck plans out on the table.

"You see here? The 'Smoking Lounge', 'Music Lounge', '1st Class' . . . This is the promenade deck, outside. Here in the centre is the gilt staircase. To the right, the smoking lounge with a view towards the bow. The music lounge is there. And just to the right of the stairs is the shipowner's cabin."

Else pointed to another of the plans.

"We've moved lower down in the ship, to the '2nd deck'," Else continued. "Do you see the numbers at the top?"

Sasha peered closer. "33, 31, 29, 27."

"They're cabin numbers. Cabin 31. That's where Vera and Wilhelm spent their last night together."

She stared at Sasha as if this should be a light-bulb moment, and Sasha nodded, trying to hide the fact that she was out of her depth. This must be something that was revealed in the second part of the manuscript, the part only Johnny had read.

"You remember the moment when Wilhelm takes off his dog tag because they're going to run away together?"

Dog tag, run away together . . . It was like listening to someone describe the final episode of a TV series before you had a chance to watch it. "Of course," she said.

"Tell your diver chap that, if he has the chance, he must check the ventilation duct in the ceiling of Cabin 31 for the cigarette case and dog tag. You will probably remember from the manuscript, alpaca silver doesn't rust in water."

"Yes, I remember," Sasha said.

She took pictures of the ship's deck plans and sent them to Johnny.

Cabin 31, if possible.

That same evening, as she passed in the fading daylight over the site of the disaster, in the plane that would take her to Bodø, she thought how crazy all this was.

A tiny little alpaca cigarette case in that gigantic ocean. But it was the same with everything, the people we meet, the lives we live, yes, the fact we exist at all, or that she was Sasha Falck from one of the wealthiest families in one of the world's most modern countries, and not a slave wife in Tsarist Russia or a Babylonian prostitute or a hunter-gatherer wandering the forests ten thousand years ago – existence itself was weird when you thought about it, and infinitely more random than a seventy-five-year-old alpaca cigarette case hidden in the dark at a depth of three hundred metres in the water far below.

42

DIVING INTO THE SHIP

The crack of dawn. Johnny was fastened to a wire rope and lifted over the rail by a winch. On terra firma, the Exosuit seemed big and shapeless. The hard aluminium armour had rotary joints at the knees, elbows and hips, but it was impossible to move about in it on dry land. It had a built-in air recycling system, and mounted on one shoulder was a camera that could record the journey down.

Even Grotle was like an excited little boy now. With an experienced eye he was checking, assisted by Rafaelsen, that the suit's surface was undamaged, that the engine and the propellers were working and that the communication equipment was correctly fitted. That done, he helped put the helmet with its glass visor over Johnny's head.

Slowly Johnny was lowered into the sea. The temperature was regulated inside the suit, and it was oppressively quiet, like a soundproofed room. He used the steering pedals in the feet to turn horizontal in the water. For a moment the visor broke the surface. To the side he glimpsed the contours of the hull of the escort boat, like a distant blue whale. Beneath him the dark depths. The wire rope was unhooked; the only thing connecting him now was the communication cable. He hovered weightlessly in the water. A diver slipped down off the escort boat and swam calmly towards him. It was Grotle. Their eyes met. Grotle looked him over one last time and stuck a thumb in the air. His silhouette – black diving suit and long flippers against an azure sea – skimmed off towards the boat until it disappeared from view.

Johnny was alone now. He turned his head. Visibility was good. The shadow of a school of fish appeared nearby, like a swarm of bees or a flock of birds across an autumn sky. Carefully he began to move downwards. The blue of the surface was gradually replaced by darker hues as he stared down into the sea's abyss. He tried to find a steady course and slowly increased the speed of the thrusters. He checked the depth gauge: thirty metres. This was where the *Prinsesse Ragnhild* had gone down. On a diagonal, like a ski slope. Seventy-five years ago. What about the passengers who did not escape? They must have lost consciousness as the water rushed in. Or maybe not, it was possible that some were trapped in air pockets, maybe they knocked desperately on the doors until they realised all hope was gone, until the portholes burst under the pressure and they too were drowned.

Death must have come as a relief.

Death was often a relief. He had never been afraid of dying, only of the moment prior, when falling from a height you would see the ground swell towards you, when the truck's grille loomed up in front of your windscreen, or when the lightning flash of the explosion was yet to turn into the supersonic wind that would rip into your internal organs. The moment when you knew it was over.

Through the darkness, he glimpsed an object on his right. It was calmly orbiting towards him. A mini submarine perhaps, but why would he encounter such a thing here? His breath quickened. He could see now that it was a fish. With a shark's tail fin. A faint light still penetrated the water, casting a soft shimmer on the grey-black creature's back.

It could not be far away now, and Johnny saw it open its mouth, a maw the size of a giant manhole. A basking shark. He had seen them in pictures. Did they eat people? No, but even in this atmospheric suit he could vanish into its gigantic mouth without it even noticing.

"I can see a basking shark," he whispered, as if the fish might hear him talking inside the suit.

"Enjoy the view," Grotle said into his ear. "Baskers are harmless."

The shark glided past.

Hanging motionless in the water, Johnny felt the backwash. When he finally dared to breathe again, his visor misted up.

He continued downwards. Daylight did not penetrate this far, and it was black as a tropical night. Onwards he went, sixty metres, ninety metres, one hundred and twenty metres beneath the surface. The sense of weightlessness made his descent feel like a dream, an alternative reality beyond the everyday.

Beneath him Johnny glimpsed some faint lights. Was he hallucinating? He blinked twice. No, it was real, and they were getting brighter, like when you fly into a big city at night. A cloud of signal-blue plankton forming a carpet on the seabed, fish with gills covered with green camouflage stripes, glassy jellyfish in fluorine blue, bright red eels, creatures with visible skeletons like on an X-ray, emerald-green starfish the size of footballs, plants with leaves edged with rows of lights like airport runways, furry yeti crabs.

He turned onto his side. A cloud of bioluminescent organisms drifted over him like snow. He had never seen anything so beautiful.

He lay at the bottom for a few minutes.

"Everything OK down there?" said Grotle.

"It's so beautiful," Johnny said. "Like entering another universe . . . Like you said . . . Times Square, only a million times brighter."

"You're thirty metres from the *Prinsesse Ragnhild*," said Grotle. "Ten o'clock to your left."

Johnny moved along the seabed. No sign of the *Prinsesse*. Strange dark shapes skimmed along the bottom, but after the basking shark, they seemed as innocuous as aquarium fish. He moved on. A few metres ahead he saw a shadow. A new rock formation, perhaps? No, the object had straight, man-made lines.

It was the hull. In the light from his headlamp, it looked white. He could see the bulwark now, the scuppers in the bow, a row of portholes.

"I've located the ship," he said into the intercom.

"Excellent," Grotle replied. "Take your time. We'll stay with you."

Little fish swarmed around the sunken ferry, buried halfway in a sandbank, like a gigantic, abandoned vehicle in a vast desert. He began inspecting the bow, working his way slowly towards the aft. Thus far the ship was intact, with red starfish suctioned to its surface here and there. Then, to the left of his field of vision, he spotted a dark patch. He swam closer. It was a large hole in the hull, perhaps a couple of metres in diameter. It was perfectly circular in shape, but it had jagged edges that did not relate to the ship's normal structure.

Before him lay the answer to what had happened to DS *Prinsesse Ragnhild*. He felt his pulse quicken.

Staying as horizontal as he could, he shone his light into the darkness, but still he found it hard to see in detail.

The edges were ripped. And they turned outwards. He prodded them with the grabber claw. There could be no doubt. And if the steel around the hole in the hull bent outwards, it meant that the explosion had come from within.

The British mine theory was a lie. Vera had told the truth.

Grotle's voice came through. "Looks like you're at the explosion site. It's hard to conclude anything from the footage we're getting. Film it from as many positions as you can."

"OK."

"When you're done, come straight back up."

Johnny moved a few metres up and to the side. The bridge wing was intact, so too was the ship's main structure. He continued past the wheelhouse and smokestack. Could he get inside?

Johnny turned off the camera; a moment later the communication system crackled.

"Johnny," said Grotle. "The picture's gone. Can you hear us?"

"Loud and clear. It's all good here."

"I don't like this," Grotle said. "We want you back at the surface now!"

"Just checking a few things," he said, turning off the intercom too.

A current lifted Johnny up and over the bow, he felt like he was flying. He floated over the mast house and on towards the command bridge. He had already found what he had come for. If he was trying to get into Cabin 31, it was for Sasha.

He entered the ship.

Johnny had memorised the ship's plans before going down. It seemed quite simple: the command bridge at the top, then the promenade deck, the superstructure deck, the main deck and so on. The staircase that Vera had described so often in her manuscript started by the lounges on the upper deck and led all the way down to the lowest passenger deck. But it was one thing to look at plans by daylight and another to find your way around in the dark. Johnny continued over the surface of the wreck. In the shaft of light from his headlamp, he could clearly see where the command bridge ended and where the sloping smoke-stack stood. He moved closer.

He was now in what must once have been the stairwell that connected the lounges in the first class to the decks below. To the right he saw a door that he presumed led to the smoking and music lounges. Where Vera had gone in her lace dress. He resisted the temptation to look inside and moved instead towards the stairs. The contours of a banister were clearly visible. In the pictures he'd seen the staircase had been decorated with mirrors, brass and teak; now only the steel skeleton of the structure remained. He dived down the first flight of stairs and stopped on the mezzanine between the decks to check that the communication cable had not got twisted. Then he descended slowly to the next deck. The space below was identical. Here, the door had led into the first-class dining room. One more deck down, and he would be there.

There was little left of the *Prinsesse Ragnhild* beyond its steel structure. Any organic material had long since been eaten away or corroded. What remained of a mirror hung on the wall. Johnny was dazzled by the light it reflected and glimpsed his own face through the glass of the Exo-suit. *What are you doing here?* Two hundred and ninety metres below the surface, according to the depth gauge. At the foot of the stairs, passageways led fore and aft. He tried to picture the deck plan.

Cabin 31, Vera had written. He needed to turn right.

The corridor went on and on. Did it lead to the front of the ship, or had he lost his way? Claustrophobia lay its clammy blanket over his face. He imagined a coffin lid closing over him and earth being scattered over it.

The door to the cabin was gone. He eased himself in. There were no longer any individual cabins, all the partitions had crumbled away. He saw the round porthole, as described in the manuscript, its steel cover still held open by a chain attached to the ceiling. He gripped the chain and pulled, and behind the cover found the ventilation duct.

A small object glinted in the light from his headlamp. *Alpaca silver can lie on the seabed for hundreds of years.* Vera's cigarette case.

He reached for it and picked it up with the grab claw, stowing it in an exterior pocket. He had had enough now. *Get yourself out.* He started to go back the way he had come. *Get yourself up.*

Suddenly he felt a massive blow to the back of his suit. He was flung about as though he was in a tumble drier. A fish must have struck him with its tail fin, and it must have been a huge fish, as powerful as a kicking horse. He groaned with pain, but pain was the least of his problems.

The light had gone out. He tried to turn the communication system back on, but it was dead. He was yelling into a dead microphone.

He peered into the darkness. Here he was, two hundred and ninety metres under the sea, inside a sunken ship. It was comfortable inside the suit, which made it all the worse. Locked-in syndrome, like the Russian soldiers in the submarine *Kursk*. He tried to think.

He remembered he had two emergency glow sticks. This gave him a modicum of hope. In the dim light of one of the sticks Johnny moved slowly back to the staircase. He saw something in front of him. It must be the communication cable, which had come loose from his suit. If he followed it, it would at least act as a guide. He began to move upwards.

When he finally emerged from the ship, he had no idea how much time had passed. Using only the emergency battery, progress was very slow. But he was at least moving. Bit by bit the wreck became a distant blur, before disappearing altogether. It was dark all around him. Was he heading upwards? He was not sure. Push on, he thought, push on. *Upwards, upwards.* An astronaut out of orbit, a submarine off course.

Was that light he saw? At first, he thought it was an illusion. He tried to speed up. No, it was getting brighter, as in the wolf hour before dawn, when a faint glow precedes the sunrise. And now he could see the sun's rays on the surface of the sea. It spurred him on. Ten metres more, twenty, thirty, forty?

When he finally broke the surface, there was no boat waiting, but he caught sight of a few jagged rocks rising above the waves a few hundred metres away. Miraculously the current was carrying him towards them. When at last he reached the reef, he clung to the shining black rocks, praying that he had not been swept too far for Grotle to find him.

43

DOG TAG

"He's asleep," said the good-natured giant of a man who met her at the lighthouse. "Best leave him till he wakes."

The red and white obelisk lighthouse stood on a little islet, just north of Landegode. Located on the top of a hill, it rose over the landscape, encircled by white houses and red-painted boat sheds, all mirrored in the water's still surface.

The man pointed towards the main house. "There's something for you at reception, by the way."

It was hard to read about Big Thor's betrayal, about Betsy's fate and Vera's desperate search for her son before the explosion. But it was the meeting between Vera and Olav in 1970 that made her hair stand on end. Their conversation about *The Sea Cemetery* had marked the start of the conflict between her father and grandmother.

Sasha walked out of the old lighthouse keeper's lodge, past the engine room, various outhouses and the workers' living quarters. She leaped over some rocks and stared into the horizon. In the distance she could make out the Lofoten Wall, while much closer, Landegode's peaks shot up before her.

Her mobile rang. She jumped. *Daddy*. She considered ignoring it, but eventually answered.

"Sasha? It's me."

She felt her stress levels rise.

"Daddy. I've read *The Sea Cemetery*."

"Alexandra." Her father spoke in a commanding tone.

"I know what Big Thor did. I know what Grandma did. I know what you said."

"Sasha. One thing at a time, please. There's something you must understand. This information was withheld for *one* reason, and *one* reason only. My mother. Vera. The notion that people need to be protected from themselves is thrown about these days, but in this case it's true."

"Have you read the manuscript?"

"No, it wasn't really something I wanted to concern myself with, though I know the story roughly. And I know what happened to it. That as a responsible publisher, Grieg seized it, along with the security services. It was best for everyone."

Sasha sighed. Sometimes he was just so bloody arrogant.

"To declare someone mentally ill when they're telling the truth is one of Nissen's master suppression techniques."

"Maybe. But in this case the person making these claims was confirmed, by the country's top psychiatrists, to be seriously ill."

"She was your mother, and you're hiding behind some bloody psychiatrists!"

"No, I am not." Olav's voice was harsh and dominating. "I'd witnessed it myself. All my life I'd witnessed it. You weren't alive then, Sasha. You don't know how awful it is when the person who by the laws of nature should take care of you, and be your safe harbour, can't fulfil that task. When you know that you could, at any moment, receive the news that your mother – the only parent you have left – has taken her life. I carried that fear from when

I was very young. I was almost relieved when you called me on that Friday you found her, Sasha. Because I knew that, no matter how terrible the news was, the thing I feared had finally happened, and that I would never have to fear it again."

For a few seconds there was complete silence.

"Come back home, Sasha."

"No," she said. "I'm tired of your lies. I'm staying here."

"Alright. I'll come to you. I'll take the first flight up."

He had read once that napalm burns under water. In his dream he was trapped in an armoured vehicle under the sea, while bombs exploded all around him and extinguished the neon lights. Then, when he thought it was over, he ventured out of the truck, and was back in the fjord as a little boy with a snorkel and diving mask, holding crabs by their shells, fingers placed behind their long claws to stop them pinching, and there, swimming beside him on the seabed, was his daughter.

When he woke up, Sasha was on a chair beside the bed.

"What's the time?" Johnny asked.

It was still light. Confused, he sat up and swung his feet to the floor.

"How was it down there?" she asked.

"Magical," he said, feeling barely conscious. "Luminous fish and glowing plankton fell like rain around me. Vera was telling the truth."

"In what way?" Sasha asked.

"The hull was blown apart from inside. I've got photographic evidence." He smiled, somewhat hazily. "Or I had, at least."

"I understand."

"I was inside the ship," he said. "In Cabin 31. What's left of it."

"What did you find?"

He reached for the bedside table.

"This," he said.

She stared at its uneven surface, ran her fingertips over it.

"Vera's cigarette case. Exactly where she said they left it on that last night."

The engraved flags of Nordenfjeldske were now vague contours in the alpaca silver.

"And look, this was inside it."

The oval object resembled a coin. Johnny put it on the table. Sasha leaned over to look. The surface, which had once been a yellowy brass colour, was dull, but the inscription was still legible.

It was a dog tag, worn by all soldiers around their necks, showing their unit number and blood type.

"My God," she said, looking at Johnny. "It must be his. Wilhelm's. You remember me telling you about our project with the Bundesarchiv in Freiburg? That's exactly the kind of information they have. We can find his identity from it. But that's not the most urgent thing right now. I know where the last chapter is."

He got up to test his balance.

"But where have you just come from?" he asked, sitting back down.

"It doesn't matter. I'm sorry I got angry with you, Johnny." She put her hand on his.

They were soon lying in each other's arms.

Next morning they travelled back to Oslo.

PART V
SUNK SOULS

EPILOGUE

Let me tell you about how the *Prinsesse Ragnhild* went down. If you have never experienced a ship's bow filling with water, then slicing down into the depths like a knife, never seen passengers clinging to booms and stays while the stern rises to become a tower, or the ship's propeller rotating in silhouette against the sky, never heard people flailing in the churning waters, never known the gravitational forces that fling you across a deck as slippery as a fish's skin, then thank your stars. Be glad you have never had to choose whether to go down with the ship into the blue-black deep until she hits the bottom, or jump into the ice-cold waves clutching an infant, *your* infant, in your arms.

Babies hold their breath under water.

It's an instinct.

Let me tell you about the sinking of a ship. It starts with an explosion so powerful that it punches the air out of me and compresses my chest so my ribs hammer against my heart. So powerful that the wooden panels in the lounges are ripped apart leaving the iron beams stripped bare, so violent that passengers are strewn, unconscious, in every direction. The shock wave is so strong that it lifts the seventy-five-metre steamship up out of the water while gravity pins down my body. Then she plunges back onto the restless sea and I am slung into the air.

I am rushing down the corridor towards the staircase when it happens. A thunderous roar and I am thrown through the air. My head hits the brass newel post.

For a moment everything goes black. Then I come to. I stare up from the floor, disorientated. My ears are ringing. Heavy smoke floods through the shattered panels and into the stairwell. The smell of cordite rips into my nose. I scrabble to my knees. My head feels like lead, as though my skull is intact but the soft tissue is swollen. My jaw drops. Coughing, I bring my hands to my temple, my palms are red with blood. I look up. I see my own face, twisted and splintered, in the broken mirrors.

As I get up to run, the ship lurches starboard. I slip and curl up helplessly as I slam into the wall of the landing. I hear boots on the stairs. The hull groans like a wounded giant. I see black boots running past on the red felt carpet, stamping on my hair, the footsteps of war. They stamp on my fingers, but I register no pain. I hear shouts in German. The fear is contagious. Passengers stream from the corridors, pushing and shoving through the bottleneck in the stairwell.

Up, up to the promenade deck, to the lifeboats!

My son is still missing.

"Where's Olav?" I get back up onto my knees. "Where's my son?!"

Nobody hears in the commotion, nobody answers.

Everything sways as I get up and start to run. I head down a passageway, push past three young Wehrmacht soldiers, two businessmen in suits and an old woman howling for help.

The ship is fast filling with water. Like in the great and terrible flood of Storofsen, rivers of wooden planks, table lamps and luggage are rushing through the corridors.

I plant my every step firmly into the floor so as not to fall.

The bulkheads between the engine room and the corridor have broken in several places. The air is heavy, as hot as an inferno.

Where is he? Olav, my little boy, who was so small when he was born, just 2.7 kilos. He smiled for the first time last week. Olav, where are you?

The ship's pistons slow down, then stop.

DS *Prinsesse Ragnhild* is about to sink, and my son is missing.

The day after the disaster, I took the ferry across the Vestfjord to the place where I grew up. Where else could I go? I had nothing left. Everything was lost. Everything was in the graveyard beneath the waves. The sky had tumbled down, the sea had risen over the earth and erased nearly all life, I floated in the narrow gap between the elements, like an air pocket in the corridor of a sinking ship.

The mountains in Moskenes rose before me as we came into the bay where the church stood. Everything was just as I remembered, the fishermen's houses standing proudly at the water's edge, the screeching of seagulls, and the strangely exhilarating smell of fish guts and sea salt.

I followed the road around the bay, past boat sheds and warehouses and gawping locals who stepped aside at the sight of my wild eyes. Minutes later I reached the village of Sørvågen, where I knocked on the door of a villa, with an engraved copper plaque I knew so well: *Schultz*.

"Vera!" Fru Schultz gasped as she opened the door. "What in heaven's name has happened?"

I could not answer, but being a wise woman, she understood the gravity of the situation as I stumbled over the
threshold and sank onto the reindeer skin in front of the
fire. She tended to me, tucked me in, and left me in peace.
Behind her skirts hid a frightened little girl. Else was her
name, she was just three. I slept long into the next day.

The second between my waking and reality sinking in
was my only moment of respite. When I looked out at the
turbulent sea and stormy sky, the world turned grey.

Dr Schultz was back, and he gave me something to
make me drowsy. I grew limp and dreamy, guilt loosened
its grip, and I floated back to a world where everything was
undone, where the ship had not sunk and I had no plans
to escape, where the war had never come, and my mother
had not died and my father not left her.

Every night for the first few weeks, little Else came into
the guest room. She sat on the floor with her dolls, and in
time she started to stroke my hair.

Winter came late to Lofoten that year, and as I grew
stronger I started to take solitary foraging trips to Sørvågen and further afield, up in the mountains. Gjertrud
grew onions and potatoes, and along with the local hare
meat and fish caught in Vestfjorden, we ate better than
most of Norway. And what an appetite I had. In the first
weeks after the shipwreck I had barely eaten any solids,
but now I devoured potato cakes for breakfast and fish for
supper.

It was on such a day that Gjertrud looked at me and
said: "You're eating like a horse, Vera."

"I need to put the weight back on."

"Are you sure you're not with child?"

"With child?" I answered. "Are you mad?"

But my increased appetite continued, and it was soon followed by morning sickness, swollen breasts and never-ending exhaustion.

That winter, a bump appeared. There was no longer any doubt.

One July evening the following summer, when the fjord lay smooth and the sun shone on Yttersia, I lay in painful labour in a small room, with Dr Schultz acting as midwife and Gjertrud and little Else squeezing my hands. I gave birth to a perfectly formed baby boy and called him Olav.

Anything else felt wrong.

I considered going to get him baptised and entered into the local register. But I decided against it, and had Olav's original birth certificate from July 1940 sent to me from Bergen.

I was given the job of caring for Olav and Else. We were a strong and healthy band, full of vitality, free of the anaemia to which southerners were martyrs. Olav grew quickly. He crawled when he was six months old and took his first steps, between the house and the woodshed, when he was a year.

I had been aboard a ship that had sunk, taking with it my entire world. Yet I never spoke of it. Back then we did not "work through" such experiences; they were hushed up, not to be discussed. And for me, this had its benefits. We got on with life. Winter was succeeded by spring, and summer fell on a Friday, as we joked up north, followed by an autumn of gales, snow and darkness. This is how the war years passed.

One day, in the late winter of 1944, Else came into my room. She was due to start school next year, but had already learned to read. Olav was sleeping. She stood there in her nightgown, with her serious and intelligent little girl's face. A sheet of paper in her hand. For a moment I froze and gasped for air. The birth certificate.

"How did you get that?" I shouted with barely suppressed rage, grabbing the document. "This is for grown-ups only!"

"It says Olav was born in Bergen in 1940," she said. "But this isn't Bergen, it's Sørvågen. And I was here the night he was born. I remember you screaming."

"Else," I began.

"Mummy!" she yelled. "Auntie Vera says that Olav was born . . . !"

I pulled her tight into me, my heart beating like ten galloping horses. Eventually she calmed down. I stroked her long hair. Whispered that everything would be alright.

"In times of war," I said, "there are things that must be kept secret. You share secrets with your friends, right? And you know that the most important thing of all is to keep them to yourself."

She nodded solemnly.

"Well, this is like that. You know what the Germans do if they find out our secrets? They burn down our houses. Take your mummy from you, from us. Which is why nobody must ever know this. You understand? Not now, not ever."

I left the next day. I had to. If I stayed, someone else might find me out, either by discovering the certificate or by demanding the truth. If, on the other hand, I left, and Else gave me away, her mother would probably dismiss the story as a childish fantasy. Else's memories would slowly fade, like writing in the sand, until she would eventually doubt their substance altogether.

I stood at the taffrail with Olav next to me. He was tall enough now to see over it when he stood on tiptoe. A fisherman took us across Vestfjord. The peaks of Moskenes shrank on the horizon. I would never return.

I took a train bound for Sulitjelma, further north and close to the Swedish border. I passed through many German checkpoints along the way, with the excuse that I was seeking catering work at the mines. From there we went to the tiny mining village of Jakobsbakken. Finally, a day or so later, some undercover border guides arrived to lead us over the mountains on skis.

It was a cold, bright morning, five or ten below zero, good weather for skiing. We started out over the first slopes, pulling Olav behind us, safely tucked in a pulk. We crossed mountain ranges and frozen lakes, skiing up steep slopes and down perilous paths.

Suddenly, the weather grew milder. On we went. Snow fell. And it was wet snow now. I wasn't the best skier, and snow at zero degrees was the worst, not only because I fell through its crust, but because it made me so wet, which was worse than the cold. But with the help and encouragement of the guides, I struggled on. I wasn't only fleeing for my life, but for Olav's.

At last, the border came into view. It was time for my guides to turn back. From here I would go on alone. Hours later I stumbled into a border reception point in northern Sweden. I was taken to see a Swedish doctor. He eyed us curiously, then looking at the birth certificate commented that my son seemed small for his age. I said that undernourishment was sadly common now in Norway. He retorted that the boy's language skills were also underdeveloped for a four-year-old, to which I replied that children developed at different rates.

Then the doctor stamped our papers. *Olav Falck, born 27.07.1940.*

It was official now: Olav was reborn.

But what was the truth?

It is October 23, 1940. The explosion has hit the ship on the starboard side, and I can't find Olav. Desperate, I turn and run up to the promenade deck. The lifeboats are about to be lowered. I spot Wilhelm holding tight to the rail. The ship is at a grotesque angle now, I cling to a stay as the stern rises towards the lowering sky. Together we rush back down, the staircase is like a waterfall now, and the passageway below is almost completely submerged, only our heads come above the surface, but Wilhelm makes one final attempt to shove the door open with his shoulder, a futile effort, before a strong current grabs him and sweeps him away down the corridor.

I reach out to him, but the next wave flings me in the opposite direction, away from him, and away from you, Olav, through the corridor, passages and stairwells. The world darkens about me, but then I see a faint light, and I'm breaking through the water's surface. I gasp for air, and am dragged up onto the freighter MK *Batnfjord.*

And for seventy-five years I have tried to keep you alive.

44

WITNESS SIGNATURE

Sasha put the epilogue gently down on Vera's old kitchen table, next to the hollowed-out copy of *The Count of Monte Cristo*. Sunlight fell through the windows onto the wooden floors that gave way slightly as you walked across them and the spines of the books on the shelves.

She went outside. It was a warm day, the fjord lay perfectly still, an outboard motor shattered the silence. Sasha followed the path from the front steps of the cottage to the clifftop. She stood there for a moment, leaning out over the edge. There below lay the skerry and the shallow bay; some stingrays floated, red and sticky, on the water's surface. She would usually have felt her stomach tighten at this height, but today she felt nothing.

What did this epilogue mean, in truth? That Olav had died in the shipwreck and was born in Moskenes in the summer of 1941. It was beyond shocking. It upended the story her father had always told of himself; the ice bather, the tough guy who had always had to fight, practically from the moment of his birth. It would break him – she knew him too well to think otherwise. Yet had she not said that the fact of the lie was worse than the lie itself?

But beyond that, did it really matter? Daddy was a German bastard child, a *tyskerunge*, even if his father was of a quite different calibre from other Germans who fathered children with Norwegian women during the occupation. But so what, she thought, filled with a sudden wave of relief; plenty of people found out, well into adulthood, that the caring father they had always known was not their actual father. This was perhaps worse in a way – but bearable.

She would tell nobody. Not her siblings, and not Olav. He would start ringing her soon. What difference did it make whether you were born seventy-four or seventy-five years ago? He would have his twilight years ruined by something that was of no real interest or meaning. No, she would say nothing, and when Sasha decided to seal her lips, they stayed sealed. She had preached about the truth, but it was a secondary concern, she understood that now.

Yet she felt for Vera. She understood her pain. After all, what she described was any parent's worst nightmare, and it must have been hard to bear, not just the trauma of what had happened, but the lie that grew until it was so big it was out of control. It was that kind of thing that people were destroyed by, that got them hospitalised, that drove them to suicide.

Johnny had hung back in the doorway of the cottage. Now he came and stood beside her. "How do you feel?"

"Better than expected, I think."

"Well, let me know if you're still up for checking that dog tag number."

The dog tag.

All thought of it had vanished in the undertow of the story they had just read. Who was Wilhelm? Sasha noticed herself jump at the thought. Who was . . .?

"Johnny. We've journeyed through this story together, and we'll finish it together."

They walked quickly through the forest, past the fountain at the junction and up the grassy slope to the main house, where she took him in through the side door. The library was open. She led Johnny into her office, opened her computer and immediately logged into the online database of German soldiers stationed in Norway during the war. Johnny stood watching. She entered the number from the Kriegsmarine dog tag in the cigarette case.

You have a match.

It was a short entry:

Hans Otto Brandt: b. 12/05/1916. Served in the Kriegsmarine, Hafenkommando, Abteilung Bergen. Missing, presumed killed in the DS Prinsesse Ragnhild *shipping accident 23/10/1940. No remains found.*

"That's Wilhelm," she said to Johnny. "We've got his real name."

There was one more thing to try. As a site administrator, Sasha could see who on the internal network had logged into this page. This was how she had caught Tollefsen, the PhD intern. She clicked on the page history for Hans Brandt.

A name came up: Siri Jacqueline Greve. She had visited it the day after Vera's death.

She could now trace the contours of what had happened. With Johnny following close behind, she rushed out of her office, up the stairs and through the living room and foyer until she reached the lawyer's office in the building's opposite wing.

She stopped, took a deep breath, and knocked.

"Have you got a minute?" said Sasha, so calmly even she was surprised.

"Come in," Siri said.

Siri looked at her watch. Johnny stood leaning against the door frame.

"I've been to Nordland," began Sasha, "and I read Vera's manuscript."

Siri nodded. She was either a good actress, or just naive.

"It answered many questions that have been bothering me," continued Sasha. "Why, for example, Grandma was so damaged, and why it was so dangerous for Daddy if this all came out."

Sasha took out a pack of cigarettes and lit one. Siri glowered at her. "But I still couldn't work out where the will was, or if it existed at all. Until Johnny, here" – she pointed back at him – "found the dog tag in the shipwreck."

The lawyer's face filled with confusion.

"Then it was simple," said Sasha. "It was just a matter of entering the serial number into the search function, and there it was: the name of Vera's old flame from *The Sea Cemetery*. But you knew that, of course. There were four hundred thousand Germans here in Norway during the occupation. But, of all of them, you chose to look up a Hans Brandt in the Kriegsmarine, Abteilung Bergen."

Siri Greve smiled stiffly. "And so?"

"It answered the question I've asked myself ever since Vera took her own life and her will went missing. Who was the other witness? It takes two signatures. The first had to be Grieg, who was given the manuscript for publication. But who was the second? I wondered about that as I hunted for the manuscript and the will melted into the background. But yes, it had to be the lawyer whose family has handled our family's affairs for three generations, who operates quietly behind the scenes, plays both ends against the middle and knows all our secrets here at Rederhaugen.

You've been lying to us all along, Siri. You've had the will ever since it was signed by Vera on the day she jumped."

"Yes. I have," Siri replied calmly.

Sasha pointed towards the filing cabinet from which Siri had taken the documents concerning Vera's Guardianship Order when she was last here.

"Would you like me to tell you why I kept it hidden?" said Siri.

"Listen, Siri. I learned today that the person my father thinks he is actually died in 1940, and that Grandma kept it a secret for seventy-five years. I think I can handle whatever this throws up too."

"I'm not so sure."

She was so calm that Sasha hesitated for the first time in the conversation. But they had come too far now, there was no turning back. Sasha nodded towards the cabinet again.

"I share all business secrets with Olav," said Siri. "But there was really no reasonable way to tell him this. Vera was also of the opinion that I should avoid telling you until you had read her manuscript. It was her way of explaining herself. You are hereby warned, for the final time."

She opened the cabinet and came back with a document, which she lay before them and read aloud.

LAST WILL AND TESTAMENT

of

Vera Margrethe Lind 20032034284
High Cliff, Rederhaugen 20/03/2015

[signature]

The Falck family has always followed the principle of "direct line" concerning the inheritance of family properties and control over companies/foundations.

The truth is that Olav Falck is the son of the German soldier Hans Otto Brandt, missing and presumed dead following the DS *Prinsesse Ragnhild* shipping disaster, 23/10/1940. For this reason, neither Olav nor his descendants have any legitimate inheritance rights.

As the oldest family survivor in direct line from Thor Falck, Hans Falck is therefore my rightful heir after my death. Rederhaugen and all other family properties are to be transferred to him.

As concerns the SAGA Group, I refer to Thor Falck's will, which states unequivocally that all his assets – including businesses, real estate and other properties – shall be managed by a person in direct line; that is, Hans Falck.

The rights to, and any future income from my books, shall without restriction be transferred to my granddaughter, Alexandra Falck.

Witness signatures:

This, the last will and testament of Vera Margrethe Lind, is signed in the presence of the following two witnesses, both being over the age of eighteen and not beneficiaries of this will.

JOHAN GRIEG

SIRI JACQUELINE GREVE

45

IT'S AN EMERGENCY

When Sasha was eight, she got her hair stuck in the drain of a jacuzzi. She had dived down under the water, when she suddenly felt an inexplicable force tug on her hair and drag her to the bottom of the metre-deep, churning water. She thrashed about, but to no avail, she was stuck, she ran out of air, her nose and mouth filled with water, until someone yanked her out.

It was Olav.

And now, as she read the will in Siri Greve's office, the emotions of that day came back to her. Not just the panic of being stuck, but of her and her father sitting on the edge afterwards, their arms wrapped round each other. They had both sobbed so much they shook. Sasha still remembered how she buried her face in his soaking wet, transparent shirt.

"It'll be alright, sweetheart," he whispered. "It'll be alright."

She suddenly missed her father. There was complete silence in the room now. Outside she could hear the hum of someone cutting a hedge with a trimmer. But Olav could offer her no comfort now.

How long she sat like that, she had no idea, but it felt like an eternity. She got up and went over to the window. Rederhaugen stretched out before her eyes, magnificent, as the estate always was in the spring, when the lawns were a vibrant green and the fjord sparkled like silver. All this had been theirs, and Vera had taken it from them with a stroke of the pen. *The truth* . . . Was this the truth, or was it revenge? Or both? Yes, it had to be. It was the voice of one who had been rendered voiceless. But whatever her motives, they were secondary. The fact was that Grandma had disinherited them.

No, that could not happen. When she was young, Sasha had been afraid of dying from cancer or in an accident, but when she had children herself, her fear of death disappeared. It was projected onto the girls. And added to that was the fear of losing what should in time be theirs.

They said she resembled her grandmother, but she was Olav's daughter.

In a flash, Sasha knew what to do. It would be the summation of everything her father and Vera had ever taught her. Reality was not something you merely documented, the real story was the one you wrote yourself.

"Siri," she said in a determined voice. "Johnny, come here."

They stepped hesitantly towards her. On the table before them lay the will.

Sasha held it up. "What do you think?" she asked them both.

"Vera writes about losing a child," Johnny said. "A child is worth more than a million properties or a billion-dollar corporation. Don't forget that."

She did not reply, but looked at the lawyer. "Siri?"

"It could be a long legal battle."

"No," said Sasha, looking at them in turn. "This will never see the light of day. I want your guarantee that it will never be made public. What happens now will never have happened. Your discretion will of course be rewarded. If you ever talk about this, no matter in what context, I'll use every means I have at my disposal to silence you. Is that understood?"

Siri nodded.

"No," said Johnny. "I can't accept that."

"You don't really care about this will," said Sasha. "That's Hans's issue. No, what you want is revenge on Daddy after what happened in Kurdistan. And I'll make sure you get it. But on one condition: that you put this will aside."

He looked at her with his green eyes and shook his head. "That goes against everything I believe in. I can't. We talked about finding the truth."

Sasha picked up the document, and before they had time to react, she had lit the will from below with a lighter. The flames curled around it, making fringes of soot before it caught fire and the ashes floated down onto Siri's office floor.

"You're just like your father," Johnny said coldly. "You both think you can burn the truth of who you really are. It works for a while. But eventually everything will go to hell. Never forget that."

Sasha walked out without answering, and did not stop until she was outside on the lawn. She was in survival mode and dialled 112.

"Sasha Falck here. I'm calling from Rederhaugen. It's an emergency."

"Go ahead?"

"It concerns a certain person. Johnny Berg, John Omar Berg. Previously a special forces soldier, recently suspected of terrorist activities in Syria and Iraq. He's here."

"Are you safe?"

"He's here on the estate. He's dangerous. You must come quickly."

"We understand," said the voice. "Stay where you are."

Soon after she heard sirens.

46

AFGHAN AIRSPACE

Sverre woke up when the plane entered Afghan airspace. The landscape of sun-scorched fields, desert and distant snowy white mountains was back. In the rows of seats around him, bearded Marine Hunters were fast asleep and barely lifted an eyebrow as they flew into Kabul and the wheels met the runway with a heavy bump.

He put on his helmet and bulletproof vest and carried his lead-heavy bag into the military terminal. The Marine Hunters treated him well. With some quiet scepticism, perhaps, but what else could one expect? He just had to do the job, and respect would come.

They drove in a column to the camp. On the surface, things had barely changed since last time. The urban landscape slipped past: barbed wire, checkpoints, houses, Eastern European-style apartment blocks, clusters of men in *shalwar kameez*, veiled women with flocks of children in tow.

The road to the camp went through several security perimeters, zigzagging between cheval traps, concrete blocks, armoured vehicles and sandbag positions. Sverre carried his personal belongings into the small enclosure of air-conditioned tents. He ate alone in the mess, but even that failed to dampen his spirits.

Afterwards there was a gathering in the operations room.

"Welcome back," said a naval captain, who was clearly the operations officer. "Your deployment starts for real as of this evening."

He laid out the night's mission in detail. Working alongside the Afghan special police they were going to arrest a bomber. A dangerous assignment. The mood in the city was, as always, tense. The Marine Hunters nodded sleepily; this was clearly routine for them, but Sverre was tingling with excitement. This was his chance to show who he was and what he was made of.

The naval captain clapped his hands. "Let's get to it then. All stops out."

The scraping of chairs when a whole troop rises simultaneously.

Sverre was heading out with the others when he heard a voice behind him.

"Falck," said the naval captain.

Sverre stopped.

"You won't be going. You'll remain here."

"Why, sir?"

The captain, a short, powerful guy his own age, with a round, bearded face, sighed irritably. "I manage the assignments down here. If your father chooses to send you to Kabul to build your character, that's on him."

The words came like a blow to the kidneys.

"But—"

"There's no *but*. It's my responsibility to allocate personnel as I see fit. You'll carry out maintenance and check the unit's weapons. Understood?"

Sverre stood there speechless.

"Good. Report back within three hours."

Sverre turned and walked away between the billeting containers.

"By the way," the naval captain called out. "Some lawyer contacted us, wanting to talk to you. Rana something. Jan Rana. Said he could do it on FaceTime. Shall I just say you're unreachable?"

"No," Sverre replied, after a moment's reflection. "Tell him I'd be happy to talk."

Sasha was an attentive mother and spouse over the next few weeks. The house was kept in impeccable order, she made dinner from scratch every day, followed up on all the girls' after-school activities, and on one magnificently sunny weekend she and Mads finally completed the trek from Finse to the Hardangerjøkulen glacier.

One warm May evening, however, shortly before Independence Day, she left her family and walked along the tree-lined avenue to the main house. Sasha had not really spoken with her father since everything had happened, but they had agreed to have dinner together that night up in the small dining room on the ground floor.

Olav was already there when she arrived. His mother's death had aged him, he was more stooped and his face paler.

"Alexandra," he said, embracing her. "You look wonderful. Did you ask Andrea to make us something?"

Sasha had given her sister strict instructions to prepare supper well in advance – the last thing she wanted was to have Andrea skulking in the wings during the conversation that would follow.

She fetched a plate of sushi and sashimi from the fridge downstairs, and coming back up she asked him, "Have you heard from Sverre lately? He told me that they're on a long assignment and he'll be unreachable for the foreseeable."

"No, it's been ages," said Olav. "I think he's angry with me. But no news is good news. Are you ready for the SAGA Arctic Challenge? Will you be speaking about Mother?"

"Yes. In fact, that's what I wanted to talk to you about," said Sasha, between mouthfuls of raw fish.

"Well, I'm going to talk about Father and the origins of the resistance movement along the coast in 1940," Olav said.

Sasha observed him, her head inclined, before eventually saying: "I wouldn't if I were you."

"Oh really?" her father replied, sounding almost amused by her stern tone. "So, remind me, do we or do we not believe in freedom of expression and openness in this family?"

Sasha stared at him thoughtfully. "Let me finish. I read Grandma's manuscript. She was right; the ship wasn't blown up by a mine, there's photographic evidence of that, captured by the camera on Rafaelsen's Exosuit. As to her claim that Big Thor collaborated with the Germans, it's true that the correspondence is missing from the archives in Bergen. But in *The Sea Cemetery* Grandma describes a meeting here at Rederhaugen that took place in the spring of 1970 during the final stages of her writing the manuscript. A meeting that sheds light on why the next forty-five years were so fraught; a meeting with *you*."

Olav said nothing.

"Of course," Sasha continued, "shoot the messenger. You could accuse your dead mother of lying, or me of conspiring against you."

She was smiling.

"But you're not going to do that. Deep down, Daddy, you know times have changed. SAGA must preserve all the good things it's achieved, but at the same time we need greater openness. So, my suggestion is that you step down and I take over as CEO and as chair of the board of the foundation. I can't think of a better opportunity to announce the change of leadership than at the SAGA Arctic Challenge."

The last of the bright evening's sunlight fell on one side of her father's face. He sat in silence for a long time, then a faint smile appeared in the corners of his mouth.

"Are you giving me the boot, Alexandra?"

Sasha smiled back. "I believe I am, Daddy."

"In that case," Olav said calmly, "you'd better call home to say you'll be late. We have a lot to discuss."

47

MUCH WRONG

The prison cell was of a very different standard from his last one, but for the first few days Johnny Berg felt lower than he remembered ever feeling before. At night he hardly slept, during the day he ate nothing. He tried to summon up the image of his daughter, but her face just dissolved like a photograph devoured in flames.

The initial court hearing was a formality. He was charged with desecrating a burial ground, in this case a "ship cemetery", a protected wreck under the Cultural Heritage Act, Section 14, and – more seriously – breaking and entering under the Penal Code, Section 184 as well as the Security Act. That he had been under suspicion as a foreign fighter was an aggravating factor, and the court saw no option but to remand him in custody.

But more than anything, he felt betrayed by Sasha. She could work with him, flirt with him, sleep with him and cling to him afterwards. But at the end of the day, she had made her choice. She had chosen the family, chosen the official version. SAGA *wrote* the official version. Not because she was evil, she had her reasons; to her mind, power was fundamentally just. Power had always treated her well. It had never stopped her at customs or taken her for a jihadist. She had never been a foreigner.

Or maybe there was something else behind it all, something beyond his understanding. In Siri Greve's office, he had felt that Sasha was driven by an impulse as foreign, incomprehensible and powerful as that behind honour killings. Families and roots always left him at a loss. From a distance he knew there were gigantic forces at play, but having not grown up with a family of his own, he failed to understand them.

Johnny was in bed. There was a rattling at his cell door, and the prison warden appeared.

"OK, Berg. How are we today?"

Johnny did not answer.

"Like that, is it?" sighed the warden. "I just came to say you've got a visitor."

When Johnny entered the visiting room ten minutes later, he found Jan I. Rana sitting there, together with HK.

"Johnny," said the older man, hugging him. "I'm to say hi from Hans and to thank you very much for your efforts. He's got cold feet as regards the book, but he'll remunerate you nevertheless."

Johnny said nothing.

"Sorry I wasn't at the hearing, Johnny," Rana said. "Dad snuffed it, poor guy. Don't worry, he'd been ill for years. Problem was he'd moved back to the Punjab. Social security export."

He laughed to himself. "When he died I had to go down there to sort a few things out. And it came at the same time as your hearing. But don't give up hope, Johnny – the whole thing was a fucking scandal. You weren't exactly equipped with OJ Simpson's defence team. Now hear this."

"You tricked me," Johnny said, glaring at HK. "You gave me that document from 1970 and set everything in motion to nail me."

"Quite the contrary," HK said.

"Case in point!" said Jan I. Rana. "The fact is, even if a third-division lawyer might not know it, a whistle-blower who reports misconduct within the secret services has the right to legal protection. The High Court is pretty hot on that. Particularly when what you're reporting dates back fifty years so there's no threat to national security. And the grave desecration? That's a joke."

Johnny shook his head. "It's all over. I'll just take my punishment and start again."

"OK," said HK. "We're on the same page. Rana?"

The lawyer took a tablet out of his bag and placed it on the table in front of them.

"Seeing as you're not allowed internet access in here," Rana said, "I brought a file for you to look at."

He inserted a USB stick in the side of his tablet, entered his password and tapped on a file.

The film was shot in a green tent of the type used in Afghanistan. Sverre Falck, wearing a desert camouflage work uniform, sat with his dog tag dangling from his neck.

A voice issued from the tablet.

"Falck? Jan Rana here. Can you hear me?"

"Loud and clear."

"Great. It is not the purpose of this conversation to record anything with legal power. This is just an introductory conversation with a view to you giving testimony that may support my client's case at a later date. You understand?"

"Understood."

"Where were you on September 6, 2014?"

"I was in Erbil, the capital of the autonomous Kurdish zone in Iraq."

"That's more than a year ago. How can you be so sure?"

"I've always had a good memory for dates. And it was my first time in Kurdistan. So, I'm absolutely certain. And it can be confirmed with plane tickets and credit card statements."

"What were you there to do?"

"My job was to transfer a sum of money to a Kurdish unit at the front and meet my contact there. It was a substantial sum. Twenty thousand dollars as far as I remember. Half up front, and half at the end of the assignment."

"Stop a moment, there are several things here. Who was your contact there?"

"His name is Miraz Barzani, but he's better known as Mike, or NordicSNIPER. We knew each other from the sniper squad. I contacted him via a fake Instagram account."

"What kind of assignment was it?"

"I never got to know. I had a sealed envelope which I was to give Mike, but it seems obvious that it related to supporting the Kurds against Daesh."

"Who gave you the money and the envelope at the Norwegian end?"

"Well, his name is Martens Magnus, but people call him MM."

"And why would this MM give you something like that?"

"Because MM is a friend of the family, that's to say, of my father."

"And you're prepared to say this under oath if it comes to it?"

"I am." Sverre Falck's eyes flickered. "Absolutely."

Rana closed the file and turned to Johnny. "Sverre Falck is willing to testify against his father. We're building a case. But if we're to move forward, you need to tell us exactly what you did in Kurdistan."

Johnny put his hands over his face, leaned back and closed his eyes.

"I'll be brief," he said. "We can go into the details later. The target was the Norwegian jihadist Abu Fellah, who had issued threats against Norway and was linked to IS's division for 'foreign operations'. He lived in a small village not far from the front line in northern Iraq. Maps and satellite pictures were studied, contact was made with the US special forces soldier and volunteers in the Assyrian militia who were going to participate.

"The trip to Kurdistan went without a hitch," he continued. "I landed, collected the money from the bank, met the American and got the weapon we were going to use. Long story short: we crossed the front line one night. It was between five hundred metres and a kilometre wide, covered with high grass. We knew where the guards were and got past them without any problem. Fellah lived in a two-storey brick house, behind an iron gate with a guardroom on the side, manned by an old Iraqi. While the American tied him up, I entered the house. There was a dog inside and I had to shoot it. I went upstairs. Fellah must have been woken by the shot with the silencer, because when I opened the bedroom door, he was already heading towards me. I fired two shots, one to his chest and one to his forehead. His wife screamed like crazy as I left. And there . . ."

Johnny paused and lowered his gaze. "There were two kids, a boy and a girl, hand in hand in the moonlight. They'd probably been woken by the noise too. They just stood there, totally petrified, like two zombies. I ran past them, down the stairs and out to where the American guy was waiting, we ran on, but the whole village was awake now, and as we came out into no man's land, he was shot. I got away and was subsequently arrested, not by IS, but by the Kurds, who thought I was a jihadist."

With that, Johnny's story came to an end.

"To be totally clear," said Rana, "was this all – everything you've described here – in line with what Martens Magnus had ordered you to do?"

"Yes," said Johnny. "*Take out Abu Fellah before he can do any harm in Norway*. Those were his exact words."

"You've been subject to the armed forces' strictest duty of confidentiality on the operations in which you've participated," Rana continued, inquisitorially. "Are you prepared to break with this and talk about the mission in open court?"

"I don't think I'd be breaking anything," said Johnny. "This is about admitting a crime. I don't think Martens Magnus and whoever he was representing were part of the armed forces at all, and if they were, this isn't a country I want to work for."

Johnny looked at HK. "As my mentor used to say, it isn't the country per se that I'm defending, it's the Constitution. And those who violate the Constitution under the pretext of protecting the country aren't worth defending."

"Brilliant, that's perfect," said Jan I. Rana, clearly pleased. "I look forward to the next episode."

Johnny looked around the visiting room and stared at HK, who sat in silence, rocking on his chair. "You promised to help me," said Johnny. "I barely remember what my daughter looks like."

"Ah yes."

HK got up and went to the door.

Rebecca entered the room, said a subdued hello. She held a little girl by the hand. Ingrid had grown into a long-legged six-year-old with tight plaits that hung down over her shoulders. Johnny took a step towards her, lifted her up and breathed in her scent before putting her back down.

"Mummy says you go to jail if you've done something wrong," she said, staring up at him with curiosity.

"That's right," Johnny said.

"Have you done something wrong?"

"I've done lots wrong."

EPILOGUE

THE SHIPOWNER'S SUITE

The Hurtigruten ship was a hybrid, so modern it hadn't yet been put into regular service. The Explorer Suite below the command deck in the fore was furnished in minimalist Scandinavian style, keeping to a palette of cool greys, beiges and browns, with a grey three-seater wool sofa behind a seating area and panoramic windows that sloped towards the bow.

Sasha stood in front of the mirror in the bathroom.

"What do you think, Mads?"

"Green's not your colour, Sasha."

She flung the jacket on a chair.

"Go for the tweed," her husband said. "It's timeless and elegant. Your words should dazzle them, not your blazer."

He crept up behind her playfully, grabbed her waist and kissed her on the neck. Sasha closed her eyes with a contented smile.

"You know, Sasha, I was worried about you – about us. After Vera's death I was seriously worried. For the first time."

She met his gaze in the mirror. "It was never about you, Mads. It was about me."

He kissed her on the top of her head.

"I need a couple of minutes to myself, Mads. Big day, you know."

It was Olav who had suggested that Sasha and her family should have the "shipowner's cabin" this time. He had winked, an insider joke made by the patriarch of a family descended from shipping magnates, but it shattered the ease that had come over her in recent weeks. Suddenly she was back in 1940. No, she was back in the weeks after Vera's death, when everything was up in the air, before the world had found its balance again. A new balance.

There was a knock on the door. Sasha opened it. Her father and Siri Greve.

"Siri, can you give Daddy and me a couple of minutes?"

The lawyer nodded politely and disappeared. She had of course kept her lips perfectly sealed after that day in her office.

Olav stepped into the suite: silver hair slicked back, intense, sunken eyes, ears that seemed to stick out when his hair was newly cut, with two lines curving from the sides of his nose to his mouth. But he was less formally dressed than usual, in jeans, moccasins and a linen shirt with turned-up sleeves. He went straight to the minibar and took out a bottle of beer.

"Don't suppose you want one?"

"Since when did you start drinking in the morning?"

Olav smiled broadly. "I'm a pensioner, Alexandra. Feel ten years younger already."

Olav took a big swig of the beer. "Should have stepped down long ago. Best decision I ever made. Escaping the meaningless chit-chat with all those international swanks who don't know which continent they're on. No more intrigues or angry board members, no more arguing with contractors, businessmen or whimpering Nobel laureates."

"Thanks for the encouragement!" Sasha said.

"That apart, this conference is important. It's time to purge the ghosts of the past."

It was a beautiful day in the middle of June. A Siberian heatwave had come in from the east and settled over northern Norway, the sun was shining day and night, small boats had gathered around the ship to admire it, sea eagles circled above, and on the horizon she saw the silhouette of the Lofoten Wall shrouded in a haze of heat. The Hurtigruten ship had left the quay in Bodø that morning. The SAGA Arctic Challenge – which had on its agenda geopolitics, climate change and other pressing questions about the region – was to be held on board. In the course of the two-day conference they would sail through Lofoten and Vesterålen before disembarking in Tromsø.

The ship reduced its speed now. The horn gave three blasts. Olav went to the rail and threw a wreath overboard. "With this we honour our family's sacrifices and, above all, *Prinsesse Ragnhild*'s final resting place. May they rest in peace, all those who were taken by the sea," he declared. "And now, my friends, I have important news for you all."

As always when he spoke publicly, he fumbled a little at the start, as though needing a few seconds to get into gear.

"As some of you probably know, this is a very symbolic place for our family. It was here that my father died beneath the waves in 1940. So, this is the perfect place to tell you that, from today, we are opening a new chapter in SAGA's history. It is my pleasure to announce that I am stepping down, and it is an honour to give the floor to our new CEO and chair of the board, Alexandra Falck."

Sasha was met with camera flashes and eager applause as she ascended the podium, feeling the adrenaline rush through her body. She took the microphone.

"My question as SAGA's leader is this: who are we, as a nation and as individuals? Few places sum up the Norwegian identity as clearly as our nation's coastline and these splendid islands of Lofoten and Vesterålen, and no place has left a stronger mark on my family than this area of the sea. This is a 'graveyard in the sea'. It was here that my grandfather Thor Falck vanished into the depths when the *Prinsesse Ragnhild* went down; it is here that a heroic skipper, Knut Indergård, and his crew rescued hundreds of people from the ice-cold waves, one of the war's greatest acts of heroism. One of those he brought to safety was my father, Olav. Olav Falck! Come up here!" said Sasha. "Come back onstage!"

Olav made a half-hearted attempt to refuse her, but the attendees whistled and cheered until he went up, smiling and waving at the crowd.

"Thankfully, you survived the shipwreck," she said seriously, addressing her father. "And since establishing SAGA you've told the story of our country. Your raison d'être: to protect the values we hold dearest – freedom and democracy – from external forces. The future is hard to predict. But I promise you, dear Olav, that this is a task I shall carry forward. We will fight for democracy against the enemies of freedom by every means we have at our disposal. For these are the values that stand above all others. If we lose our freedom, we lose everything. I shall dedicate my life to continuing the fight for what you believe in."

She thought she saw a tear in the corner of his eye.

"It's difficult to know what to give a man who has everything, and has experienced almost everything," she continued. "But I think I have the answer in this: a leather-bound copy of your mother's manuscript of *The Sea Cemetery*!"

There was thunderous applause and more flashing lights as she handed him the book. It contained no epilogue.

Following Sasha's speech, there was a reception up on the promenade deck. Hans Falck wove his way through the dignitaries as they gossiped and quaffed their champagne. Nobody had greater double standards than these parasites, flying round the world in first class, charging million-dollar fees to moralise about how other people's diesel cars and barbecued burgers were destroying the planet. He saw them wherever he went . . . There was something so fake about the whole business. He had felt it strongly when he had given a lecture about the brave Kurdish women who fought against IS. It had not been the truth as it really was, but as people wanted it to be.

Craving solitude, Hans went up onto the viewing deck. The ship had crossed the fjord now and was entering the narrow Raftsund Strait. He leaned over the rail as it made a slow turn to port. Here the mountains plunged steeply down into the fjord.

His moment of peace was short-lived, as the dignitaries trooped up from the reception to admire the dramatic view.

An elegant and athletic woman in her forties leaned over the ship's rail beside him.

"Siri Greve, how nice to see you," exclaimed Hans.

"Do you have a moment?"

"Falcks come and go, but not you. The tenacity of the Greve family has always impressed me."

"You need to listen carefully now," said Siri. She was clearly not interested in small talk.

"Why?"

"Because of this," she said, discreetly pulling out an envelope from her blazer pocket. "I was a witness to Vera Lind's will. The other was Johan Grieg. I was present when Sasha Falck burned it, and I can no longer endorse the actions of the Falck family. Sasha has proven even more ruthless than her father. This is a copy."

Before them lay the mouth of the Trollfjord, with mountains soaring up on both sides in a V shape, leading to snow-capped peaks at the end of the fjord. The ship glided over the sea's surface, the midnight sun shone on the peaks.

Hans turned and walked through the ship, back to his cabin.

Once inside, he flung his dinner jacket on the bed. His instincts told him this was going to change the course of his life, just as his encounter with Vera at Hordnes in the winter of 1970 and that fateful September night in Beirut in 1982 had done. Yes, that in particular. Hans opened a picture on his mobile, an old photograph he had kept and scanned. All that remained of *them*. He was leaning proudly over an iron bed. In it lay Mouna Khouri, with the exhausted but happy gaze of a woman who has just given birth. On her lap was a newborn baby with green eyes. His firstborn. "His name will be Yahya," the mother had whispered. "That's Arabic for John the Baptist."

ACKNOWLEDGEMENTS

Although this is a novel, there are many who deserve thanks for helping me with the truth. They include the journalist Christian Lyder Marstrander, who by chance put me on to the fate of DS *Prinsesse Ragnhild*. His series *Norske skipsforlis* (*Norwegian Shipwrecks*), broadcast on NRK Radio in the autumn of 2017, contains an episode about this shipwreck, and is available as a podcast on NRK's website.

During my research into the shipwreck, Rune Thomas Ege, communications manager at Hurtigruten, put me in contact with Lina Vibe at the Hurtigruten Museum in Stokmarknes, and Sten Magne Engen, who gave me a private tour and found the old floor plans of and timetables for the *Prinsesse Ragnhild*. Without these drawings, the job of reconstructing the last October days before the shipwreck would have been much harder, and I hope for forgiveness for having the ship begin its last voyage in Bergen, and not Trondheim, as was the case. I have nevertheless striven to follow Hurtigruten's route and timetable in October 1940.

A decisive thank you goes also to Jørgen Strand at the Skipsfartshistorisk Selskap Nordmøre (The Shipping History Society, Nordmøre), which found the skipper Knut Indergård's testimony and let me use it. The best-written entry for the shipwreck can be found in the compendium of texts related to the disaster, *En samling av tekst omkring Prinsesse Ragnhilds forlis den 23. oktober 1940* (ed. Åge Johansen), which can be found at the Norwegian National Library and contains among other things the Salten District Court report.

It was Professor Terje Emberland at the Norwegian Centre for Holocaust and Minority Studies (The HL Centre) who advised me to take a closer look at the under-investigated question of resistance fighters in the German armed forces during the war. I also discussed the matter with historian Dr Bjørn Tore Rosendahl at the Stiftelsen Arkivet in Kristiansand, where the two Germans were imprisoned before the execution. To claim that I got to the bottom of this case would be an exaggeration, however. Just as in this novel, there may be future academic work hidden there.

For more general questions about the Hurtigruten and shipping during the war, I thank Per Kristian Sebak of the Bergen Sjøfartsmuseum (Bergen Maritime Museum), the author Asgeir Ueland and above all Pål Espolin Johnsen, the author of the classic *Hurtigruta* (Cappelen, 1978), who has patiently answered my questions about the ships and coastal culture.

I have also relied heavily on Dag Bakka Jr's *Livslinje of eventyrreise: Historien om Hurtigruten* (Bedoni, 2017), *I storm og still på alle hav: Nordenfjeldske 125 år* (F. Beyer, 1982) by Leif B. Lillegård, and *Hurtigruta: EN litterær reise* by Øystein Rottem (Press, 2002), the latter being one of the few Norwegian writers who has tried to give Norway's coastal culture the place in literary history that I think it deserves.

As for the coast itself, I am naturally strongly inspired by Morten A. Strøksnes's *Havboka, eller Kunsten å fange en kjempehai fra en gummibåt på et stort hav gjennom fire årstider* (October 2015). Before and during my travels in Lofoten I talked to William Hakvaag at the Lofoten War Memorial Museum in Svolvær and the historian Gro Røde, author of *På et berg eg kalla mett* (Orkana, 1994), a powerful and fascinating narrative about the eviction from the fishing villages on Yttersia in Lofoten.

For the more contemporary aspects of this book, I have relied less on research. Thanks go to Mohammed Usman Rana, Matias L'Abée-Lund, Adele Matheson Mestad, Inger Zadig, Kim Heger and Lasse Gallefoss for answers to questions big and small. Thanks also to Guri Hjeltnes, Director of the Centre for Studies of the Holocaust and Religious Minorities, Oslo, who kindly gave me a private tour of the Villa Grande, a property that may have some shared features with Rederhaugen.

The parts of the book set in Kurdistan could hardly have been written had I not travelled there myself. A warm thank you to Mike Peshmerganor (pseudonym), whose book *Min kamp mot Kalifatet* (Kagge, 2017) I edited some years ago. Mike read through the relevant parts of this book, and has been kind enough to let me use a fictionalised version in this story. My friends in the special forces and the intelligence services will be allowed to remain anonymous.

I thank Aschehoug Publishing and my editors Nora Campbell and Marius Fossøy Mohaugen for crucial input, enormous effort and indomitable faith in the project, even when I have sometimes wanted to give up. Benedicte Treider, Trygve Åslund and Sarah Natasha Melbye also read the manuscript and made important comments. Anne-Laure Albessard may not read Norwegian, but intuitively understands how a story should be screwed together. Writers are lucky when they have a friendly sounding board such as screenwriter Petter Skavlan, who can solve tangles in a plot almost on the hoof. I owe many of the ideas in this book to his creativity. I also owe author Ruth Lillegraven a big thank you. I have edited her crime novels. Now the tables have been turned, and without her readings, linguistic sensitivity and thoughtfulness, that might have proved difficult.

I remain solely responsible for the contents of this book.

Aslak Nore
Marseille, August 2021

ASLAK NORE grew up in Oslo. Educated at the University of Oslo and the New School for Social Research in New York, he then served in Norway's elite Telemark Battalion in Bosnia. A modern-day adventurer, Nore has lived in Latin America and worked as a journalist in the Middle East and Afghanistan. He has published several non-fiction books and three novels, including *Ulvefellen*, which was a bestseller and won the Riverton Prize for best crime novel in Norway in 2018. *The Sea Cemetery* is an international bestseller. He lives in Provence, France.

DEBORAH DAWKIN originally trained in theatre at Drama Centre, London, before turning to translation. Her translations include *The Blue Room* by Hanne Orstavik and *Buzz Aldrin: What Happened to You in All the Confusion* by Johan Harstad, as well as Lars Mytting's Sister Bells Trilogy. She is the co-translator of eight plays by Ibsen for Penguin Classics, and is presently working on a PhD about the life and work of the Ibsen translator Michael Meyer.